HARRAP'S
YES YOU CAN!

A Mind to Murder

P. D. JAMES

First published in 1963
by Faber and Faber Limited
Bloomsbury House, 74-77 Great Russell Street,
London WC1B 3DA

All characters in this publication are fictitious and any resemblance to real persons, living or dead, is purely coincidental.

Pour les notes en marge du texte
© Larousse, 2013
21, rue du Montparnasse
75283 Paris Cedex 06

HARRAP's® est une marque de Larousse SAS
www.harrap.com

ISBN 978 2 81 870273 4

About the author

P. D. James was born in Oxford in 1920 and educated at Cambridge High School for Girls. From 1949 to 1968 she worked in the National Health Service[1] and subsequently[2] in the Home Office[3], first in the Police Department and later in the Criminal Policy Department. All that experience has been used in her novels. She is a Fellow[4] of the Royal Society of Literature and of the Royal Society of Arts and has served as a Governor[5] of the BBC, a member of the Arts Council[6], where she was Chairman of the Literary Advisory Panel[7], on the Board[8] of the British Council[9] and as a magistrate in Middlesex and London. She has won awards[10] for crime writing in Britain, America, Italy and Scandinavia, including the Mystery Writers of America Grandmaster Award and The National Arts Club Medal of Honor for Literature (US). She has received honorary degrees[11] from seven British universities, was awarded an OBE[12] in 1983 and was created a life peer[13] in 1991. In 1997 she was elected President of the Society of Authors.

She lives in London and Oxford and has two daughters, five grandchildren and seven great-grandchildren.

1. service national de santé
2. ensuite
3. le ministère britannique de l'intérieur
4. membre
5. membre du conseil d'administration
6. organisme public britannique de promotion des arts
7. présidente du panel littéraire
8. membre du conseil d'administration
9. organisme public chargé de promouvoir la langue et la culture anglaises
10. prix
11. diplômes honoris causa
12. Officer of the Order of the British Empire = distinction honorifique britannique
13. pair (membre de la Chambre des lords) à vie

DIRECTION DE LA PUBLICATION : Carine Girac-Marinier

DIRECTION ÉDITORIALE : Claude Nimmo

NOTES EN MARGE : Émilie Bourdarot

RÉVISION DES NOTES : Giovanni Picci

RELECTURE : Dominique Chevalier

INFORMATIQUE ÉDITORIALE : Philippe Cazabet, Willemine Jaspars, Marion Pépin

CONCEPTION GRAPHIQUE : Uli Meindl

MISE EN PAGES : Jérôme Faucheux

FABRICATION : Rebecca Dubois

Mot de l'Éditeur

Vous aimeriez lire en langue originale, mais le vocabulaire, les expressions figurées ou la syntaxe vous arrêtent parfois ?

Cette collection est faite pour vous !

Vous trouverez en effet, en note dans la marge, une traduction de certains mots et expressions qui vous permettra d'avancer facilement dans votre lecture.

Nous n'avons pas cherché à vous donner une traduction littéraire de l'ouvrage et nous nous sommes parfois écartés du sens littéral pour vous fournir celui qui convient le mieux à l'histoire. Aussi les mots sont-ils traduits dans le contexte du texte original.

Les expressions figées anglaises sont, bien entendu, rendues par une expression équivalente en français.

Les allusions à des réalités culturelles du monde anglo-saxon sont expliquées également dans la marge, pour vous aider à mieux comprendre la trame de l'histoire.

Vous aurez ainsi, en regard du texte original, tout le savoir-faire d'un dictionnaire rien que pour vous et adapté à ce livre !

Notre objectif est de vous mener jusqu'au mot FIN en vous donnant les clés nécessaires à la compréhension du récit.

Laissez-vous gagner par l'angoisse, l'humour et le suspense qui règnent chez les maîtres de la littérature anglo-saxonne.

Lire en VO ? You can indeed!

For Edward Gordon James

Author's Note

There is only a small number of autonomous psychiatric out-patient clinics[1] in London and it is obvious that these units, dealing as they do with[2] the same medical specialty and organized within a unified National Health Service[3], must inevitably have some methods of treatment and administrative procedures in common. A number of these they share[4] with the Steen Clinic. It is the more important to state[5] clearly that the Steen is an imaginary clinic situated in an imaginary London square[6], that none of its patients or staff[7], medical or lay[8], represent living people, and that the deplorable events which took place in its basement[9] have their origin only in that curious psychological phenomenon – the imagination of the crime novelist[10].

P. D. J

1. services de consultation externe
2. puisqu'ils s'occupent de
3. service national de santé
4. ils partagent
5. déclarer
6. place
7. personnel
8. non médical
9. sous-sol
10. auteur(e.) de romans noirs

Coup de pouce pour vous aider à bien comprendre le début de l'histoire...

Le livre que vous tenez entre vos mains est un roman policier (*crime novel* en anglais), le deuxième roman de la « baronne » du crime, P. D. James. Un crime va bouleverser la vie ordinaire d'un hôpital psychiatrique, la clinique *Steen*. Nous sommes au début de l'histoire... un vendredi soir tiède du mois d'octobre, Paul Steiner, psychiatre, écoute assis dans son cabinet M. Burge, un de ses patients. Un peu plus loin, le Dr James Baguley soigne un malade à coups d'électrochocs pendant qu'Amy Shorthouse, la femme de ménage, papote bruyamment avec des patients. Du bruit, des pas, des voix, Paul Steiner est agacé, impossible de se concentrer dans ce brouhaha quand soudain... un hurlement ! Trop, c'est trop ! Que se passe-t-il encore ?

CHAPTER ONE

Dr Paul Steiner, consultant psychiatrist at the Steen Clinic, sat in the front ground-floor[1] consulting-room[2] and listened to his patient's highly rationalized explanation of the failure[3] of his third marriage. Mr Burge lay[4] in comfort on a couch[5] the better to expound[6] the complications of his psyche[7]. Dr Steiner sat at his head in a chair of the carefully documented type which the Hospital Management Committee had decreed for the use of consultants[8]. It was functional and not unattractive but it gave no support to the back of the head. From time to time a sharp jerk[9] of his neck[10] muscles recalled Dr Steiner from momentary oblivion[11] to the realities of his Friday evening psychotherapy clinic. The October day had been very warm. After a fortnight of sharp frosts[12] during which the staff of the clinic had shivered[13] and pleaded[14], the official date for starting the central heating had coincided with one of those perfect autumn days when the city square outside had brimmed with[15] yellow light and the late dahlias in the railed[16] garden, bright as a paintbox[17], had shone like the gauds of high summer[18]. It was now nearly seven o'clock. Outside, the warmth of the day had long given way[19], first to mist[20] and then to chilly[21] darkness. But here, inside the clinic, the heat of noon was trapped, the

1. au rez-de-chaussée
2. cabinet de consultation
3. échec
4. était allongé
5. divan
6. exposer
7. psychisme
8. avait décidé d'allouer aux médecins spécialistes
9. brusque tiraillement
10. cou
11. absence
12. après deux semaines de fortes gelées
13. grelotté
14. supplié
15. était inondée de
16. clôturé
17. aussi éclatants qu'une palette de peintre
18. jetaient leurs derniers feux de plein été
19. avait depuis longtemps cédé la place
20. brume
21. très fraîche

air, heavy and still, seemed spent with[1] the breath of too much talking.

Mr Burge enlarged on[2] the immaturity, coldness and insensitivity of his wives in a querulous falsetto[3]. Dr Steiner's clinical judgement, not uninfluenced by the late effects of a large lunch and the unwise[4] choice of a cream doughnut with his afternoon tea, told him that the time was not yet ripe[5] to point out[6] that the one defect shared by the three mesdames Burge had been a singular lack of judgement in their choice of husband. Mr Burge was not yet ready to face[7] the truth of his own inadequacy[8].

Dr Steiner felt no moral indignation about his patient's behaviour. It would indeed have been most unethical[9] had any such improper emotion clouded his judgement[10]. There were few things in life which aroused[11] Dr Steiner's moral indignation and most of them affected his own comfort. Many of them were, indeed, concerned with the Steen Clinic and its administration. He disapproved strongly of the administrative officer, Miss Bolam, whose preoccupation with the number of patients he saw in a session and the accuracy[12] of his travelling expense form[13] he saw as part of a systematic policy of persecution. He resented[14] the fact that his Friday evening clinic coincided with Dr James Baguley's electro-convulsive therapy session so that his psychotherapy patients, all of them of high intelligence and sensible of the privilege[15] of being treated by him, had to sit in the waiting-room with the motley crowd[16] of depressed suburban housewives[17] and ill-educated psychotics that Baguley seemed to delight in collecting[18]. Dr Steiner had refused the use of one of the third-floor consulting-

1. saturé de
2. s'étendait sur
3. d'une voix plaintive de fausset
4. peu judicieux
5. le moment n'était pas venu
6. faire remarquer
7. admettre
8. incapacité
9. contraire à l'éthique
10. laisser une émotion si déplacée obscurcir son jugement
11. provoquer
12. exactitude
13. note de frais de déplacement
14. était contrarié par
15. conscients du privilège
16. foule de patients de tous types
17. femmes au foyer dépressives vivant en banlieue
18. aimait collectionner

rooms. These had been formed by partitioning the large and elegant Georgian rooms and he despised[1] them as badly proportioned and unpleasing cells[2], ill-suited either to[3] his grade or to the importance of his work. Nor had he found it convenient[4] to change the time of his session. Baguley, therefore[5], should change his. But Dr Baguley had stood firm[6] and in this, too, Dr Steiner had seen the influence of Miss Bolam. His plea[7] that the ground-floor consulting-rooms should be sound-proofed[8] had been turned down[9] by the Hospital Management Committee on the grounds of[10] expense. There had, however, been no demur[11] over providing Baguley with a new and highly expensive contraption[12] for shocking his patients out of the few wits[13] they still possessed. The matter[14] had, of course, been considered by the Clinic Medical Committee, but Miss Bolam had made no secret of where her sympathies lay[15]. In his diatribes against the administrative officer, Dr Steiner found it convenient to forget that her influence over the Medical Committee was non-existent.

It was difficult to forget the irritations of the ECT session[16]. The clinic building had been put up when men built to last, but even the sturdy oak door[17] of the consulting room could not muffle[18] the comings and goings[19] of a Friday night. The front door was closed at 6 p.m. and patients at the evening clinics were booked in and out[20] since the time, over five years ago, when a patient had entered unobserved, secreted herself[21] in the basement lavatory and chosen that insalubrious place in which to kill herself. Dr Steiner's psychotherapy sessions were punctuated by the ringing of the front-door bell,

1. méprisait
2. cellules
3. ne convenant pas à
4. opportun
5. par conséquent
6. n'avait pas cédé
7. demande insistante
8. insonorisés
9. rejetée
10. en raison de
11. objection
12. truc
13. le peu d'intelligence
14. affaire
15. où allait sa préférence
16. séances d'électrochocs
17. robuste porte en chêne
18. atténuer le bruit causé par
19. allées et venues
20. étaient enregistrés
21. s'était cachée

the passing of feet as patients came and went, the hearty[1] voices of relatives[2] and escorts exhorting the patient or calling goodbyes to Sister Ambrose. Dr Steiner wondered why relatives found it necessary to shout at the patients as if they were deaf as well as psychotic. But possibly after a session with Baguley and his diabolic machine they were. Worst of all was the clinic domestic assistant[3], Mrs Shorthouse. One might imagine that Amy Shorthouse could do the cleaning[4] early in the mornings as was surely the normal arrangement. That way there would be the minimum of disturbance[5] to the clinic staff. But Mrs Shorthouse maintained[6] that she couldn't get through[7] the work without an extra two hours in the evenings and Miss Bolam had agreed[8]. Naturally, she would[9]. It appeared to Dr Steiner that very little domestic work was done on Friday evenings. Mrs Shorthouse had a predilection for the ECT patients – indeed, her own husband had once been treated by Dr Baguley – and she was usually to be seen hanging around[10] the hall and the ground-floor general office while the session was being held. Dr Steiner had mentioned it at the Medical Committee more than once and had been irritated by his colleagues' general uninterest in the problem. Mrs Shorthouse should be kept out of sight and encouraged to get on with[11] her work, not permitted to stand around gossiping[12] with the patients. Miss Bolam, so unnecessarily strict with other members of the staff, showed no inclination to discipline Mrs Shorthouse. Everyone knew that good domestic workers were hard to get[13] but an administrative officer who knew her job would recruit them[14] somehow. Weakness[15] solved nothing.

1. chaleureuses
2. famille
3. femme de service
4. faire le ménage
5. dérangement
6. soutenait
7. terminer
8. accepté
9. on n'en attendait pas moins d'elle
10. traîner dans
11. continuer
12. rester là à papoter
13. trouver
14. arriverait toujours à les recruter
15. la faiblesse

But Baguley could not be persuaded to complain[1] about Mrs Shorthouse and Bolam would never criticize Baguley. The poor woman was probably in love with him. It was up to Baguley to take a firm line[2] instead of sloping around[3] the clinic in that ridiculously long white coat which made him look like a second-rate dentist. Really, the man had no idea of the dignity with which a consultant clinic should be conducted.

Clump[4], clump went someone's boots along the passage. It was probably old Tippett, a chronic schizophrenic patient of Baguley's who for the past nine years had regularly spent Friday evenings carving[5] wood in the art therapy department. The thought of Tippett increased[6] Dr Steiner's petulance[7]. The man was totally unsuitable[8] for the Steen. If he were well enough[9] to be out of hospital, which Dr Steiner doubted, he ought to[10] attend a Day Hospital or one of the County Council's sheltered workshops[11]. It was patients like Tippett who gave the clinic a dubious[12] reputation and obscured its real function as an analytically orientated centre of psychotherapy. Dr Steiner felt positively embarrassed when one of his own carefully selected patients encountered[13] Tippett creeping[14] about the clinic on a Friday evening. Tippett wasn't even safe to be out. One day there would be an incident and Baguley would find himself in trouble.

Dr Steiner's happy contemplation of his own colleague in trouble was punctured[15] by the ring of the front-door bell. Really, it was impossible! This time it was apparently a hospital car service driver calling for a patient. Mrs Shorthouse went to the door to speed them away. Her eldritch[16] screech[17]

1. se plaindre
2. faire preuve de fermeté
3. traînasser dans
4. clop
5. à sculpter
6. renforça
7. irritabilité
8. ne convenait absolument pas
9. s'il se sentait assez bien
10. il aurait dû
11. atelier protégé
12. douteuse
13. rencontrait
14. marchant à pas de loup
15. brutalement interrompue
16. étrange
17. cri strident

echoed through the hall. 'Cheerio, ducks[1]. See you next week. If you can't be good, be careful.'

Dr Steiner winced[2] and shut[3] his eyes. But his patient, happily engaged in his favourite hobby of talking about himself, seemed not to have heard. Mr Burge's high whine[4] had not, in fact, faltered[5] for the past twenty minutes.

'I don't pretend I'm an easy person. I'm not, I'm a complicated devil. That's something which Theda and Sylvia have never understood. The roots of it go deep of course. You remember that session we had in June? Some pretty basic stuff came out then I thought.'

His therapist did not recall the session in question but was unconcerned. With Mr Burge pretty basic stuff was invariably near the surface and could be trusted to emerge. An unaccountable[6] peace fell. Dr Steiner doodled[7] on his notepad[8], regarded his doodle with interest and concern, looked at it again with the pad held upside down[9] and became for a moment more preoccupied with his own subconscious than with that of his patient. Suddenly he became aware of[10] another sound from outside, faint[11] at first and then becoming louder[12]. Somewhere a woman was screaming. It was a horrible noise, high, continuous, and completely animal. Its effect on Dr Steiner was peculiarly[13] unpleasant. He was naturally timid and highly strung[14]. Although his job involved him in the occasional emotional crises he was more adept at circumventing[15] than coping with[16] an emergency. Fear gave vent to[17] irritation and he sprang from[18] his chair exclaiming.

'No! Really, this is too bad! What's Miss Bolam doing? Isn't anyone supposed to be in charge here?'

1. À plus, mes poussins
2. grimaça
3. ferma
4. gémissement
5. n'avait pas faibli
6. inexplicable
7. griffonna
8. bloc-notes
9. à l'envers
10. il prit conscience de
11. faible
12. plus fort
13. particulièrement
14. nerveux
15. il préférait contourner
16. faire face à
17. se transforma en
18. il se leva d'un bond de

'What's up?[1]' inquired Mr Burge, sitting up like a jack-in-the-box[2] and dropping his voice half an octave to its more normal tone.

'Nothing. Nothing. Some woman having an attack of hysteria[3] that's all. Stay where you are. I'll be back,' commanded Dr Steiner.

Mr Burge collapsed[4] again but with eye and ear cocked[5] for the door. Dr Steiner found himself in the hall.

Immediately a little group swung round[6] to face him. Jennifer Priddy, the junior typist[7], was clinging to[8] one of the porters[9], Peter Nagle, who was patting her shoulder[10] in embarrassed pity and looking puzzled[11]. Mrs Shorthouse was with them. The girl's screams were subsiding[12] into whimpers[13] but her whole body was shaking, and she was deathly pale.

'What's the matter?' asked Dr Steiner sharply. 'What's wrong with her?[14]'

Before anyone had a chance to reply, the door of the ECT room opened and Dr Baguley came out followed by Sister Ambrose and his anaesthetist, Dr Mary Ingram. The hall seemed suddenly full of people. 'Calm down, that's a good girl,' said Dr Baguley mildly. 'We're trying to run a clinic' He turned to Peter Nagle and asked in a low voice: 'What's the matter anyway?'

Nagle seemed about to speak when, suddenly, Miss Priddy gained control. Breaking free[15] she turned to Dr Baguley and said with absolute clearness:

'It's Miss Bolam. She's dead. Someone's killed her. She's in the basement record-room[16] and she's murdered. I found her. Enid's been murdered!'

1. qu'est-ce qui se passe ?

2. comme un diable à ressort

3. crise de nerfs

4. s'effondra

5. tout yeux, tout oreilles

6. se retourna

7. dactylographe

8. se cramponnait à

9. portiers

10. qui lui tapotait l'épaule

11. perplexe

12. se calmaient

13. gémissements

14. qu'est-ce qu'elle a ?

15. en se libérant

16. aux archives

She clung to Nagle and began to cry again but more quietly. The dreadful[1] shaking had ceased[2]. Dr Baguley said to the porter:

'Take her into the treatment-room. Make her lie down[3]. Better give her something to drink. Here's the key. I'll be back.'

He made for[4] the basement stairs and the rest, abandoning the girl to Nagle's ministrations[5], followed in a jostling bunch[6]. The basement at the Steen was well lit; all its rooms were used by the clinic which, like most psychiatric units, was chronically short of space. Here, below stairs, in addition to the boiler-room[7], the telephone equipment-room and the porters' quarters, was the art therapy department, a medical records storeroom and, at the front of the building, a treatment-room for the lysergic acid[8] patients. As the little group reached the bottom of[9] the stairs the door of this room opened and Nurse[10] Bolam, Miss Bolam's cousin, looked out briefly[11] – a shadowy wraith[12] in her white uniform against the darkness of the room behind. Her gentle, puzzled voice floated[13] to them down the corridor. 'Is there anything wrong? I thought I heard a scream a few minutes ago.'

Sister Ambrose said with brusque authority:

'There's nothing wrong, Nurse. Get back to your patient.'

The white figure disappeared and the door was shut. Turning to Mrs Shorthouse, Sister Ambrose went on[14]:

'And there's nothing for you to do here, Mrs Shorthouse. Please stay upstairs. Miss Priddy might like a cup of tea.'

1. horrible
2. avait cessé
3. s'allonger
4. se dirigea vers
5. soins
6. en se bousculant
7. chaufferie
8. acide lysergique, L. S. D.
9. arrivait au pied de
10. infirmière
11. un court instant
12. une apparition spectrale
13. flotta
14. ajouta

Mrs Shorthouse was heard to mutter[1] rebelliously but beat a reluctant retreat[2]. The three doctors, with Sister in tow[3], pressed on[4].

The medical record-room was on their right, between the porters' rest-room[5] and the art therapy department. The door was ajar[6] and the light was on.

Dr Steiner, who had become unnaturally aware of every small detail, noticed the key was in the lock[7]. No one was about. The steel racks[8], with their tight-packed rows[9] of manilla folders[10], ran ceiling high[11] and at right angles to the door forming a series of narrow aisles[12], each lit by a fluorescent light. The four high windows were barred and dissected[13] by the racks; it was an airless little room rarely visited and seldom dusted[14]. The little group pushed its way down[15] the first passage and turned left to where there was a small windowless space clear of shelving[16] and furnished with[17] a table and chair where records[18] could be sorted for filing[19] or information copied from the notes without the need to take the file away. Here was chaos. The chair was overturned. The floor was littered with[20] records. Some had their covers wrenched apart[21] and their pages torn[22], others lay dumped[23] in shifting layers[24] beneath gaps on the shelves[25] which looked too narrow[26] to have held[27] such a weight of paper. And in the middle of this confusion, like a plump[28] and incongruous Ophelia afloat[29] on a tide of paper, was the body of Enid Bolam. On her chest rested a heavy and grotesque image carved in wood, her hands folded about[30] its base so that she looked, horribly, like a parody of

1. grommeler
2. battre en retraite à contrecœur
3. dans leur sillage
4. continuèrent leur chemin
5. salle de repos
6. entrouverte
7. serrure
8. casiers
9. rangées
10. chemises en papier kraft
11. arrivaient jusqu'au plafond
12. couloirs
13. coupées
14. rarement époussetée
15. se fraya un chemin le long de
16. sans étagères
17. meublé de
18. dossiers
19. triés et classés
20. jonché de
21. arrachées
22. déchirées
23. étaient abandonnés
24. formaient des piles instables
25. sous des étagères vides
26. étroites
27. pu soutenir
28. dodue
29. flottant
30. serraient

motherhood with her creature ritually laid to her breast.

There could be no doubt that she was dead. Even in the midst of his fear and repugnance Dr Steiner could not miss that final diagnosis. Staring at the wooden figure he cried:

'Tippett! That's his fetish! That's the carving he's
1. fier so proud[1] of. Where is he? Baguley, he's your pa-
2. tu ferais mieux de t'en occuper tient! You'd better handle this[2]!'

He looked round nervously as if expecting Tippett to materialize, arm raised to strike, the very personification of violence.

Dr Baguley was kneeling by the body. He said quietly:

'Tippett isn't here this evening.'

'But he's always here on Fridays! That's his fetish!
3. hurla That's the weapon!' Dr Steiner wailed[3] against such
4. stupidité obtuseness[4].

5. souleva Dr Baguley gently lifted[5] Miss Bolam's left eyelid[6]
6. paupière with his thumb[7]. Without looking up he said:
7. pouce

'We had a phone call from St Luke's this morning. Tippett's been admitted with pneumonia. Last Monday, I think. Anyway, he wasn't here this evening.'
Suddenly he gave an exclamation. The two women
8. se penchèrent bent[8] closer to the body. Dr Steiner, who could not bring himself to watch the examination, heard him say:

9. poignardée 'She's been stabbed[9], too. Through the heart by
10. on dirait the look of it[10] and with a black-handled chisel[11].
11. ciseau Isn't this one of Nagle's, Sister?' There was a pause and Dr Steiner heard Sister's voice:

'It looks very like it, Doctor. All his tools have
12. manches black handles[12]. He keeps them in the porters' rest-

room.' She added defensively. 'Anyone could get at them.'

'It looks as if someone has.' There was the sound of Dr Baguley getting to his feet[1]. Still keeping his eyes on the body he said: 'Phone Cully on the door[2], will you, Sister. Don't alarm him, but tell him that no one is to be admitted or to leave the building. That includes the patients. Then get Dr Etherege and ask him to come down. He'll be in his consulting-room I imagine.'

'Oughtn't we to[3] phone the police?' Dr Ingram spoke nervously and her pink face, so ridiculously like that of an angora rabbit, flushed[4] pinker. It was not only in moments of high drama that one was apt to overlook[5] the presence of Dr Ingram, and Dr Baguley stared blankly at her[6] as if he had momentarily forgotten her existence.

'We'll wait for the medical director,' he said.

Sister Ambrose disappeared with a rustle[7] of starched linen[8]. The nearest telephone was just outside the record-room door but, insulated[9] by tiers[10] of paper from every outside noise, Dr Steiner strained his ears[11] in vain to hear the lift[12] of the receiver[13] or the murmur of Sister's voice. He forced himself to look once more at Miss Bolam's body. In life he had thought of her as graceless and unattractive, and death had lent[14] her no dignity. She lay on her back[15], her knees[16] raised and parted[17] so that there was an expanse of[18] pink woollen knicker[19] clearly visible, looking far more indecent than naked flesh. Her round, heavy face was quite peaceful. The two thick plaits[20] which she wore wound[21] above her forehead were undisturbed. But then, nothing had ever been known to disturb

1. se relever
2. à la réception
3. ne devrions-nous pas
4. devint
5. ne pas remarquer
6. la regarda d'un air absent
7. froissement
8. linge amidonné
9. isolé
10. rangées
11. tendit l'oreille
12. déclic
13. combiné
14. conféré
15. dos
16. genoux
17. écartés
18. on voyait
19. culotte
20. nattes
21. enroulées

Miss Bolam's archaic hair style. Dr Steiner was reminded of his private fantasy that the thick, lifeless plaits exuded[1] their own mysterious secretion and were fixed for ever, immutably, about that placid brow[2]. Looking at her in the defenceless indignity of death, Dr Steiner tried to feel pity and knew that he felt fear. But he was fully conscious only of repugnance. It was impossible to feel tenderly towards something so ridiculous, so shocking, so obscene. The ugly word spun unbidden[3] to the surface of thought. Obscene! He felt a ridiculous urge to pull down her skirt, to cover that puffy[4], pathetic face, to replace the spectacles[5] which had slipped[6] from her nose and hung, askew[7], from her left ear. Her eyes were half closed, her small mouth pursed[8] as if in disapproval of so undignified and unmerited an end. Dr Steiner was not unfamiliar with that look: he had seen it on her face in life. He thought, 'She looks as if she's just confronting me with my travelling expense form.'

Suddenly he was seized with an intolerable need to giggle[9]. Laughter welled up[10] uncontrollably. He recognized that this horrible urge[11] was the result of nervousness and shock but understanding did not bring control. Helplessly, he turned his back on his colleagues and fought for composure[12], grasping[13] the edge of a filing rack[14] and pressing his forehead[15] for support against the cold metal, his mouth and nostrils[16] choked with[17] the musty smell[18] of old records.

He was not aware of Sister Ambrose's return but, suddenly, he heard her speaking.

1. produisaient
2. front
3. émergea spontanément
4. bouffi
5. lunettes
6. glissé
7. de travers
8. pincée
9. ricaner
10. montait
11. envie
12. calme
13. agrippé à
14. casier
15. front
16. narines
17. emplies de
18. odeur de renfermé

'Dr Etherege is on his way down. Cully is on the door and I've told him that no one is to leave. Your patient is making rather a fuss[1], Dr Steiner.'

'Perhaps I'd better go up to him.' Faced with the need for decision, Dr Steiner regained control. He felt that it was somehow important that he should stay with the others and be there when the medical director arrived; that it would be wise[2] to ensure[3] that nothing important was said or done out of his hearing. On the other hand[4] he was not anxious to stay with the body. The record-room, brightly lit[5] as an operating theatre[6], claustrophobic and overheated[7], made him feel like a trapped animal. The heavy close-packed shelves seemed to press upon him, compelling[8] his eyes again and again to that lumpen[9] figure on its paper bier[10].

'I'll stay here,' he decided. 'Mr Burge must wait like everyone else.'

They stood together without speaking. Dr Steiner saw that Sister Ambrose, white-faced but otherwise apparently unmoved, stood stockily[11] calm with her hands loosely clasped[12] over her apron[13]. So must she have stood time without number in nearly forty years of nursing, waiting at the bedside of a patient, quietly deferential[14], for the doctor's orders. Dr Baguley pulled out[15] his cigarettes, looked at the packet for a moment as if surprised to find it in his hand, and replaced it in his pocket. Dr Ingram seemed to be silently crying. Once Dr Steiner thought he heard her murmur: 'Poor woman. Poor woman!'

Soon they heard footsteps[16] and the medical director was with them followed by the senior psychologist, Fredrica Saxon. Dr Etherege knelt down[17]

1. fait des histoires
2. sage
3. s'assurer
4. d'un autre côté
5. éclairé
6. salle d'opération
7. surchauffé
8. forçant
9. informe
10. cercueil
11. trapue
12. tranquillement croisées
13. tablier
14. révérencieuse
15. sortit
16. des pas
17. s'agenouilla

beside the body. He did not touch it but put his face close to Miss Bolam's as if he were about to kiss her[1]. Dr Steiner's sharp[2] little eyes did not miss the glance[3] that Miss Saxon gave Dr Baguley, that instinctive move towards each other and the quick withdrawal[4].

'What happened?' she whispered[5]. 'Is she dead?'

'Yes. Murdered apparently.' Baguley's tone was flat[6]. Miss Saxon made a sudden gesture. For one unbelievable moment Dr Steiner thought that she was going to cross herself[7].

'Who did it? Not poor old Tippett? That's his fetish, surely.'

'Yes, but he isn't here. He's in St Luke's with pneumonia.'

'Oh, my God! Then who?' This time she moved close to Dr Baguley and they did not draw apart[8]. Dr Etherege scrambled to his feet[9].

'You're right, of course. She's dead. Stunned[10] first apparently and then stabbed through the heart. I'll go upstairs to phone the police and let the rest of the staff know. We'd better[11] keep people together[12]. Then we three had better search the building. Nothing must be touched of course.'

Dr Steiner dared not meet Dr Baguley's eyes[13]. Dr Etherege in his role of the calm, authoritative administrator had always struck him[14] as slightly ridiculous. He suspected that Baguley felt the same.

Suddenly they heard footsteps and the senior psychiatric social worker Miss Ruth Kettle appeared from behind the filing racks, peering at them short-sightedly[15].

'Ah, there you are[16], Director,' said Miss Kettle, in her fluting[17], breathless voice. (She was the only staff

1. comme s'il allait l'embrasser
2. perçants
3. coup d'œil
4. rapide mouvement de recul
5. murmura
6. éteint
7. se signer
8. restèrent à côté l'un de l'autre
9. se releva tant bien que mal
10. assommée
11. nous ferions mieux de
12. rassembler tout le monde
13. n'osa pas regarder le docteur Baguley dans les yeux
14. lui avait toujours paru
15. les scrutant d'un regard myope
16. vous voilà
17. flûtée

member, thought Dr Steiner, to give Dr Etherege that ridiculous title and God only knew why. It made the place sound like a nature-cure clinic[1].)

'Cully told me you were down here. Not busy, I hope? I'm so distressed[2], I don't want to make trouble[3] but it really is too bad! Miss Bolam has booked me[4] a new patient for ten on Monday. I've just seen the appointment in my diary, No consultation with me[5] of course. She knows I always see the Worrikers then. It's quite deliberate, I'm afraid[6]. You know, Director, someone has really got to do something about Miss Bolam.'

Dr Baguley stood aside[7] and said grimly[8]: 'Someone has.'

At the other end of the square Superintendent[9] Adam Dalgliesh of the Criminal Investigation Department was attending[10] the ritual autumn sherry party given by his publishers which had coincided with the third reprint[11] of his first book of verse[12]. He didn't overestimate[13] his talent or the success of his book. The poems, which reflected his detached, ironic and fundamentally restless[14] spirit, had happened to catch a public mood[15]. He did not believe that more than half a dozen would live even in his own affections. Meanwhile he found himself awash[16] on the shallows of an unfamiliar sea[17] in which agents, royalties[18] and reviews were agreeable hazards[19]. And now there was this party. He had thought of it without enthusiasm as something to be endured[20], but it had proved unexpectedly enjoyable. Messrs Hearne and Illingworth were as incapable of providing poor sherry as they were of publishing poor work; Dalgliesh estimated that

1. centre de médecine douce

2. affligée

3. causer des ennuis

4. m'a fixé un rendez-vous avec

5. elle l'a fait sans me consulter

6. je crains

7. s'écarta

8. d'un ton sérieux

9. commissaire

10. participait à

11. réimpression

12. poésie

13. ne surestimait pas

14. toujours en ébullition

15. correspondaient au goût du public

16. à fleur d'eau

17. au-dessus des hauts-fonds d'une mer inconnue

18. droits d'auteur

19. dangers

20. à subir

his publishers' share of his own book's profits had been drunk in the first ten minutes. Old Sir Hubert Illingworth had made his brief appearance in the course of it, had shaken[1] Dalgliesh sadly by the hand, and had shuffled off[2] muttering under his breath as if deploring that yet another writer on the firm's list was exposing himself and his publisher to the doubtful gratifications[3] of success. To him all writers were precocious children; creatures to be tolerated and encouraged but not overexcited in case they cried before bedtime[4].

There were less welcome diversions[5] than the brief appearance of Sir Hubert. Few of the[6] guests knew that Dalgliesh was a detective and not all of them expected him to talk about his job. But there were inevitably those who thought it inappropriate that a man who caught murderers[7] should also write verse and who said so with varying degrees of tact[8]. Presumably they wanted murderers caught[9] however much they might argue about[10] what should happen to them afterwards; but they displayed a typical ambivalence towards those who did the catching. Dalgliesh was used to[11] this attitude and found it less offensive[12] than the common assumption[13] that there was a particular glamour in being a member of the murder squad[14]. But if there had been the expected quota of furtive curiosity and the inanities[15] common to all such parties, there had also been agreeable people saying agreeable things. No writer, however apparently detached about his talent, is immune to[16] the subtle reassurance of disinterested praise[17] and Dalgliesh, fighting the suspicion that few of those who admired had actually read and fewer still had bought,

1. secoué
2. avait disparu
3. satisfactions douteuses
4. de peur qu'ils ne pleurent avant d'aller se coucher
5. des diversions moins agréables
6. peu de
7. attrapait les meurtriers
8. avec plus ou moins de tact
9. ils voulaient sans doute que les meurtriers soient attrapés
10. même s'il leur arrivait de ne pas être d'accord au sujet de
11. était habitué à
12. offensante
13. l'idée commune
14. brigade criminelle
15. inepties
16. insensible à
17. éloge désintéressé

found that he was quietly enjoying himself and was honest enough to admit why.

The first hour had been hectic[1] but, soon after seven o'clock, he found himself standing alone glass in hand beside the ornate James Wyatt chimney-piece[2]. A thin wood fire was burning, filling the room with a faint[3] country smell. It was one of those inexplicable moments when one is suddenly[4] completely alone in the middle of a crowd[5], when the noise is muted[6] and the pressing bodies seem to recede[7] and become remote and mysterious as actors on some distant stage. Dalgliesh leaned[8] the back of his head against the mantelpiece[9], savouring this momentary privacy and noting appreciatively the elegant proportions of the room. Suddenly he saw Deborah Riscoe. She must have come into the room very quietly. He wondered[10] how long[11] she had been there. Immediately his diffuse sense of peace and happiness gave way to[12] a pleasure as keen[13] and painful as that of a boy in love for the first time. She saw him at once and, glass in hand, edged her way[14] across the room to him.

Her appearance was wholly[15] unexpected and he did not deceive himself[16] that she was there on his account[17]. After their last encounter that would hardly be likely[18].

He said, 'It's very pleasant to see you here.'

'I should have come anyway,' she replied. 'But actually I work here. Felix Hearne got me the job after Mummy died. I'm quite useful. I'm the general dogsbody[19]. Shorthand and typing[20], too. I took a course.'

He smiled.

'You make it sound like a cure.'

1. mouvementée
2. manteau de cheminée
3. légère
4. soudain
5. foule
6. atténué
7. s'éloigner
8. appuya
9. le rebord de la cheminée
10. il se demanda
11. depuis combien de temps
12. firent place à
13. vif
14. se faufila
15. complètement
16. n'eut pas l'illusion de croire
17. pour lui
18. n'était guère probable
19. la bonne à tout faire
20. sténographie et dactylographie

'Well, in a way it was.'

He did not pretend not to understand. They were both silent. Dalgliesh knew that he was morbidly[1] sensitive to any allusion to the case which nearly three years ago, had led to their first meeting. That sore[2] could not stand[3] even the gentlest of probes[4]. He had seen the announcement of her mother's death in the paper about six months ago, but it had seemed impossible and impertinent then to send her a message or to speak the customary[5] words of condolence. After all, he was partly responsible for her death. It was no easier now. Instead they talked of his verse and of her job. Taking his share of this casual undemanding small talk[6] he wondered what she would say if he asked her to have dinner with him. If she didn't turn him down flat[7] – and she probably would – it could be for him the beginning of involvement. He didn't deceive himself that he only wanted[8] an agreeable meal with a woman he happened to think beautiful. He had no idea what she thought of him, but, ever since their last meeting, he had known himself to be on the brink of love[9]. If she accepted – for this or for any evening – his solitary life would be threatened[10]. He knew this with complete certainty and the knowledge frightened him[11]. Ever since the death of his wife in childbirth he had insulated himself carefully against[12] pain[13]: sex little more than an exercise in skill[14]; a love affair merely an emotional pavan[15], formalized, danced according to the rules, committing[16] one to nothing. But, of course, she wouldn't accept. He had absolutely no reason to think that she was interested in him. It was only this certainty that gave him the confidence to in-

1. de façon malsaine
2. plaie
3. supporter
4. le plus doux des examens
5. habituels
6. tout en échangeant des banalités
7. si elle ne refusait pas tout net
8. il ne prétendait pas avoir seulement envie de
9. à deux doigts de tomber amoureux
10. menacée
11. l'effrayait
12. s'était soigneusement protégé de
13. douleur
14. un exercice technique
15. une simple pavane
16. n'engageant

dulge his thoughts[1]. But he was tempted to try his luck[2]. As they talked he mentally rehearsed[3] the words, wryly amused to recognize[4] after so many years the uncertainties of adolescence.

The light tap on his shoulder took him by surprise. It was the chairman[5]'s secretary to say that he was wanted on the telephone. 'It's the Yard[6], Mr Dalgliesh,' she said, with well-controlled interest as if Hearne and Illingworth's authors were accustomed to calls from the Yard.

He smiled his excuses at Deborah Riscoe and she gave a little resigned shrug of her shoulders[7].

'I won't be a moment[8],' he said. But even as he threaded his way through the crush of chatterers[9] he knew that he wouldn't be back.

He took the call in a small office next to the boardroom[10], struggling to the telephone through chairs heaped with[11] manuscripts, rolled galley proofs[12] and dusty files. Hearne and Illingworth fostered an air of[13] old-fashioned leisureliness[14] and general muddle[15] which concealed[16] – sometimes to their authors' discomfiture[17] – a formidable efficiency and attention to detail.

The familiar voice boomed[18] in his ear.

'That you, Adam? How's the party? Good. Sorry to break it up but I'd be grateful if you'd look in over the way[19]. The Steen Clinic, Number 31. You know the place. Upper-class neuroses catered for only[20]. It seems that their secretary or administrative officer or what have you has got herself murdered. Bashed on the head[21] in the basement and then stabbed expertly through the heart. The boys are on their way. I've sent you Martin, of course. He'll have your gear[22] with him.'

1. la confiance de laisser libre cours à ses pensées
2. tenter sa chance
3. répétait
4. reconnaissant avec une ironie amusée
5. président
6. Scotland Yard, siège de la police à Londres
7. haussa un peu les épaules d'un air résigné
8. je n'en ai pas pour longtemps
9. la foule de bavards
10. la salle de réunion
11. couvertes de
12. épreuves en placard enroulées
13. adoptaient une apparence de
14. détente
15. désordre
16. cachaient
17. gêne
18. résonna
19. si vous regardiez en face
20. soins réservés aux névroses huppées
21. assommée
22. votre matériel

'Thank you, sir. When was it reported[1]?'

'Three minutes ago. The medical director rang[2]. He gave me a concise account[3] of practically everyone's alibi for the supposed time of death and explained why it couldn't possibly be one of the patients. He was followed by a doctor called Steiner. He explained that we met about five years ago at a dinner party given by his late brother-in-law[4]. Dr Steiner explained why it couldn't have been him and favoured me with[5] his interpretation of the psychological make-up[6] of the killer. They've read all the best detective fiction. No one has touched the body, they're not letting anyone in or out of the building and they've all collected[7] into one room to keep an eye on[8] each other. You'd better hurry over[9], Adam, or they'll solve the crime before you arrive.'

'Who is the medical director?' asked Dalgliesh.

'Dr Henry Etherege. You must have seen him on television. He's the establishment psychiatrist, dedicated to making the profession respectable. Distinguished looking, orthodox and earnest[10].'

'I've seen him in court[11],' said Dalgliesh.

'Of course. Remember him in the Routledge case? He practically had me weeping into my hankie[12] and I knew Routledge better than most. Etherege is the natural choice of any defence counsel[13] – if he can get him. You know their bleat[14]. Find me a psychiatrist who looks respectable, speaks English and won't shock the jury or antagonize the judge[15]. Answer, Etherege. Ah, well, good luck!'

The AC[16] was optimistic in supposing that his message could break up[17] the party. It had long reached the stage when the departure of a solitary

1. signalé
2. a appelé
3. résumé
4. feu son beau-frère
5. m'a fait la faveur de me donner
6. portrait psychologique
7. Ils se sont rassemblés
8. surveiller
9. de vous dépêcher
10. sérieux
11. au tribunal
12. il m'a quasiment fait pleurer dans mon mouchoir
13. tout avocat de la défense
14. leurs jérémiades
15. ne se mettra pas le juge à dos
16. préfet de police adjoint
17. interrompre

guest disconcerted no one. Dalgliesh thanked his host, waved a casual goodbye[1] to the few people who caught his eye[2] and passed almost unnoticed out of the building. He did not see Deborah Riscoe again, and made no effort to find her. His mind was already on the job ahead and he felt that he had been saved, at best from a snub[3] and, at worst, from folly[4]. It had been a brief, tantalizing[5], inconclusive[6] and unsettling[7] encounter but, already, it was in the past.

Walking across the square to the tall Georgian building[8] that housed the Steen Clinic, Dalgliesh recalled some of the scant items of information[9] about the place that had come his way. It was a well-known witticism[10] that you had to be exceptionally sane to be accepted for treatment at the Steen. Certainly it had a reputation – Dalgliesh thought probably undeserved[11] – for selecting its patients with more regard to their intelligence and social class than their mental condition, subjecting them to diagnostic procedures designed to deter[12] all but the most enthusiastic, and then placing them on a waiting list for treatment long enough to ensure that the curative effects of time could exert their maximum influence before the patient actually attended for his first psychotherapy session. The Steen, Dalgliesh remembered, had a Modigliani. It was not a well-known painting, nor did it represent the artist at his best, but it was, undeniably[13], a Modigliani. It hung[14] in the first-floor boardroom[15], the gift[16] of a former[17] grateful[18] patient, and it represented much that the clinic stood for[19] in the public eye. Other National Health Service clinics brightened their walls with reproductions from the Red

1. fit rapidement au revoir de la main
2. qui se trouvaient dans son champ de vision
3. une rebuffade
4. une sottise
5. excitante
6. peu concluante
7. troublante
8. immeuble de style géorgien (1714-1830)
9. le peu d'information
10. bon mot
11. imméritée
12. dissuader
13. indéniablement
14. était accroché
15. salle de réunion
16. cadeau
17. ancien
18. reconnaissant
19. représentait

Cross picture library. The Steen staff made no secret that they preferred a second-rate[1] original to a first-class reproduction any day. And they had a second-rate original to prove it.

The house itself was one of a Georgian terrace[2]. It stood at the south corner of the square, comfortable, unpretentious and wholly[3] pleasing. At the rear[4] a narrow[5] passage ran into Lincoln Square Mews. There was a railed[6] basement; in front of the house the railings curved[7] on each side of the broad steps[8] which led to the door and supported two wrought-iron[9] lamp standards[10]. On the right of the door an unpretentious bronze plaque bore[11] the name of the Hospital Management Committee which administered the unit and, underneath[12], the words, 'The Steen Clinic.' No other information was given. The Steen did not advertise its function to a vulgar world nor did it wish to invite an influx[13] of the local psychotics seeking[14] treatment or reassurance. There were four cars parked outside but no signs yet of the police. The house looked very quiet. The door was shut but a light shone from the elegant Adam fanlight[15] above[16] the door and between the folds of drawn curtains[17] in the ground-floor rooms.

The door was opened almost before he had taken his finger from the bell. They had been waiting for him. A stockily built[18] young man in porter's uniform opened the door and let him in without speaking. The hall blazed with light and struck very warm after the coolness of the autumn night. To the left of the door was a glass-panelled reception kiosk[19] with a telephone switchboard[20]. A second, and much older, porter sat at the board in

1. de second choix
2. rangée de maisons
3. tout à fait
4. à l'arrière
5. étroit
6. clôturé
7. la grille s'incurvait
8. des larges marches
9. en fer forgé
10. lampadaires
11. portait
12. en dessous
13. afflux
14. recherchant
15. l'élégante imposte semi-circulaire
16. au-dessus de
17. entre les plis des rideaux
18. trapu
19. une réception en panneaux de verre
20. standard téléphonique

an attitude of utter misery. He looked round and glanced briefly at[1] Dalgliesh with rheumy[2] eyes, then returned to his contemplation of the board as if the arrival of the superintendent was the last straw of an intolerable burden[3] which, if ignored, might be lifted from him. In the main body[4] of the hall the reception committee[5] came forward, the medical director with outstretched[6] hand as if welcoming a guest. 'Superintendent Dalgliesh? We're very glad to see you. May I introduce my colleague, Dr James Baguley, and the secretary of the Hospital Management Committee, Mr Lauder.'

'You got here very promptly[7], sir,' said Dalgliesh to Lauder. The group secretary said:

'I didn't know about the murder until I arrived two minutes ago. Miss Bolam telephoned me at lunchtime today and said she wanted to see me urgently. Something was going on at the clinic and she needed advice[8]. I came as soon as I could and found that she'd been murdered. In the circumstances, I had more reasons than one for deciding to stay around[9]. It looks as if[10] she needed advice more than she knew.'

'Whatever it was, you've come too late, I'm afraid,' said Dr Etherege.

Dalgliesh saw that he was much shorter than his television appearances suggested. His large, high-domed[11] head with its aureole of white hair soft and fine as a baby's looked too weighty[12] for the slight[13] supporting body which seemed to have aged independently giving him an oddly disintegrated appearance[14]. It was difficult to guess[15] his age but Dalgliesh thought that he must be nearer seventy than sixty-five, the normal retiring age[16]

1. jeta un bref coup d'œil à
2. chassieux
3. fardeau
4. la partie principale
5. le comité d'accueil
6. tendue
7. rapidement
8. un conseil
9. rester
10. on dirait que
11. bombée
12. lourde
13. mince
14. apparence étrangement hétéroclite
15. deviner
16. âge de la retraite

for a consultant. He had the face of an indestructible gnome, the cheeks mottled[1] with high colour so that they looked painted, the eyebrows[2] springing above eyes of a piercing blue. Dalgliesh felt that those eyes and the soft, persuasive voice were not the least of the medical director's professional assets[3].

In contrast, Dr James Baguley was six feet tall, nearly as tall as Dalgliesh, and the immediate impression he gave was of intense weariness[4]. He was wearing a long white coat[5] which hung loosely[6] from his bowed shoulders[7]. Although he was much the younger man he had none of the medical director's vitality. His hair was straight[8] and turning iron-grey. From time to time he swept it out of his eyes[9] with long nicotine-stained[10] fingers. His was a handsome, bony[11] face, but the skin and eyes were dulled[12] as if with permanent tiredness[13].

The medical director said:

'You will, of course, want to see the body straight away[14]. I'll ask Peter Nagle, our second porter, to come down with us if you've no objection. His chisel was one of the weapons used – not that he could help that[15], poor fellow – and no doubt you will want to ask him questions.'

'I shall want to question everyone here in due course[16],' replied Dalgliesh.

It was apparent that the medical director had taken charge[17]. Dr Baguley, who had not yet spoken, seemed glad to accept that position. Lauder had apparently decided to adopt a watching brief[18]. As they moved towards the basement stairs at the back of the hall he caught Dalgliesh's eye. The momentary glance[19] was hard to analyse, but Dalgliesh

1. joues marbrées
2. sourcils
3. atouts
4. lassitude
5. blouse
6. pendait lâchement
7. dos courbé
8. raides
9. écartait les mèches tombant devant ses yeux
10. jaunis par la nicotine
11. osseux
12. ternis
13. fatigue
14. tout de suite
15. il n'y est pour rien
16. en temps voulu
17. avait pris les choses en main
18. jouer un rôle d'observateur
19. coup d'œil

thought he detected an amused gleam[1] and a certain wry detachment[2].

They stood in silence as Dalgliesh knelt by the body. He did not touch it except to part the cardigan and blouse, both of which were unbuttoned, and expose the handle of the chisel. It had been driven in up to the hilt[3]. There was very little bruising[4] of the tissues and no blood. The woman's vest[5] had been rolled up[6] above her breasts[7] to expose the flesh for that vicious[8], calculated thrust[9]. Such deliberation suggested that the killer had a confident knowledge of anatomy. There were easier ways of killing than to pierce the heart with one thrust. But for those with the knowledge and the strength there were few ways so sure.

He got to his feet[10] and turned to Peter Nagle.

'Is that your chisel?'

'Apparently. It looks like[11] it and mine isn't in the box.' Despite[12] the omission of the usual 'sir' the voice, educated and unemphatic, held no trace of insolence or resentment. Dalgliesh asked:

'Any idea how it got here?'

'None at all. But I'd hardly be likely to say if I had[13], would I?'

The medical director gave Nagle a quick frown of warning or admonition[14] and placed his hand briefly on the porter's shoulder[15]. Without consulting Dalgliesh he said gently:

'That will be all for the present[16], Nagle. Just wait outside, will you?'

Dalgliesh made no demur[17] as the porter quietly detached himself from the group and left without another word.

1. une lueur d'amusement

2. un certain détachement ironique

3. enfoncé jusqu'au manche

4. très peu d'ecchymoses

5. maillot de corps

6. enroulé

7. seins

8. pervers

9. coup

10. se releva

11. ressemble

12. malgré

13. et même si je savais, il y aurait peu de chances que je le dise

14. fronça brièvement les sourcils pour avertir ou réprimander Nagel

15. épaule

16. pour le moment

17. n'opposa pas d'objection

'Poor boy! The use of his chisel has naturally shocked him. It looks unpleasantly like an attempt[1] to implicate him. But you will find, Superintendent, that Nagle is one of the few members of the staff with a complete alibi for the presumed time of death.' Dalgliesh did not point out[2] that this was, in itself, highly[3] suspicious.

'Did you make any estimate of the time of death?' he asked.

Dr Etherege replied:

'I thought that it must have been very recent. That is Dr Baguley's view[4] too. The clinic is very warm today – we've just started our central heating – so that the body would cool[5] very slowly. I didn't try for rigor.[6] I am, of course, little more than a layman[7] in such matters[8]. Subsequently[9] I knew that she must have died within the hour[10]. Naturally we have been talking among ourselves[11] while waiting for you and it appears that Sister Ambrose was the last person to see Miss Bolam alive. That was at twenty past six. Cully, our senior porter, tells me that Miss Bolam rang him on the internal phone at about six-fifteen to say that she was going down to the basement and that Mr Lauder should be directed to her office if he arrived. A few minutes later, as far as she can judge[12], Sister came out of the ECT[13] room on the ground floor and crossed[14] the hall to the patients' waiting-room to let a husband know that his wife was ready to be taken home. Sister saw Miss Bolam going down the hall towards the basement stairs. No one saw her alive again after that.'

'Except her murderer,' said Dalgliesh.

Dr Etherege looked surprised.

1. une tentative
2. ne fit pas remarquer
3. extrêmement
4. opinion
5. se refroidir
6. testé sa rigidité cadavérique
7. un profane
8. en la matière
9. par la suite
10. il y a moins d'une heure
11. entre nous
12. pour autant qu'elle puisse en juger
13. traitement par électrochocs
14. a traversé

'Yes, that would be so, of course. I mean that none of us saw her alive again. I have asked Sister Ambrose about the time and Sister is quite sure ...'

'I shall be seeing Sister Ambrose and the other porter.'

'Of course. Naturally you will want to see everybody. We expect that. While waiting we telephoned our homes to say that we would be delayed[1] tonight but gave no explanation[2]. We had already searched[3] the building and ascertained that[4] the basement door and the ground-floor rear[5] entrance were both bolted[6]. Nothing has been touched in here naturally. I arranged for[7] the staff to stay together in the front[8] consulting-room except for Sister and Nurse Bolam who were with the remaining[9] patients in the waiting-room. No one but Mr Lauder and you have been allowed in[10].'

'You seem to have thought of everything, Doctor,' said Dalgliesh. He got up from his knees and stood looking down at the body.

'Who found her?' he asked.

'One of our medical secretaries, Jennifer Priddy. Cully, the senior porter, has been complaining of[11] stomach-ache[12] most of the day and Miss Priddy went to find Miss Bolam to ask if he could go home early. Miss Priddy is very upset[13] but she was able to tell me[14] ...'

'I think it would be better if I heard it from her direct. Was this door kept locked[15]?'

His tone was perfectly courteous but he felt their surprise. The medical director's tone did not change as he replied:

1. retardés

2. nous n'avons pas donné d'explication

3. fouillé

4. nous nous sommes assurés que

5. arrière

6. fermées à clé

7. j'ai donné des ordres pour que

8. de devant

9. derniers

10. personne n'est entré à part vous et Mr Lauder

11. s'est plaint de

12. maux de ventre

13. bouleversée

14. elle a pu me dire

15. fermée à clé

'Usually it is. The key is kept on a board[1] with other clinic keys in the porters' duty-room[2] here in the basement. The chisel was kept there, too.'

'And this fetish?'

'Taken from the basement art therapy room across[3] the passage. It was carved[4] by one of our patients.'

It was still the medical director who replied. So far Dr Baguley hadn't spoken a word. Suddenly he said:

'She was knocked out[5] with the fetish and then stabbed[6] through the heart by someone who was either knowledgeable[7] or damned lucky[8]. That much is obvious. What isn't obvious is why they had this free-for-all[9] with the medical records[10]. She's lying on them[11] so it must have happened before the murder.'

'The result of a struggle[12], perhaps,' suggested Dr Etherege.

'It doesn't look like it. They were pulled out[13] of the shelves[14] and deliberately chucked about[15]. There must have been a reason. There wasn't anything impulsive about this murder.'

It was then that Peter Nagle, who had apparently been standing outside the door, came into the room.

'There's been a ring at the door, sir. Would that be the rest of the police?'

Dalgliesh noted that the record-room was almost[16] sound-proof[17]. The front-door bell was strident but he had not heard it.

'Right,' he said. 'We'll go up.'

As they moved together towards the stairs Dr Etherege said:

1. accrochée à un tableau
2. salle de permanence
3. de l'autre côté de
4. sculpté
5. assommée
6. poignardée
7. expert
8. sacrément chanceux
9. cette mêlée
10. dossiers médicaux
11. sur les dossiers
12. une lutte
13. tirés
14. casiers
15. éparpillés
16. presque totalement
17. insonorisée

'I wonder[1], Superintendent, if you could see the patients fairly soon[2]. We have only two still[3] with us, a male psychotherapy patient of my colleague Dr Steiner, and a woman who has been receiving lysergic acid treatment down here in the basement front treatment-room. Dr Baguley will be able to explain the treatment to you – she is his patient – but you can be assured that she wasn't capable of leaving her bed until a few minutes ago and certainly wouldn't know anything about the murder. These patients become quite disorientated during treatment. Nurse Bolam was with her all the evening.'

'Nurse Bolam? She is a relation of[4] the dead woman?'

'Her cousin,' said Dr Baguley briefly.

'And your disorientated patient, Doctor. Would she know if Nurse Bolam left her alone during treatment?'

Dr Baguley said curtly[5]:

'Nurse Bolam would not have left her.'

They mounted[6] the stairs together to meet the murmur of voices in the hall.

That ring at the door brought[7] into the Steen Clinic the paraphernalia[8] and skills[9] of an alien world[10]. Quietly and without fuss[11] the experts in violent death got busy[12]. Dalgliesh disappeared into the record-room with the police surgeon[13] and photographer. The print man[14], small and plump-cheeked[15] as a hamster, with tiny[16] delicate hands, gave his attention to door handles, locks[17], the tool case[18] and Tippett's fetish. Plain-clothes[19] men, looking disconcertingly[20] like television actors playing plainclothes men, made their methodical

1. je me demande
2. assez rapidement
3. encore
4. a-t-elle un lien de parenté avec
5. sèchement
6. montèrent
7. introduisit
8. l'attirail
9. les techniques
10. monde inconnu
11. discrètement
12. se mirent au travail
13. le médecin de la police
14. le spécialiste des empreintes digitales
15. joufflu
16. minuscules
17. serrures
18. boîte à outils
19. en civil
20. d'une manière déconcertante

search of every room and cupboard[1] in the clinic verifying that there was indeed no unauthorized person on the premises[2] and that the back doors both of the ground floor and the basement were securely locked from the inside. The clinic staff, excluded from these activities and congregated[3] in the front ground-floor consulting-room, which had been hastily[4] furnished with additional easy chairs[5] from the patients' waiting-room, felt that their familiar ground had been taken over by strangers and that they were caught up in the inexorable machinery of justice and being ground forward to God knew what embarrassments and disasters. Only the group secretary appeared unperturbed. He had stationed himself in the hall like a watchdog[6] and sat there patient and alone until his turn came to be interviewed.

Dalgliesh took Miss Bolam's office for his use. It was a small room on the ground floor situated between the large general office at the front of the building and the ECT treatment-room and recovery-room at the rear. Opposite it was a suite of two consulting-rooms and the patients' waiting-room. The office had been formed by partitioning[7] the end of a larger room so that it was oddly proportioned[8] and unattractively narrow for its height[9]. It was sparsely furnished[10] and lacked all evidence of personal taste[11] except for a large bowl[12] of chrysanthemums set on one of the filing cabinets. There was an old-fashioned safe[13] against one wall and the other was lined[14] with green metal filing cabinets. The desk was unostentatious[15] and held nothing but[16] a stationery office[17] desk calendar, a jotting pad[18] and a small stack[19] of manilla folders.

1. placard
2. sur les lieux
3. se rassembla
4. précipitamment
5. fauteuils
6. chien de garde
7. en cloisonnant
8. avait des dimensions étranges
9. hauteur
10. contenait peu de meubles
11. ne disposait d'aucune touche personnelle
12. vase
13. coffre
14. aligné
15. sobre
16. rien que
17. de l'imprimerie nationale
18. bloc-notes
19. pile

Dalgliesh looked through them[1] and said, 'This is odd[2]. These are staff dossiers apparently, but only of the female staff. Her own isn't here incidentally. I wonder why she got these out?'

'Checking on people's annual leave entitlement[3] or something like that perhaps,' suggested Sergeant Martin.

'Could be, I suppose. But why only the women? Oh well, it's hardly of[4] immediate importance. Let's have a look at that jotter[5].'

Miss Bolam was apparently one of those administrators who prefer not to trust to memory. The top leaf[6] of the jotter, headed with the date, was well filled with notes in a sloping[7], rather childish handwriting.

Medical Committee – speak MD[8] re[9] proposed Adolescent Dept.

Speak Nagle – broken sash cord[10] Miss Kallinski's room.

Mrs Shorthouse –? leave[11].

These notes were at least self-explanatory but the jottings[12] below them[13] – written it appeared in some hurry[14] – were less explicit.

Woman. Here eight years. To arrive 1st Monday.

Dalgliesh said: 'These look like the jottings of a telephone call. It could have been a private call, of course, and nothing to do with the clinic. It could have been a doctor trying to trace[15] a patient, or vice versa. Something, or someone, is apparently expected to arrive on the first Monday or on Monday the first. There are a dozen possible interpretations and none of them relevant to the murder. Still, someone phoned recently about a woman and Miss Bolam was obviously examining the dossiers

1. les feuilleta
2. bizarre
3. congés annuels
4. ça n'a pas de
5. bloc-notes
6. la première feuille
7. penchée
8. médecins
9. au sujet de
10. cordon de fenêtre
11. congé
12. notes
13. en dessous
14. à la hâte
15. retrouver les traces de

of every woman on the staff except herself. Why? To check which of them were here eight years ago? It's all pretty farfetched[1]. We'll leave the pleasures of conjecture for the moment and get down to seeing these people. I'd like that typist in first, the girl who found the body. Etherege said she was upset. Let's hope she's calmed down by now or we'll be here half the night.'

But Jennifer Priddy was perfectly calm. She had obviously been drinking and her grief[2] was overlaid with[3] a barely suppressed excitement[4]. Her face, still swollen[5] from crying, was blotched with high colour[6] and her eyes were unnaturally bright[7]. But the drink had not fuddled her[8] and she told her story well. She had been busy in the ground-floor general office for most of the evening and had last seen Miss Bolam at about five-forty-five when she had gone into the AO's office[9] with a query[10] about a patient's appointment[11]. Miss Bolam had seemed the same as usual to her. She had returned to the general office and had been joined[12] by Peter Nagle at about six-ten[13]. He was wearing his coat and had come to collect[14] the outgoing post[15]. Miss Priddy had registered the last few letters in the post book and handed them to him[16]. At about quarter or twenty past six Mrs Shorthouse had joined them. Mrs Shorthouse had mentioned that she had just come from Miss Bolam's office where she had been settling[17] a query about her annual leave entitlement. Peter Nagle had gone out with the post and she and Mrs Shorthouse had stayed together until his return some ten minutes later. Nagle had then gone down to the basement porters' room to hang up[18] his coat and feed[19] Tigger, the office cat,

1. tiré par les cheveux
2. chagrin
3. était occulté par
4. une excitation à peine dissimulée
5. enflé
6. écarlate
7. brillants
8. ne lui avait pas fait perdre la tête
9. le bureau du responsable administratif
10. question
11. rendez-vous
12. rejointe
13. six heures dix
14. était venu chercher
15. courrier sortant
16. les lui avait données
17. elle avait réglé
18. suspendre
19. donner à manger à

and she had followed him down almost immediately. She had helped him feed Tigger and they had returned to the general office together. At about seven the senior porter, Cully, complained again about his stomach-ache[1] which had been troubling him all day. Miss Priddy, Mrs Bostock, the other medical secretary, and Peter Nagle had all had to take Cully's place at the switchboard[2] from time to time[3] because of his stomach-ache, but he had refused to go home. Now he was willing to[4] go and Miss Priddy had gone to the AO's office to ask Miss Bolam if he could leave early. Miss Bolam wasn't in her office so she had looked in the nurses' duty-room[5] on the ground floor. Sister Ambrose told her that she had seen the AO passing down the hall towards the basement stairs about thirty minutes or so earlier, so Miss Priddy had looked in the basement. The record-room was usually kept locked but the key was in the lock and the door just ajar[6], so she had looked inside. The light was on[7]. She had found the body – here Miss Priddy's voice faltered[8] – and had rushed[9] upstairs at once to get help. No, she hadn't touched anything. She didn't know why the medical records were strewn around[10]. She didn't know how she had known that Miss Bolam was dead. It was just that Miss Bolam had looked so very dead. She didn't know why she had been so sure it was murder. She thought she had seen a bruise[11] on Miss Bolam's head. And, then, there had been Tippett's fetish lying on the body. She was afraid that Tippett was hiding among the record racks[12] and would jump out at her[13]. Everyone said that he wasn't dangerous – at least everyone except Dr Steiner – but he had been in a mental

1. maux d'estomac
2. standard
3. de temps à autre
4. était disposé à
5. salle de permanence
6. entrouverte
7. allumée
8. faiblit
9. s'était précipitée
10. jonchaient le sol
11. contusion
12. casiers
13. se jetât sur elle

hospital[1] and, after all, you couldn't be really sure, could you? No, she hadn't known that Tippett wasn't in the clinic. Peter Nagle had taken the call from the hospital and had told Miss Bolam but he hadn't told her. She hadn't seen the chisel in Miss Bolam's chest[2] but Dr Etherege had told the staff about the stabbing[3] when they were gathered together[4] in the front consulting-room waiting for the police. She thought that most of the staff knew where Peter Nagle kept his tools[5] and also which key opened the door of the basement record-room. It hung on hook[6] number 12 and was shinier[7] than the other keys, but it wasn't labelled[8]. Dalgliesh said:

'I want you to think very hard and very carefully. When you went downstairs to help Mr Nagle feed the cat was the record-room door ajar and the light on as it was when you went down later and found Miss Bolam?'

The girl pushed back[9] her dank[10] blonde hair and said with sudden weariness[11]:

'I ... I can't remember. I didn't go past[12] that door you see. I went straight[13] into the porters' room at the bottom of the stairs. Peter was there clearing up[14] Tigger's plate. He hadn't eaten all of his last meal so we scraped it off his plate[15] and washed it at the sink[16]. We didn't go near the record-room.'

'But you could see the door as you came down the stairs. Would you be likely to notice if the door were ajar?[17] The room isn't often used, is it?'

'No, but anyone might go there if they wanted a record. I mean, if the door were open I wouldn't go to see who was there or anything like that. I think I would notice if the door was wide open[18]

1. hôpital psychiatrique
2. poitrine
3. qu'on l'avait poignardée
4. étaient rassemblés
5. outils
6. crochet
7. plus brillante
8. étiquetée
9. repoussa
10. humide
11. fatigue
12. je ne suis pas passée devant
13. directement
14. en train de nettoyer
15. nous avons raclé son assiette
16. évier
17. croyez-vous que vous auriez remarqué si la porte était entrouverte ?
18. grande ouverte

so I suppose it wasn't, but I can't remember, honestly I can't.'

Dalgliesh ended by asking her about Miss Bolam. It appeared that Miss Priddy knew her outside the clinic, that the Priddy family attended[1] the same church and that Miss Bolam had encouraged her to take the job at the clinic.

'I shouldn't have got[2] this job if it hadn't been for Enid. Of course, I never called her that inside the clinic. She wouldn't have liked it.' Miss Priddy gave the impression that she had only reluctantly[3] brought herself to use the Christian name[4] outside the clinic. She went on[5]: 'I don't mean she actually appointed me[6]. I had to be interviewed by Mr Lauder and by Dr Etherege, but I know she spoke up for me[7]. My shorthand[8] and typing[9] weren't very good then – it was nearly two years ago when I came – and I was lucky to get here. I didn't see very much of Enid at the clinic but she was always very kind and keen for me to get on[10]. She wanted me to take the Institute of Hospital Administration Diploma so that I needn't be a shorthand typist[11] all my life.'

This ambition for Miss Priddy's future career struck Dalgliesh as a little odd[12]. The child gave no impression of being ambitious and she would surely marry in time[13]. It hardly[14] needed the Institute's diploma, whatever that might be, to save her from being a shorthand typist for life. He felt a little sorry for Miss Bolam who could scarcely[15] have picked[16] a less promising[17] protégée. She was pretty, honest and naïve, but not, he thought, particularly intelligent. He had to remind himself that she had given her age as twenty-two not seventeen.

1. fréquentait
2. je n'aurais pas eu
3. à contrecœur
4. prénom
5. continua
6. m'a nommée
7. a parlé en ma faveur
8. sténo
9. dactylographie
10. tenait à ce que je continue
11. sténodactylo
12. lui sembla un peu étrange
13. le moment venu
14. guère
15. à peine
16. pu choisir
17. moins prometteuse

She had a shapely[1] and oddly mature body, but her thin[2] face with its frame[3] of long, straight[4] hair was the face of a child.

There was little she could tell him about the administrative officer. She hadn't noticed any change recently in Miss Bolam. She didn't know that the AO had sent for Mr Lauder and had no idea what could be worrying[5] Miss Bolam at the clinic. Everything was going on very much as usual. Miss Bolam had no enemies as far as she knew[6], certainly no one who would wish to kill her.

'She was happy here, then, as far as you know? I was wondering whether[7] she had asked for a move[8]. A psychiatric clinic can't be the easiest unit to administer.'

'Oh, it isn't! I don't know how Enid carried on[9] sometimes. But I'm sure she would never ask for a move. Someone must have given you the wrong impression. She was never one to give up[10]. If she thought people wanted her to go she'd dig her toes in[11]. The clinic was a kind of challenge to her.'

It was probably the most illuminating thing she had said about Miss Bolam. As he thanked her and asked her to wait with the rest of the staff until his preliminary interviews were over, Dalgliesh pondered on the possible nuisance value of[12] an administrator who regarded her job as a challenge, a battleground[13] from which she would never willingly retreat[14]. He asked next to see Peter Nagle.

If the junior porter was worried by the killer's choice of his chisel as a weapon he gave no sign. He answered Dalgliesh's questions calmly and politely, but so dispassionately[15] that they might have been discussing some minor point of clinic procedure

1. bien fait
2. mince
3. cadre
4. raides
5. inquiéter
6. autant qu'elle sache
7. si
8. demandé à être mutée
9. s'en sortait
10. abandonner
11. se serait braquée
12. médita sur le fléau que pouvait représenter
13. champ de bataille
14. battre en retraite de son plein gré
15. froidement

which was only doubtfully his concern.[1] He gave his age as twenty-seven and an address in Pimlico[2] and confirmed that he had been employed at the clinic for just over two years and was previously at a provincial art school. His voice was level[3] and educated[4], his mud-brown eyes were large, almost expressionless. Dalgliesh noticed that he had unusually long arms which, held loosely from[5] his short and powerful body, gave an impression of simian strength[6]. His hair was black, coiling tightly over the scalp[7]. It was an interesting face, withdrawn[8] but intelligent. There could scarcely have been[9] a greater contrast with poor old Cully, long since despatched home[10] to nurse[11] both his stomach-ache and his grievance at being kept late[12].

Nagle confirmed Miss Priddy's story. He again identified his chisel with no more emotion than a brief moue of distaste[13] and said that he had last seen it at eight o'clock that morning when he had arrived on duty[14] and – for no particular reason – had made a check of[15] his toolbox. Everything was in order then. Dalgliesh asked whether it was generally known where the box was kept. Nagle replied:

'I'd be a fool[16] if I said no, wouldn't I?'

'You'd be a fool to say anything but the truth[17] now or later.'

'I suppose most of the staff knew. Those who didn't could find out[18] easily enough. We don't keep the porters' room locked.'

'Isn't that rather unwise[19]? What about the patients?'

'They don't go down to the basement on their own[20]. The lysergic acid patients are always escorted

1. qui ne le concernait que de très loin
2. quartier résidentiel de Londres faisant partie de la cité de Westminster
3. posée
4. cultivée
5. pendaient le long de
6. d'être fort comme un singe
7. frisés
8. renfermée
9. il n'y aurait pas pu y avoir
10. qui avait été renvoyé chez lui depuis un moment
11. soigner
12. mécontentement d'avoir été retenu si tard
13. dégoût
14. pris son service
15. vérifié le contenu de
16. stupide
17. autre chose que la vérité
18. le découvrir
19. imprudent
20. seuls

and the art therapy people usually have someone keeping an eye on them[1]. The department hasn't been down there for long[2]. The light's bad and it isn't really suitable[3]. It's a temporary department.'

'Where used it to be, then?[4]'

'On the third floor. Then the clinic Medical Committee decided they wanted the large room there for the marital[5] problems discussion groups, so Mrs Baumgarten – she's the art therapist – lost it. She's been agitating to get it back[6], but the MPD[7] patients say it would be psychologically disturbing for them to meet in the basement.'

'Who runs[8] the MPD?'

'Dr Steiner and one of the psychiatric social workers[9], Miss Kallinski. It's a club where the divorced and the single[10] tell the patients how to be happy though married[11]. I don't see how it can concern the murder.'

'Nor do I[12]. I asked about it to satisfy my curiosity as to why the art therapy department was so unsuitably[13] housed. When did you hear that Tippett wasn't attending today by the way[14]?'

'At about nine o'clock this morning. The old boy had been worrying[15] St Luke's Hospital to telephone and let us know what had happened. So they did. I told Miss Bolam and Sister.'

'Anyone else?'

'I think I mentioned it[16] to Cully when he came back on the board[17]. He's had a belly-ache[18] for most of the day[19].'

'So I'm told[20]. What's wrong with him?[21]'

'Cully? Miss Bolam made him go to hospital for an examination but nothing was found. He gets these

1. qui les surveille
2. depuis longtemps
3. appropriée
4. où se trouvait-il, avant ?
5. conjugaux
6. elle a fait campagne pour le récupérer
7. marital problems discussion
8. dirige
9. assistantes sociales
10. les célibataires
11. tout en étant mariés
12. moi non plus
13. de manière si peu appropriée
14. à propos
15. tourmentait
16. j'en ai parlé
17. standard
18. mal au ventre
19. presque toute la journée
20. c'est ce qu'on m'a dit
21. qu'est-ce qu'il a ?

belly-aches if anyone upsets him[1]. They say here it's psychosomatic.'

'What upset him this morning?'

'I did. He got here before me this morning and started sorting the post[2]. That's my job. I told him to concentrate on his own work.'

Dalgliesh took him patiently over the events of the evening. His story agreed[3] with Miss Priddy's and, like her, he was unable to say whether the door of the basement record-room had been ajar when he returned from posting the letters. He admitted that he had passed the door when he went to ask Nurse Bolam if the laundry[4] was sorted[5]. It was usual for the door to be closed as the room was seldom[6] visited and he thought he would have noticed had it been open[7]. It was frustrating and maddening[8] that this crucial point could not be cleared up[9], but Nagle stood firm[10]. He hadn't noticed. He couldn't say. He hadn't noticed, either[11], whether the record-room key was on the board in the porters' rest-room. This was easier to understand. There were twenty-two hooks on the board and most of the keys were in use and missing[12]. Dalgliesh said:

'You realize that Miss Bolam's body was almost certainly lying in the record-room when you and Miss Priddy were together feeding the cat? You realize how important it is to remember whether the door was open or shut[13]?'

'It was ajar when Jenny Priddy went down later. That's what she says and she's no liar[14]. If it was shut when I got back from the post someone must have opened it between six-twenty-five and seven. I don't see what's so impossible about that. It would

1. l'énerve
2. trier le courrier
3. concordait
4. le linge
5. trié
6. rarement
7. si elle avait été ouverte
8. exaspérant
9. éclairci
10. ne revint pas sur sa position
11. non plus
12. ne se trouvaient pas sur les crochets
13. fermée
14. menteuse

be better for me if I could remember about the door, but I can't. I hung up[1] my coat in my locker[2], went straight to ask Nurse Bolam about the clean laundry, and then returned to the rest-room. Jenny met me at the bottom of the stairs.'

He spoke without heat[3], almost unemotionally[4]. It was as if[5] he said, 'That's what happened. Like it or not[6], it happened that way[7].' He was too intelligent not to see that he was in some danger. Perhaps he was also intelligent enough to know that the danger was minimal to an innocent man who kept his head[8] and told the truth[9].

Dalgliesh told him to let the police know at once if he remembered anything fresh and let him go.

Sister Ambrose was seen next. She strutted into[10] the room, armour-plated in white linen[11], belligerent as a battleship[12]. The bib[13] of her apron[14], starched rigid as a board[15], curved against a formidable bosom[16] on which she wore[17] her nursing badges like medals of war. Grey hair spurted from each side of her cap[18] which she wore low on her forehead above a face of uncompromising plainness[19]. Her colour was high; Dalgliesh thought that she was finding it difficult to control her resentment and distrust[20]. He dealt with her gently[21], but his questions were answered in an atmosphere of rigid disapproval. She confirmed briefly that she had last seen Miss Bolam walking through the hall towards the basement stairs at about twenty past six. They had not spoken and the administrative officer had looked the same as usual. Sister Ambrose was back in the ECT room before Miss Bolam was out of sight[22] and had been there with Dr Ingram until the body was found. In reply to Dalgliesh's ques-

1. j'ai suspendu
2. casier
3. chaleur
4. sans émotion
5. comme si
6. que vous le vouliez ou non
7. ainsi
8. qui gardait la tête froide
9. vérité
10. entra en se pavanant dans
11. vêtue d'une armure de linge blanc
12. belliqueuse comme un cuirassé
13. bavette
14. tablier
15. que l'amidon avait rendu dur comme une planche
16. une redoutable poitrine
17. elle portait
18. des mèches grises s'échappaient de sa coiffe
19. un visage parfaitement quelconque
20. méfiance
21. il la traita avec ménagement
22. ait disparu de sa vue

tion whether Dr Baguley had also been with them for the whole of that time[1], Sister Ambrose suggested that he should ask the doctor direct. Dalgliesh replied mildly[2] that this was his intention. He knew that the Sister could give him a great deal of useful information about the clinic if she chose[3] but, apart from a few questions about Miss Bolam's personal relationships from which he gained nothing[4], he did not press her[5]. He thought that she was probably more shocked by the murder, by the calculated violence of Miss Bolam's death, than anyone he had yet seen. As sometimes happens with unimaginative and inarticulate[6] people, this shock gave vent to ill-temper[7]. She was very cross[8]: with Dalgliesh because his job gave him the right to ask impertinent and embarrassing questions; with herself because she could not conceal[9] her feelings; with the victim, even[10], who had involved the clinic in this bizarre predicament[11]. It was a reaction Dalgliesh had met before and no good came of trying to force co-operation on such a witness[12]. Later on[13] Sister Ambrose might be induced to[14] talk more freely; at present, it was a waste of time to do more than elicit[15] the facts which she was prepared to give. One fact at least was crucial. Miss Bolam was alive and making her way towards the basement stairs at about twenty past six. At seven o'clock her body was discovered. Those forty minutes were vital and any member of the staff who could produce an alibi covering them could be eliminated from the inquiry[16]. On the face of it[17] the case presented little difficulty. Dalgliesh did not believe that an outsider[18] had somehow gained access[19] to the clinic and lain in wait for[20] Miss Bolam. The killer was

1. pendant tout ce temps
2. avec douceur
3. si elle voulait
4. qui ne lui apprirent rien
5. il n'insista pas
6. dépourvus d'imagination et qui ont du mal à s'exprimer
7. avait fait éclater sa mauvaise humeur
8. très en colère
9. cacher
10. même
11. situation
12. témoin
13. plus tard
14. persuadée de
15. obtenir
16. enquête
17. à première vue
18. une personne étrangère à la clinique
19. avait réussi à entrer dans
20. avait guetté l'arrivée de

almost certainly still in the building. It was now a matter of careful questioning[1], of the methodical checking of alibis, of the seeking out[2] of a motive[3]. Dalgliesh decided to talk to the one man whose alibi appeared unassailable[4] and who would have the detached, outsider's view of the clinic and its varied personalities. He thanked Sister Ambrose for her valuable cooperation – a flicker[5] of the eyes behind the steel-rimmed spectacles[6] suggested that the irony was not lost on her[7] – and asked the constable[8] at the door to send in Mr Lauder.

1. interrogatoires
2. la recherche
3. mobile
4. imprenable
5. lueur
6. lunettes à monture d'acier
7. l'ironie de ces remerciements ne lui avait pas échappé
8. agent de police

CHAPTER TWO

It was the first chance[1] Dalgliesh had had to observe the group secretary closely[2]. He saw a thickset[3], chubby-featured[4] man, mild-eyed[5] behind the heavy square[6] spectacles, who looked, in his well-cut[7] tweeds, more like a country doctor or small-town solicitor[8] than a bureaucrat. He was completely at ease[9] and bore himself[10] like a man confident of[11] his powers, unwilling to[12] be hurried[13], keeping always something in reserve, including, Dalgliesh thought, a keener intelligence[14] than his appearance might suggest.

He seated himself opposite[15] Dalgliesh, drew his chair comfortably forward and, without either apology or excuse[16], took a pipe from one pocket and sought[17] in the other for his tobacco pouch[18]. Nodding towards[19] Martin and his open notebook he said, in a slow voice with a trace of north-country accent:

'Reginald Iven Lauder. Date of birth, 21st April 1905. Address, 42 Makepeace Avenue, Chigwell, Essex. Occupation, Group Secretary, East Central Hospital Management Committee. And now, Superintendent, what do you want to know?'

'A great deal[20], I'm afraid,' said Dalgliesh. 'And firstly, have you any idea at all who could have killed Miss Bolam?' The group secretary established

1. occasion
2. de près
3. trapu
4. joufflu
5. aux yeux doux
6. carrées
7. bien coupé
8. avocat de province
9. à l'aise
10. se comportait
11. sûr de
12. peu disposé à
13. bousculé
14. une intelligence plus vive
15. en face de
16. sans daigner s'excuser
17. chercha
18. blague à tabac
19. désignant d'un signe de la tête
20. pas mal de choses

his pipe and, leaning his elbows on the desk[1], regarded its glowing head[2] with satisfaction.

'I wish I had[3]. I'd have been in here to tell you before now, never fear[4]. But, no. I've no help of that kind for you.'

'Miss Bolam had no enemies as far as you were aware[5]?'

'Enemies? Well now[6], Superintendent, that's a strong word! She had people who didn't much like her, the same as I have. You, too, no doubt. But we don't go in fear of being murdered. No, I wouldn't have said she had enemies. Mind you[7], I know nothing of her private life. That's not my concern.'

'Could you tell me something about the Steen and the position she held[8]? I know something of the clinic's reputation, of course, but it would be helpful if I could have a clear picture of what goes on[9] here.'

'A clear picture of what goes on?' It might have been imagination, but Dalgliesh thought he saw the group secretary's mouth twitch[10].

'Well, the medical director could tell you more about that than I – on the medical side, that is. But I can give you a gist[11]. The place was founded between the wars by the family of a Mr Hyman Stein. The story goes that[12] the old man suffered from impotence[13], got himself some psychotherapy and subsequently fathered[14] five children. So far from impoverishing him[15] they all did well[16] and when papa died they put the clinic on a sound financial footing[17] as a memorial to him[18]. After all, they did owe[19] the place something. The sons all changed their name to Steen – for the usual reason I suppose – and the clinic was given the angli-

1. appuyant ses coudes sur le bureau
2. foyer rougeoyant
3. j'aimerais bien le savoir
4. n'ayez crainte
5. à votre connaissance
6. eh bien
7. remarquez
8. qu'elle avait
9. ce qui se passe
10. se contracter
11. l'essentiel
12. on dit que
13. impuissance
14. engendra
15. bien loin de l'appauvrir
16. ils ont tous réussi dans la vie
17. ils ont donné une solide base financière à la clinique
18. en son honneur
19. devaient

cized name. I often wonder what old Hyman would have thought.'

'Is it well endowed[1]?'

'It was. The state got the endowments[2] of course on the Appointed Day[3] following the 1946 Act. A bit has come in[4] since, but not much. People aren't so keen to will money[5] to institutions run[6] by the Government. But the place was quite well off[7] before 1948 as these places go[8]. They did themselves well in the way of equipment and facilities[9]. The Hospital Management Committee's had quite a job[10] providing for them[11] in the way to which they'd become accustomed.'

'Is the clinic difficult to administer? I imagine there may be personality problems.'

'No more difficult than any other small unit. You get personality problems anywhere. I'd rather deal with[12] a difficult psychiatrist than a difficult surgeon[13] any day[14]. They're the real prima donnas[15].'

'Did you consider Miss Bolam a successful administrative officer?'

'Well … she was efficient[16]. I hadn't really any complaints. She was a bit rigid, I suppose. After all, Ministry circulars[17] haven't even the force of law, so there's no sense in treating them as if they are personally dictated by God Almighty[18]. I doubt whether Miss Bolam would have got much further[19]. Mind you, she was a competent, methodical and highly conscientious officer. I don't think she ever sent in an inaccurate return[20].'

'Poor devil!' thought Dalgliesh, stung by the bleak anonymity of that official epitaph[21]. He asked:

'Was she popular here? With the medical staff, for example?'

1. bien dotée
2. dotations
3. 5 juillet 1948, date de l'entrée en vigueur du « National Health Service », service national de santé britannique
4. il y a eu quelques rentrées
5. léguer de l'argent
6. administrées
7. riche
8. comparée à d'autres
9. installations
10. n'a pas eu la tâche facile
11. subvenir à leurs besoins
12. je préférerais avoir affaire à
13. chirurgien
14. de loin
15. divas
16. efficace
17. circulaires ministérielles
18. dictées par Dieu tout-puissant
19. plus loin (dans sa carrière)
20. déclaration inexacte
21. troublé par la triste banalité de cette épitaphe officielle

'Well, now, Superintendent, you'll have to ask them. I can't think of any reason why she shouldn't be.'

'You were not then under any pressure from the medical committee to remove her from the clinic[1]?'

The mild grey eyes grew suddenly blank[2]. There was a momentary pause before the group secretary calmly replied:

'I have had no official request of that kind made to me.'

'But unofficially[3]?'

'There has been a feeling here from time to time, I believe, that a change of job might be helpful[4] to Miss Bolam. Now that's not such a bad idea, Superintendent! Any officer in a small unit, particularly a psychiatric clinic, can benefit from[5] a change of experience. But I don't transfer[6] my staff at the whim[7] of medical committees. Bless me[8], no! And, as I said, no official request was made. If Miss Bolam herself had asked for a transfer, that would have been a different matter[9]. Even so[10], it wouldn't have been easy. She was a general administrative officer and we haven't many posts in that grade[11].'

Dalgliesh then asked again about Miss Bolam's telephone call and Lauder confirmed that he had spoken to her at about ten to one. He remembered the time because he was just about to[12] go for lunch. Miss Bolam had asked to speak to him personally and had been put through by his secretary[13]. She had asked whether she could see him urgently.

'Can you remember the exact conversation?'

'More or less. She said: "Can I have an appointment to see you as soon as possible[14]? I think there may be something going on here that you ought

1. lui imposer une mutation
2. devinrent soudain absents
3. officieusement
4. bénéfique
5. tirer profit de
6. mute
7. sur un caprice
8. mon dieu
9. ça aurait été une autre histoire
10. même ainsi
11. niveau
12. il s'apprêtait à
13. sa secrétaire lui avait transmis l'appel
14. dès que possible

to know about[1]. I should like your advice[2]. Something that started well before my time here[3]." I said that I couldn't see her this afternoon as I would be in the Finance and General Purposes Committee from two-thirty onwards[4] and had a Joint Consultative Committee[5] immediately afterwards[6]. I asked whether she could give me any idea what it was all about[7] and whether it couldn't wait until Monday. She hesitated, so, before she could reply, I said I'd drop in[8] on my way home[9] this evening. I knew they had a late clinic on Fridays. She said that she would arrange to be alone in her office from six-thirty onwards, thanked me, and rang off[10]. The JCC lasted[11] longer than I expected[12] – that Committee always does – and I got here just before seven-thirty. But you know that. I was still in Committee at the time they found the body, as no doubt you'll be checking in due course.'

'Did you take Miss Bolam's message seriously? Was she the sort of woman who ran to you with trifles[13] or would a request to see you really mean that something serious was wrong?'

The group secretary thought for a moment before replying: 'I took it seriously. That's why I came round[14] tonight.'

'And you have no idea at all what it might be?'

'None, I'm afraid. It must have been something that she learned about[15] since Wednesday. I saw Miss Bolam then at the House Committee meeting in the late afternoon and she told me afterwards that things were pretty quiet[16] here at present. That is the last time I saw her, incidentally[17]. She was looking rather well[18] I thought. Better than for some time.'

1. vous devriez savoir
2. j'aimerais savoir ce que vous en pensez
3. mon arrivée à la clinique
4. à partir de deux heures et demie
5. commission mixte de consultation
6. après
7. de quoi il s'agissait
8. je passerais
9. en rentrant
10. raccrocha
11. a duré
12. prévu
13. qui se précipitait vers vous pour des broutilles
14. je suis passé
15. qu'elle a appris
16. il n'y avait pas de problème particulier
17. au fait
18. elle avait l'air d'aller plutôt bien

Dalgliesh asked the group secretary what, if anything, he knew of Miss Bolam's private life.

'Very little. I believe she has no near relations and lives alone in a flat in Kensington. Nurse Bolam will be able to tell you more about her. They're cousins, and Nurse Bolam is probably the nearest living relative[1]. I've got an idea that she had private means[2]. All the official information about her career will be on her dossier. Knowing Miss Bolam, I expect her file will be as meticulously kept as any other staff dossier. It'll be here no doubt.'

Without moving from his chair he leaned sideways[3], jerked open[4] the top drawer[5] of the filing cabinet and inserted a chubby[6] hand between the manilla folders.

'Here we are. Bolam, Enid Constance. I see she came to us in October 1949 as a shorthand typist. She spent eighteen months in Group Headquarters[7], was transferred to one of our chest clinics[8] on 19th April 1951 on Grade[9] B and applied[10] for the vacant post of administrative officer here on 14th May 1957. The post was then Grade D and she was lucky to get it. We hadn't a very strong field[11], I remember. All administrative and clerical jobs[12] were regraded[13] in 1958 following the Noel Hall report[14] and, after some argument with the Regional Board[15], we managed to[16] get this one graded as general administrative. It's all down here. Date of birth, 12th December 1922. Address, 37a Ballantyne Mansions, SW8. Then come details about her tax code[17], national insurance number and incremental date[18]. She's only had one week off sick[19] since she came here and that was in 1959 when she had flu[20]. There isn't much more here. Her original

1. la plus proche parente qui lui reste
2. une fortune personnelle
3. se pencha sur le côté
4. ouvrit d'un coup sec
5. le tiroir supérieur
6. potelée
7. au siège du groupe
8. centres de pneumologie
9. échelon
10. postulé
11. notre travail n'était pas vraiment reconnu
12. emplois de bureau
13. reclassés
14. rapport Noel Hall (3 mars 1958)
15. après avoir plaidé notre cause auprès du conseil régional
16. nous avons réussi à
17. numéro fiscal
18. la date de sa prochaine augmentation de salaire
19. une semaine de congé maladie
20. la grippe

application form[1] and letters of appointment[2] will be on her main dossier at Group Headquarters.'

He handed the file to Dalgliesh who looked through it[3] and then said:

'This states that her previous employers[4] were the Botley Research Establishment. Isn't that Sir Mark Etherege's show?[5] They dabble in[6] aeronautical research. He's Dr Etherege's brother, isn't he?'

'I think Miss Bolam did mention to me when she was appointed to this post that she knew Dr Etherege's brother slightly[7]. Mind you now, it can't have been more than that. She was only a shorthand typist at Botley. It's a bit of a coincidence, I suppose, but then she had to come from somewhere. I seem to remember it was Sir Mark who gave her a reference[8] when she applied to us. That will be on her Group dossier, of course.'

'Would you mind telling me[9], Mr Lauder, what arrangements you propose making[10] here now that she's dead?'

The group secretary replaced the file in the cabinet.

'I don't see why not. I shall have to consult my Committee, of course, as the circumstances[11] are unusual, but I shall recommend that the senior medical stenographer here, Mrs Bostock, takes over in an acting capacity[12]. If she can do the job – and I think she can – she'll be a strong candidate for the vacancy[13], but the post will be advertised[14] in the usual way[15].'

Dalgliesh did not comment but he was interested. Such a quick[16] decision on Miss Bolam's successor could only mean that Lauder had earlier given some thought to it[17]. The approaches of the medical staff

1. formulaire de candidature
2. lettres de nomination
3. y jeta un coup d'œil
4. ses employés précédents
5. c'est bien l'entreprise dirigée par Sir Mark Etherege ?
6. ils font un peu de
7. un peu
8. lettre de recommandation
9. puis-je vous demander
10. quelles dispositions vous avez l'intention de prendre
11. la situation
12. assure l'intérim
13. poste à pourvoir
14. l'offre d'emploi sera publiée
15. de la manière habituelle
16. aussi rapide
17. y avait déjà réfléchi auparavant

may have been unofficial, but they had probably been more effective than the group secretary cared to admit[1]. Dalgliesh returned to the telephone call which had brought Mr Lauder to the clinic. He said:

'The words Miss Bolam used strike me as significant[2]. She said that there may be something very serious going on here which you ought to know about and that it started before her time[3]. That suggests, firstly that she wasn't yet certain but only suspicious[4], and secondly that she wasn't worried about a particular incident but about something of long standing[5]. A systematic policy of thieving[6], for example, as opposed to[7] one isolated theft[8].'

'Well now, Superintendent, it's odd[9] you should mention theft. We have had a theft recently, but it was an isolated incident, the first we've had here for years[10], and I can't see how it could be connected with murder. It was just over a week ago, last Tuesday if I remember rightly. Cully and Nagle were the last to leave the clinic as usual and Cully asked Nagle to have a drink with him at the Queen's Head. You know it, I expect. It's the pub on the far corner of Beefsteak Street. There are one or two odd things about this story and one of the strangest[11] is that Cully should invite Nagle for a drink. They've never struck me as buddies[12]. Anyway, Nagle accepted and they were in the Queen's Head together from about seven. At about half past, a pal of Cully's[13] came in and said he was surprised to see Cully there as he had just passed the clinic and there was a faint light[14] in one of the windows – as if someone was moving around with a torch, he said. Nagle and Cully went off to investigate and found one of the back basement windows broken,

1. ne voulait l'admettre
2. me semblent significatifs
3. avant qu'elle ne soit embauchée à la clinique
4. elle avait des soupçons
5. ayant commencé il y a longtemps
6. des vols à répétition
7. par opposition à
8. un seul vol
9. étrange
10. depuis des années
11. l'une des plus étranges
12. je n'ai jamais eu l'impression qu'ils étaient copains
13. un copain de Cully
14. une faible lumière

or rather, cut out[1]. Quite a clever job it was[2]. Cully didn't feel inclined to[3] investigate further without reinforcements[4] and I'm not sure that I blame him[5]. He's sixty-five, remember, and not strong. After some whispering together[6], Nagle said that he'd go in[7] and Cully had better telephone the police from the kiosk[8] on the corner[9]. Your people came pretty smartly[10] but they didn't get the intruder[11]. He gave Nagle the slip[12] inside the building, and when Cully got back from telephoning he was just in time to see the man slip out of the mews[13].'

'I'll check how far our people have got with the investigation,' said Dalgliesh. 'But I agree that a connection between the crimes seems unlikely[14] on the face of it[15]. Was much taken?[16]'

'Fifteen pounds from a drawer[17] in the psychiatric social worker's office. The door was locked but he wrenched it open[18]. The money was in an envelope addressed in green ink[19] to the administrative secretary of the clinic and had been received a week earlier. There was no letter with it, only a note to say that the money was from a grateful[20] patient. The other contents of the drawer were torn[21] and scattered[22] but nothing else was stolen[23]. Some attempt had been made to force open the cabinets of records in the general office and Miss Bolam's desk drawers had been forced but nothing taken.'

Dalgliesh asked whether the fifteen pounds should have been placed in the wall safe[24].

'Well now, Superintendent, you're right[25], of course. It should have been. But there was a little difficulty about using the money. Miss Bolam phoned me about its arrival and said that she thought it should be paid immediately into the clinic's free

1. découpée
2. c'était du beau travail !
3. n'avait pas envie de
4. renforts
5. on ne peut pas vraiment lui reprocher
6. après qu'ils en eurent parlé à voix basse
7. il irait voir à l'intérieur
8. cabine
9. coin
10. très rapidement
11. intrus
12. faussa compagnie à Nagle
13. se glisser hors de la ruelle
14. peu probable
15. à première vue
16. On a pris beaucoup de choses ?
17. tiroir
18. il l'a forcée
19. encre
20. reconnaissant
21. déchirés
22. dispersés
23. volé
24. coffre mural
25. vous avez raison

money account[1] to be used in due course on the authority of the House Committee. That was a very proper[2] course of action, and so I told her. Shortly afterwards the medical director phoned me to ask if he could have authority to spend the money on some new flower vases for the patients' waiting-room. The vases were certainly needed and it seemed a correct use for non-Exchequer funds[3], so I rang the chairman[4] of the House Committee and got his approval. Apparently Dr Etherege wanted Miss Kettle to choose the vases and asked Miss Bolam to hand over[5] the cash[6]. I had already notified[7] Miss Bolam of the decision so she did so[8], expecting that the vases would be bought at once[9]. Something happened to change Miss Kettle's plans and, instead of returning the cash to the AO for safe custody[10], she locked it in her drawer.'

'Do you know how many of the staff knew that it was there?'

'That's what the police asked. I suppose most people knew that the vases hadn't been bought or Miss Kettle would have shown them around[11]. They probably guessed[12] that, having been handed the cash, she wouldn't be likely to return it even temporarily. I don't know. The arrival of that fifteen pounds was mysterious. It caused nothing but trouble[13] and its disappearance was equally mysterious. Anyway, Superintendent, no one here stole it. Cully only saw the thief[14] for a second but he was certain that he didn't know the man. He did say, though, that he thought the chap[15] looked like a gentleman. Don't ask me how he knew or what his criteria are. But that's what he said.'

1. dans le compte de la clinique
2. approprié
3. fonds non officiels
4. président
5. remettre
6. l'argent
7. informé
8. c'est ce qu'elle fit
9. immédiatement
10. pour qu'elle le mette en lieu sûr
11. les aurait montrés
12. deviné
13. des ennuis
14. voleur
15. type

Dalgliesh thought that the whole incident[1] was odd and would bear further investigation[2] but he could see no apparent connection between the two crimes. It was not even certain that Miss Bolam's call to the group secretary for advice was related to[3] her death, but here the presumption[4] was much stronger. It was very important to discover, if possible, what she had suspected. He asked Mr Lauder once more whether he could help.

'I told you, Superintendent, I haven't an idea what she meant[5]. If I suspected that anything was wrong I shouldn't wait for Miss Bolam to phone me. We're not quite so remote[6] from the units at group offices as some people think and I usually get to know anything I ought to know. If the murder is connected with that phone message something pretty serious must be happening here. After all, you don't kill just to prevent[7] the group secretary knowing that you've fiddled your travelling claim[8] or overspent your annual leave[9]. Not that anyone has as far as I know.'

'Exactly,' said Dalgliesh. He watched the group secretary's face very closely[10] and said, without emphasis[11]:

'It suggests something that might ruin a man professionally. A sexual relationship with a patient perhaps – something as serious as that.' Mr Lauder's face did not change.

'I imagine every doctor knows the seriousness of that, particularly psychiatrists. They must have to be pretty careful[12] with some of the neurotic[13] women they treat. Frankly, I don't believe it. All the doctors here are eminent men, some of them with world-wide reputations[14]. You don't get that sort of

1. tout cet incident
2. il faudrait poursuivre les recherches
3. lié à
4. présomption
5. ce qu'elle voulait dire
6. déconnectés
7. pour empêcher
8. falsifié vos notes de frais de déplacement
9. dépassé votre droit aux congés annuels
10. avec beaucoup d'attention
11. sans changer de ton
12. prudents
13. névrosées
14. de renommée internationale

reputation if you're a fool[1], and men of that eminence don't commit murder.'

'And what about the rest of the staff? They may not be eminent, but presumably you consider them honest?'

Unruffled[2], the group secretary replied:

'Sister Ambrose has been here for nearly twenty years and Nurse Bolam for five. I would trust them both absolutely[3]. All the clerical staff[4] came with good references and so did[5] the two porters, Cully and Nagle.' He added wryly[6]: 'Admittedly[7] I didn't check that they hadn't committed murder but none of them strike me as homicidal maniacs[8]. Cully drinks a bit and is a pathetic fool[9] with only another four months' service to complete. I doubt whether he could kill a mouse without making a hash of it[10]. Nagle is a cut above[11] the usual hospital porter. I understand he's an art student and works here for pocket money. He's only been with us a couple of years so he wasn't here before Miss Bolam's time. Even if he's been seducing[12] all the female staff, which seems unlikely, the worst that could happen to him would be the sack[13] and that wouldn't worry him as things are today. Admittedly she was killed with his chisel but anyone could have got their hands on that.'

'I'm afraid this was an inside job[14], you know,' said Dalgliesh gently. 'The murderer knew where Tippett's fetish and Nagle's chisel were kept, knew which key opened the old record-room, knew where that key was hung on the board in the porters' duty-room, probably wore one of the rubber[15] aprons from the art therapy room as a protection, certainly had medical knowledge. Above all, of

1. un imbécile
2. imperturbable
3. elles sont tout à fait dignes de confiance
4. personnel administratif
5. de même que
6. avec ironie
7. je dois admettre que
8. maniaque à tendance meurtrière
9. un pauvre diable
10. sans que cela se termine en un parfait désastre
11. un cran au-dessus
12. même s'il avait séduit
13. d'être mis à la porte
14. je crois hélas que le meurtrier se trouve parmi le personnel de la clinique
15. en caoutchouc

course, the murderer couldn't have left[1] the clinic after the crime. The basement door was bolted[2] and so was the ground-floor back door. Cully was watching the front door.'

'Cully had a belly-ache. He could have missed someone.'

'Do you really believe that's possible?' asked Dalgliesh. And the group secretary did not reply.

At first sight[3] Marion Bolam could be thought beautiful. She had the fair, classical good looks[4] which, enhanced[5] by her nurse's uniform, gave an immediate impression of serene loveliness[6]. Her blonde hair, parted[7] above a broad forehead[8] and twisted into a high roll at the back of her head[9], was bound[10] by the simple white cap[11]. It was only at second glance[12] that the illusion faded[13] and beauty gave way to prettiness[14]. The features[15], individually analysed, were unremarkable[16], the nose a little too long, the lips[17] a little too thin. In ordinary clothes, hurrying home perhaps at the end of the day, she would be undistinguished[18]. It was the combination of the starched[19] formal linen[20] with that fair[21] skin and yellow hair which dazzled the eye[22]. Only in the broad forehead and the sharpness of the nose[23] could Dalgliesh detect any likeness[24] to her dead cousin. But there was nothing ordinary about the large grey eyes which met his fully[25] for a brief second before she lowered her glance[26] and gazed fixedly at[27] the clasped hands in her lap[28].

'I understand that you are Miss Bolam's next of kin[29]. This must be a terrible shock for you.'

'Yes. Oh, yes, it is! Enid was my cousin.'

1. quitté
2. verrouillée
3. à première vue
4. beauté
5. mise en valeur
6. charme
7. séparés par une raie
8. un front haut
9. relevés en un haut chignon torsadé
10. retenus
11. coiffe
12. quand on la regardait plus attentivement
13. disparaissait
14. elle n'était plus belle, mais seulement jolie
15. traits
16. n'avaient rien de particulier
17. lèvres
18. quelconque
19. amidonné
20. linge
21. claire
22. éblouissait
23. le nez pointu
24. ressemblance
25. le regardèrent intensément
26. baisse le regard
27. regarde fixement
28. les mains jointes sur ses genoux
29. la parente la plus proche

'You have the same name. Your fathers were brothers?'

'Yes, they were. Our mothers were sisters, too. Two brothers married two sisters so that we were doubly related.'

'Had she no other relations living?'

'Only Mummy and me.'

'I shall have to see Miss Bolam's solicitor[1], I expect,' said Dalgliesh, 'but it would be helpful if you would tell me as much as you know about her affairs. I'm afraid I have to ask these personal questions. Usually they have no bearing[2] on the crime, but one must know as much as possible about everyone concerned. Had your cousin any income apart from her salary[3]?'

'Oh, yes. Enid was quite well off[4]. Uncle Sydney left her mother about £25,000 and it all came to Enid. I don't know how much was left, but I think she had about £1,000 a year coming in apart from her salary here. She kept on Auntie[5]'s flat in Ballantyne Mansions and she ... she was always very good to us.'

'In what way, Miss Bolam? Did she make you an allowance[6]?'

'Oh, no! Enid wouldn't want to do that. She gave us presents[7]. Thirty pounds at Christmas and fifty in July for our summer holiday. Mummy has disseminated sclerosis[8] and we couldn't go away to an ordinary hotel.'

'And what happens to Miss Bolam's money now?'

The grey eyes lifted[9] to meet his with no trace of embarrassment. She answered simply:

'It will come to Mummy and me. There wasn't anyone else to leave it to, was there? Enid always

1. notaire
2. pas de rapport
3. des revenus en dehors de son salaire
4. riche
5. tante
6. Est-ce qu'elle vous donnait régulièrement de l'argent ?
7. des cadeaux
8. sclérose en plaques
9. se levèrent

said it would come to us if she died first. But, of course, it wasn't likely[1] that she would die first; not while Mummy was alive anyway.'

It was indeed[2] unlikely, in the ordinary course of events, that Mrs Bolam would ever have benefited from that £25,000 or what was left of it, thought Dalgliesh. Here was the obvious[3] motive, so understandable[4], so universal, so dear[5] to any prosecuting counsel[6]. Every juryman[7] understood the lure[8] of money. Could Nurse Bolam really be unaware of[9] the significance of the information which she was handing him with such unembarrassed candour? Could innocence be so naïve or guilt[10] so confident? He said suddenly:

'Was your cousin popular, Miss Bolam?'

'She hadn't many friends. I don't think she would have called herself popular. She wouldn't want that. She had her church activities and the Guides[11]. She was a very quiet[12] person really.'

'But you know of no enemies?'

'Oh, no! None at all[13]. Enid was very much respected.'

The formal, old-fashioned[14] epithet was almost inaudible.

Dalgliesh said:

'Then it looks as if this is a motiveless, unpremeditated[15] crime. Normally that would suggest one of the patients. But it hardly seems[16] possible, and you are all insistent that it isn't likely.'

'Oh, no! It couldn't be a patient! I'm quite sure none of our patients would do a thing like that. They aren't violent.'

'Not even Mr Tippett?'

1. il était peu probable
2. effectivement
3. évident
4. compréhensible
5. cher
6. procureur de la Couronne
7. chaque juré
8. l'attrait
9. n'avait-elle pas conscience de
10. culpabilité
11. les Éclaireuses
12. tranquille
13. aucun
14. démodée
15. non prémédité
16. ne semble pas

'But it couldn't have been Mr Tippett. He's in hospital.'

'So I'm told[1]. How many people here knew that Mr Tippett wouldn't be coming to the clinic this Friday?'

'I don't know. Nagle knew because he took the message and he told Enid and Sister. Sister told me. You see, I usually try to keep an eye on[2] Tippett when I'm specialling[3] the LSD patients on Fridays. I can't leave my patient for more than a second, of course, but I do pop out[4] occasionally to see if Tippett is all right[5]. Tonight it wasn't necessary. Poor Tippett, he does love[6] his art therapy! Mrs Baumgarten has been away ill for[7] six months now, but we couldn't stop Tippett from coming. He wouldn't hurt a fly[8]. It's wicked[9] to suggest that Tippett could have anything to do with it. Wicked!'

She spoke with sudden vehemence. Dalgliesh said mildly[10]:

'But no one is suggesting anything of the sort. If Tippett is in hospital – and I haven't the least[11] doubt we shall find that he is – then he couldn't have been here.'

'But someone put his fetish on the body, didn't they?[12] If Tippett had been here you would have suspected him straight away[13] and he would have been so upset[14] and confused. It was a wicked thing to do. Really wicked!'

Her voice broke[15] and she was very near to tears[16]. Dalgliesh watched the thin fingers twisting[17] in her lap[18]. He said gently:

'I don't think we need worry about Mr Tippett. Now I want you to think carefully and tell me everything that you know happened in the clinic

1. c'est ce qu'on m'a dit
2. surveiller
3. je m'occupe spécialement de
4. je m'absente quelques instants
5. va bien
6. aime vraiment
7. est en congé maladie depuis
8. il ne ferait pas de mal à une mouche
9. monstrueux
10. doucement
11. le moindre
12. n'est-ce pas ?
13. immédiatement
14. bouleversé
15. se brisa
16. au bord des larmes
17. s'agiter nerveusement
18. sur ses genoux

from the time you came on duty[1] this evening. Never mind about other people[2], I just want to know what you did.'

Nurse Bolam remembered very clearly what she had done and, after a second's hesitation, she gave a careful and logical account. It was her job on Friday evenings to 'special[3]' any patient undergoing treatment[4] with lysergic acid. She explained that this was a method of releasing deep-seated inhibitions[5] so that the patient was able to recall[6] and recount[7] the incidents which were being repressed in his subconscious[8] and were responsible for his illness[9]. As she spoke about the treatment Nurse Bolam lost her nervousness and seemed to forget that she was talking to a layman[10]. But Dalgliesh did not interrupt.

'It's a remarkable drug and Dr Baguley uses it quite a lot. It's name is lysergic acid diethylamide and I think it was discovered by a German in 1942. We administer it orally, and the usual dose is 0.25 mg. It's produced in ampoules of 1 mg and mixed with from 15 to 30 ccs of distilled water. The patients are told not to have any breakfast. The first effects are noticed after about half an hour and the more disturbing subjective experiences occur[11] from one to one and a half hours after administration. That's when Dr Baguley comes down[12] to be with the patient. The effects can last[13] for as long as four hours and the patient is flushed[14] and restless[15] and quite withdrawn from reality[16]. They're never left alone, of course, and we use the basement room because it's secluded[17] and quiet and other patients aren't distressed[18] by the noise[19]. We

1. vous avez pris votre service
2. ne vous préoccupez pas des autres
3. assister
4. suivant un traitement
5. cela consistait à débloquer des inhibitions profondes
6. se souvenir de
7. raconter
8. réprimés dans son subconscient
9. maladie
10. non-initié
11. ont lieu
12. descend
13. durer
14. rougit
15. est agité
16. profondément déconnecté de la réalité
17. à l'écart
18. dérangés
19. bruit

usually give LSD treatments on Friday afternoon and evening, and I always "special" the patient.'

'I suppose that, if any noise, such as a cry, were heard on Fridays in the basement most of the staff would assume[1] that it was the LSD patient?'

Nurse Bolam looked doubtful[2].

'I suppose they might. Certainly these patients can be very noisy. My patient today was more disturbed[3] than usual which was why I stayed close to her[4]. Usually I spend a little time in the linen-room[5] which adjoins[6] the treatment-room sorting the clean laundry as soon as the patient is over the worst[7]. I keep the door open between the rooms, of course, so that I can watch the patient from time to time.'

Dalgliesh asked what exactly had happened during the evening.

'Well, the treatment began just after three-thirty and Dr Baguley looked in[8] shortly after four to see if all was well. I stayed with the patient until four-thirty when Mrs Shorthouse came to tell me that tea was made[9]. Sister came down while I went upstairs to the nurses' duty-room and drank tea. I came down again at a quarter to five and rang for Dr Baguley at five. He was with the patient for about three-quarters of an hour. Then he left to return to his ECT clinic. I stayed with the patient, and as she was so restless[10] I decided to leave the laundry until later in the evening. At about twenty to seven Peter Nagle knocked on the door[11] and asked for the laundry. I told him that it wasn't sorted and he looked a bit surprised but didn't say anything. A little time after that I thought I heard[12] a scream[13]. I didn't take any notice[14] at first as it didn't seem very

1. supposeraient
2. avait l'air peu convaincu
3. perturbée
4. près d'elle
5. blanchisserie
6. attenante à
7. a surmonté le pire
8. a passé une tête
9. prêt
10. très agitée
11. a frappé à la porte
12. j'ai cru entendre
13. cri
14. je n'y ai pas prêté attention

close[1] and I thought it was children playing in the square. Then I thought I ought to make sure[2] and I went to the door. I saw Dr Baguley and Dr Steiner coming into the basement with Sister and Dr Ingram. Sister told me that nothing was wrong[3] and to go back to my patient, so I did[4].'

'Did you leave the treatment-room at all after Dr Baguley left you at about quarter to six?'

'Oh, no! There wasn't any need. If I'd wanted to go to the cloakroom[5] or anything like that (Nurse Bolam blushed faintly[6]) I would have phoned for Sister to come and take my place.'

'Did you make any telephone calls from the treatment-room at all during the evening?'

'Only the one to the ECT room at five to call Dr Baguley.'

'Are you quite sure you didn't telephone Miss Bolam?'

'Enid? Oh, no! There wouldn't be any reason to call Enid. She … that is[7], we, didn't see very much of each other in the clinic. I am responsible to[8] Sister Ambrose, you see, and Enid wasn't concerned with the nursing staff[9].'

'But you saw quite a lot of her outside the clinic?'

'Oh, no! I didn't mean that[10]. I went to her flat once or twice[11], to collect[12] the cheque at Christmas and in the summer, but it isn't easy for me to leave Mummy. Besides[13], Enid had her own life to live. And then she's quite a lot older than me. I didn't really know her very well.'

Her voice broke and Dalgliesh saw that she was crying[14]. Fumbling under her apron for the pocket in her nurse's dress[15], she sobbed[16]:

1. tout près
2. vérifier
3. tout allait bien
4. ce que j'ai fait
5. toilettes
6. rougit un peu
7. je veux dire
8. responsable devant
9. le personnel infirmier
10. ce n'est pas ce que je voulais dire
11. une fois ou deux
12. pour recevoir
13. en plus
14. elle pleurait
15. en tentant maladroitement de trouver la poche de sa robe sous son tablier
16. sanglota

'It's so dreadful[1]! Poor Enid! Putting that fetish on her body as if he was making fun of her[2], making it look as if she was nursing a baby[3]!'

Dalgliesh hadn't realized that she had seen the body and said so.

'Oh, I didn't! Dr Etherege and Sister wouldn't let me go in to her[4]. But we were all told what had happened.'

Miss Bolam had indeed looked as if she were nursing a baby. But he was surprised that someone who hadn't seen the body should say so. The medical director must have given a graphic[5] description of the scene.

Suddenly Nurse Bolam found her handkerchief[6] and drew it out[7] of her pocket. With it came a pair of thin, surgical gloves[8]. They fell at Dalgliesh's feet. Picking them up[9] he asked:

'I didn't realize that you used surgical gloves here.'

Nurse Bolam seemed unsurprised by his interest. Checking her sobs[10] with surprising control she replied:

'We don't use them very often but we keep a few[11] pairs. The whole Group's gone over to[12] disposable[13] gloves now, but there are a few of the old kind about[14]. That's one of them. We use them for odd cleaning jobs[15].'

'Thank you,' said Dalgliesh. 'I'll keep this pair if I may[16]. And I don't think I need worry[17] you any more at present.'

With a murmured word which could have been 'thank you,' Nurse Bolam almost backed out of the room[18].

1. horrible
2. se moquait d'elle
3. allaitait un bébé
4. ne m'auraient pas laissée entrer pour la voir
5. très précise
6. mouchoir
7. le sortit
8. gants chirurgicaux
9. en les ramassant
10. contrôlant ses sanglots
11. quelques
12. se sert de
13. jetables
14. qui circulent encore
15. travaux de nettoyage divers
16. si vous me le permettez
17. déranger
18. faillit sortir de la pièce à reculons

*

The minutes dragged heavily[1] to the clinic staff waiting in the front consulting-room to be interviewed. Fredrica Saxon had fetched[2] some papers from her room on the third floor and was scoring[3] an intelligence test. There had been some discussion about whether she ought to go upstairs alone, but Miss Saxon had stated firmly[4] that she didn't intend to[5] sit there wasting time[6] and biting her nails[7] until the police chose to see her, that she hadn't the murderer hidden upstairs, nor was she proposing to destroy incriminating evidence[8] and that she had no objection to any member of the staff accompanying her to satisfy themselves on this point. This distressing frankness[9] had provoked a murmur of protests and reassurance, but Mrs Bostock had announced abruptly[10] that she would like to fetch a book from the medical library and the two women had left the room and returned together. Cully had been seen[11] early, having established his right to be classed as a patient, and had been released[12] to cosset his stomach-ache[13] at home. The only remaining[14] patient, Mrs King, had been interviewed and allowed to depart[15] with her husband in attendance[16]. Mr Burge had also left, protesting loudly[17] at the interruption of his session and the trauma of the whole experience.

'Mind you, he's enjoying himself, you can see that,' confided[18] Mrs Shorthouse to the assembled staff. 'The superintendent had a job getting rid of him[19], I can tell you.'

There was a great deal[20] which Mrs Shorthouse seemed able to tell them. She had been given per-

1. s'écoulaient lentement
2. était allée chercher
3. comptait les points de
4. avait déclaré fermement
5. n'avait pas l'intention de
6. à perdre son temps
7. à se ronger les ongles
8. preuves compromettantes
9. franchise désespérante
10. brusquement
11. interrogé
12. relâché
13. dorloter son ventre douloureux
14. qui restaient
15. avait été autorisée à partir
16. accompagnée de son mari
17. avec force
18. confia
19. a eu bien du mal à se débarrasser de lui
20. beaucoup de choses

mission to make coffee and prepare sandwiches in her small ground-floor kitchen at the rear of the building, and this gave her an excuse for frequent trips up and down[1] the hall. The sandwiches were brought in almost singly[2]. Cups were taken individually to be washed. This coming and going gave her an opportunity of reporting the latest situation[3] to the rest of the staff who awaited each instalment[4] with an anxiety and eagerness[5] which they could only imperfectly conceal[6]. Mrs Shorthouse was not the emissary they would have chosen but any news, however obtained and by whomever delivered[7], helped to lighten[8] the weight of suspense and she was certainly unexpectedly[9] knowledgeable[10] about police procedure.

'There's several of them searching the building now and they've got their own chap on the door. They haven't found anyone, of course. Well, it stands to reason[11]! We know he couldn't have got out of the building. Or in for that matter[12]. I said to the sergeant[13]: "This clinic has had all the cleaning from me that it's getting today[14], so tell your chaps to mind where they plant[15] their boots ..."'

'The police surgeon's seen[16] the body. The fingerprint man is still downstairs and they're taking everyone's prints. I've seen the photographer. He went through the hall with a tripod[17] and a big case[18], white on top and black at the bottom ...

'Here's a funny thing now. They're looking for prints in the basement lift[19]. Measuring it up[20], too.'

Fredrica Saxon lifted her head, seemed about to say something, then went on with her work. The basement lift, which was about four feet square[21] and operated by a rope pulley[22], had been used

1. allées et venues
2. un par un
3. rapporter les dernières nouvelles
4. épisode
5. impatience
6. dissimuler
7. quelle que fût la façon dont on l'avait obtenue et la personne qui la transmettait
8. alléger
9. étonnamment
10. bien informée
11. cela va de soi
12. ni entrer dans le bâtiment d'ailleurs
13. brigadier
14. j'ai fini de nettoyer pour aujourd'hui
15. mettent
16. a vu
17. trépied
18. valise
19. monte-charge
20. ils le mesurent
21. mesurait environ 1,2 mètres carrés
22. était actionné à l'aide d'une poulie et d'une corde

to transport food from the basement kitchen to the first-floor dining-room when the clinic was a private house. It had never been taken out[1]. Occasionally medical records from the basement record-room were hoisted[2] in it to the first- and second-floor consulting-rooms, but it was otherwise little used[3]. No one commented on a possible reason why the police should test it for prints[4].

Mrs Shorthouse departed with two cups to be washed. She was back within five minutes.

'Mr Lauder's in the general office phoning the chairman. Telling him about the murder, I suppose. This'll give the HMC something to natter about and no mistake[5]. Sister is going through the linen inventory with one of the police. Seems there's a rubber apron from the art therapy room missing. Oh, and another thing. They're letting the boiler out[6]. Want to rake it through[7], I suppose. Nice for us, I must say. This place'll be bloody cold[8] on Monday ...

'The mortuary van[9]'s arrived. That's what they call it, the mortuary van. They don't use an ambulance, you see. Not when the victim's dead. You probably heard it arrive. I dare say if you draw the curtains back a bit[10] you'll see her being took in.'

But no one cared to draw back the curtains and as the soft, careful feet of the stretcher-bearers[11] shuffled past the door[12] no one spoke. Fredrica Saxon laid down[13] her pencil[14] and bowed[15] her head as if she were praying. When the front door closed their relief[16] was heard in the soft hiss[17] of breath released. There was a brief silence and then the van drove off[18]. Mrs Shorthouse was the only one to speak.

1. enlevé

2. hissés

3. à part ça, il était peu utilisé

4. y cherchait des empreintes digitales

5. va donner au comité de gestion de l'hôpital l'occasion de papoter un peu, ça c'est sûr

6. ils ont éteint la chaudière

7. la passer au peigne fin

8. terriblement froid

9. fourgon mortuaire

10. si vous ouvrez un peu les rideaux

11. brancardiers

12. franchirent la porte d'un pas traînant

13. déposa

14. crayon

15. pencha

16. soulagement

17. sifflement

18. démarra

1. pauvre femme
2. après tout ce qui s'est passé
3. elle partirait les pieds devant
4. au bord
5. à la voix grave
6. il n'avait pas pris la peine de lui témoigner sa sympathie
7. compréhensif
8. mensonge
9. simple
10. environ
11. ça n'avait pas pris beaucoup de temps
12. même si c'était rapide
13. rêveries
14. gâchées par
15. fâché
16. elle s'était comportée

'Poor little blighter[1]! Mind you I only gave her another six months here what with one thing and another[2], but I never thought she'd leave feet first[3].'

Jennifer Priddy sat apart from the rest of the staff on the edge[4] of the treatment couch. Her interview with the superintendent had been unexpectedly easy. She didn't know quite what she had expected but certainly it wasn't this quiet, gentle, deep-voiced[5] man. He hadn't bothered to commiserate with her[6] on the shock of finding the body. He hadn't smiled at her. He hadn't been paternal or understanding[7]. He gave the impression that he was interested only in finding out the truth as quickly as possible and that he expected everyone else to feel the same. She thought that it would be difficult to tell him a lie[8] and she hadn't tried. It had all been quite easy to remember, quite straightforward[9]. The superintendent had questioned her closely about the ten minutes or so[10] she had spent in the basement with Peter. That was only to be expected. Naturally he was wondering whether Peter could have killed Miss Bolam after he returned from the post and before she joined him. Well, it wasn't possible. She had followed him downstairs almost immediately and Mrs Shorthouse could confirm it. Probably it hadn't taken long[11] to kill Enid – she tried not to think about that sudden, savage, calculated violence – but however quickly it was done[12], Peter hadn't had time.

She thought about Peter. Thinking about him occupied most of her few solitary hours. Tonight, however, the familiar warm imaginings[13] were needled with[14] anxiety. Was he going to be cross[15] about the way she had behaved[16]? She remembered with shame[1] her delayed scream[2] of terror after finding the body, the way she had thrown herself[3] into his arms[4]. He had been very kind[5] and considerate[6], of course, but then he always was considerate when he wasn't working and remembered she was there. She knew that he hated fuss[7] and that any demonstration of affection irked him[8]. She had learned to accept that their love, and she dared no longer doubt that it was love, must be taken on his terms[9]. Since their brief time together in the nurses' duty-room after the finding of Miss Bolam she had scarcely[10] spoken to him. She couldn't guess what he felt[11]. She was only sure of one thing. She couldn't possibly pose[12] for him tonight. It hadn't anything to do with shame or guilt; he had long since cut her free[13] of those twin encumbrances[14]. He would expect her to arrive at the studio as planned[15]. After all, her alibi was fixed[16] and her parents would accept that she was at her evening class[17]. He would see no reasonable grounds[18] for altering their arrangements and Peter was a great one for reason[19]. But she couldn't do it! Not tonight. It wasn't so much the posing as what would follow. She wouldn't be able to refuse him. She wouldn't want to refuse him. And tonight, with Enid dead, she felt that she couldn't bear[20] to be touched.

When she returned from her talk[21] with the superintendent, Dr Steiner had come to sit beside her[22] and had been very kind. But then Dr Steiner was kind. It was easy enough to criticize his indolence or laugh at his odd patients. But he did care about people[23], whereas[24] Dr Baguley, who worked so hard and wore himself out[25] with his heavy clinics[26], didn't really like people at all, but only wished

1. honte
2. son cri de terreur à retardement
3. elle s'était jetée
4. bras
5. gentil
6. plein d'égards
7. la panique
8. l'agaçait
9. comme il l'entendait
10. à peine
11. il ressentait
12. poser
13. délivrée
14. fardeaux indissociables
15. comme prévu
16. solide
17. cours
18. raison
19. avait toujours besoin de bonnes raisons
20. supporter
21. conversation
22. à côté d'elle
23. il s'intéressait vraiment aux gens
24. alors que
25. s'épuisait
26. nombreuses consultations

that he did[1]. Jenny wasn't sure how she knew this so clearly. She hadn't really thought about it before. Tonight, however, now that the first shock of finding the body had passed, her mind was unnaturally clear. And not only her mind. All her perceptions were sharpened[2]. The tangible objects about her[3], the chintz covering[4] on the couch[5], the red blanket folded[6] at its foot, the bright varied greens and golds[7] of the chrysanthemums on the desk, were clearer, brighter, more real to her than ever before[8]. She saw the line[9] of Miss Saxon's arm as it rested on the desk curved around the book she was reading and the way in which the small hairs on her forearm were tipped with light from the desk lamp[10]. She wondered whether Peter always saw the life around him with this wonder[11] and clarity as if one were born into[12] an unfamiliar[13] world with all the first bright hues[14] of creation fresh upon it. Perhaps this was what it felt like to be a painter[15].

'I suppose it's the brandy,' she thought, and giggled[16] a little. She remembered hearing the muttered grumblings[17] of Sister Ambrose half an hour earlier.

'What's Nagle been feeding to[18] Priddy? That child's half drunk[19].' But she wasn't drunk and she didn't really believe it was the brandy.

Dr Steiner had drawn his chair close to her[20] and had laid his hand briefly on her shoulder. Without thinking, Miss Priddy had said:

'She was kind to me and I didn't like her.'

She no longer felt sad or guilty[21] about it. It was a statement of fact[22].

'You mustn't worry about it,' he said gently, and patted[23] her knee. She didn't resent the pat[24]. Peter

1. voulait pouvoir les aimer
2. plus intenses
3. les objets qui l'entouraient
4. housse de chintz
5. canapé
6. couverture pliée
7. ors
8. que jamais
9. contour
10. la lampe de bureau éclairait l'extrémité des poils de son avant-bras
11. émerveillement
12. était né dans
13. étrange
14. nuances
15. ce que ressentaient les peintres
16. ricana
17. ronchonnements
18. donné à
19. à moitié soûle
20. avait approché sa chaise
21. coupable
22. état de fait
23. tapota
24. la tape ne lui déplut pas

would have said: 'Lecherous old goat[1]! Tell him to keep his paws[2] to himself.' But Peter would have been wrong[3]. Jenny knew that it was a gesture of kindliness[4]. For a moment she was tempted to put her hand over his to show that she understood. He had small and very white hands for a man, so different from Peter's long, bony[5], paint-stained[6] fingers. She saw how the hairs curled beneath his shirt cuffs[7], the stubble of black along the knuckles[8]. On his little finger he wore a gold signet ring[9], heavy as a weapon[10].

'It's natural to feel as you do,' he said. 'When people die we always wish that we had been kinder to them, had liked them better[11]. There is nothing to be done[12] about it. We shouldn't pretend about[13] our feelings. If we understand them we learn in time to accept them and to live with them.'

But Jenny was no longer listening[14]. For the door had opened quietly and Peter Nagle had come in.

Bored with[15] sitting in the reception desk and exchanging commonplace remarks[16] with the uncommunicative policeman on duty there, Nagle sought[17] diversion in the front consulting-room. Although his formal interview was over he wasn't yet free to leave the clinic. The group secretary obviously expected him to stay until the building could be locked for the night and it would be his job to open it again on Monday morning. The way things were going[18] it looked as if he would be stuck[19] in the place for another couple of hours at least. That morning he had planned to get home early and work on the picture, but it was no use thinking of that[20] now. It might well be[21] after eleven o'clock before the business was settled[22] and he was free to

1. vieux cochon
2. pattes
3. aurait eu tort
4. gentillesse
5. osseux
6. tachés de peinture
7. ses poils frisés sous les manchettes de sa chemise
8. les poils drus sur ses phalanges
9. chevalière
10. arme
11. de ne pas les avoir aimés davantage
12. à faire
13. camoufler
14. n'écoutait plus
15. las de
16. des banalités
17. cherchait
18. au rythme où allaient les choses
19. il serait probablement coincé
20. il était inutile d'y penser
21. il pourrait bien être
22. l'affaire soit réglée

go home. But even if they could go to the Pimlico flat together Jenny wouldn't pose for him tonight. One glance at her face told him that. She did not come across to him[1] as he entered the room and he was grateful[2] for that amount of restraint[3] at least. But she gave him her shy[4], elliptical glance, half conspiratorial and half pleading[5]. It was her way of asking him to understand, of saying sorry. Well, he was sorry, too. He had hoped to put in[6] a good three hours tonight and time was getting short[7]. But if she was only trying to convey[8] that she wasn't in the mood for[9] making love, well, that suited him all right[10]. It suited him most nights if she only knew. He wished that he could take her – since she was so tiresomely insistent[11] on being taken – as simply and quickly as he took a meal, a means of satisfying an appetite that was nothing to be ashamed of[12] but nothing to fuss about[13] either[14]. But that wasn't Jenny. He hadn't been as clever[15] as he thought and Jenny was in love. She was hopelessly, passionately and insecurely in love, demanding a constant reassurance, facile tenderness and time-consuming[16] technique which left him exhausted and barely[17] satisfied. She was terrified of becoming pregnant[18] so that the preliminaries to love-making were irritatingly clinical, the aftermath[19], more often than not, her wild sobbing[20] in his arms. As a painter he was obsessed by her body. He couldn't think of changing his model now and he couldn't afford[21] to change. But the price of Jenny was getting too high.

He was almost untouched[22] by Miss Bolam's death. He suspected that she had always known just how little work he did[23] for his money. The rest

1. vers lui
2. reconnaissant
3. retenue
4. timide
5. mi-complice, mi-implorant
6. travailler
7. il lui restait peu de temps
8. communiquer
9. d'humeur à
10. cela lui allait très bien
11. elle insistait de manière tellement agaçante
12. dont il n'y avait pas à avoir honte
13. s'agiter
14. non plus
15. malin
16. chronophage
17. très peu
18. tomber enceinte
19. conséquence
20. ses sanglots convulsifs
21. se permettre
22. indifférent
23. qu'il travaillait très peu

of the staff, deluded by[1] comparing him with that poor fool, Cully, thought they had a paragon of industry[2] and intelligence. But Bolam had been no fool. It was not that he was lazy[3]. One could have an easy life at the Steen – and most people, including some psychiatrists, did – without risking that imputation. Everything required of him[4] was well within his capabilities and he gave no more than was required. Enid Bolam knew that all right, but it worried neither of them. If he went she could only hope to replace him by a porter who did less and did it less efficiently. And he was educated, personable[5] and polite. That had meant a great deal to Miss Bolam. He smiled as he remembered how much it had meant. No, Bolam had never bothered him[6]. But he was less confident about her successor.

He glanced across the room to where Mrs Bostock sat alone, gracefully relaxed in one of the more comfortable patients' chairs that he had brought in from the waiting-room. Her head was studiously bent over[7] a book, but Nagle had little doubt that her mind was otherwise[8] occupied. Probably working out[9] her incremental date as AO, he thought. This murder was a break for her all right[10]. You couldn't miss[11] compulsive ambition in a woman. They burnt with it[12]. You could almost smell it sizzling their flesh[13]. Underneath that air of calm unflappability[14] she was as restless and nervous as a cat on heat[15]. He sauntered across the room to her[16] and lounged against[17] the wall beside her chair, his arm just brushing[18] her shoulder.

'Nicely timed for you[19], isn't it?' he said.

She kept her eyes on the page but he knew that she would have to answer. She could never resist

1. trompés par
2. modèle d'application
3. paresseux
4. tout ce qu'on lui demandait
5. il présentait bien
6. ne l'avait jamais importuné
7. penchée sur
8. ailleurs
9. en train de calculer
10. un sacré coup de chance pour elle
11. il était impossible de ne pas remarquer
12. elle les enflamme
13. embraser leur chair
14. imperturbabilité
15. en chaleur
16. il traversa la pièce d'un pas nonchalant jusqu'à se retrouver près d'elle
17. s'appuya paresseusement contre
18. frôlant
19. Ça tombe à point pour vous

defending herself even when defence only made her more vulnerable. She's like the rest of them[1], he thought. She can't keep her bloody mouth shut[2].

'I don't know what you mean, Nagle.'

'Come off it[3]. I've been admiring your performance for the last six months. Yes, Doctor. No, Doctor. Just as you like, Doctor. Of course, I'd like to help, Doctor, but there are certain complications here … You bet there were[4]! She wasn't giving up[5] without a struggle[6]. And now she's dead. Very nice for you. They won't have to look far for their new AO.'

'Don't be impertinent and ridiculous. And why aren't you helping Mrs Shorthouse with the coffee?'

'Because I don't choose to[7]. You're not the AO yet, remember.'

'I've no doubt the police will be interested in knowing where you were this evening. After all, it was your chisel.'

'I was out with the post and fetching my evening paper. Disappointing, isn't it?[8] And I wonder where you were at six-twenty-two.'

'How do you know she died at six-twenty-two?'

'I don't. But Sister saw her going down to the basement at six-twenty and there wasn't anything in the basement to keep her as far as I know. Not unless[9] your dear Dr Etherege was there, of course. But surely he wouldn't demean himself[10] cuddling[11] Miss Bolam. Not quite his type I'd have said[12]. But you know his tastes[13] in that direction better than I do, of course.'

Suddenly she was out of her chair[14] and, swinging her right arm[15], she slapped[16] his cheek[17] with a force that momentarily rocked him[18]. The sharp

1. comme les autres
2. elle ne sait pas fermer sa putain de gueule
3. pas de ce petit jeu avec moi
4. et comment !
5. elle ne cédait pas
6. sans se battre
7. je n'en ai pas envie
8. comme c'est décevant
9. sauf si
10. il ne se serait pas abaissé à
11. faire un câlin à
12. je dirais
13. goûts
14. bondit de sa chaise
15. avec un large mouvement du bras droit
16. elle le frappa sur
17. joue
18. le fit chanceler

crack of the blow[1] echoed in the room. Everyone looked at them. Nagle heard Jennifer Priddy's gasp[2], saw Dr Steiner's worried frown[3] as he looked from one to the other in puzzled inquiry[4], saw Fredrica Saxon's contemptuous[5] glance at them before her eyes fell again to her book. Mrs Shorthouse, who was piling plates on to a tray[6] at a side[7] table, looked round a second too late. Her sharp[8] little eyes darted from one to the other[9], frustrated at having missed something worth seeing[10]. Mrs Bostock, her colour heightened[11], sank back[12] in her chair and picked up her book. Nagle, holding his hand to his cheek, gave a shout of laughter[13].

'Is anything the matter?[14]' asked Dr Steiner. 'What happened?'

It was then that the door opened and a uniformed policeman put his head in and said:

'The superintendent would like to see Mrs Shorthouse now, please.'

Mrs Amy Shorthouse had seen no reason why she should stay in her working clothes while waiting to be interviewed so that, when called in to Dalgliesh, she was dressed ready to go home. The metamorphosis was striking[15]. Comfortable working slippers[16] had been replaced by a modish pair of high-heeled court shoes[17], white overall[18] by a fur[19] coat, and head scarf[20] by the latest idiocy in hats[21]. The total effect was curiously old-fashioned. Mrs Shorthouse looked like a relic[22] of the gay twenties[23], an effect which was heightened[24] by the shortness of her skirt and the careful curls of peroxided[25] hair which lay cunningly[26] arranged on forehead and cheeks. But there was nothing false about her voice

1. le claquement cinglant du coup
2. retenir son souffle
3. froncement de sourcils
4. d'un regard interrogateur
5. méprisant
6. plateau
7. sur le côté
8. vifs
9. passaient rapidement de l'un à l'autre
10. qui valait la peine d'être vu
11. le visage cramoisi
12. s'affala
13. explosa de rire
14. y a-t-il un problème ?
15. frappante
16. les confortables mules de travail
17. une paire d'escarpins à talons hauts dernier cri
18. tunique et pantalon blancs
19. en fourrure
20. foulard
21. la dernière folie en matière de chapeaux
22. un vestige
23. des années folles
24. accentué
25. décolorés
26. habilement

and little, Dalgliesh suspected, about her personality. The little grey eyes were shrewd[1] and amused. She was neither frightened[2] nor distressed[3]. He suspected that Amy Shorthouse craved[4] more excitement than her life customarily afforded and was enjoying herself. She would not wish anyone violently dead but, since it had happened, one might as well make the most of it[5].

When the preliminaries were over and they got down to the events of the evening, Mrs Shorthouse came out with her prize[6] piece of information.

'No good[7] saying I can tell you who did it because I can't. Not that I haven't got my own ideas. But there's one thing I can tell you. I was the last person to talk to her, no doubt about that. No, scrub that out[8]! I was the last person to talk to her, face to face. Excepting the murderer, of course.'

'You mean that she subsequently[9] spoke on the telephone? Hadn't you better[10] tell me about it plainly[11]? I've got enough mystery here for one evening.'

'Smart, aren't you?[12]' said Mrs Shorthouse without rancour. 'Well, it was in this room. I came in at about ten past six to ask how much leave[13] I'd got left on account of wanting[14] a day off[15] next week. Miss Bolam got out my dossier – leastwise[16] it was already out come to think of it[17] – and we fixed that up[18] and had a bit of a chat about the work. I was on my way out really, just standing at the door for a few last words as you might say[19], when the phone rang.'

'I want you to think very carefully, Mrs Shorthouse,' said Dalgliesh. 'That call may be important. I wonder if you can remember what Miss Bolam said?'

1. rusés
2. effrayée
3. affligée
4. avait envie de
5. en profiter
6. capitale
7. pas la peine de
8. effacez ça
9. par la suite
10. ne vaudrait-il pas mieux que vous
11. clairement
12. on ne vous la fait pas à vous, hein ?
13. combien de jours de congé
14. parce que je veux
15. de congé
16. du moins
17. maintenant que j'y pense
18. on a arrangé ça
19. pour ainsi dire

'Think someone was enticing her down[1] to her death, do you?' said Mrs Shorthouse with alliterative relish[2]. 'Well, could be, come to think of it[3].'

Dalgliesh thought that his witness[4] was far from being a fool. He watched while she screwed up her face[5] in a simulated agony of effort[6]. He had no doubt that she remembered very well what had been said.

After a nicely judged pause for suspense, Mrs Shorthouse said:

'Well, the phone rang like I said. That would be about six-fifteen, I suppose. Miss Bolam picked up the receiver and said, "Administrative Officer speaking[7]." She always answered like that. Very keen on[8] her position[9] she was. Peter Nagle used to say[10], "Who the hell[11] does she think we're expecting to hear? Khrushchev?" Not that he said it to her. No fear! Anyway, that's what she said. Then there was a little pause and she looked up at me and said: "Yes, I am." Meaning[12], I suppose, that she was alone, not counting me. Then there was a longer pause while the chap at the other end[13] spoke. Then she said: "All right, stay where you are. I'll be down." Then she asked me to show Mr Lauder into her office if I was about[14] when he arrived, and I said I would and pushed off[15].'

'You're quite sure about her conversation on the telephone?'

'Sure as I'm sitting here. That's what she said all right.'

'You talked about the chap at the other end. How could you tell it was a man?'

'Never said I could. Just assumed[16] it was a chap, I suppose. Mind you, if I'd been closer I might

1. essayait de l'attirer au sous-sol
2. en se délectant de ses allitérations
3. si on y pense
4. témoin
5. grimaçait
6. comme si on lui demandait un terrible effort
7. au téléphone
8. très attachée à
9. place dans la hiérarchie
10. avait l'habitude de dire
11. qui diable
12. ce qui voulait dire
13. à l'autre bout
14. si j'étais dans les parages
15. j'ai filé
16. j'ai juste supposé

have known. You can sometimes get an idea who's speaking from the crackly noise[1] the phone makes. But I was standing against the door.'

'And you couldn't hear the other voice at all?'

'That's right. Suggests he was talking low[2].'

'What happened then, Mrs Shorthouse?'

'I said cheerio[3] and toddled off[4] to do a bit[5] in the general office. Peter Nagle was there taking young Priddy's mind off her work[6] as usual, and Cully was in the reception kiosk, so it wasn't them. Peter went out with the post as soon as I arrived. He always does at about a quarter past six.'

'Did you see Miss Bolam leaving her office?'

'No, I didn't. I told you. I was in with Nagle and Miss Priddy. Sister saw her, though[7]. You ask her. Sister saw her going down the hall.'

'So I understand. I have seen Sister Ambrose. I wondered whether Miss Bolam followed you out of the room.'

'No, she didn't. Not at once anyway. Perhaps she thought it would do the chap good to be kept waiting[8].'

'Perhaps,' said Dalgliesh. 'But she would have gone down promptly I expect if a doctor had phoned for her.'

Mrs Shorthouse gave a shriek of laughter[9].

'Maybe. Maybe not. You didn't know Miss Bolam.'

'What was she like, Mrs Shorthouse?'

'All right. We got on[10]. She liked a good worker and I'm a good worker. Well – you can see how the place is kept.'

'I can indeed.'

'Her yea[11] was yea and her nay[12], nay. I'll say that for her[13]. Nothing unpleasant behind your back[14].

1. le grésillement
2. bas
3. bye-bye
4. je suis partie tranquillement
5. un peu de ménage
6. en train d'empêcher la petite Priddy de penser à son travail
7. en fait
8. c'était bien que le type attende un peu
9. hurla de rire
10. on s'entendait bien
11. oui
12. non
13. il faut le dire
14. par derrière

Mind you, quite a bit of unpleasantness in front of your face sometimes if you didn't watch out[1]. Still[2], I'd rather have it that way[3]. She and me understood each other.'

'Had she any enemies – anyone who bore her a grudge?[4]'

'Must have had, mustn't she?[5] That wasn't no playful tap[6] on the head. Carrying a grudge a bit far[7], if you ask me.' She planted her feet apart[8] and leaned[9] towards Dalgliesh confidentially.

'Look, ducks[10],' she said. 'Miss B put people's backs up[11]. Some people do. You know how it is. They can't make no allowances[12]. Right was right and wrong was wrong and nothing in between. Rigid. That's what she was. Rigid.' Mrs Shorthouse's tone and tightened mouth[13] expressed the ultimate in virtuous inflexibility. 'Take the little matter of[14] the attendance book[15] now. All the consultants are supposed to sign it so that Miss Bolam could make her monthly return[16] to the Board. All very right and proper[17]. Well, the book used to be kept[18] on a table in the doctors' cloakroom[19] and no trouble to anyone[20]. Then Miss B gets to noticing[21] that Dr Steiner and Dr McBain are coming in late, so she moves the book to her office and they all have to go in there to sign. Mind you, as often as not Dr Steiner won't do it[22]. "She knows I'm here," he says. "And I'm a consultant not a factory hand[23]. If she wants her stupid book signed she can put it back in the medical cloakroom." The doctors have been trying to get rid of[24] her for a year or more, I do know that.'

'How do you know, Mrs Shorthouse?'

1. si on ne faisait pas attention
2. cela dit
3. je préfère ça
4. quelqu'un qui lui en voulait ?
5. sans doute
6. une petite tape innocente
7. une vieille rancune
8. écarta les jambes
9. se pencha
10. écoutez, mon vieux
11. se mettait les gens à dos
12. faire des exceptions
13. bouche serrée
14. prenons par exemple l'histoire de
15. registre de présence
16. rapport mensuel
17. juste
18. était
19. vestiaire
20. ça ne dérangeait personne
21. remarque
22. souvent Steiner ne voulait pas le faire
23. ouvrier d'usine
24. se débarrasser de

'Let's just say that I know. Dr Steiner couldn't stand her[1]. He goes in for[2] psychotherapy. Intensive psychotherapy. Ever heard of it?'

Dalgliesh admitted that he had. Mrs Shorthouse gave him a look in which disbelief[3] fought with[4] suspicion. Then she leaned forward[5] conspiratorially[6] as if about to divulge[7] one of Dr Steiner's less reputable idiosyncrasies[8].

'He's analytically orientated, that's what he is. Analytically orientated. Know what that means?'

'I've some idea.'

'Then you know that he doesn't see many patients. Two a session, three if you're lucky[9], and a new patient once every eight weeks. That doesn't push up the figures[10].'

'The figures?'

'The attendance figures[11]. They go to the Hospital Management Committee and the Regional Board every quarter[12]. Miss Bolam was a great one for pushing up the figures.'

'Then she must have approved thoroughly[13] of Dr Baguley. I understand that his ECT sessions are usually very busy.'

'She approved all right[14]. Not about his divorce, though.'

'How could that affect[15] the figures?' asked Dalgliesh, innocently obtuse[16]. Mrs Shorthouse looked at him pityingly[17].

'Who said anything about the figures? We were talking about the Baguleys. Getting a divorce, they were, on account of[18] Dr Baguley having an affair with Miss Saxon. It was in all the papers[19], too. Psychiatrist's wife cites[20] psychologist. Then suddenly Mrs Baguley withdrew the case[21]. Never said why.

1. ne pouvait pas la voir en peinture
2. est adepte de
3. incrédulité
4. se mélangeait avec
5. se pencha en avant
6. avec un air de conspiration
7. sur le point de révéler
8. une caractéristique peu flatteuse du Docteur Steiner
9. à tout casser
10. fait pas monter les chiffres
11. les chiffres de fréquentation
12. tous les trimestres
13. elle devait avoir une très bonne opinion
14. elle n'en avait pas une mauvaise opinion
15. avoir une influence sur
16. en faisant semblant de ne pas comprendre
17. avec pitié
18. à cause du fait que
19. dans tous les journaux
20. assigne
21. a retiré sa demande de divorce

No one said why. Didn't make any difference here, though. Dr B and Miss Saxon went on working together easy as you please[1]. Still do.'

'And Dr Baguley and his wife were reconciled[2]?'

'Who said anything about reconciled? They stayed married, that's all I know. Miss Bolam couldn't say a good word for Miss Saxon after that. Not that she ever talked about it; she wasn't one for gossip I'll give her that[3]. But she let Miss Saxon see what she felt. She was against that sort of thing Miss Bolam was[4]. No carrying on with her[5], I can tell you!'

Dalgliesh inquired whether anyone had tried[6]. It was a question he usually put with the maximum of tact, but he felt that subtlety[7] would be lost on Mrs Shorthouse. She gave a scream of laughter.

'What do you think? She wasn't one for the men. Not as far as I know, anyway. Mind you, some of the cases[8] they have here would put you off sex for life[9]. Miss Bolam went to the medical director once to complain about[10] some of the reports Miss Priddy was given to type. Said they weren't decent[11]. Of course, she was always a bit odd about[12] Priddy. Tried to fuss round the kid too much[13] if you ask me. Priddy used to be in Miss Bolam's Guide Company or something when she was young, and I suppose Bolam wanted to keep an eye on her in case she forgot what captain had taught her. You could see the kid was embarrassed by it. There wasn't anything wrong, though. Don't you go believing it if they hint[14] that there was. Some of them here have dirty minds[15] and there's no denying it[16].'

Dalgliesh asked whether Miss Bolam had approved of Miss Priddy's friendship with Nagle.

1. comme si de rien n'était
2. réconciliés
3. il faut le reconnaître
4. elle était réellement opposée à ce genre de choses
5. elle n'était pas du tout du genre à avoir une liaison
6. avait essayé de la séduire
7. subtilité
8. cas
9. vous dégoûteraient du sexe pour toujours
10. se plaindre de
11. convenables
12. bizarre avec
13. elle en faisait trop
14. l'insinuent
15. ont l'esprit mal tourné
16. il n'y a pas à dire

'Oh, you're on to that[1], are you? Nothing to approve of, if you ask me. Nagle's a cold fish[2] and as mean as hell[3]. Just try getting his tea money[4] out of him! He and Priddy play around[5] a bit and I dare say Tigger could tell a thing or two if cats could speak. I don't think Bolam noticed though. She kept pretty much to her own office. Anyway, Nagle isn't encouraged in the general office and the medical stenogs[6] are kept pretty busy, so there isn't much time for hanky-panky[7]. Nagle took good care[8] to keep in Miss B's good books[9]. Quite the little blue-eyed boy he was. Never absent, never late, that's our Peter. Leastways[10], he got stuck[11] in the Underground one Monday and wasn't he in a state about it[12]! Spoilt his record[13], you see. He even came in on May first when he had the flu because we had a visit from the Duke and, naturally, Peter Nagle had to be here to see everything was done proper[14]. Temperature of 103[15] he had. Sister took it[16]. Miss Bolam sent him home pretty soon, I can tell you. Dr Steiner took him in his car.'

'Is it generally known that Mr Nagle keeps his tools in the porters' duty-room?'

'Of course it is! Stands to reason[17]. People are always wanting him to mend[18] this or that and where else would he keep his tools? A proper old woman he is about them[19], too. Talk about fussy[20]. Cully isn't allowed to touch them. Mind you they aren't clinic tools. They belong to Nagle. There wasn't half a row[21] about six weeks ago when Dr Steiner borrowed a screwdriver[22] to do something to his car. Being Dr Steiner he mucked up the job[23] and bent[24] the screwdriver. Talk about trouble[25]! Nagle thought it was Cully and they had

1. vous êtes au courant
2. froid
3. très près de ses sous
4. l'argent pour le thé
5. s'amusent
6. sténos
7. des galipettes
8. a pris soin de
9. être toujours bien vu par Miss B
10. du moins
11. est resté bloqué
12. il était dans un état pas possible
13. c'était mauvais pour son dossier
14. pour que tout soit parfait
15. 40 de fièvre
16. a pris sa température
17. ça va de soi
18. réparer
19. il se comporte comme une vieille maniaque
20. c'est un vrai maniaque
21. il y a eu une belle dispute
22. a emprunté un tournevis
23. a tout bousillé
24. a tordu
25. ça a fait toute une histoire

one hell of a row[1] which brought on Cully's belly-ache again, poor old blighter[2]. Then Nagle found out that someone had seen Dr Steiner coming out of the porters' duty-room with the tool so he complained to Miss Bolam and she spoke to Dr Steiner and made him buy another screwdriver. We do see life here[3], I can tell you. Never a dull moment[4]. Never had a murder before, though[5]. That's something new. Nice goings-on, I don't think[6].'

'As you say. If you've any idea who did it, Mrs Shorthouse, now's the time to say so.'

Mrs Shorthouse adjusted one of the curls on her forehead with a licked[7] finger, wriggled[8] more comfortably into her coat and got to her feet, thus indicating that, in her opinion, the interview was over.

'No fear! Catching murderers is your job, mate[9], and you're welcome to it[10]. I'll say this much, though. It wasn't one of the doctors. They haven't the guts[11]. These psychiatrists are a timid lot[12]. Say what you like about this killer, the chap has nerve[13].'

Dalgliesh decided to question the doctors next. He was surprised and interested by their patience, by their ready acceptance of his role. He had kept them waiting because he judged it more important to his inquiry to see other people first, even such an apparently less important witness as the domestic assistant. It looked as if they appreciated that he wasn't trying to irritate them or keep them unnecessarily in suspense. He wouldn't have hesitated to do either[14] if it would have served his purpose[15], but it was his experience that useful information could most often be obtained when a witness hadn't

1. une sacrée dispute
2. pauvre bougre
3. on en voit de toutes les couleurs
4. on ne s'ennuie jamais
5. par contre
6. ce n'est pas très folichon, si vous voulez mon avis
7. léché
8. se tortilla
9. mon vieux
10. je vous le laisse volontiers
11. ils n'ont pas assez de cran
12. sont timides
13. ne manque pas de courage
14. à faire ni l'un ni l'autre
15. but

been given time to think and could be betrayed by shock or fear[1] into garrulity and indiscretion[2]. The doctors had not kept themselves apart. They had waited in the front consulting-room with the others, quietly and without protest. They gave him the credit of knowing his job[3] and let him get on with it. He wondered whether consultant surgeons[4] or physicians[5] would have been so accommodating[6] and felt with the group secretary that there were worse people to deal with than psychiatrists.

Dr Mary Ingram was seen first by request of the medical director. She had three young children at home and it was important that she get back to them as soon as possible. She had been crying spasmodically[7] while waiting, to the embarrassment of her colleagues who had difficulty in comforting[8] a grief which seemed to them unreasonable and ill-timed[9]. Nurse Bolam was bearing up well[10], after all, and she was a relative[11]. Dr Ingram's tears[12] added to the tension and provoked an irrational guilt[13] in those whose emotions were less uncomplicated[14]. There was a general feeling that she should be allowed[15] to go home to her children without delay[16]. There was little she could tell Dalgliesh. She attended[17] the clinic only twice weekly[18] to help with the ECT sessions and had hardly known[19] Miss Bolam. She had been in the ECT room with Sister Ambrose for the whole of[20] the crucial time from six-twenty until seven. In reply to Dalgliesh's question she admitted that Dr Baguley might have left them for a short time after six-fifteen, but she couldn't remember when exactly or for how long[21]. At the end of the interview she looked at Dalgliesh from reddened eyes[22] and said:

1. pouvait être amené à se trahir sous l'effet du choc ou de la peur
2. et devenir loquace ou se compromettre
3. il lui supposait une bonne connaissance de son métier
4. chirurgiens
5. médecins généralistes
6. conciliants
7. de façon intermittente
8. du mal à consoler
9. déplacé
10. tenait le coup
11. une parente
12. larmes
13. sentiment de culpabilité
14. dont les émotions étaient moins évidentes
15. on devait lui permettre
16. sans tarder
17. fréquentait
18. deux fois par semaine
19. connaissait à peine
20. pendant toute
21. pour combien de temps
22. yeux rougis

'You will find out[1] who did it, won't you? That poor, poor girl.'

'We shall find out,' replied Dalgliesh.

Dr Etherege was interviewed next. He gave the necessary personal details without waiting to be asked and went on:

'As regards[2] my own movements this evening, I'm afraid I can't be very helpful[3]. I arrived at the clinic just before five and went into Miss Bolam's office to speak to her before going upstairs. We had a little general conversation. She seemed perfectly all right to me and didn't tell me that she had asked to see the group secretary. I rang the general office for Mrs Bostock at about five-fifteen and she was with me taking dictation[4] until about ten to six when she went downstairs with the post. She came back after ten minutes or so and we continued with the dictation, until some time before half past six, when she went next door to type material directly from a tape machine[5]. Some of my treatment sessions are recorded[6] and the material subsequently[7] played back[8] and a typescript[9] made either for research purposes or for the medical record. I worked alone in my consulting-room except for one brief visit to the medical library[10] – I can't remember when, but it was very shortly after[11] Mrs Bostock left me – until she returned to consult me on a point. That must have been just before seven because we were together when Sister rang to tell me about Miss Bolam. Miss Saxon came down from her room on the third floor to go home and caught us up[12] on the stairs[13], so she and I went to the basement. You know what we found and the subsequent steps I took[14] to ensure that no one left the clinic.'

1. vous découvrirez
2. en ce qui concerne
3. je ne pourrai pas vous être très utile
4. écrivant sous ma dictée
5. machine à écrire
6. enregistrées
7. ensuite
8. réécouté
9. texte dactylographié
10. bibliothèque
11. peu de temps après
12. elle nous a rattrapés
13. escalier
14. les mesures que j'ai ensuite prises

'You seem to have acted with great presence of mind[1], Doctor,' said Dalgliesh. 'As a result the field of inquiry[2] can be considerably narrowed[3]. It looks, doesn't it, as if the murderer is still in this building?'

'Certainly Cully has assured me that no one got past him[4] after 5 p.m. without being entered in his register[5]. That is our system here. The implication of that locked back door is disturbing, but I'm sure you are too experienced an officer to jump to conclusions[6]. No building is impregnable[7]. The … the person responsible could have got in at any time, even early this morning, and lain hidden[8] in the basement.'

'Can you suggest where such a person lay concealed[9] or how he got out of the clinic?'

The medical director did not reply.

'Have you any idea who that person might be?'

Dr Etherege slowly traced the line of his right eyebrow[10] with his middle finger[11]. Dalgliesh had seen him do this on television and reflected, now as then[12], that it served to draw[13] attention to a fine[14] hand and a well-shaped[15] eyebrow even if as an indication of serious thought the gesture[16] seemed slightly spurious[17].

'I have no idea at all. The whole tragedy is incomprehensible. I'm not going to claim[18] that Miss Bolam was an altogether easy person to get on with[19]. She sometimes aroused[20] resentment.' He smiled deprecatingly[21]. 'We're not always very easy to get on with ourselves and the most successful administrator of a psychiatric unit is probably someone far more tolerant than Miss Bolam, less obsessional perhaps. But this is murder! I can't think of anyone, patient or staff, who would want to kill her.

1. présence d'esprit
2. le champ d'investigation
3. réduit
4. personne n'est passé devant lui
5. registre
6. tirer des conclusions hâtives
7. impénétrable
8. être restée cachée
9. cachée
10. sourcil
11. majeur
12. maintenant comme à moment-là
13. attirer
14. belle
15. bien dessiné
16. le geste
17. spécieux
18. prétendre
19. était facile à vivre
20. provoquait
21. avec désapprobation

It's very horrible to me as medical director to think that there might be someone as disturbed[1] as that working at the Steen and I never knew.'

'As disturbed or as wicked[2],' said Dalgliesh, unable to resist the temptation.

Dr Etherege smiled again, patiently explaining a difficult point to an obtuse[3] member of the television panel[4]. 'Wicked? I'm not competent to discuss this in theological terms.'

'Nor am I[5], Doctor,' replied Dalgliesh. 'But this crime doesn't look like the work of a madman[6]. There's an intelligence behind it.'

'Some psychopaths are highly intelligent, Superintendent. Not that I am knowledgeable about psychopathy. It's a most interesting field but not mine. We have never claimed at the Steen to be able to treat the condition[7].'

Then the Steen was in good company, thought Dalgliesh. The Mental Health Act, 1959, may have defined psychopathy as a disorder[8] requiring or susceptible to medical treatment[9], but there appeared little enthusiasm on the part of doctors to treat it. The word seemed little more than a psychiatrist's term of abuse[10] and he said as much[11]. Dr Etherege smiled, indulgent, unprovoked[12].

'I have never accepted a clinical entity because it is defined in an Act of Parliament. However, psychopathy exists. I'm not convinced at present that it is susceptible to medical treatment. What I am sure is that it is not susceptible to a prison sentence[13]. But we have no certainty that we're looking for a psychopath.'

1. dérangé
2. méchant
3. obtus
4. débat télévisé
5. moi non plus
6. fou
7. traiter ce trouble mental
8. trouble
9. nécessitant ou susceptible de réagir à un traitement médical
10. injure
11. il ne se gêna pas pour le dire
12. il ne se sentait pas provoqué
13. peine

Dalgliesh asked Dr Etherege whether he knew where Nagle kept his tools and which key opened the door of the record-room.

'I knew about the key. If I'm working late and alone I sometimes need one of the old files and I fetch it[1] myself. I do a certain amount of research and, of course, lecturing[2] and writing, and it's important to have access to the medical records. I last fetched a file about ten days ago. I don't think I've ever seen the box of tools in the porters' room, but I knew that Nagle had his own set and was particular about them[3]. I suppose if I'd wanted a chisel I should have looked in the porters' room. The tools would hardly be kept anywhere else[4]. Obviously, too, I should expect Tippett's fetish to be in the art therapy department. It was a most[5] curious choice of weapons! What I find interesting is the apparent care[6] taken by the murderer to fix suspicion on[7] the clinic staff.'

'Suspicion can hardly rest elsewhere in the face of[8] those locked doors.'

'That's what I meant, Superintendent. If a member of the staff present this evening did kill Miss Bolam surely he would want to divert[9] suspicion from the relatively few people[10] known to be in the building at the time. The easiest way to do that would be to unlock[11] one of the doors. He'd need to wear gloves[12], of course, but then, I gather[13] that he did wear them.'

'There are no prints[14] on either of the weapons, certainly. They were wiped[15], but it is probable that he did wear gloves.'

'And yet, those doors were kept locked, the strongest evidence[16] that the murderer was still in

1. je vais le chercher
2. je donne des conférences
3. y faisait très attention
4. ailleurs
5. très
6. soin
7. faire peser les soupçons sur
8. à cause de
9. détourner
10. peu de gens
11. déverrouiller
12. gants
13. j'imagine
14. empreintes
15. elles ont été essuyées
16. preuve

the building. Why? It would be risky to unlock the back door on the ground floor. That, as you know, is between the ECT room and the medical staff-room[1] and it leads into[2] a well-lit[3] road. It would be difficult to unlock it without the risk of being seen, and a murderer would hardly make his exit that way. But there are the two fire-escape doors[4] on the second and third floors and the door in the basement. Why not unlock one of those? It can only be, surely, because the murderer hadn't the opportunity between the time of the crime and the finding of the body, or that he deliberately wished to throw suspicion on[5] the clinic staff even at the inevitable cost of increasing[6] his own danger.'

'You talk about "he", Doctor. Do you think, as a psychiatrist, that we should be looking for a man?'

'Oh yes! I would expect this to be the work of a man.'

'Although it didn't require great strength[7]?' asked Dalgliesh.

'I wasn't thinking primarily of the strength required but of the method and the choice of weapon. I can only give my opinion, of course, and I'm not a criminologist. I would expect it to be a man's crime. But, of course, a woman could have done it. Psychologically, it's unlikely. Physically, it's perfectly possible.'

It was indeed, thought Dalgliesh. It required merely[8] knowledge and nerve[9]. He pictured[10] for a moment an intent[11], pretty face bent over[12] Miss Bolam's body; a thin, girlish hand slipping open[13] the sweater[14] buttons and rolling up[15] the fine cashmere jumper[16]. And then, that clinical selection of exactly the right place to pierce[17], and the grunt[18]

1. salle du personnel médical
2. donne sur
3. bien éclairée
4. sorties de secours
5. que les soupçons se portent sur
6. même si cela augmentait inévitablement
7. force
8. seulement
9. courage
10. il s'imagina
11. attentif
12. penché sur
13. défaisant
14. du pull
15. retroussant
16. tricot
17. à transpercer
18. grognement

of effort as the blade went home[1]. And, last of all, the sweater drawn[2] lightly back to conceal[3] the chisel handle, the ugly fetish placed in position on the still twitching body[4] in an ultimate gesture of derision and defiance[5]. He told the medical director about Mrs Shorthouse's evidence of the phone call.

'No one has admitted to making that call. It looks very much as if she were tricked down to the basement[6].'

'That is mere supposition, Superintendent.'

Dalgliesh pointed out mildly that it was also common sense[7], the basis of all sound[8] police work. The medical director said:

'There is a card hung beside the telephone outside the record-room. Anyone, even a stranger to the clinic, could discover Miss Bolam's number.'

'But what would be her reaction to an internal call from a stranger? She went downstairs without question. She must have recognized the voice.'

'Then it was someone she had no reason to fear, Superintendent. That doesn't tie up with[9] the suggestion that she was in possession of some dangerous knowledge and was killed to prevent her passing it on to[10] Lauder. She went down to her death without fear or suspicion. I can only hope that she died quickly and without pain[11].'

Dalgliesh said that he would know more when he got the autopsy report but that death was almost certainly instantaneous. He added:

'There must have been one dreadful[12] moment when she looked up and saw her murderer with the fetish raised[13], but it happened very quickly. She would feel nothing after she was stunned[14]. I doubt whether she even had time to cry out[15]. If she did

1. la lame atteignait son but
2. tiré
3. cacher
4. alors que le corps s'agitait encore convulsivement
5. défi
6. c'était une ruse pour l'attirer vers le sous-sol
7. du bon sens
8. solide
9. ne cadre pas avec
10. l'empêcher de la transmettre à
11. sans souffrir
12. atroce
13. levé
14. assommée
15. crier

the sound would be muffled[1] by the tiers[2] of paper and I'm told that Mrs King was being rather noisy[3] during her treatment.' He paused for a moment, then said quietly: 'What made you describe to the staff just how Miss Bolam died? You did tell them?'

'Of course. I called them together in the front consulting-room – the patients were in the waiting-room – and made a brief statement[4]. Are you suggesting that the news could have been kept from them[5]?'

'I am suggesting that they need not have been told the details[6]. It would have been useful to me if you hadn't mentioned the stabbing[7]. The murderer might have given himself away[8] by showing more knowledge than an innocent person could have possessed.'

The medical director smiled.

'I'm a psychiatrist not a detective. Strange as it may seem to you[9], my reaction to this crime was to assume that the rest of the staff would share my horror and distress, not to lay traps for them[10]. I wanted to break the news to them[11] myself, gently and honestly. They have always had my confidence and I saw no reason for withholding that confidence[12] now.'

That was all very well, thought Dalgliesh, but an intelligent man must surely have seen the importance of saying as little as possible. And the medical director was a very intelligent man. As he thanked his witness and drew the interview to its close[13], his mind busied itself[14] with the problem. How carefully had Dr Etherege considered the position[15] before he spoke to the staff? Had his disclosure of[16] the stabbing been as thoughtless[17] as it ap-

1. étouffé
2. rangées
3. bruyante
4. j'ai exposé brièvement la situation
5. on aurait pu leur cacher la nouvelle
6. il n'aurait pas été nécessaire de leur donner des détails
7. le fait qu'elle a été poignardée
8. se trahir
9. aussi étrange que cela puisse vous paraître
10. leur tendre des pièges
11. leur annoncer la nouvelle
12. ne plus leur faire confiance
13. mit fin à l'entretien
14. s'occupa
15. la situation
16. le fait de révéler
17. irréfléchi

peared? It would, after all, have been impossible to deceive[1] most of the staff. Dr Steiner, Dr Baguley, Nagle, Dr Ingram and Sister Ambrose had all seen the body. Miss Priddy had seen it but had apparently fled[2] without a second look. That left Nurse Bolam, Mrs Bostock, Mrs Shorthouse, Miss Saxon, Miss Kettle and Cully. Possibly Etherege was satisfied that none of these was the murderer. Cully and Shorthouse both[3] had an alibi. Had the medical director been reluctant to[4] lay a trap for Nurse Bolam, Mrs Bostock or Miss Saxon? Or was he so certain in his own mind that the murderer must be a man that any subterfuge to mislead[5] the women seemed a waste of time[6], likely to result only in embarrassment and resentment? The medical director had certainly been almost blatant in his hints[7] that anyone working on the second or third floor could be eliminated since they would have had the opportunity of opening one of the fire-escape doors. But, then, he himself had been in his consulting-room on the second floor. In any case, the obvious door for the killer to unlock was the one in the basement and it was hard to believe that he had lacked the opportunity[8]. It would be a second's work only to draw back that lock[9] and provide evidence that the murderer could have left the clinic that way. Yet the basement door had been fast bolted[10]. Why?

Dr Steiner came in next, short, dapper[11], outwardly self-composed[12]. In the light from Miss Bolam's desk lamp his pale smooth[13] skin looked slightly luminous. Despite his calmness he had been sweating heavily[14]. The heavy smell[15] hung about his clothes, about the well-cut[16], conventional black coat of a consultant. Dalgliesh was surprised when

1. tromper
2. s'était enfuie
3. tous deux
4. avait-il été réticent à l'idée de
5. induire en erreur
6. une perte de temps
7. avait fait des allusions quasi manifestes
8. il n'en avait pas eu l'opportunité
9. ouvrir la serrure
10. bien fermée à clé
11. fringant
12. apparemment calme
13. lisse
14. il avait beaucoup transpiré
15. la forte odeur de transpiration
16. bien taillé

he gave his age as forty-two. He looked older. The smooth skin, the sharp black eyes, the bouncy[1] walk gave a superficial impression of youth but he was already thickening[2] and his dark hair, cunningly sleeked back[3], could not quite conceal the tonsure-like patch on the crown of the head[4].

Dr Steiner had apparently decided to treat his encounter with a policeman as a social occasion. Extending[5] a plump, well-kept[6] hand, he smiled a benign[7] 'how d'you do?[8]' and inquired whether he was speaking to the writer, Adam Dalgliesh.

'I have read your verse,' he announced complacently[9]. 'I congratulate you[10]. Such a deceptive[11] simplicity. I started at the first poem and read straight through[12]. That is my way of experiencing verse. At the tenth page I began to think that we might have a new poet.'

Dalgliesh admitted to himself that Dr Steiner had not only read the book but showed some critical insight[13]. It was at the tenth page that he, too, sometimes felt they might have a new poet. Dr Steiner inquired whether he had met Ernie Bales, the new young playwright[14] from Nottingham. He looked so hopeful[15] that Dalgliesh felt positively unkind[16] as he disclaimed acquaintance with[17] Mr Bales and steered the conversation from literary criticism back to[18] the purpose of the interview. Dr Steiner at once assumed an air of shocked gravity.

'The whole affair is dreadful, quite dreadful. I was one of the first people to see the body as you may know and it has distressed me greatly. I have always had a horror of violence. It is an appalling[19] business. Dr Etherege, our medical director, is due

1. pleine d'entrain
2. il commençait à engraisser
3. astucieusement lissés vers l'arrière
4. la calvitie semblable à une tonsure au sommet de sa tête
5. tendant
6. soignée
7. bienveillant
8. enchanté
9. d'un ton suffisant
10. je vous félicite
11. si trompeuse
12. j'ai tout lu d'une traite
13. faisait preuve d'un certain discernement critique
14. dramaturge
15. plein d'espoir
16. vraiment désobligeant
17. nia connaître
18. redirigea la conversation vers
19. épouvantable

to retire[1] at the end of the year. This is a most unfortunate thing[2] to happen in his last months here.'

He shook his head sadly, but Dalgliesh fancied[3] that the little black eyes held something very like satisfaction.

Tippett's fetish had yielded[4] its secrets to the fingerprint expert and Dalgliesh had stood it on the desk before him. Dr Steiner put out his hand[5] to touch it then drew back and said:

'I had better not handle it[6], I suppose, because of fingerprints.' He darted a quick look[7] at Dalgliesh and getting no response went on: 'It's an interesting carving, isn't it? Quite remarkable. Have you ever noticed, Superintendent, what excellent art the mentally ill[8] can produce, even patients without previous training or experience? It raises[9] interesting questions on the nature of artistic achievement[10]. As they recover[11], their work deteriorates[12]. The power and originality go. By the time they are well again the stuff they produce is valueless[13]. We've got several interesting examples of patients' work in the art therapy department, but this fetish is outstanding[14]. Tippett was very ill when he carved it and went to hospital shortly afterwards. He's a schizophrenic. The fetish has the typical facies[15] of the chronic disease[16], the frog-like[17] eyes and spreading nostrils[18]. Tippett looked very like that himself at one time.'

'Everyone knew where this thing was kept, I suppose?' said Dalgliesh.

'Oh, yes! It was kept on the shelf in the art therapy department. Tippett was very proud[19] of it and Dr Baguley often showed it to House Committee members when they made visits of inspection.

1. doit prendre sa retraite
2. événement particulièrement fâcheux
3. pensa
4. livré
5. avança la main
6. y toucher
7. lança un regard rapide
8. les malades mentaux
9. soulève
10. réussite artistique
11. guérissent
12. se détériore
13. sans valeur
14. remarquable
15. faciès
16. maladie
17. de grenouille
18. narines élargies
19. fier

Mrs Baumgarten, the art therapist, likes to keep some of the best work on show[1]. That's why she had the shelves put up[2]. She's on sick leave[3] at the present but you've been shown[4] the department, I expect?'

Dalgliesh said that he had.

'Some of my colleagues feel that the art therapy is a waste of money,' confided Dr Steiner. 'Certainly I never use Mrs Baumgarten. But one must be tolerant. Dr Baguley refers[5] patients now and again[6], and it probably does them less harm[7] to dabble about[8] down there than to be subjected to ECT[9]. But to pretend that the patients' artistic efforts can help towards a diagnosis seems very far fetched[10] to me. Of course that claim[11] is all part of the effort to get Mrs Baumgarten graded as[12] a lay psychotherapist, quite unwarrantably[13], I'm afraid. She has no analytical training[14].'

'And the chisel? Did you know where that was kept, Doctor?'

'Well, not really, Superintendent. I mean, I knew that Nagle had some tools and presumably[15] kept them in the porters' dutyroom, but I didn't know exactly where.'

'The toolbox is large and clearly labelled[16] and is kept on the small table in the duty-room. It would be difficult to miss[17].'

'Oh, I'm sure it would! But then, I have no reason to go into the porters' duty-room. That is true of all the doctors. We must get a key for that box now and see that it's kept somewhere safe. Miss Bolam was very wrong to allow Nagle to keep it unlocked. After all, we do occasionally have disturbed patients and some tools can be lethal[18].'

1. pour les exposer
2. elle a fait installer les étagères
3. en congé maladie
4. vous avez visité
5. y envoie
6. de temps en temps
7. il est probablement moins nocif pour eux
8. faire un peu de peinture
9. subir un traitement par électrochocs
10. tiré par les cheveux
11. prétention
12. lui accorder le statut de
13. de façon injustifiable
14. aucune formation en psychologie analytique
15. probablement
16. porte une étiquette très claire
17. de ne pas la voir
18. meurtriers

'So it appears[1].'

'This clinic wasn't intended to treat grossly[2] psychotic patients, of course. It was founded to provide a centre for analytically orientated psychotherapy, particularly for middle-class and highly intelligent patients. We treat people who would never dream of[3] entering a mental hospital[4] – and who would be just as out of place[5] in the ordinary psychiatric outpatient department. In addition, of course, there is a large research element in our work.'

'What were you doing between six o'clock and seven this evening, Doctor?' inquired Dalgliesh.

Dr Steiner looked pained[6] at this sudden intrusion of sordid curiosity into an interesting discussion but answered, meekly enough[7], that he had been conducting his Friday night psychotherapy session.

'I arrived at the clinic at five-thirty when my first patient was booked[8]. Unfortunately he defaulted[9]. His treatment has arrived at a stage when poor attendance is to be expected[10]. Mr Burge was booked for six-fifteen and he is usually very prompt[11]. I waited for him in the second consulting-room on the ground floor and joined him in my own room at about ten past six. Mr Burge dislikes[12] waiting with Dr Baguley's patients in the general waiting-room and I really don't blame him. You've heard of Burge, I expect. He wrote that interesting novel *The Souls of the Righteous*[13], a quite brilliant exposure of[14] the sexual conflicts concealed beneath the conventionality of a respectable English suburb[15]. But I'm forgetting. Naturally you have interviewed Mr Burge.'

1. on dirait
2. réellement
3. à qui il ne viendrait jamais à l'idée de
4. hôpital psychiatrique
5. ne se sentiraient pas non plus à leur place
6. peiné
7. docilement
8. avait rendez-vous
9. il n'est pas venu
10. il faut s'attendre à un manque d'assiduité
11. à l'heure
12. n'aime pas
13. justes
14. qui révèle brillamment
15. banlieue

Dalgliesh had indeed. The experience had been tedious[1] and not unenlightening[2]. He had also heard of Mr Burge's book, an opus[3] of some two hundred thousand words in which the scabrous[4] episodes are inserted with such meticulous deliberation that it only requires an exercise in simple arithmetic to calculate on what page the next will occur[5]. Dalgliesh did not suspect Burge of any part in the murder. A writer who could produce such a hotchpotch[6] of sex and sadism was probably impotent and certainly timid. But he was not necessarily a liar[7]. Dalgliesh said:

'Are you quite sure of your times, Doctor? Mr Burge says that he arrived at six-fifteen and Cully has booked him in at that time. Burge says he went straight into your own consulting-room, having checked[8] with Cully that you weren't seeing a patient, and that it was a full ten minutes before you joined him. He was getting impatient and was thinking of going to inquire[9] where you were.'

Dr Steiner did not appear either frightened[10] or angry[11] at his patient's perfidy. He did, however, look embarrassed[12].

'It's interesting Mr Burge should say that. I'm afraid he may be right. I thought he seemed a little put out[13] when we began the session. If he says that I joined him at six-twenty-five I have no doubt he's telling the truth. The poor man has had a very short and interrupted session this evening. It's very unfortunate[14] at this particular stage in his treatment.'

'So, if you weren't in the front consulting-room when your patient arrived, where were you?' persisted Dalgliesh gently.

1. fastidieuse
2. non dépourvue d'intérêt
3. ouvrage
4. scabreux
5. se trouve le suivant
6. salmigondis
7. menteur
8. après avoir vérifié
9. se renseigner
10. effrayé
11. fâché
12. gêné
13. contrarié
14. fâcheux

An astonishing[1] change came over Dr Steiner's face. Suddenly he looked as shamefaced[2] as a small boy who has been caught in the middle of mischief[3]. He didn't look frightened but he did look extremely guilty[4]. The metamorphosis from consultant psychiatrist to embarrassed delinquent was almost comical.

'But I told you, Superintendent! I was in number two consulting-room, the one between the front one and the patients' waiting-room.'

'Doing what, Doctor?'

Really, it was almost laughable[5]! What could Steiner have been up to to[6] produce this degree of embarrassment? Dalgliesh's mind toyed with[7] bizarre possibilities. Reading pornography? Smoking hemp[8]? Seducing Mrs Shorthouse? It surely couldn't be anything so conventional as planning murder. But the doctor had obviously decided that the truth must be told. He said with a burst[9] of shamefaced[10] candour:

'It sounds silly[11], I know, but … well … it was rather warm and I'd had a busy day and the couch was there.' He gave a little giggle[12]. 'In fact, Superintendent, at the time Miss Bolam is thought to have died, I was, in the vulgar parlance[13], having a kip[14]!'

Once[15] this embarrassing confession was off his chest[16] Dr Steiner became happily voluble[17] and it was difficult to get rid of him[18]. But at last[19] he was persuaded that he could help no more for the present and his place was taken by Dr Baguley.

Dr Baguley, like his colleagues, made no complaint[20] of his long wait, but it had taken its toll[21].

1. étonnant
2. honteux
3. qui a été pris en train de faire des bêtises
4. coupable
5. risible
6. qu'avait-il pu faire pour
7. s'imagina diverses
8. marijuana
9. explosion
10. penaude
11. stupide
12. ricanement
13. comme on dit vulgairement
14. je piquais un roupillon
15. une fois que
16. il fut débarrassé de cette confession délicate
17. loquace
18. se débarrasser de lui
19. enfin
20. ne se plaignit pas
21. l'attente avait laissée des traces

He was still wearing his white coat and he hugged it around himself[1] as he drew the chair under him. He seemed to have difficulty in settling comfortably, twitching[2] his lean[3] shoulders and crossing and recrossing his legs. The clefts[4] from nose to mouth looked deeper[5], his hair was dank[6], his eyes black pools[7] in the light of the desk lamp. He lit[8] a cigarette and, fumbling[9] in his coat pocket, produced a slip[10] of paper and passed it to Martin.

'I've written down my personal details. It'll save time.'

'Thank you, sir,' said Martin stolidly[11].

'I may as well say now that I haven't an alibi for the twenty minutes or so after six-fifteen. I expect you've heard that I left the ECT clinic a few minutes before Sister saw Miss Bolam for the last time. I went into the medical staff cloakroom at the end of the hall and had a cigarette. The place was empty[12] and no one came in. I didn't hurry back to the clinic so I suppose it was about twenty to seven before I rejoined[13] Dr Ingram and Sister. They were together for the whole of that time, of course.'

'So Sister tells me.'

'It's ridiculous even to consider that either of them would be involved[14] but I'm glad[15] they happened to stick[16] together. The more people you can eliminate the better[17] from your point of view, I suppose. I'm sorry not to be able to produce an alibi. I can't help in any other way either, I'm afraid. I heard and saw nothing.'

Dalgliesh asked the doctor how he had spent the evening.

'It was the usual pattern[18], until seven o'clock that is. I arrived just before four and went into Miss Bolam's

1. le serrait autour de lui
2. il bougeait
3. maigres
4. ridules
5. plus profondes
6. poisseux
7. flaques
8. alluma
9. fouillant
10. en retira un morceau
11. flegmatiquement
12. vide
13. j'ai rejoint
14. impliquée
15. content
16. étaient restées
17. mieux c'est
18. comme d'habitude

office to sign the medical attendance book. It used to be kept in the medical staff cloakroom until recently when she moved it into her office. We talked for a short time – she had some queries[1] about the servicing arrangements[2] for my new ECT machine – and then I went to start my clinic[3]. We were pretty busy[4] until just after six and I also had my lysergic acid patient to visit periodically. She was being specialled by Nurse Bolam in the basement treatment-room. But I'm forgetting. You've seen Mrs King.'

Mrs King and her husband had been sitting in the patients' waiting-room on Dalgliesh's arrival[5] and he had taken very little time to satisfy himself that they could have had nothing to do with the murder. The woman was still weak[6] and a little disorientated and sat holding tightly to[7] her husband's hand. He had not arrived at the clinic to escort her home until a few minutes after Sergeant Martin and his party[8]. Dalgliesh had questioned the woman briefly and gently and had let her go. He had not needed the assurances of the medical director to be satisfied that this patient could not have left her bed to murder anyone. But he was equally sure that she was in no state to give an alibi to anyone else. He asked Dr Baguley when he had last visited his patient.

'I looked in on her[9] shortly after I arrived, before I started the shock treatment actually. The drug[10] had been given at three-thirty and the patient was beginning to react. I ought to say that LSD is given in an effort to make the patient more accessible to psychotherapy by releasing[11] some of the more deep-seated[12] inhibitions. It's only given under

1. questions
2. dispositions nécessaires à l'entretien
3. consultation
4. très occupés
5. à l'arrivée de Dalgliesh
6. faible
7. en tenant fermement
8. équipe
9. je suis passé la voir
10. médicament
11. en libérant
12. profondément enracinées

close supervision[1] and the patient is never left[2]. I was called down again by Nurse Bolam at five and stayed for about forty minutes. I went back upstairs and gave my last shock treatment at about twenty to six. The last ECT patient actually left the clinic a few minutes after Miss Bolam was last seen. From about six-thirty I was clearing up[3] and writing my notes.'

'Was the door of the medical record-room open when you passed it at five o'clock?'

Dr Baguley thought for a moment or two and then said:

'I think it was shut. It's difficult to be absolutely certain, but I'm pretty[4] sure I should have noticed[5] if it had been open or ajar.'

'And at twenty to six when you left your patient?'

'The same.'

Dalgliesh asked again the usual, the inevitable, the obvious questions. Had Miss Bolam any enemies? Did the doctor know of any reason why someone might wish her dead[6]? Had she seemed worried[7] lately[8]? Had he any idea why she might have sent for[9] the group secretary? Could he decipher[10] the notes on her jotting pad[11]? But Dr Baguley could not help. He said:

'She was a curious woman in some ways, shy[12], a little aggressive, not really happy with us. But she was perfectly harmless[13], the last person I'd have said to invite[14] violence. One can't go on saying how shocking it is. Words seem to lose their meaning with repetition. But I suppose we all feel the same. The whole thing[15] is fantastic! Unbelievable[16]!'

'You said she wasn't happy here. Is this a difficult clinic to administer? From what I've heard[17],

1. sous étroite surveillance
2. laissé seul
3. je rangeais
4. presque
5. j'aurais remarqué
6. souhaiter sa mort
7. inquiète
8. ces derniers temps
9. elle aurait fait venir
10. déchiffrer
11. bloc-notes
12. timide
13. inoffensive
14. inciter à
15. toute cette affaire
16. incroyable
17. d'après ce que j'ai entendu

Miss Bolam wasn't particularly skilled[1] at dealing with[2] difficult personalities.'

Dr Baguley said easily[3]:

'Oh, you don't want to believe[4] all you hear. We're individualists, but we get along with each other pretty well[5] on the whole[6]. Steiner and I scrap[7] a bit but it's all quite amiable[8]. He wants the place to become a psychotherapy training unit with registrars[9] and lay professional staff running around[10] like mice[11] and a bit of research on the side. One of those places where time and money are spent lavishly[12] on anything but[13] actually treating patients – especially psychotics. There's no danger he'll get his way[14]. The Regional Board wouldn't wear it[15] for one thing[16].'

'And what were Miss Bolam's views, Doctor?'

'Strictly speaking she was hardly competent to hold any[17], but that didn't inhibit her. She was anti-Freudian and pro-eclectic. Anti-Steiner and pro-me if you like. But that didn't mean anything. Neither Dr Steiner nor I were likely to knock her on the head because of our doctrinal differences. As you see we haven't even taken a knife to each other yet[18]. All this is utterly irrelevant[19].'

'I'm inclined to agree with you,' said Dalgliesh. 'Miss Bolam was killed with great deliberation and considerable expertise. I think the motive was a great deal more positive[20] and important than a mere difference of opinion or clash of personality. Did you know, by the way[21], which key opens the record-room?'

'Of course. If I want one of the old records I usually fetch it myself. I also know, if it's any help to you[22], that Nagle keeps his box of tools in the por-

1. douée
2. traiter
3. avec aisance
4. il vaut mieux ne pas croire
5. on s'entend plutôt bien
6. dans l'ensemble
7. nous nous bagarrons
8. de façon amicale
9. chefs de clinique
10. courant partout
11. des souris
12. sans compter
13. tout sauf
14. il n'y a aucun risque qu'il parvienne à ses fins
15. ne le tolèrerait pas
16. pour commencer
17. avoir une opinion
18. nous ne nous sommes même pas encore menacés d'un couteau
19. totalement hors de propos
20. réel
21. au fait
22. si cela peut vous aider

ters' rest-room. Furthermore, when I arrived this afternoon, Miss Bolam told me about Tippett. But that's hardly relevant[1], is it? You can't seriously believe that the murderer hoped to implicate Tippett.'

'Perhaps not. Tell me, Doctor. From your knowledge of Miss Bolam what would be her reaction to finding those medical records strewn about[2] the floor?'

Dr Baguley looked surprised for a second then gave a curt laugh[3].

'Bolam? That's an easy one[4]! She was obsessionally neat[5]. Obviously she'd start to pick them up[6]!'

'She wouldn't be more likely to ring for a porter to do the work or to leave the records where they were as evidence until the culprit[7] was discovered?'

Dr Baguley thought for a moment and seemed to repent of his first categorical opinion.

'One can't possibly know for certain what she'd do[8]. It's all conjecture. Probably you're right and she'd ring for Nagle. She wasn't afraid of work but she was very conscious of[9] her position as AO. I'm sure of one thing, though. She wouldn't have left the place in a mess like that[10]. She couldn't pass a rug[11] or a picture[12] without straightening it[13].'

'And her cousin? Are they alike?[14] I understand that[15] Nurse Bolam works for you more than for any other consultant.'

Dalgliesh noticed the quick frown[16] of distaste[17] that this question provoked. Dr Baguley, however co-operative and frank about his own motives, was not disposed to comment on those of anyone else. Or was it that Nurse Bolam's gentle defencelessness[18] had aroused his protective instincts?

1. guère pertinent
2. éparpillés
3. eut un petit rire brusque
4. c'est facile
5. maniaque de l'ordre et de la propreté
6. les ramasser
7. coupable
8. ce qu'elle aurait fait
9. tenait à
10. dans un tel désordre
11. tapis
12. tableau
13. sans les remettre en place
14. se ressemblent-elles ?
15. si j'ai bien compris
16. grimace
17. dégoût
18. vulnérabilité

1. sèchement
2. je ne dirais pas que
3. une confiance totale
4. héritière
5. la conclusion était trop évidente pour ne pas s'imposer
6. pour elle
7. une sacrée belle somme
8. pourront
9. plus tôt
10. résolu
11. mieux ce sera
12. dernière
13. toilettes
14. ne savait pas mentir
15. ne tremblaient pas
16. manque d'intérêt
17. il se força à

Dalgliesh waited for a reply. After a minute the doctor said curtly[1]:

'I shouldn't have said[2] the cousins were alike. You will have formed your own impression of Nurse Bolam. I can only say that I have complete trust[3] in her, both as a nurse and a person.'

'She is her cousin's heir[4]. Or perhaps you knew that?'

The inference was too plain to be missed[5] and Dr Baguley too tired to resist the provocation.

'No, I didn't. But I hope for her sake[6] that it's a bloody great sum[7] and that she and her mother will be allowed to[8] enjoy it in peace. And I hope, too, that you won't waste time suspecting innocent people. The sooner[9] this murder is cleared up[10] the better[11]. It's a pretty intolerable position for all of us.'

So Dr Baguley knew about Nurse Bolam's mother. But, then, it was likely that most of the clinic staff knew. He asked his last[12] question:

'You said, Doctor, that you were alone in the medical staff cloakroom from about six-fifteen until twenty to seven. What were you doing?'

'Going to the lavatory[13]. Washing my hands. Smoking a cigarette. Thinking.'

'And that was absolutely all you did during the twenty-five minutes?'

'Yes – that was all, Superintendent.'

Dr Baguley was a poor liar[14]. The hesitation was only momentary; his face did not change colour; the fingers holding his cigarette were quite steady[15]. But his voice was a little too nonchalant, the disinterest[16] a little too carefully controlled. And it was with a palpable effort that he made himself[17] meet

Dalgliesh's eyes. He was too intelligent to add to his statement but his eyes held those of the detective as if willing[1] Dalgliesh to repeat his question, and bracing himself[2] to meet it[3].

'Thank you, Doctor,' said Dalgliesh calmly. 'That will be all for the present[4].'

1. comme s'il voulait
2. rassemblait ses forces
3. pour y faire face
4. pour le moment

CHAPTER THREE

And so it went on: the patient questioning, the meticulous taking of notes, the close watch[1] of suspects' eyes and hands for the revealing flicker of fear[2], the tensed[3] reaction to an unwelcome change of emphasis[4]. Fredrica Saxon followed[5] Dr Baguley. As they passed each other[6] in the doorway[7] Dalgliesh saw that they were careful not to meet each other's eyes. She was a dark, vital[8], casually dressed[9] woman of twenty-nine who would do no more than give brief but straightforward[10] answers to his questions and who seemed to take a perverse pleasure in pointing out[11] that she had been alone scoring[12] a psychological test in her own room from six until seven and could neither claim an alibi for herself nor give one to anyone else. He got little help or information from Fredrica Saxon but did not, on that account[13], assume that she had none to give.

She was followed by a very different witness. Miss Ruth Kettle had apparently decided that the murder was none of her affair[14] and, although she was willing[15] to answer Dalgliesh's questions, it was with a vague lack of interest which suggested that her thoughts were on higher[16] things. There is only a limited number of words to express horror and surprise and the clinic staff had used most of

1. surveillance étroite
2. signe de peur
3. crispée
4. fâcheux changement de sujet
5. succéda à
6. se croisèrent
7. dans l'embrasure de la porte
8. dynamique
9. habillée de façon décontractée
10. franches
11. affirmer avec un plaisir pervers
12. elle corrigeait
13. pour autant
14. ne la concernait pas du tout
15. disposée
16. plus importantes

them during the evening. Miss Kettle's reaction was less orthodox. She gave her opinion that the murder was peculiar[1] … really very odd indeed, and sat blinking[2] at Dalgliesh through her thick spectacles in gentle bewilderment[3] as if she did indeed find it odd, but hardly sufficiently odd to be worth discussing at length[4]. But at least two pieces of information which she was able to give were interesting. Dalgliesh could only hope that they were reliable[5].

She had been vague about her own movements during the evening, but Dalgliesh's persistence elicited[6] that she had been interviewing the wife of one of the ECT patients until about twenty to six when Sister had telephoned to say that the patient was ready to be taken home. Miss Kettle had walked downstairs with her client, said 'good night' in the hall and had then gone straight down to the record-room to fetch a file. She had found the room in perfect order and had locked it after her. Despite[7] her gentle[8] incertitude about most of the evening's activities she was positive[9] about the time. In any case[10], thought Dalgliesh, it could probably be verified by Sister Ambrose. The second clue[11] was more nebulous[12] and Miss Kettle mentioned it with apparent indifference to its importance. Some half-hour after returning to her room on the second floor she had heard the unmistakable sound of the service lift thumping to a stop[13].

Dalgliesh was tired now. Despite the central heating he felt spasms of cold and recognized the familiar malaise that preceded an attack of neuralgia[14]. The right side of his face already felt stiff[15] and heavy, and the needling pain was beginning to

1. bizarre
2. à cligner des yeux
3. en signe de perplexité
4. pour que cela vaille la peine d'en discuter dans les détails
5. fiables
6. lui permit d'apprendre
7. malgré
8. légère
9. certaine
10. quoi qu'il en soit
11. indice
12. vague
13. le bruit sourd caractéristique que l'ascenseur de service faisait en s'arrêtant
14. névralgie
15. engourdi

stab spasmodically behind his eyeball[1]. But his last witness was here.

Mrs Bostock, the senior medical stenographer, had none of the doctors' tolerant acceptance of a long wait. She was angry and her anger came into the room with her like a chill[2] wind. She seated herself without speaking, crossed a pair of long and remarkably shapely[3] legs, and looked at Dalgliesh with frank dislike[4] in her pale eyes. She had a striking and unusual head. Her long hair, golden as a guinea[5], was coiled in intricate folds[6] above a pale, arrogant, sharp-nosed face. With her long neck, poised[7], colourful head and slightly protuberant eyes, she looked like some exotic bird. Dalgliesh had difficulty in concealing his shock when he saw her hands. They were as huge[8], red and raw-boned[9] as the hands of a butcher[10] and looked as if they had been incongruously grafted[11] on to the slim wrists[12] by some malignant fate[13]. It was almost a deformity[14]. She made no attempt to conceal them, but her nails[15] were short and she wore no polish[16]. She had a beautiful figure[17] and was well and expensively dressed, an object lesson[18] in the art of minimizing one's defects[19] and emphasizing[20] one's advantages. She probably lived her life, thought Dalgliesh, on much the same principle.

She gave details of her movements since six o'clock that evening briefly and with no apparent reluctance[21]. She had last seen Miss Bolam at six o'clock when, as was usual, she had taken in the post for the administrative officer to sign. There were only five letters. Most of the post consisted of medical reports and letters to general practitioners[22] from the psychiatrists and Miss Bolam was

1. des coups d'épingle commencèrent à lui taper le fond de l'œil
2. glacial
3. bien galbées
4. antipathie
5. guinée (pièce de 21 shillings)
6. relevés en un savant chignon
7. immobile
8. énormes
9. décharnées
10. boucher
11. greffées de manière incongrue
12. poignets minces
13. par quelque mauvais coup du sort
14. difformité
15. ongles
16. vernis
17. jolie silhouette
18. illustration
19. défauts
20. accentuer
21. réticence
22. médecins généralistes

not, of course, concerned with these. All the outgoing mail was registered in the post book by either Mrs Bostock or Miss Priddy, and was then taken across the road by Nagle[1] to catch the six-thirty[2] from the pillar-box. Miss Bolam had seemed her usual self[3] at six o'clock. She had signed her own letters and Mrs Bostock had returned to the general office, handed[4] them with the doctors' post to Miss Priddy, and had then gone upstairs to take dictation from Dr Etherege for the last hour of the day. It was an understood thing[5] that she helped Dr Etherege on Friday evenings for one hour with his research project. She and the medical director had been together except for a few short periods. Sister rang at about seven o'clock with the news of Miss Bolam's death. As she and Dr Etherege left the consulting-room they met Miss Saxon who was just leaving[6]. She went down to the basement with the medical director. Mrs Bostock, at Dr Etherege's request[7], had gone to join Cully at the front door to ensure[8] that the instructions were followed about no one leaving the building. She had stayed with Cully until the party from the basement[9] appeared and they had then all collected in the waiting-room to await[10] the arrival of the police, except for the two porters who remained on duty[11] in the hall.

'You said that you were with Dr Etherege from just after six onwards[12] except for short periods. What were you both doing?'

'We were both working, naturally.' Mrs Bostock managed to[13] suggest that the question had been both stupid and a little vulgar. 'Dr Etherege is writing a paper on the treatment of twin[14] schizophrenic women by psychoanalysis. As I said, it has been

1. Nagle l'emmenait ensuite à la boîte aux lettres de l'autre côté de la rue
2. avant la levée de 18 h 30
3. avait l'air dans son état normal
4. donné
5. il avait été entendu
6. sortait à ce moment-là
7. à la demande de Dr Etherege
8. s'assurer
9. le groupe de ceux qui étaient allés au sous-sol
10. attendre
11. de service
12. à partir de six heures à peu près
13. parvint à
14. jumelles

agreed[1] that I shall assist him for one hour on Friday evenings. That is quite inadequate[2] for his needs[3], but Miss Bolam took the view[4] that the work wasn't strictly a clinic concern and that Dr Etherege should do it in his own consulting-room with the help of his private secretary. Naturally that's impossible. All the material, including some on tape[5], is here. My part of the job is varied[6]. For some of the time I take dictation. Sometimes I work in the little office typing directly from the tape. Sometimes I look up[7] references in the staff library[8].'

'And what did you do this evening?'

'I took dictation for about thirty minutes. Then I went into the adjoining office[9] and worked from the tape. Dr Etherege rang me to come in at about ten to seven. We were working together when the phone rang.'

'That would mean that you were with Dr Etherege taking dictation until about six-thirty-five.'

'Presumably[10].'

'And for the whole of that time[11] you were together?'

'I think Dr Etherege went out for a minute or so to verify a reference.'

'Why should you be uncertain[12], Mrs Bostock? Either[13] he did or[14] he didn't.'

'Naturally, Superintendent. As you say, either he did or he didn't. But there is no reason why I should particularly remember. This evening was in no way remarkable[15]. My impression is that he did go out for a short time but I really couldn't recall[16] exactly when. I expect[17] he may be able to help you.'

1. on s'était mis d'accord
2. tout à fait insuffisant
3. pour ses besoins
4. était d'avis
5. enregistrements sur bande magnétique
6. variée
7. je cherche
8. la bibliothèque du personnel
9. bureau voisin
10. sans doute
11. pendant tout ce temps-là
12. incertaine
13. soit
14. soit
15. n'avait rien de particulier
16. je ne pourrais pas me souvenir
17. je présume

Suddenly Dalgliesh changed the course of questioning. He paused for a full half-minute and then asked quietly:

'Did you like Miss Bolam, Mrs Bostock?'

It was not a welcome[1] question. Under the patina[2] of make-up he saw a flush of anger or embarrassment die along her neck[3].

'She wasn't an easy person to like. I tried to be loyal to her[4].'

'By loyal you mean, no doubt, that you tried to smooth down[5] rather than exacerbate her difficulties with the medical staff and refrained from[6] any overt[7] criticism of her as an administrator?'

The tinge[8] of sarcasm in his voice awoke[9], as was intended, all her latent hostility. Behind the mask of hauteur and detachment he glimpsed[10] the insecure schoolgirl. He knew that she would have to justify herself even against an implied criticism. She did not like him but she could not bear to be underrated[11] or ignored.

'Miss Bolam wasn't really a suitable[12] administrator for a psychiatric unit. She hadn't any sympathy with[13] what we're trying to do here.'

'In what way was she unsympathetic?'

'Well, for one thing, she didn't like neurotics.'

Neither do I, God help me, thought Dalgliesh. Neither do I. But he said nothing and Mrs Bostock went on:

'She was difficult, for example, about paying out some of the patients' travelling expenses. They only get them if they're on National Assistance[14], but we help other cases from the Samaritan Fund[15]. We have one girl, a most intelligent person, who comes here twice a week[16] from Surrey to work in the art

1. appréciée
2. patine
3. il la vit brièvement rougir de colère ou d'embarras
4. faire preuve de loyauté envers elle
5. atténuer
6. vous abstenir
7. manifestes
8. pointe
9. éveilla
10. aperçut
11. sous-estimée
12. n'était pas vraiment à sa place en tant que
13. elle n'appréciait pas
14. bénéficient de l'assistance publique
15. organisation caritative
16. deux fois par semaine

therapy department. Miss Bolam thought she ought to get treatment nearer home[1] – or go without[2]. Actually she made it pretty plain that[3], in her view[4], the patient ought to be discharged[5] to do a job of work[6], as she put it[7].'

'She didn't say this sort of thing to the patient.'

'Oh, no! She was careful enough[8] what she actually said. But I could see that the sensitive ones[9] weren't at ease[10] with her. Then she was very critical of intensive psychotherapy. It's a time-consuming[11] procedure. It has to be[12]. Miss Bolam tended to judge a psychiatrist's worth[13] by the number of patients he saw in a session. But that was less important than her attitude to the patients. There was a reason for it, of course. Her mother was mentally ill and in analysis[14] for years before she died. I understand that she killed herself. Miss Bolam can't have had an easy time[15]. Naturally she couldn't allow herself to[16] hate her mother, so she projected her resentment on to the patients here. She was subconsciously afraid of her own neurosis[17] too. That was pretty obvious.'

Dalgliesh did not feel qualified to comment on these theories. He was prepared to believe that there was truth in them but not that Mrs Bostock had thought them out for herself[18]. Miss Bolam may have irritated the psychiatrists by her lack of sympathy, but here, at least, they had a believer[19].

'Do you know who treated Mrs Bolam?' he asked.

Mrs Bostock uncrossed her elegant legs and settled herself more comfortably in the chair before deigning[20] to reply.

'I do, as a matter of fact[21]. But I hardly see its relevance to[22] this inquiry.'

1. plus près de chez elle
2. se passer de traitement
3. elle nous a bien fait comprendre que
4. à son avis
5. devrait arrêter son traitement à l'hôpital
6. pour travailler
7. selon ses termes
8. faisait suffisamment attention
9. les personnes sensibles
10. à l'aise
11. qui prend beaucoup de temps
12. il ne peut en être autrement
13. valeur
14. a fait une analyse
15. n'a pas dû avoir une vie facile
16. n'était pas capable de
17. névrose
18. les avaient élaborées elle-même
19. une adepte
20. daigner
21. à vrai dire
22. en quoi cela pourrait être pertinent pour

'Shall we leave that to me to decide[1]? I can find out quite easily. If you don't know or aren't sure it would save time[2] if you said so.'

'It was Dr Etherege.'

'And who do you think will be appointed[3] to succeed Miss Bolam?'

'As administrative officer? Really,' said Mrs Bostock coolly[4], 'I've no idea.'

*

At last the main work of the evening was over for Dalgliesh and Martin. The body had been taken away and the record-room sealed[5]. All the clinic staff had been questioned and most of them had left for their homes. Dr Etherege had been the last doctor to leave and had hung around[6] uneasily[7] for some time after Dalgliesh had said he might go. Mr Lauder and Peter Nagle were still in the clinic and were waiting together in the hall where two uniformed policemen were on duty. The group secretary had said with quiet determination that he preferred to be on the premises[8] while the police were still there, and Nagle could not leave until the front door had been locked and the key handed over[9] since it was his job to open the clinic at eight o'clock on Monday morning.

Dalgliesh and Martin made their last round of the premises[10] together. Watching them at work a casual observer[11] might have been misled into the facile assumption[12] that Martin was merely a foil[13] for the younger, more successful man. Those at the Yard[14] who knew them both judged differently. In appearance they were certainly unalike[15]. Martin was a big man, nearly six feet[16] and broad-

1. vous voulez bien me laisser le loisir d'en décider

2. cela nous permettrait de gagner du temps

3. nommé

4. froidement

5. scellée

6. attendu

7. avec inquiétude

8. sur les lieux

9. remise

10. parcoururent une dernière fois le bâtiment

11. observateur peu attentif

12. aurait pu facilement avoir l'illusion

13. servait seulement de faire-valoir

14. Scotland Yard

15. ils ne se ressemblaient pas du tout

16. 1,80 mètres

shouldered[1], and looking, with his open ruddy[2] face, more like a successful farmer[3] than a detective. Dalgliesh was even taller[4], dark, lean[5] and easy moving. Beside him Martin seemed ponderous[6]. No one watching Dalgliesh at work could fail to recognize his intelligence. With Martin one was less sure. He was ten years older than his chief and it was unlikely now that he would gain further promotion[7]. But he had qualities that made him an admirable detective. He was never tormented by doubt of his own motives. Right and wrong stood for him as immutable[8] as the two poles. He had never wandered[9] in that twilight country[10] where the nuances of evil and good cast their perplexing shadows[11]. He had great determination and infinite patience. He was kind[12] without being sentimental and meticulous for detail without losing sight of the whole[13]. Looking at his career, no one could have called him brilliant. But if he was incapable of high intelligence he was equally incapable of stupidity. Most police work consists of the boring, repetitive and meticulous checking[14] of detail. Most murders are sordid little crimes bred out of[15] ignorance and despair[16]. It was Martin's job to help solve them and, patiently and uncensoriously[17], that is what he did. Faced with[18] the murder at the Steen Clinic with its frightening undertones of[19] a trained intelligence at work, he remained unimpressed[20]. Methodical attention to detail had solved other murders and would solve this one. And murderers, intelligent or subnormal[21], devious[22] or impulsive[23] had to be caught. He walked, as was usual, a pace[24] or two behind Dalgliesh and said little. But when he spoke it was usually to the point[25].

1. large d'épaules
2. rougeaud
3. fermier
4. plus grand
5. mince
6. lourd
7. obtiendrait encore de l'avancement
8. immuable
9. il ne s'était jamais aventuré
10. zone nébuleuse
11. projetaient leurs ombres mystérieuses
12. gentil
13. sans perdre de vue l'ensemble
14. vérification
15. engendrés par
16. désespoir
17. sans sévérité
18. confronté à
19. qui laissait supposer
20. il ne se laissa pas impressionner
21. arriérés
22. retors
23. impulsifs
24. un pas
25. il disait des choses pertinentes

They went through the building for the last time that evening, starting on the third floor. Here the eighteenth-century rooms had been divided to provide accommodation for psychiatric social workers, psychologists and lay therapists, together with two larger treatment-rooms for the use of psychiatrists. There was one pleasant and unconverted[1] room at the front of the building furnished[2] comfortably with easy chairs and a number of small tables. This, apparently, was the rendezvous of[3] the marital problem group who could enjoy an agreeable view over the square in the intervals of analysing their domestic and sexual incompatibilities. Dalgliesh could understand the chagrin[4] of the absent Mrs Baumgarten. The room was admirably suited for the art therapy department.

The more important rooms were on the floor below and here there had been little alteration[5] or adaptation so that ceilings[6], doors and windows could contribute their own graciousness to the atmosphere of elegance and calm. The Modigliani was out of place in the boardroom but not aggressively so. The smaller medical library next door with its antique bookcases[7], each bearing[8] the name of the donor[9], could have been an eighteenth-century gentleman's library until one looked at the titles on the books. There were low bowls of flowers set on the bookcases and a number of armchairs[10] which looked right together although they had obviously come originally from half a dozen different houses.

On this floor, too, the medical director had his consulting-room and it was one of the most elegant in the clinic. The treatment couch which stood against the far wall[11] was the same pattern[12] as that

1. qui n'avait pas été transformée

2. meublée

3. c'est là que se réunissait

4. déception

5. peu de modifications

6. plafonds

7. bibliothèques d'époque

8. portant

9. donateur

10. fauteuils

11. le mur du fond

12. motif

in each of the other psychiatrists' rooms, a low single divan, covered in chintz and with a red blanket folded at its foot and one pillow. But no HMC had provided the rest of the furniture. The eighteenth-century desk was uncluttered by[1] cardboard[2] calendars or stationery office diaries and held merely a leather-bound blotter[3], a silver inkstand[4] and a tray[5] for papers. There were two leather armchairs and a mahogany[6] corner cupboard[7]. It appeared that the medical director collected[8] old prints[9] and was particularly interested in mezzotints[10] and eighteenth-century engravings[11]. Dalgliesh inspected a collection of works by James MacArdell and Valentine Green, arranged on either side of the chimney-piece, and noted that Dr Etherege's patients unburdened[12] their subconscious beneath a couple of fine lithographs by Hullmandel. He reflected that the unknown clinic thief might have been a gentleman if Cully's opinion was to be trusted, but he was certainly no connoisseur[13]. It was more typical of the small-time professional[14] to neglect two Hullmandels for fifteen pounds in cash. It was certainly a pleasant room, proclaiming its owner as a man with taste and the money to indulge it[15], the room of a man who sees no reason why his working life should be spent in less agreeable surroundings[16] than his leisure[17]. And yet it was not wholly successful. Somewhere there was a lack[18]. The elegance was a little too contrived[19], the good taste a little too orthodox. Dalgliesh felt that a patient might well be happier in the warm, untidy[20], oddly shaped cell upstairs where Fredrica Saxon worked in a litter[21] of papers, pot-plants[22] and the paraphernalia of tea-brewing[23]. Despite the engravings

1. n'était pas encombré de
2. en carton
3. un sous-main relié en cuir
4. encrier d'argent
5. casier
6. en acajou
7. encoignure
8. collectionnait
9. estampes
10. mezzo-tinto
11. gravures
12. déchargeaient
13. connaisseur
14. un voleur à la petite semaine
15. pour se faire plaisir
16. cadre
17. temps libre
18. il manquait quelque chose
19. recherchée
20. mal rangée
21. fouillis
22. plantes en pot
23. tout l'attirail nécessaire à la préparation du thé

the room lacked the nuances of personality. In that it was somehow typical of its owner. Dalgliesh was reminded of a recent conference which he had attended on mental illness and the law at which Dr Etherege had been one of the speakers. At the time his paper[1] had seemed a model of felicitous wisdom[2]; afterwards Dalgliesh was unable accurately to recall a single word.

They went down to the ground floor where the group secretary and Nagle, chatting quietly to the police constables[3], turned to watch but made no move to join them. The four waiting figures were standing together in a sad group like mourners[4] after a funeral[5], uncertain and disorganized in the hiatus[6] that follows grief[7]. When they talked together their voices sounded muted[8] in the silence of the hall.

The ground-floor plan was simple. Immediately inside the front door and to the left as one entered was the glass-panelled[9] reception kiosk. Dalgliesh noted again that it commanded a good view of[10] the whole hall[11], including the great curved[12] staircase[13] at the end. Yet Cully's observations during the evening had been curiously selective. He was positive that everyone entering or leaving the clinic after 5 p.m. had been seen by him and entered in his book, but many of the comings and goings in the hall had passed unnoticed[14]. He had seen Mrs Shorthouse come out of Miss Bolam's office and into the front general office but had not seen the administrative officer passing down the hall to the basement stairs. He had seen Dr Baguley coming out of the medical staff cloakroom but not entering it. Most of the movements of patients

1. communication
2. authentique sagesse
3. agents de police
4. proches du défunt
5. un enterrement
6. vide
7. chagrin
8. assourdies
9. vitré
10. donnait sur
11. l'ensemble du hall
12. qui s'incurvait
13. escalier
14. il n'avait pas remarqué

and their relations had not escaped him and he was able to confirm the comings and goings of Mrs Bostock. He was certain that Dr Etherege, Miss Saxon and Miss Kettle had not passed through the hall after 6 p.m. If they had, he hadn't noticed. Dalgliesh would have felt more confidence in Cully's evidence if it were not apparent that the pathetic little man was terrified. When they arrived at the clinic he had been merely depressed and a little surly[1]. By the time he was allowed to go home he was in a state of terror. At some stage of the investigation, thought Dalgliesh, he would have to find out why[2].

Behind[3] the reception kiosk and with windows facing[4] the square was the general office, part of which had been partitioned[5] to form a small filing-room[6] for the current[7] medical records. Next to the general office was Miss Bolam's room and, beyond that[8], the ECT suite[9] with its treatment-room, nurses' duty-room and male and female recovery bays[10]. This suite was separated by a hallway[11] from the medical staff cloakroom[12], clerical staff lavatories[13] and the domestic assistant's pantry[14]. At the end of the hallway was the locked side door, seldom used except by members of the staff who had been working late and who did not want to give Nagle the trouble of undoing[15] the more complicated locks[16], bolts[17] and chains on the front door.

At the opposite side of the main hall were two consulting-rooms and the patients' waiting-room, and lavatories. The front room had been divided to form two fairly large[18] psychotherapy-rooms which were separated from the waiting-room by a passage. Dr Steiner could, therefore, move from one to the other without coming within Cully's view[19]. But

1. maussade
2. découvrir pourquoi
3. derrière
4. donnant sur
5. séparée par une cloison
6. pièce pour les archives
7. courants
8. au-delà
9. l'ensemble des pièces réservées au traitement par électrochocs
10. salles de repos
11. couloir
12. vestiaire
13. toilettes
14. garde-manger
15. ouvrir
16. serrures
17. verrous
18. plutôt grandes
19. sans être vu par Cully

he could hardly move down the hall to the basement stairs without risk of being seen. Had he been seen? What was Cully keeping back[1] and why?

Together, Dalgliesh and Martin examined the basement rooms for the last time that night. At the rear was the door which led[2] to the area steps. Dr Etherege had said that this door was bolted when he and Dr Steiner had examined it after finding the body. It was still bolted. It had been tested for fingerprints, but the only decipherable ones had been Peter Nagle's. Nagle had said that he was probably the last person to touch the lock since it was his habit to check that the door was securely bolted before he locked up at night. It was rare for him or for any member of the staff to use the basement exit and the door was usually opened only when the coal[3] or other heavy supplies[4] were delivered[5]. Dalgliesh shot back[6] the bolt. There was a short flight of iron steps[7] leading to the rear railings[8]. Here, again, the wrought-iron[9] door was bolted and fitted with[10] a lock and chain. But an intruder would have no difficulty in getting into the basement area, particularly as the mews[11] at the back was ill lit[12] and unoccupied. The clinic itself would be less easy of access. All the basement windows, except the small lavatory window, were barred[13]. It was through that window the clinic thief had cut his way.

Dalgliesh bolted the door again and they went into the porters' rest-room which occupied most of the back of the building. Nothing was changed since they had first examined it. Two clothes lockers[14] stood against one wall. The centre of the floor was occupied by a heavy square table. There was a

1. taisait
2. menait
3. charbon
4. fournitures
5. livrés
6. repoussa
7. quelques marches en fer
8. grille
9. en fer forgé
10. équipée de
11. ruelle
12. mal éclairée
13. avaient des barreaux
14. casiers

small old-fashioned gas cooker[1] in one corner and, beside it, a cupboard containing cups and saucers[2] and tins[3] of tea, sugar and biscuits. Two shabby[4] leather chairs were drawn up[5] one on either side of the gas fire. To the left of the door was a keyboard[6] with the hooks numbered but not named. On this board had hung, among others, the key to the basement record-room. That key was now in the possession of the police.

A large striped[7] cat was curled[8] in a basket before the unlit gas fire. When the light was switched on it stirred[9] and, lifting its heavy barred[10] head, gave the intruders a stare, blank and expressionless[11], from immense yellow eyes. Dalgliesh knelt beside the basket and stroked[12] the top of its head. The cat shivered[13] then sat immobile under his touch. Suddenly it rolled on its back, and stretched out[14] its legs, rigid as poles[15], to display a ridge[16] of soft belly hair for Dalgliesh's ministrations[17]. The superintendent stroked and talked while Martin, whose preference was for dogs, looked on in tolerant patience. He said: 'I've heard about him from Mrs Shorthouse. It's Tigger, Miss Bolam's cat.'

'We deduce that Miss Bolam read A. A. Milne as a child. Cats are nocturnal. Why isn't he let out at night?[18]'

'I heard about that, too. Miss Bolam thought he'd keep the mice down[19] if he were shut in[20]. Nagle goes out at lunch time for a beer and a sandwich, but Cully eats his grub[21] here and Miss B was always on to him[22] about crumbs[23]. The cat is shut in here every night and let out during the day. He's got his food and his scratch tin[24].'

1. gazinière
2. des tasses et des soucoupes
3. boîtes en fer-blanc
4. élimées
5. rangées
6. panneau à clés
7. rayé
8. en boule
9. bougea
10. rayée
11. fixa les intrus d'un regard vide et sans expression
12. caressa
13. frissonna
14. étira
15. bâtons
16. crête
17. soins
18. pourquoi ne le laisse-t-on pas sortir la nuit ?
19. il tuerait quelques souris
20. si on l'enfermait
21. casse la croûte
22. était toujours après lui
23. à propos des miettes
24. son bac

'So I see. Furnished[1] with cinders[2] from the boiler[3].'

'Pity[4] he can't talk, sir. He was in here for most of the evening waiting to be fed[5]. He was probably here when the murderer came in for the record-room key.'

'And for the chisel. Oh, yes, Tigger saw it all right. But what makes you think he'd tell you the truth?'

Sergeant Martin didn't reply. People who went for cats in a big way[6] were like that, of course. Childish you might call it. Unusually talkative[7], he said:

'Miss B had him doctored[8] at her own expense[9]. Mrs Shorthouse told PC Holliday that Dr Steiner was very upset about it. He likes cats seemingly[10]. They had words over it. Dr Steiner told Mrs Bostock that Miss Bolam would like everything male at the clinic doctored if she had her way. He put it rather crudely[11], I gather[12]. Of course, it wasn't meant to get back to[13] Miss Bolam but Mrs Bostock saw that it did[14].'

'Yes,' said Dalgliesh shortly. 'She would[15].'

They continued their inspection.

It was not an uncomfortable room. It smelled of food and leather and, just perceptibly, of gas. There were a number of pictures[16] which looked as if they had found a home with the porters when their previous owners had seen enough of them. One was of the founder[17] of the Steen surrounded[18], appropriately enough, by his five sons. It was a faded[19] sepia photograph in a gilt frame[20] more indicative[21], Dalgliesh thought, of old Hyman's character than the more orthodox commemorative oil[22] which hung[23] upstairs in the hall.

1. rempli
2. cendres
3. chaudière
4. dommage
5. qu'on lui donne à manger
6. qui aiment beaucoup les chats
7. bavard
8. l'a fait castrer
9. à ses frais
10. apparemment
11. il l'a dit assez crûment
12. d'après ce que j'ai cru comprendre
13. censé arriver aux oreilles de
14. a fait en sorte que ce soit le cas
15. c'était à prévoir
16. tableaux
17. fondateur
18. entouré
19. vieille
20. cadre doré
21. qui en disait plus
22. peinture à l'huile
23. accrochée

On a smaller table against the rear wall[1] lay Nagle's box of tools. Dalgliesh lifted the lid[2]. The tools, meticulously cared for[3], lay each in its correct place. There was only one missing[4] and that one was unlikely ever again to find its place in Nagle's toolbox.

'He could have come in through that rear door if he left it unlocked,' said Martin, voicing[5] Dalgliesh's thought[6].

'Of course. I admit to a perverse disposition to suspect the one person who was apparently not even in the building when the murder was committed. There's little doubt, though[7], that Nagle was with Miss Priddy in the general office when Mrs Shorthouse left Miss Bolam. Cully confirms that. And Miss Priddy states that she never left the general office except momentarily to fetch a file from the next room. What did you think of Shorthouse by the way[8]?'

'I thought she was telling the truth, sir. I wouldn't put her above a bit of lying when it suited her[9]. She's the sort who likes things to happen and isn't averse to giving them a bit of a shove in the right direction[10]. But she had plenty to tell us without adding any frills[11].'

'She had, indeed,' agreed Dalgliesh. 'There isn't any reasonable doubt that Miss Bolam came down to the basement as a result of that call which fixes the approximate time of death for us very satisfactorily. It ties up[12] with the police surgeon[13]'s view[14], too, but we shall know more about that when we get the result of the PM[15]. The call could have been genuine[16], of course. It's possible that someone phoned from the basement, spoke to Miss Bolam

1. mur du fond
2. souleva le couvercle
3. entretenus
4. il n'en manquait qu'un
5. exprimant
6. ce que Dalgliesh pensait tout bas
7. cependant
8. d'ailleurs
9. je ne la crois pas incapable de mentir un peu si elle le juge opportun
10. n'est pas contre le fait de leur donner un petit coup de pouce
11. fioritures
12. cela correspond
13. médecin légiste
14. avis
15. autopsie
16. authentique

somewhere down here, then left her to go back to his or her own room and is now too afraid to admit making the call. As I say, it's possible, but I don't think it's likely[1].'

'If the call was genuine it could have been someone calling her down to look at the mess[2] in the record-room. Those files were certainly chucked about[3] before the murder. Some of them were under the body. It looked to me as if she was struck[4] as she crouched[5] to pick them up[6].'

'That's how it looked to me,' said Dalgliesh. 'Well, let's press on[7].'

They passed the service lift door without comment and went next into the basement treatment-room at the front of the building. Here Nurse Bolam had sat with her patient through the early hours of the evening[8]. Dalgliesh switched on the lights. The heavy curtains had been drawn back but the windows were hung with thin net[9], presumably to give privacy[10] during the day. The room was simply furnished. There was a low stretcher bed[11] in one corner with a hospital screen[12] at its foot and a small armchair at its head. Against the front wall was a small table and chair, apparently for the use of the nurse in attendance[13]. The table held a rack[14] of nursing report forms[15] and blank medical record sheets[16]. The left-hand wall was lined with cupboards where the clinic's clean linen was stored[17]. Some attempt had been made to soundproof the fourth wall. It had been lined with acoustic panels[18] and the door, strong and well built, was hung with a heavy curtain.

Dalgliesh said:

1. probable
2. désordre
3. éparpillés
4. frappée
5. s'est accroupie
6. les ramasser
7. continuons
8. en début de soirée
9. fin voilage
10. préserver une certaine intimité
11. brancard
12. paravent
13. de service
14. casier
15. formulaires de rapport de soins infirmiers
16. fiches vierges destinées aux dossiers médicaux
17. rangé
18. panneaux acoustiques

'If her patient were noisy I doubt whether Nurse Bolam would hear much that went on outside. Walk down the passage will you, Martin, and make a call on the telephone, the one just outside the medical record-room.'

Martin closed the door behind him and Dalgliesh was alone with the heavy silence. His hearing[1] was acute and Martin's heavy tread[2] was just[3] audible. He doubted whether he would have heard it against the noise of a distressed[4] patient. He could not hear the faint ring[5] as Martin took off[6] the receiver[7] nor the swing of the dial[8]. In a few seconds he heard the footsteps again and Martin was back. He said:

'There's a card giving the internal numbers so I rang 004. That's Miss Bolam's room. Funny how eerie[9] a telephone bell[10] sounds when there's no one to answer. Then someone did. It gave me quite a shock when the ringing[11] stopped. It was Mr Lauder, of course. He sounded a bit surprised, too. I told him we wouldn't be long now.'

'Nor shall we[12]. I couldn't hear you, by the way. And yet Nurse Bolam did hear the Priddy child scream[13]. Or so she says.'

'She took her time doing anything about it, didn't she, sir? What's more she apparently heard the doctors and Sister when they came down.'

'That's reasonable enough[14]. There were four of them clattering about[15]. She's the obvious suspect[16], of course. She could have telephoned her cousin from this room, saying perhaps that someone had been creating chaos[17] in the record-room. Her patient would be far too disorientated to hear or understand. I saw her with Dr Baguley and it was obvious that she wasn't capable of giving any-

1. ouïe
2. pas lourd
3. à peine
4. agité
5. léger tintement
6. décrocha
7. combiné
8. le bruit du cadran qui tournait
9. angoissante
10. sonnerie
11. sonnerie
12. en effet
13. hurler
14. cela me semble tout à fait plausible
15. ils étaient quatre à faire du raffut
16. suspect numéro 1
17. avait mis le bazar

one an alibi. Nurse Bolam could have left the treatment-room and waited for her cousin in the record-room with a fair degree of safety[1]. She had the best opportunity to kill, she has the necessary medical knowledge, she has an obvious motive. If she is the murderer the crime probably had nothing to do with the phone call to Lauder. We shall have to find out what Bolam did think was going on here, but it needn't necessarily have anything to do with[2] her death. If Nurse Bolam knew that the group secretary was coming she might have decided to kill now with the idea of obscuring[3] the real motive.'

'She doesn't strike me as clever enough[4] for that kind of planning, sir.'

'She doesn't strike me as a murderer, Martin, but we've known less likely ones. If she is innocent then her being down here alone was very convenient[5] for the murderer. Then there are those rubber gloves[6]. Of course, she had an explanation for them. There are plenty of pairs about[7] and it's perfectly reasonable for a member of the nursing staff to have a used pair in her apron[8] pocket. But the fact remains that we haven't found any dabs[9] on either of the weapons nor on the door key, not even old prints. Someone wiped them[10] first[11] and handled[12] them with gloves. And what more suitable[13] than thin surgical gloves. Driving that chisel in[14] was practically a surgical operation.'

'If she had the sense to[15] use the gloves, then she'd have the sense to destroy[16] them afterwards. The boiler was alight[17]. What about that missing[18] rubber apron from the art department? If the killer used that as possible protection and disposed

1. en toute sécurité

2. ça n'a sans doute rien à voir avec

3. cacher

4. elle ne me paraît pas assez intelligente

5. commode

6. gants en caoutchouc

7. un peu partout

8. tablier

9. empreintes digitales

10. les a essuyées

11. d'abord

12. touchées

13. approprié

14. enfoncer ce ciseau

15. assez de bon sens pour

16. détruire

17. allumée

18. manquant

of it[1] in the boiler, it would be daft[2] to hang on to[3] the gloves.'

'So daft that we're probably meant to think that no sane[4] person would do it. I'm not sure about that apron, anyway. Apparently there's one missing and it's possible that the killer wore it[5]. But this was a clean death and it was planned that way. Anyway, we'll know tomorrow when the boiler's cold and can be raked out[6]. Those aprons have metal studs[7] on the shoulder straps[8] and, with luck, we might find them.'

They closed the treatment door behind them and went upstairs. Dalgliesh began to be conscious of his tiredness and the stabbing pain[9] behind his eye was now almost continuous. It had not been an easy week and the sherry party, which promised an agreeable relaxing finish[10] to a busy day, had proved[11] an unsettling preliminary to an even busier night. He wondered briefly where Deborah Riscoe had dined, and with whom. Their meeting now seemed part of a different world. Perhaps because he was tired he felt none of the confidence with which he usually began a case. He did not seriously believe that the crime would defeat him[12]. Professionally he had never yet known the taste of failure[13]. It was all the more irritating, therefore, to be visited by this vague sensation of inadequacy[14] and unrest[15]. For the first time he felt unsure of his own mastery[16], as if he were opposed by an intelligence actively working against him and equal[17] to his own. And he did not think that Nurse Bolam had that intelligence.

The group secretary and Nagle were still waiting in the hall. Dalgliesh handed over[18] the clinic keys

1. l'a jeté
2. stupide
3. conserver
4. saine d'esprit
5. l'ait porté
6. examiné
7. boutons
8. bretelles
9. douleur lancinante
10. conclusion
11. s'était avéré
12. il ne réussirait pas à résoudre ce crime
13. défaite
14. incapacité
15. agitation
16. maîtrise
17. égale
18. remit

and was promised that an additional set[1], now held at group headquarters[2], would be delivered[3] to the police next day. Martin and he, with the two constables, waited while Nagle checked that all lights were out[4]. Soon the whole clinic was in darkness[5] and the six men stepped into the foggy[6] chill of the October night and went their separate ways[7].

1. un jeu supplémentaire
2. bureau central
3. livré
4. éteintes
5. dans le noir
6. brumeux
7. s'en allèrent chacun de leur côté

CHAPTER FOUR

Dr Baguley knew that he couldn't in decency[1] neglect to offer Miss Kettle a lift home[2]. She lived in Richmond and her house was directly on the route to his Surrey village. Usually he managed to avoid her[3]; her attendance at the clinic was so erratic[4] that they seldom[5] left at the same time and he could usually drive alone without compunction[6]. He enjoyed driving. Even the frustrations of getting through the city in the rush hour[7] were a small price to pay for those few miles[8] of straight road[9] before he reached home when he could feel the power of the car like a physical thrust[10] in his back and the tensions of the day were ripped from him[11] in the singing air[12]. Just before he reached Stalling it was his custom[13] to stop at a quiet pub for a pint of beer. He never drank more nor less. This nightly ritual, the formal division of day from night, had become necessary to him since he had lost Fredrica. The night brought no relief from the strain[14] of coping with[15] neurosis. He was accustoming himself to a life in which the greatest demands on his patience and professional skill[16] were made in his own home. But it was good to sit alone and in peace, savouring the brief interlude between two different but essentially similar worlds.

1. décemment
2. proposer à Miss Kettle de la raccompagner chez elle en voiture
3. l'éviter
4. irrégulière
5. rarement
6. remords
7. à l'heure de pointe
8. quelques kilomètres
9. route en ligne droite
10. poussée
11. s'envolaient
12. l'air sifflant
13. habitude
14. l'effort
15. faire face à
16. compétence professionnelle

He drove slowly at first since Miss Kettle was known to dislike speed[1]. She sat beside him, close-wrapped[2] in a heavy tweed coat, her grey cropped head[3] incongruously[4] crowned[5] with a knitted red cap[6]. Like many professional social workers she had little instinctive understanding of people, a lack[7] which had gained her an undeserved[8] reputation for insensitivity. It was, of course, different if they were her clients – and how Baguley hated[9] that word! Once they were securely caged[10] behind the bars of a professional relationship she gave them a dedicated[11] and meticulous attention which left few of their privacies intact. They were understood whether they liked it or not, their weaknesses exposed and condoned[12], their efforts applauded and encouraged, their sins forgiven[13]. Apart from her clients the rest of the Steen Clinic hardly existed for Miss Kettle. Baguley did not dislike her. He had long come to the melancholy conclusion that psychiatric social work held a strong attraction for those least suited to it, and Miss Kettle was better than most. The reports she provided for him[14] were over-long[15] and spattered[16] with the peculiar jargon of the job, but at least she provided them. The Steen Clinic had its share of[17] those PSWs[18] who, driven[19] by their irresistible urge[20] to treat patients, were restless until they had trained as lay psychotherapists and left behind such lesser excitements as the writing of social reports and the arranging of recuperative[21] holidays. No, he did not dislike Ruth Kettle, but tonight, of all nights[22], he would have been happier to drive alone.

1. vitesse
2. bien enveloppée
3. ses cheveux gris coupés courts
4. incongrûment
5. couronnés
6. bonnet rouge tricoté
7. manque
8. imméritée
9. détestait
10. emprisonnés
11. dévouée
12. excusées
13. leurs péchés pardonnés
14. lui fournissait
15. trop longs
16. parsemés
17. avait eu son lot de
18. assistantes sociales
19. guidées
20. envie
21. régénératrices
22. particulièrement

She did not speak until they had reached Knightsbridge, then her high breathy[1] voice fluted in his ear.

'Such a very complicated murder, wasn't it? And so oddly timed. What did you think of the superintendent?'

'He's efficient, I suppose,' replied Dr Baguley. 'My attitude to him is a little ambivalent, probably because I haven't an alibi. I was alone in the medical staff cloakroom when Miss Bolam is thought to have died.'

He knew that he was hoping for reassurance, expecting to hear her eager[2] protestations that, naturally, no one could think of suspecting him. Despising himself[3] he added quickly:

'It's a nuisance[4], of course, but not important. I expect he'll clear the matter up[5] pretty quickly.'

'Oh, do you think so? I wonder. I thought he seemed rather puzzled[6] by the whole thing. I was alone in my room most of the evening so I probably haven't an alibi either. But then I don't know when she's supposed to have died.'

'Probably at about six-twenty,' said Baguley briefly.

'Is that so?[7] Then I most certainly haven't an alibi.' Miss Kettle spoke with the liveliest[8] satisfaction. After a moment she said: 'I shall be able to arrange a country holiday from Free Money for the Worrikers now – Miss Bolam was always so difficult about spending Free Money on patients. Dr Steiner and I feel that if the Worrikers can have a quiet[9] fortnight[10] together in some pleasant country[11] hotel they may be able to sort things out[12]. It may save the marriage.'

1. voilée
2. vives
3. en se méprisant
4. c'est ennuyeux
5. il tirera cette affaire au clair
6. plutôt perplexe
7. vraiment ?
8. la plus vive
9. tranquilles
10. deux semaines
11. à la campagne
12. faire la part des choses

Dr Baguley was tempted to say that the Worriker marriage had been in jeopardy[1] for so many years that its salvation[2] or otherwise was hardly likely to be settled in a fortnight, however pleasant the hotel[3]. Being precariously married was the Worrikers' main emotional preoccupation and one they were unlikely to relinquish[4] without a struggle[5]. He asked:

'Isn't Mr Worriker in work then?[6]'

'Oh, yes! He's in work,' replied Miss Kettle, as if that fact could have no relevance to his ability to pay for a holiday. 'But his wife is a poor manager[7], I'm afraid, although she does her best[8]. They can't really afford[9] to go away unless the clinic pays. Miss Bolam wasn't very sympathetic[10], I'm sorry to say. There was another matter, too. She would make appointments for me to see patients without telling me. It happened today. When I looked at my diary[11] just before I left there was a new patient booked[12] for ten on Monday. Mrs Bostock had written it in, of course, but she added "on Miss Bolam's instructions". Mrs Bostock would never do a thing like that herself. She's a very pleasant and efficient secretary.'

Dr Baguley thought that Mrs Bostock was an ambitious trouble-maker[13], but saw no point in[14] saying so. Instead, he asked how Miss Kettle had got on during her interview with Dalgliesh.

'I wasn't able to help him very much, I'm afraid, but he was interested to hear about the lift[15].'

'What about the lift, Miss Kettle?'

'Someone was using it this evening. You know how it creaks[16] when someone's using it and then bangs[17] when it reaches[18] the second floor? Well,

1. en péril
2. salut
3. quelle que soit la qualité de l'hôtel
4. à laquelle il était peu probable qu'ils renonceraient
5. sans opposer de résistance
6. il ne travaille pas ?
7. une piètre gestionnaire
8. bien qu'elle fasse de son mieux
9. se permettre
10. ne s'est pas montrée très compréhensive
11. agenda
12. inscrit
13. élément perturbateur
14. il jugea inutile de
15. monte-charge
16. grince
17. fait du bruit
18. arrive à

I heard it bang. I don't know exactly when, of course, as it didn't seem important at the time. It wasn't very early in the evening. I suppose it could have been at about six-thirty.'

'Surely Dalgliesh isn't seriously thinking that someone used the lift to get down to the basement. It's large enough, of course, but it would need two people.'

'Yes, it would, wouldn't it? No one could hoist himself up in it[1]. It would need an accomplice[2].' She spoke the word conspiratorially[3] as if it were part of some criminal patois, a naughty[4] expression which she was daring to[5] use. She went on: 'I can't imagine dear Dr Etherege squatting[6] in the lift like a plump[7] little Buddha while Mrs Bostock heaved on[8] the ropes[9] with her strong red hands, can you?'

'No,' said Dr Baguley curtly[10]. The description had been unexpectedly[11] vivid[12]. To change the image he said:

'It would be interesting to know who was last in the medical record-room. Before the murder, I mean. I can't remember when I last used the place.'

'Oh, can't you? How strange! It's such a dusty[13] claustrophobic room that I can always remember when I have to go down there. I was there at a quarter to six this evening.'

Dr Baguley nearly[14] stopped the car in his surprise.

'At five-forty-five this evening? But that was only thirty-five minutes before the time of death!'

'Yes, it must have been, mustn't it, if she died at about six-twenty? The superintendent didn't tell me that. But he was interested to hear that I'd been in the basement. I fetched one of the old Worriker

1. se hisser à l'intérieur
2. complice
3. d'un air de conspiration
4. vilaine
5. osait
6. accroupi
7. rondelet
8. tiraient sur
9. cordes
10. sèchement
11. étonnamment
12. vivante
13. poussiéreuse
14. presque

records. It must have been about five-forty-five when I went down and I didn't stay[1]; I knew just where the record was.'

'And the room was as usual? The records weren't chucked[2] on the floor[3]?'

'Oh, no, everything was perfectly tidy[4]. The room was locked, of course, so I got the key from the porters' rest-room and locked the room again when I'd finished. I put the key back on the board.'

'And you didn't see anyone?'

'No, I don't think so. I could hear your LSD patient, though. She seemed very noisy, I thought. Almost as if she were alone.'

'She wasn't alone. She never is[5]. As a matter of fact[6] I was with her myself up to[7] about five-forty. If you'd been a few minutes earlier we should have seen each other.'

'Only if we'd happened to pass on the basement stairs or if you'd come into the record-room. But I don't think I saw anyone. The superintendent kept asking me[8]. I wonder if he's a capable[9] man. He seemed very puzzled by the whole thing. I thought.'

They did not speak again about the murder although, to Dr Baguley, the air of the car was heavy with unspoken[10] questions. Twenty minutes later he drew up[11] outside[12] Miss Kettle's flat off Richmond Green and leaned over[13] to open the car door for her with a sense of relief. As soon as she had disappeared from view he got out of the car and, in defiance of the chilly dampness[14], opened the roof[15]. The next few miles fled in a gold thread[16] of winking cats'-eyes[17] marking the crown[18] of the road, a rush of cold autumnal air. Outside Stalling he turned from the main road to where the

1. je ne suis pas restée longtemps
2. éparpillés
3. par terre
4. parfaitement bien rangé
5. elle ne l'est jamais
6. d'ailleurs
7. jusqu'à
8. n'a pas arrêté de me poser la question
9. compétent
10. non prononcées
11. s'arrêta
12. devant
13. se pencha
14. humidité
15. toit
16. fil d'or
17. le clignotement des catadioptres
18. bombement

dark, uninviting little pub was set well back among its surrounding elms[1]. The bright boys[2] of Stalling Coombe had never discovered it or had rejected it in favour of the smart[3] pubs edging[4] the green belt[5]; their Jaguars were never seen parked against its black brick walls. The saloon bar was empty as usual, but there was a murmur of voices across the wooden partition which separated it from the public bar. He took his seat by the fire which burned summer and winter, evidently stocked[6] with malodorous chunks[7] of the publican's old furniture[8]. It was not a welcoming room. The chimney smoked in an east wind, the stone floor was bare[9] and the wooden benches[10] lining[11] the walls were too hard and narrow for comfort. But the beer was cold and good, the glasses clean, and there was a kind of peace about the place bred out of[12] its bareness[13] and the solitude.

George brought over[14] his pint.

'You're late this evening, Doctor.'

George had called him that since his second visit. Dr Baguley neither knew nor cared[15] how George had discovered what his job was.

'Yes,' he replied. 'I was kept late[16] at the clinic.'

He said no more and the man went back to his bar. Then he wondered whether he had been wise[17]. It would be in all the papers tomorrow. They would probably be talking about it in the public bar. It would be natural for George to say:

'The doctor was in as usual on Friday. He didn't say anything about the murder ... Looked upset[18], though.'

Was it suspicious to say nothing? Wasn't it more natural for an innocent man to want to talk about

1. ormes
2. la jeunesse dorée
3. chics
4. qui bordaient
5. ceinture verte
6. alimenté
7. morceaux nauséabonds
8. de vieux meubles du patron
9. dépouillé
10. bancs
11. le long de
12. qui naissait de
13. son dépouillement
14. apporta
15. ne savait pas et ne voulait pas savoir
16. on m'a retenu
17. sage
18. bouleversé

a murder case in which he was involved? Suddenly the little room became unbearably stuffy[1], the peace dissolved in an uprush[2] of anxiety and pain. He had got to tell Helen somehow, and the sooner she knew the better.

But although he drove fast it was well after ten before he reached home and saw through the tall beech hedge[3] the light in Helen's bedroom. So she had gone up without waiting for him; that was always a bad sign. Garaging the car[4] he braced himself[5] for whatever lay ahead[6]. Stalling Coombe was very quiet. It was a small private estate[7] of architect-designed houses[8], built in the traditional manner, and set each in a spacious garden. It had little contact with the neighbouring village of Stalling and was, indeed, an oasis of prosperous suburbia[9] whose inhabitants, bound by ties of[10] common prejudices[11] and snobberies[12], lived like exiles[13] determinedly preserving the decencies of civilization in the midst of[14] an alien culture. Baguley had bought[15] his house fifteen years ago, soon after his marriage. He had disliked the place then and the past years had taught[16] him the folly of disregarding[17] first impressions. But Helen had liked it; and Helen had been pregnant then so that there was an additional reason for trying to make her happy. To Helen, the house, spacious mock Tudor[18], had promised much. There was the huge oak[19] in the front lawn[20] ('just the place for the pram[21] on hot days'), the wide entrance hall ('the children will love it for parties later on'), the quiet of the estate ('so peaceful for you, darling, after London and all those dreadful patients').

1. le manque d'air devint intolérable

2. montée soudaine

3. haie de hêtres

4. en mettant sa voiture dans le garage

5. se prépara

6. à toutes les éventualités

7. lotissement privé

8. composé de maisons d'architecte

9. banlieue prospère

10. liés par

11. préjugés

12. snobismes

13. exilés

14. au milieu de

15. acheté

16. appris

17. à ne pas tenir compte de

18. de style Tudor

19. l'immense chêne

20. le gazon devant la maison

21. landau

But the pregnancy had ended in a miscarriage[1] and there had never again been the hope of children. Would it have made any difference if there had? Would the house have been any less an expensive repository[2] of lost hopes? Sitting quietly in the car and watching that ominous[3] square of lighted window, Dr Baguley reflected that all unhappy marriages were fundamentally alike. He and Helen were no different from the Worrikers. They stayed together because they expected to be less miserable[4] together than apart[5]. If the strain[6] and miseries[7] of marriage became greater than the expense, the inconvenience and the trauma of a legal separation, then they would part[8]. No sane person continued to endure[9] the intolerable. For him there had been only one valid and overriding[10] need for a divorce, his hope of marrying Fredrica Saxon. Now that the hope was over for ever he might as well continue to endure a marriage which, for[11] all its strain, at least gave him the comfortable illusion of being needed. He despised his private image, the stock predicament[12] of the psychiatrist unable to manage his own personal relationships. But at least something remained from the marriage; a fugitive surge[13] of tenderness and pity which for most of the time enabled him to be kind.

He locked the garage gates[14] and crossed the wide lawn to the front door. The garden was looking unkempt[15]. It was expensive to maintain[16] and Helen took little interest in it. It would be better in every way[17] if they sold and bought a smaller place. But Helen wouldn't talk of selling. She was as happy at Stalling Coombe as she could hope to be anywhere. Its narrow[18] and undemanding[19] social life gave her

1. fausse couche
2. réceptacle
3. inquiétant
4. malheureux
5. séparés
6. tensions
7. souffrances
8. se sépareraient
9. supporter
10. primordial
11. en dépit de
12. problème classique
13. accès
14. portes
15. mal entretenu
16. entretenir
17. à tous égards
18. limitée
19. peu exigeante

at least a semblance of security. This cocktail-and-canapé existence, the bright chatter[1] of its smart[2], lean[3], acquisitive[4] women, the gossip over the iniquities[5] of foreign maids[6] and au pair girls, the lamentations over school fees[7] and school reports[8] and the boorish[9] ingratitude of the young, were preoccupations which she could sympathize with[10] or share. Baguley had long known with pain that it was in her relationship with him that she was least at home.

He wondered how he could best break the news[11] of Miss Bolam's murder. Helen had only met her once, that Wednesday at the clinic, and he had never learned what they had said to each other. But that brief, catalytic[12] encounter had established some kind of intimacy between them[13]. Or was it perhaps an offensive alliance directed against himself? But not on Bolam's part, surely? Her attitude to him had never altered[14]. He could even believe that she approved of him more than of most psychiatrists. He had always found her co-operative, helpful[15] and correct. It was without malice[16], without vindictiveness[17], without even disliking him particularly, that she had called Helen into her office that Wednesday afternoon and, in half an hour's conversation, destroyed the greatest happiness he had ever known. It was then that Helen appeared at the top of the stairs.

'Is that you, James?' she called.

For fifteen years he had been greeted[18] every night with that unnecessary[19] question.

'Yes. I'm sorry I'm late. I'm sorry, too, that I couldn't tell you more on the phone. But something pretty dreadful has happened at the Steen

1. brillant bavardage
2. intelligentes
3. minces
4. âpres au gain
5. immoralité
6. bonnes
7. frais de scolarité
8. bulletins
9. grossière
10. comprendre
11. annoncer la nouvelle
12. catalytique
13. les avait rapprochées
14. n'avait jamais changé
15. serviable
16. méchanceté
17. rancune
18. salué
19. superflue

and Etherege thought it better to say as little as possible. Enid Bolam has been killed.'

But her mind had seized[1] on the medical director's name.

'Henry Etherege! He would, of course. He lives in Harley Street with an adequate staff[2] and about twice our income[3]. He might consider me a little[4] before keeping you at the clinic until this hour. His wife isn't stuck[5] in the country alone until he chooses to come home.'

'It wasn't Henry's fault[6] that I was kept. I told you. Enid Bolam's been killed. We've had the police at the clinic most of the evening.'

This time she heard. He sensed her sharp intake of breath[7], saw her eyes narrow[8] as she came down the stairs to him, clutching[9] her dressing-gown[10] around her.

'Miss Bolam killed?'

'Yes, murdered.'

She stood motionless[11], seeming to consider, then asked calmly: 'How?'

As he told her she still didn't speak. Afterwards they stood facing each other. He wondered uneasily[12] whether he ought to go to her, to make some gesture[13] of comfort or sympathy. But why sympathy? What, after all, had Helen lost? When she spoke her voice was as cold as metal.

'You none of you liked her, did you? Not one of you!'

'That's ridiculous, Helen! Most of us hardly came into touch with her[14] except briefly and in her capacity as AO.'

'It looks like an inside job[15], doesn't it?'

1. s'était emparé
2. suffisamment de personnel
3. revenus
4. penser un peu à moi
5. coincée
6. faute
7. retenir son souffle
8. la vit plisser les yeux
9. serrant
10. robe de chambre
11. immobile
12. avec gêne
13. geste
14. la plupart d'entre nous n'avait aucun contact avec elle
15. on dirait que c'est quelqu'un de la clinique qui a fait le coup

He winced[1] at the crude, police-court[2] jargon, but said curtly: 'On the face of it[3], yes. I don't know what the police think.'

She laughed bitterly.

'Oh, I can guess what the police think!'

Again she stood silent, then suddenly asked:

'Where were you?'

'I told you. In the medical staff cloakroom.'

'And Fredrica Saxon?'

It was hopeless now to wait for that spring[4] of pity or tenderness. It was useless, even, to try to keep control. He said with a deadly calm:

'She was in her room, scoring a Rorschach[5]. If it's any satisfaction to you, neither of us had an alibi. But if you're hoping to pin this murder on Fredrica or me[6] you'll need more intelligence than I give you credit for[7]. The superintendent's hardly likely to listen to a neurotic woman, acting out of spite[8]. He's seen too many of that type. But make an effort! You might be lucky! Why not come and examine my clothes for blood?'

He threw out[9] his hands towards her, his whole body shaking with anger. Terrified, she gave him one glance, then turned and stumbled up the stairs[10], tripping over[11] her dressing-gown and crying like a child. He gazed after her[12], his body cold from tiredness, hunger and self-disgust. He must go to her. Somehow it must be put right[13]. But not now, not at once. First, he must find a drink. He leaned for a moment against the banister[14] and said with infinite tiredness:

'Oh, Fredrica. Darling Fredrica. Why did you do it? Why? Why?'

1. grimaça
2. tribunal de police
3. à première vue
4. sursaut
5. en train d'évaluer les résultats d'un test de Rorschach
6. faire endosser ce crime à Fredrica ou à moi
7. celle que je sais que tu as
8. par dépit
9. tendit
10. grimpa maladroitement les escaliers
11. en trébuchant sur
12. la regarda
13. il fallait qu'il répare les dégâts tant bien que mal
14. rampe

Sister Ambrose lived with an elderly[1] nurse friend who had trained[2] with her thirty-five years ago and who had recently retired. Together they had bought a house in Gidea Park where they had lived together for the last twenty years on their joint income[3], in comfort and happy accord. Neither of them had married and neither of them regretted it. In the past they had sometimes wished for children, but observation of the family life of their relations had convinced them that marriage, despite a common belief to the contrary[4], was designed to benefit men at the expense of women, and that even motherhood was not an unmixed blessing[5]. Admittedly[6] this conviction had never been put to the test[7] since neither of them had ever received a proposal[8]. Like any professional worker in a psychiatric clinic, Sister Ambrose was aware of the dangers of sexual repression[9], but it had never once occurred to her[10] that these might apply to herself and, indeed, it would be difficult to imagine anyone less repressed. It is possible that she would have dismissed[11] most of the psychiatrists' theories as dangerous nonsense[12] if she had ever considered them critically[13]. But Sister Ambrose had been trained to think of consultants as only one degree lower than God. Like God they moved in mysterious ways their wonders to perform[14] but, like God, they were not subject to open criticism[15]. Some, admittedly, were more mysterious in their ways than others, but it was still the privilege of a nurse to minister[16] to these lesser deities[17], to encourage the patients to have confidence in their treatment, especially when its suc-

1. âgée
2. suivi sa formation
3. deux revenus
4. bien que l'on pense souvent le contraire
5. pure bénédiction
6. il est vrai que
7. mise à l'épreuve
8. demande en mariage
9. refoulement
10. il ne lui était jamais venu à l'esprit
11. considéré
12. absurdités
13. d'un œil critique
14. pour accomplir leurs miracles
15. on ne pouvait pas les critiquer ouvertement
16. servir
17. ces sous-dieux

cess appeared most doubtful[1], and to practise the cardinal professional virtue[2] of complete loyalty[3].

'I've always been loyal to the doctors,' was a remark frequently heard at Acacia Road, Gidea Park. Sister Ambrose often noted that the young nurses who occasionally worked at the Steen as holiday reliefs[4] were trained in a less accommodating tradition, but she had a poor opinion[5] of most young nurses, and an even poorer opinion of modern training.

As usual she took the Central Line to Liverpool Street, changed to an electric train on the eastern suburban line, and twenty minutes later was letting herself into the neat[6] semi-detached house[7] which she shared with Miss Beatrice Sharpe. Tonight, however, she fitted[8] her key in the lock without her customary inspection of the front garden, without running a critical eye over the paintwork on the door, and even without reflecting as was her custom on the generally satisfactory appearance of the property and on the gratifying[9] capital investment[10] that its purchase[11] had proved to be.

'Is that you, Dot?' called Miss Sharpe from the kitchen. 'You're late.'

'It's a wonder[12] I'm not later. We've had murder at the clinic and the police have been with us for most of the evening. As far as I know they're still there. I've had my fingerprints taken and so have the rest of the staff.'

Sister Ambrose deliberately kept her voice level[13] but the effect of the news was gratifying. She had expected no less[14]. It is not every day one has such excitement to relate[15] and she had spent some time

1. improbables
2. vertu professionnelle cardinale
3. loyauté
4. pour effectuer des remplacements lors des congés
5. une piètre opinion
6. jolie
7. maison jumelée
8. glissa
9. très satisfaisant
10. investissement de capitaux
11. achat
12. miracle
13. parla d'un ton neutre
14. elle ne s'attendait pas à moins
15. raconter

in the train rehearsing[1] how most effectively to break the news. The selected sentence expressed concisely[2] the salient[3] details. Supper[4] was temporarily forgotten. Murmuring that a casserole[5] could always wait, Miss Sharpe poured[6] her friend and herself a glass of sherry, specific against shock, and settled down[7] with it in the sitting-room[8] to hear the full story. Sister Ambrose, who had a reputation at the clinic for discretion and taciturnity[9], was a great deal more forthcoming[10] at home, and it wasn't long before Miss Sharpe knew as much about the murder as her friend was able to tell.

'But who do you think did it, Dot?' Miss Sharpe refilled their glasses – an unprecedented extravagance – and applied her mind to analysis.

'As I see it the murder must have been done between six-twenty when you saw Miss Bolam going towards the basement stairs and seven o'clock when the body was discovered.'

'Well, that's obvious! That's why the superintendent kept asking me whether I was sure about the time. I was the last person to see her alive, there's no doubt about that. Mrs Belling had finished treatment and was ready to go home at about six-fifteen and I went across to the waiting-room to let her husband know. He's always fussed[11] about time because he's on night duty[12] and has to be fed[13] and at work by[14] eight. So I looked at my watch and saw that it was just six-twenty. As I came out of the ECT room door Miss Bolam passed me[15] and went towards the basement stairs. The superintendent asked me what she looked like and whether we spoke. Well, we didn't and, as far as I could see, she looked the same as usual.'

1. à répéter
2. avec concision
3. principaux
4. souper
5. ragoût
6. versa
7. s'installa
8. salon
9. d'être discrète et taciturne
10. communicative
11. il se tracasse toujours
12. il travaille de nuit
13. il faut qu'il ait mangé
14. avant
15. est passée à côté de moi

'What's he like?' asked Miss Sharpe, visions of Maigret and Inspector Barlow crowding[1] her mind.

'The superintendent? Perfectly polite, I must say. One of those lean, bony[2] faces. Very dark. I didn't say a great deal. You could see he's used to[3] smarming things[4] out of people. Mrs Shorthouse was with him for hours and I bet he got plenty out of her. Well, I wasn't playing that game. I've always been loyal to the clinic.'

'All the same[5], Dot, it is murder.'

'That's all very well[6], Bea, but you know what the Steen is. There's enough gossip without adding to it. None of the doctors liked her and nor did anyone else as far as I know. But that's no reason for killing her. Anyway, I kept my mouth shut[7] and if the others have any sense[8] they'll do the same.'

'Well, you're all right[9], anyway[10]. You've got an alibi if you and Dr Ingram were together in the ECT room all the time.'

'Oh, we're all right. So are Shorthouse and Cully and Nagle and Miss Priddy. Nagle was out with the post after six-fifteen and the others were together. I'm not sure about the doctors, though[11], and it's a pity that Dr Baguley left the ECT room after the Belling treatment. Mind you, no one in their senses could suspect him, but it's unfortunate[12] all the same. While we were waiting for the police, Dr Ingram came over[13] to suggest that we ought not to say anything about it. A nice mess we'd get Dr Baguley into[14] with that kind of hanky-panky[15]! I pretended[16] not to understand. I just gave her one of my looks[17] and said: "I'm sure that if we all tell the truth, Doctor, the innocent will have nothing to fear." That shut her up all right[18]. And that's

1. se précipitaient dans
2. osseux
3. il a l'habitude de
4. soutirer des informations
5. quand même
6. je sais
7. j'ai fermé ma bouche
8. bon sens
9. hors de cause
10. de toute façon
11. en revanche
12. regrettable
13. est venue
14. on mettrait le docteur Baguley dans un beau pétrin
15. entourloupes
16. j'ai fait semblant
17. un regard dont j'ai le secret
18. ça lui a bien fermé le clapet

what I did. I told the truth. But I wasn't going any further[1]. If the police want gossip they can go to Mrs Shorthouse.'

'What about Nurse Bolam?' inquired Miss Sharpe.

'It's Bolam I'm worried about. She was on the spot[2] all right and you can't say an LSD patient is an alibi for anyone. The superintendent was on to her[3] quick enough. He tried to pump me[4]. Were she and her cousin friendly[5]? No doubt they worked at the Steen to be together? You can tell that to the Marines[6], I thought, but I kept my mouth shut. He didn't get much change out of me[7]. But you could see which way his mind was working. You can't wonder[8], really. We all know Miss Bolam had money and if she hasn't willed[9] it to a cats' home it will go to her cousin. There's no one else to leave it to after all.'

'I can't see her leaving it to a cats' home,' said Miss Sharpe, who had a literal mind[10].

'I didn't mean that exactly. As a matter of fact she never took much notice of Tigger although he's supposed to be her cat. I always thought that was typical of Miss Bolam. She found Tigger practically starving[11] in the square and took him into the clinic. Ever since then she's bought three tins of cat meat for him every week. But she never petted[12] him or fed him or let him into any of the upstairs rooms. On the other hand, that fool Priddy is always down in the porters' room with Nagle making a fuss of[13] Tigger, but I've never seen either of them bringing in food for him. I think Miss Bolam just bought the food out of a sense of duty[14]. She didn't really care for[15] animals. But she might leave

1. plus loin
2. sur les lieux
3. l'a suspectée
4. me cuisiner
5. amies
6. à d'autres
7. je ne lui ai pas dit grand-chose
8. il n'y a rien d'étonnant
9. légué
10. prenait tout au premier degré
11. affamé
12. caressait
13. aux petits soins avec
14. par sens du devoir
15. n'aimait pas vraiment

her money to that church she's so keen on[1], or to the Guides, for that matter[2].'

'You'd think she'd leave it to her own flesh and blood[3],' said Miss Sharpe. She herself had a poor opinion of her own flesh and blood, and found much to criticize in the conduct of her nephews and nieces[4], but her small and slowly accumulated capital had been carefully willed between them[5]. It was beyond her understanding that money should be left out of the family.

They sipped[6] their sherry in silence. The two bars of the electric fire glowed[7] and the synthetic coals shone[8] and flickered[9] as the little light behind them revolved[10]. Sister Ambrose looked around at the sitting-room and found it good. The standard lamp[11] threw a soft light on the fitted carpet[12] and the comfortable sofa and chairs. In the corner a television set stood, its small twin aerials[13] disguised as two flowers on their stems[14]. The telephone nestled[15] beneath the crinolined skirt[16] of a plastic doll[17]. On the opposite wall, above the piano, hung a cane basket from which an indoor plant, cascading streamers of green[18], almost concealed the wedding group of Miss Sharpe's eldest niece which had pride of place[19] on the piano. Sister Ambrose took comfort from the unchanged homeliness[20] of these familiar things. They at least were the same. Now that the excitement of telling her news was over she felt very tired. Planting her stout[21] legs apart she bent to loosen the laces[22] of her regulation black shoes[23], grunting a little with the effort. Usually she changed out of uniform as soon as she got home. Tonight she couldn't be bothered[24]. Suddenly she said:

1. à laquelle elle tient tant
2. d'ailleurs
3. famille
4. neveux et nièces
5. leur serait équitablement distribué après sa mort
6. sirotaient
7. brillaient
8. luisaient
9. vacillaient
10. tournait
11. lampadaire
12. moquette
13. deux antennes
14. tiges
15. était niché
16. jupe à crinoline
17. poupée
18. dont les serpentins verts tombaient en cascade
19. place d'honneur
20. simplicité
21. robustes
22. défaire les lacets
23. chaussures noires réglementaires
24. cela lui était égal

'It isn't easy to know what to do for the best. The superintendent said that anything, however small, might be important. That's all very well. But suppose it's important in the wrong way? Suppose it gives the police the wrong ideas?'

Miss Sharpe was not imaginative nor sensitive, but she had not lived in the same house as her friend for twenty years without recognizing a plea for help[1].

'You'd better tell me what you have in mind[2], Dot.'

'Well, it happened on Wednesday. You know what the ladies' cloakroom is like at the Steen? There's the large outside room with the wash-basin[3] and the lockers and two lavatories. The clinic was rather later than usual. I suppose it was well after seven when I went to wash. Well, I was in the lavatory when Miss Bolam came into the outer room[4]. Nurse Bolam was with her. I thought they'd both gone home, but I suppose Miss Bolam must have wanted something from her locker and Nurse just followed her in. They must have been in the AO's office together because they'd obviously been talking and were just carrying on with the argument[5]. I couldn't help hearing[6]. You know how it is. I could have coughed[7] or flushed the pan[8], I suppose, to show I was there but, by the time[9] I thought of it, it was too late.'

'What were they arguing about?[10]' inquired her friend. 'Money?'

In her experience this was the most frequent cause of family dissension.

'Well, that's what it sounded like. They weren't talking loudly[11] and I certainly didn't try to hear. I think they must have been having words about

1. appel à l'aide
2. ce à quoi tu penses
3. lavabo
4. première pièce
5. continuaient leur conversation
6. je n'ai pas pu m'empêcher d'entendre
7. tousser
8. tirer la chasse d'eau
9. au moment où
10. quel était le sujet de leur dispute
11. à haute voix

Nurse Bolam's mother – she's a DS[1], you know, and more or less confined to bed[2] now – because Miss Bolam said she was sorry, but she was doing as much as she could and that it would be wiser if Marion accepted the situation and placed her mother's name on a waiting list[3] for a hospital bed.'

'That's reasonable enough[4]. You can't nurse[5] these cases at home indefinitely[6]. Not without giving up[7] outside work and staying at home all the time.'

'I don't suppose Marion Bolam could afford that. Anyway, she started arguing and saying that her mother would only end up in a geriatric ward[8] with a lot of senile old women and Enid had a duty to help them because that's what her mother would have wanted. Then she said something about the money coming to her if Enid died and how much better to have some now when it would make such a difference to them.'

'What did Miss Bolam reply to that?'

'That's what's worrying me[9],' said Sister Ambrose. 'I can't remember the actual words[10], but what it amounted to was[11] that Marion shouldn't rely[12] on getting any of the money because she was going to change her will[13]. She said that she meant to tell her cousin quite openly as soon as she had really made up her mind[14]. She talked about what a great responsibility the money was and how she had been praying for guidance to do the right thing[15].'

Miss Sharpe sniffed[16]. She found it impossible to believe that the Almighty[17] would ever counsel leaving cash away from the family[18]. Miss Bolam was either an ineffectual petitioner[19] or had wilfully misinterpreted[20] the divine instructions. Miss Sharpe was not even sure that she approved of the

1. elle a une sclérose en plaques
2. grabataire
3. liste d'attente
4. ça me paraît raisonnable
5. soigner
6. à l'infini
7. renoncer à
8. service de gériatrie
9. ce qui m'inquiète
10. ce qu'elle a dit exactement
11. cela revenait à dire
12. compter
13. testament
14. pris sa décision
15. prié pour que Dieu l'aide à faire le bon choix
16. renifla
17. le Tout-puissant
18. puisse jamais conseiller de ne pas donner d'argent à la famille
19. soit elle ne savait pas poser des questions
20. délibérément mal interprété

praying. There are some things, surely, which one ought to be able to decide on one's own[1]. But she saw her friend's difficulty.

'It would look bad if it came out,' she admitted. 'No doubt about that.'

'I think I know Bolam pretty well, Bea, and that child wouldn't lay hands on a fly[2]. The idea of her murdering anyone is ridiculous. You know what I think about young nurses generally. Well, I wouldn't mind Bolam taking over[3] when I retire next year and that's saying something[4]. I'd trust her completely[5].'

'Maybe, but the police wouldn't. Why should they? She's probably their first suspect already. She was on the spot; she hasn't an alibi; she has medical knowledge and would know where the skull[6] is most vulnerable; and where to put that chisel in. She was told that Tippett wouldn't be in the clinic. And now this!'

'And it's not as if it's a small sum.' Sister Ambrose leaned forward and dropped[7] her voice. 'I thought I heard Miss Bolam mention thirty thousand pounds. Thirty thousand, Bea! It would be like winning the pools[8]!'

Miss Sharpe was impressed[9] despite herself, but remarked merely[10] that people who went on[11] working when they had thirty thousand wanted their brains examined[12].

'What would you do, Bea? Do you think I ought to say anything?'

Sister Ambrose, sturdily[13] independent and used to settling[14] her own affairs, recognized that this decision was beyond her[15] and threw half the burden[16] on her friend. Both of them knew that the

1. tout seul
2. ne ferait pas de mal à une mouche
3. je ne verrais pas d'inconvénient à ce que Bolam prenne ma place
4. ce qui n'est pas peu dire
5. je lui ferais entièrement confiance
6. crâne
7. baissa
8. gagner au loto
9. impressionnée
10. fit simplement la remarque
11. continuaient
12. n'avaient pas toute leur tête
13. vigoureusement
14. habituée à gérer
15. au-delà de ses capacités
16. fardeau

moment was unique. Never had two friends made fewer demands on each other. Miss Sharpe sat in silence for a moment or two, then said:

'No. Not yet, anyway. After all she is your colleague and you trust her. It wasn't your fault that you overheard[1] the conversation, but it was only overhearing. It was only chance[2] that you happened to be in the loo[3]. I should try to forget it. The police will find out how Bolam has left her money anyway and whether the will[4] has been changed. Either way Nurse Bolam will be suspected. And if it should come to a trial[5] – I'm only saying "if", remember – well, you don't want to get involved unnecessarily. Remember those nurses in the Eastbourne case, the hours they spent in the box[6]. You wouldn't want that kind of publicity[7].'

Indeed she wouldn't, thought Sister Ambrose. Her imagination set the scene only too vividly. Sir Somebody or Other would be prosecuting[8], tall, beak-nosed[9], bending his terrifying gaze on her, thumbs[10] hooked[11] in the bands of his gown[12].

'And now, Sister Ambrose, perhaps you will tell his Lordship[13] and the jury what you were doing when you overheard this conversation between the accused and her cousin.'

Titters in court[14]. The judge, terrifying in scarlet[15] and white wig[16], leans down from his seat.

'If there is any more of this laughter I shall clear the court[17].'

Silence. Sir Somebody on the ball[18] again.

'Well, Sister Ambrose ...?'

No, she certainly wouldn't want that kind of publicity.

1. surpris
2. hasard
3. aux toilettes
4. testament
5. procès
6. à la barre
7. faire parler de toi de cette façon
8. représenterait le parquet
9. avec un nez crochu
10. pouces
11. glissés
12. robe
13. Monsieur le Juge
14. on entend des ricanements dans la salle d'audience
15. sa robe rouge écarlate
16. perruque blanche
17. suspendre l'audience
18. très réactif

'I think you're right, Bea,' she said. 'After all, it's not as if the superintendent actually asked me whether I'd ever overheard them quarrelling[1].' Certainly he hadn't and, with luck[2], he never would[3].

Miss Sharpe felt that it was time to change the subject.

'How did Dr Steiner take it?' she asked. 'You always said that he was working to get Bolam moved to another unit.'

'That's another extraordinary thing! He was terribly upset[4]. You know I told you that he was with us when we first saw the body? D'you know he could hardly control himself? He had to turn his back on us and I could see his shoulders shaking[5]. He was actually crying[6], I think. I've never seen him so upset. Aren't people extraordinary, Bea?'

It was a vehement cry[7] of resentment and protest. People were extraordinary! You thought you knew them. You worked with them, sometimes for years. You spent more time with them than you would with family or close friends[8]. You knew every line[9] of their faces. And all the time they were private[10]. As private as Dr Steiner who cried over the dead body of a woman he had never liked. As private as Dr Baguley who had been having a love affair[11] with Fredrica Saxon for years with no one knowing until Miss Bolam found out and told his wife. As private as Miss Bolam, who had taken God knows what secrets to the grave[12]. Miss Bolam, dull[13], ordinary, unremarkable[14] Enid Bolam, who had inspired so much hate[15] in someone that she had ended with a chisel in her heart. As private as that unknown member of the staff who would be at the clinic on Monday morning, dressed as usual,

1. se disputer
2. avec un peu de chance
3. il ne le ferait jamais
4. bouleversé
5. trembler
6. il pleurait
7. un cri véhément
8. amis proches
9. ride
10. ils vous restaient étrangers
11. liaison
12. tombe
13. ennuyeuse
14. peu intéressante
15. haine

looking the same as usual, speaking and smiling as usual and who was a murderer.

'Damned smiling[1] villain[2]!' said Sister Ambrose suddenly. She thought that the phrase was a quotation[3] from some play[4] or other. Shakespeare probably. Most quotations were. But its terse[5] malevolence[6] suited[7] her mood.

'What you need is food,' said Miss Sharpe positively[8]. 'Something light[9] and nourishing[10]. Suppose we leave the casserole until tomorrow night and just have boiled eggs[11] on a tray?'

She was waiting for him at the entrance to St James's Park just as he had expected her to be. As he crossed the Mall and saw the slight figure[12] drooping[13] a little disconsolately[14] by the war memorial Nagle could almost feel sorry[15] for her. It was the hell of a raw night[16] to be standing about[17]. But her first words killed any impulse to pity.

'We should have met somewhere else. This is all right for you, of course. You're on the way home.'

She sounded as peevish[18] as a neglected wife.[19]

'Come back to the flat, then,' he taunted her softly[20]. 'We can get a bus down.'

'No. Not the flat. Not tonight.'

He smiled into the darkness and they moved together into the black shadow of the trees. They walked a little way apart[21] and she made no move towards him. He glanced down at the calm, uplifted[22] profile cleansed[23] now of all traces of crying. She looked desperately tired. Suddenly she said:

'That superintendent is very good-looking[24], isn't he? Do you think he suspects us?'

1. souriant
2. scélérat
3. citation
4. pièce de théâtre
5. laconique
6. animosité
7. s'accordait bien avec
8. catégoriquement
9. léger
10. nourrissant
11. œufs durs
12. mince silhouette
13. affaissée
14. à l'air abattu
15. eut presque pitié
16. nuit sacrément froide
17. pour rester debout à attendre
18. irritable
19. épouse délaissée
20. dit-il pour la taquiner un peu
21. un peu éloignés l'un de l'autre
22. haut
23. lavé
24. très beau

So here it was, the grasping at reassurance, the childish[1] need to be protected. And yet she had sounded almost uncaring[2]. He said roughly:

'For God's sake why should he? I was out of the clinic when she died. You know that as well as I do.'

'But I wasn't. I was there.'

'No one's going to suspect you for long. The doctors will see to that[3]. We've had all this out before[4]. Nothing can go wrong if you keep your head[5] and listen to me. Now this is what I want you to do.'

She listened as meekly[6] as a child, but watching that tired, expressionless face he felt that he was in the company of a stranger. He wondered idly[7] whether they would ever get free of each other again. And suddenly he felt that it was not she who was the victim.

As they came to the lake she stopped and gazed out over the water. Out of the darkness came the subdued cry and shuffle of ducks[8]. He could smell the evening breeze[9], salty as a sea wind, and shivered[10]. Turning to study her face, ravaged now with fatigue, he saw, in his mind's eye, another picture: a broad brow[11] under a white nurse's cap, a swathe[12] of yellow hair, immense grey eyes which gave nothing away[13]. Tentatively he pondered a new idea[14]. It might come to nothing[15], of course. It might easily come to nothing. But the picture would soon be finished and he could get rid of Jenny. In a month he would be in Paris, but Paris was only an hour's flight away[16] and he would be coming back often. And with Jenny out of the way and a new life in his grasp it would be worth trying[17]. There were worse

1. puéril
2. froide
3. feront en sorte que ce soit le cas
4. on a déjà dit tout ça
5. garde ton sang-froid
6. humblement
7. négligemment
8. on entendait au loin les cris et mouvements des canards
9. brise
10. frissonna
11. front large
12. bande
13. qui ne trahissaient rien
14. il eut l'idée furtive d'un nouveau projet
15. n'aboutir à rien
16. à une heure de vol
17. vaudrait la peine d'être essayé

fates[1] than marrying the heiress[2] to thirty thousand pounds.

Nurse Bolam let herself into the narrow terraced house at 17 Rettinger Street, NW 1, and was met by the familiar ground-floor smell compounded of frying fat[3], furniture polish[4] and stale[5] urine. The twins' pram stood behind the door with its stained under-blanket[6] thrown across the handle[7]. The smell of cooking was less strong than usual. She was very late tonight and the ground-floor tenants[8] must long have finished their evening meal. The wail[9] of one of the babies sounded faintly from the back of the house, almost drowned[10] by the noise of the television. She could hear the National Anthem[11]. The BBC service was closing for the day.

She mounted to the first floor. Here the smell of food was fainter and was masked by the tang[12] of a household disinfectant. The first-floor tenant was addicted to cleanliness[13] as the basement tenant was to drink[14]. There was the usual note[15] on the landing window ledge[16]. Tonight it read[17]: 'Do not stand your dirty milk bottles here. This ledge is private. This means you.' From behind the brown polished door, even at this late hour, came the roar[18] of a vacuum cleaner[19] in full throttle[20].

Up now to the third floor, to their own flat. She paused on the bottom step[21] of the last flight[22] and saw, as if with a stranger's eyes, the pathetic attempt she had made to improve the look of the place. The walls here were painted with white emulsion paint[23]. The stairs were covered with a grey drugget[24]. The door was painted a bright citrus yellow[25] and sported[26] a brass knocker[27] in the

1. destins
2. héritière
3. huile de friture
4. encaustique
5. vieille
6. alaise sale
7. guidon
8. locataires du rez-de-chaussée
9. hurlement
10. couvert
11. l'hymne national
12. odeur piquante
13. accro à la propreté
14. l'était à l'alcool
15. il y avait comme d'habitude un mot
16. sur le rebord de la fenêtre du palier
17. ce soir, on pouvait y lire
18. grondement
19. aspirateur
20. tournant à plein régime
21. la première marche
22. du dernier palier
23. peinture mate
24. tapis en toile de jute
25. jaune citron éclatant
26. arborait
27. un heurtoir en laiton

shape of a frog's head. On the wall, carefully disposed one above the other, were the three flower prints she had picked up in Berwick Street market. Until tonight she had been pleased with the result of her work. It really had given the entrance quite an air. There had been times when she had felt that a visitor, Mrs Bostock from the clinic, perhaps, or even Sister Ambrose, might safely be invited home for coffee without the need to apologize[1] or explain. But tonight, freed[2], gloriously freed for ever, from the self-deceit[3] of poverty, she could see the flat for what it was, sordid, dark, airless, smelly[4] and pathetic. Tonight, for the first time, she could safely recognize how much she hated every brick of 17 Rettinger Street.

She trod[5] very softly, still not ready to go in. There was so little time in which to think, in which to plan. She knew exactly what she would see when she opened the door of her mother's room. The bed stood against the window. In summer evenings Mrs Bolam could lie[6] and watch the sun setting[7] behind a castellation of[8] sloping roofs[9] and twisting[10] chimneys with, in the distance, the turrets[11] of St Pancras Station darkening against a flaming[12] sky. Tonight the curtains would be drawn[13]. The district nurse would have put her mother to bed, would have left the telephone and portable wireless[14] on the bedside table[15], together with the handbell[16] which could, if necessary, summon aid[17] from the tenant of the flat below. Her mother's bedside lamp would be lit, a small pool of light[18] in the surrounding gloom[19]. At the other end of the room one bar of the electric fire would be burning, one bar only, the nicely calculated allocation of comfort

1. s'excuser
2. libérée
3. aveuglement
4. malodorant
5. marchait
6. rester allongée
7. se coucher
8. les créneaux que formaient
9. toits en pente
10. torsadées
11. tourelles
12. flamboyant
13. fermés
14. poste de TSF
15. table de chevet
16. clochette
17. appeler à l'aide
18. rond de lumière
19. obscurité environnante

for an October evening. As soon as she opened the door her mother's eyes would meet her, brightened by pleasure and anticipation. There would be the same intolerably bright greeting, the same minute inquiries[1] about the doings of the day.

'Did you have a good day at the clinic, darling? Why were you late? Did anything happen?'

And how did one answer that?

'Nothing of any importance, Mummy, except that someone has stabbed Cousin Enid through the heart and we're going to be rich after all.'

And what did that mean? Dear God, what didn't it mean? No more smell of polish[2] and napkins[3]. No more need to propitiate[4] the second-floor harpy[5] in case she were needed to answer[6] that bell. No more watching[7] the electricity meter[8] and wondering whether it was really cold enough for that extra bar of the fire. No more thanking Cousin Enid for her generous cheque twice a year, the one in December that made such a difference to Christmas, the one late in July that paid for the hired[9] car and the expensive hotel which catered for[10] invalids who could afford to pay for being a nuisance. No longer any need to count the days, to watch the calendar, to wonder whether Enid was going to oblige[11] this year. No need to take the cheque with becoming[12] gratitude to conceal behind lowered[13] eyes the hate and resentment that longed to tear it up[14] and throw[15] it in that smug[16], plain[17], condescending face. No need to climb these stairs any more. They could have the house in a suburb which her mother talked about. One of the better-class suburbs[18], of course, near enough to London for easy travelling to the clinic – it wouldn't be wise

1. questionnement précis
2. encaustique
3. couches
4. se concilier
5. harpie
6. pour qu'elle réponde, en cas de besoin
7. plus besoin de surveiller
8. compteur
9. louée
10. accueillait
11. aura l'amabilité de faire un chèque
12. convenable
13. baissés
14. donnaient envie de le déchirer
15. jeter
16. suffisant
17. quelconque
18. banlieues résidentielles ayant bonne réputation

to give up the job before she really had to – but far enough out for a small garden, perhaps, even for a country view[1]. They might even afford a little car. She could learn to drive. And then, when it was no longer possible for her mother to be left, they could be together. It meant the end of this nagging[2] anxiety about the future. There was no reason now to picture[3] her mother in a chronic sick ward[4], cared for by overworked[5] strangers, surrounded by the senile and incontinent, waiting hopelessly for the end. And money could buy less vital but not unimportant pleasures. She would get some clothes. It would no longer be necessary to wait for the biennial sales[6] if she wanted a suit[7] with some evidence of quality[8]. It would be possible to dress well[9], really well, on half the amount[10] Enid had spent on those unattractive skirts[11] and suits. There must be wardrobes[12] full of them in the Kensington flat. Someone would have the job of sorting them out[13]. And who would want them? Who would want anything that had belonged[14] to Cousin Enid? Except her money. Except her money. Except her money. And suppose she had already written to her solicitor[15] about changing the will. Surely that wasn't possible! Nurse Bolam fought down[16] panic and forced herself once again to consider the possibility rationally. She had thought it out[17] so many times[18] before. Suppose Enid had written on Wednesday night. All right, suppose she had. It would be too late to catch the post that evening so the letter would have been received only this morning. Everyone knew how long solicitors took to do anything. Even if Enid had stressed the urgency, had caught the Wednesday post, the new will couldn't

1. une vue sur la campagne
2. tenace
3. s'imaginer
4. service pour les malades chroniques
5. surmenés
6. soldes bisannuelles
7. tailleur
8. d'une certaine qualité
9. s'habiller bien
10. avec la moitié
11. jupes
12. armoires
13. les trier
14. appartenu
15. notaire
16. tenta de réprimer
17. elle avait réfléchi à ça
18. fois

possibly be ready for signature yet. And if it were ready, if it were waiting to be posted in its solid official-looking envelope, what did it matter?[1] Cousin Enid wouldn't sign it now with that round, upright, unadult hand[2] which had always seemed so typical of her. Cousin Enid would never sign anything again.

She thought again about the money. Not about her own share[3]. That was hardly likely to bring her happiness now. But even if they arrested her for murder they couldn't stop Mummy inheriting her share. No one could stop that. But somehow she must get hold of some cash[4] urgently. Everyone knew that a will took months to prove[5]. Would it look very suspicious or heartless[6] if she went to Enid's solicitor to explain how poor they were and to ask what could be arranged? Or would it be wiser to approach the bank? Perhaps the solicitor would send for her[7]. Yes, of course he would. She and her mother were the next of kin[8]. And as soon as the will was read she could tactfully[9] raise the question of an advance[10]. Surely that would be natural enough? An advance of one hundred pounds wouldn't be much to ask by someone who was going to inherit a share of thirty thousand.

Suddenly she could bear it no longer. The long tension broke. She wasn't conscious of covering those last few stairs[11], of putting her key in the lock. At once she was in the flat and through to her mother's room. Howling[12] with fear and misery[13], crying as she had not cried since childhood, she hurled herself[14] on her mother's breast and felt around her the comfort and the unexpected strength of those brittle[15], shaking arms. The arms rocked her[16] like

1. cela n'avait aucune importance
2. écriture arrondie, droite et enfantine
3. sa propre part
4. obtenir de l'argent
5. homologuer
6. cruel
7. la ferait venir
8. les plus proches parents
9. avec tact
10. acompte
11. monter les dernières marches
12. hurlant
13. détresse
14. se rua
15. fragiles
16. la bercèrent

a baby. The beloved voice cooed[1] its reassurance. Under the cheap nightdress[2] she smelt the soft familiar flesh.

'Hush[3], my darling. My baby. Hush. What is it? What's happened. Tell me, darling.'

And Nurse Bolam told her.

Since his divorce two years earlier Dr Steiner had shared a house in Hampstead with his widowed[4] sister. He had his own sitting-room and kitchen, an arrangement which enabled Rosa and him to see little of each other, thus fostering[5] the illusion that they got on well together. Rosa was a culture snob[6]. Her house was the centre for a collection of resting[7] actors, one-volume poets, aesthetes posing on the fringe of[8] the ballet world, and writers more anxious[9] to talk about their craft[10] in an atmosphere of sympathetic[11] understanding than to practise it. Dr Steiner did not resent them[12]. He merely ensured that they ate and drank at Rosa's expense, not his. He was aware that his profession had a certain cachet for his sister and that to introduce 'my brother Paul – the famous psycho-analyst' was in some measure a compensation for the low rent[13] which he spasmodically paid and the minor irritations of propinquity[14]. He would hardly have been housed[15] so economically and comfortably had he been[16] a bank manager.

Tonight Rosa was out. It was exasperating and inconsiderate of her[17] to be missing on the one evening when he needed her company, but that was typical of Rosa. The German maid[18] was out, too, presumably illicitly[19], since Friday was not her half-day. There was soup and salad put ready for him

1. roucoula
2. chemise de nuit
3. chut
4. devenue veuve
5. entretenait
6. faisait preuve de snobisme culturel
7. faisant une pause
8. en marge de
9. désireux
10. métier
11. bienveillant
12. n'était pas hostile à leur présence
13. faible loyer
14. proximité
15. logé
16. s'il avait été
17. signe d'un manque de considération de sa part
18. bonne
19. illicitement

in his kitchen, but even the effort of heating[1] the soup seemed beyond him. The sandwiches he had eaten without relish[2] at the clinic had taken away his appetite but left him hungry for protein, preferably hot and properly cooked. But he did not want to eat alone. Pouring himself[3] a glass of sherry he recognized his need to talk to someone – anyone – about the murder. The need was imperative. He thought of Valda.

His marriage to Valda had been doomed[4] from the start, as any marriage must be when husband and wife have a basic ignorance of[5] each other's needs coupled with the illusion[6] that they understand each other perfectly. Dr Steiner had not been desolated[7] by his divorce, but he had been inconvenienced[8] and distressed[9], and had been harried[10] afterwards by an irrational sense of failure and guilt[11]. Valda, on the other hand[12], apparently throve[13] on freedom. When they met he was always struck with[14] her glow[15] of physical well-being. They did not avoid each other[16], since meeting her ex-husband and discarded lovers[17] with the greatest appearance of friendliness and good humour was what Valda meant when she talked about civilized behaviour[18]. Dr Steiner did not like or admire her. He liked the company of women who were well-informed, well-educated, intelligent and fundamentally serious. But these were not the kind of women he liked to go to bed with. He knew all about this inconvenient dichotomy. Its causes had occupied many expensive hours with his analyst. Unfortunately, knowing is one thing and changing is another, as some of his patients could have told him. And there had been times with Valda

1. réchauffer
2. sans plaisir
3. en se versant
4. condamné
5. ignorent totalement
6. tout en ayant l'illusion
7. affligé
8. gêné
9. désolé
10. tourmenté
11. culpabilité
12. de son côté
13. s'épanouissait
14. frappé par
15. éclat
16. ils ne s'évitaient pas
17. amants éconduits
18. comportement

(christened[1] Millicent) when he hadn't really wanted to be different.

The telephone rang for about a minute before she answered and he told her about Miss Bolam against a background[2] noise of music and clinking glasses[3]. The flat was apparently full of people. He wasn't even sure she had heard him.

'What is it?' he asked irritably. 'Are you having a party?'

'Just a few chums[4]. Wait while I turn down[5] the gramophone. Now, what did you say?'

Dr Steiner said it again. This time Valda's reaction was entirely satisfactory.

'Murdered! No! Darling, how too frightful[6] for you! Miss Bolam. Isn't she that dreary[7] old AO you hated so much? The one who kept trying to do you down[8] over your travelling claims[9]?'

'I didn't hate her, Valda. In some ways[10] I respected her. She had considerable integrity. Of course, she was rather obsessional, frightened of her own subconscious aggressions, possibly sexually frigid …'

'That's what I said, darling. I knew you couldn't bear[11] her. Oh, Paulie, they won't think you did it, will they?'

'Of course not,' said Dr Steiner, beginning to regret his impulse to confide.

'But you always did say that someone should get rid of[12] her.'

The conversation was beginning to have a nightmare quality[13]. The gramophone thudded its insistent bass to the treble cacophony of[14] Valda's party and the pulse[15] in Dr Steiner's temple[16] beat in unison[17]. He was going to start one of his headaches[18].

1. baptisée
2. fond
3. tintement de verres
4. copains
5. baisse le son de
6. atroce
7. ennuyeuse
8. te rouler
9. frais de déplacement
10. quelque part
11. supporter
12. se débarrasser de
13. devenait cauchemardesque
14. les basses obsédantes du gramophone se superposaient à la cacophonie des sons aigus de
15. pouls
16. tempe
17. à l'unisson
18. maux de tête

'I meant that she should be transferred to another clinic, not bashed[1] on the head with a blunt instrument[2].'

The hackneyed phrase[3] sharpened[4] her curiosity. Violence had always fascinated her. He knew that she saw in imagination a spatter[5] of blood and brains.

'Darling, I must hear all about it. Why not come over?'

'Well, I was thinking of it,' said Dr Steiner. He added cunningly[6]: 'There are one or two details I can't give you over the phone. But if you've got a party it's rather difficult. Frankly, Valda, I'm not capable of being sociable just now. I've got one of my heads[7] starting. This has all been a terrible shock. After all, I did more or less discover the body.'

'You poor sweet[8]. Look[9], give me half an hour and I'll get rid of the chums.'

The chums sounded to Dr Steiner as if they were well entrenched[10] and he said so.

'Not really. We were all going on to Toni's[11]. They can manage[12] without me. I'll give them a shove[13] and you set off[14] in about half an hour. All right?'

It was certainly all right. Replacing the receiver[15], Dr Steiner decided that he would just have time to bathe and change in comfort[16]. He pondered[17] on a choice of tie[18]. The headache unaccountably[19] seemed to have gone. Just before he left the house the telephone rang. He felt a spasm of apprehension. Perhaps Valda had changed her mind about seeing off the chums and having some time alone together. That, after all, had been a recurring pattern[20] in his marriage. He was irritated to find that the hand reaching for the receiver was not quite

1. frappée
2. instrument contondant
3. expression éculée
4. aiguisa
5. les éclaboussures
6. astucieusement
7. maux de tête
8. pauvre chéri
9. écoute
10. n'avaient pas l'intention de partir
11. chez Toni
12. ils pourront continuer leur soirée
13. je vais les pousser à la porte
14. tu te mets en route
15. en raccrochant
16. prendre un bain et se changer tranquillement
17. hésita
18. cravate
19. mystérieusement
20. un scénario récurrent

steady[1]. But the caller was only Dr Etherege to say that he was calling an emergency meeting of the clinic Medical Committee for 8 p.m. the following evening. In his relief Dr Steiner, momentarily forgetting Miss Bolam, just saved himself in time from the folly[2] of asking why.

If Ralfe and Sonia Bostock had lived in Clapham their flat would have been called a basement. Since, however, it was in Hampstead, half a mile in fact from Dr Steiner's house, a small wooden notice[3], lettered[4] with impeccable taste[5], directed one[6] to the garden flat. Here they paid nearly twelve pounds a week for a socially acceptable address and the privilege of seeing a green sloping lawn[7] from the sitting-room window. They had planted this lawn with crocuses[8] and daffodils[9] and in spring those plants which managed to bloom[10] in the almost complete lack[11] of sun, at least fostered the illusion that the flat had access to a garden. In autumn, however, the view was less agreeable and dampness[12] from the sloping soil seeped[13] into the room. The flat was noisy. There was a nursery school[14] two houses away and a young family in the ground-floor flat. Ralfe Bostock, dispensing[15] drinks to their carefully selected friends and raising[16] his voice against the wail of bath-time tantrums[17], would say:

'Sorry for the row[18]. I'm afraid the intelligentsia have taken to breeding[19] but not – alas – to controlling their brats[20].' He was given to[21] malicious remarks, some of which were clever, but he overworked them[22]. His wife lived in constant apprehension that he would make the same witticism[23]

1. tremblait un peu
2. sottise
3. panneau en bois
4. gravé
5. avec beaucoup de goût
6. indiquait la direction
7. pelouse en pente
8. crocus
9. jonquilles
10. fleurir
11. absence
12. humidité
13. suintait
14. école maternelle
15. en distribuant
16. élevant
17. les hurlements des enfants piquant une crise à l'heure du bain
18. vacarme
19. se sont mis à faire des enfants
20. petits morveux
21. il avait le don de
22. elles étaient trop recherchées
23. trait d'esprit

twice to the same people. There were few things more fatal to a man's chances than the reputation for repeating his jokes[1].

Tonight he was out at a political meeting. She approved of the meeting which might be an important one for him and she did not mind being alone. She wanted time to think. She went into the bedroom and took off[2] her suit, shaking it carefully and hanging it in the wardrobe, then put on a housecoat[3] of brown velvet[4]. Next she sat at her dressing-table[5]. Binding a crêpe bandage about her brow she began to cream the make-up from her face[6]. She was more tired than she had realized and needed a drink, but nothing would deter her from[7] her evening ritual. There was much to think about, much to plan. The grey-green eyes, ringed[8] with cream, gazed calmly back at her from the glass. Leaning forward she inspected the delicate folds[9] of skin beneath each eye, watching for the first lines of age[10]. She was only twenty-eight after all. There was no need to worry yet. But Ralfe was thirty this year. Time was passing. If they were to achieve anything there was no time to lose.

She considered tactics. The situation would need careful handling[11] and there was no room[12] for mistakes. She had made one already. The temptation to slap[13] Nagle's face had proved irresistible, but it was still a mistake and possibly a bad one, too like vulgar exhibitionism to be safe. Aspiring[14] administrative officers did not slap[15] a porter's face, even when under strain, particularly if they wanted to create an impression of calm, authoritative[16] competence. She remembered the look on Miss Saxon's face. Well, Fredrica Saxon was in no position to[17]

1. blagues
2. enleva
3. robe de chambre
4. velours
5. coiffeuse
6. se démaquiller
7. l'empêcher de s'adonner à
8. entourés
9. plis
10. rides
11. manœuvre
12. place
13. gifler
14. quand on souhaite devenir
15. on ne gifle pas
16. qui fait autorité
17. n'était pas en mesure de

be censorious[1]. It was a pity that Dr Steiner was there, but it had all happened so quickly that she couldn't be sure that he had really seen. The Priddy child was of no importance.

Nagle would have to go, of course, once she was appointed[2]. Here, too, she would have to be careful. He was an insolent devil, but the clinic could do much worse and the consultants knew it. An efficient porter made quite a difference to their comfort, especially when he was willing and able to carry out the many small repair jobs[3] that were needed. It wouldn't be a popular move if they had to wait for someone to come from the group engineer's department every time a sash cord[4] broke or a fuse needed replacing[5]. Nagle would have to go, but she would put out feelers[6] for a good replacement[7] before taking any action.

The main concern[8] at present must be to get the consultants' support for her appointment. She could be sure of Dr Etherege and his was the most powerful voice. But it wasn't the only one. He would be retiring in six months' time and his influence would be on the wane[9]. If she were offered an acting appointment[10], and all went well, the Hospital Management Committee might not be in too much of a hurry[11] to advertise the post[12]. Almost certainly they would wait until the murder was either solved or the police shelved the case[13]. It was up to her[14] to consolidate her position in the intervening months[15]. It wouldn't do to take anything for granted[16]. When there had been trouble at a unit, Committees tended to make an outside appointment[17]. There was safety in bringing in a stranger uncontaminated by[18] the previous upset[19].

1. se montrer critique
2. nommée
3. travaux de réparation
4. un cordon de fenêtre
5. un fusible devait être remplacé
6. tâterait le terrain
7. remplaçant
8. préoccupation
9. en déclin
10. nomination temporaire
11. être pressé
12. publier l'annonce
13. classe l'affaire
14. c'était à elle
15. les mois qui suivraient
16. il ne fallait pas tenir quoi que ce soit pour acquis
17. nommer quelqu'un d'extérieur à la clinique
18. qui n'avait rien à voir avec
19. bouleversement

The group secretary would be an influence there. It had been a wise move to see him last month and ask his advice about working for the diploma of the Institute of Hospital Administrators. He liked his staff to qualify and, being a man, he was flattered[1] to be asked for advice[2]. But he wasn't a fool. He didn't have to be. She was as suitable a candidate as the HMC were likely to find, and he knew it.

She lay back[3], relaxed, on her single bed, her feet raised on a pillow[4], her mind busy with the images of success. 'My wife is administrative officer of the Steen Clinic.' So much more satisfactory than, 'Actually, my wife is working as a secretary at present. The Steen Clinic, as a matter of fact[5].'

And less than two miles away, in a mortuary[6] in north London, Miss Bolam's body, tight-packed as a herring in an ice box[7], stiffened[8] slowly through the autumn night.

1. flatté
2. conseil
3. s'allongea
4. coussin
5. en fait
6. morgue
7. serré comme un hareng dans un compartiment à glace
8. se raidissait

CHAPTER FIVE

If there had to be a murder at the Steen, Friday was the most convenient day for it. The clinic did not open on Saturday so that the police were able to work in the building without the complications presented by the presence of patients and staff. The staff, presumably, were glad[1] of two days' grace[2] in which to recover[3] from the shock, determine at leisure[4] what their official reaction should be and seek[5] the comfort and reassurance of their friends.

Dalgliesh's day began early. He had asked for a report from the local CID[6] about the Steen burglary[7] and this, together with typescripts of the previous day's interviews, was waiting on his desk. The burglary had puzzled[8] the local men[9]. There could be no doubt that someone had broken[10] into the clinic and that the £15 was missing. It was not so certain that these two facts were related[11]. The local sergeant thought it odd that a casual thief had picked the one drawer which held cash while neglecting the safe[12] and leaving untouched the silver inkstand[13] in the medical director's office. On the other hand, Cully had undoubtedly[14] seen a man leaving the clinic and both he and Nagle had alibis for the time of entry. The local CID were inclined to suspect Nagle of having helped himself to the cash[15] while he was alone in the building,

1. content
2. de répit
3. se remettre
4. quand bon leur semblerait
5. chercher
6. P.J.
7. cambriolage
8. laissé perplexe
9. policiers
10. s'était introduit
11. liés
12. coffre-fort
13. encrier
14. indubitablement
15. avoir volé l'argent

but it had not been found on him and there was no real evidence[1]. Besides, the porter had plenty of opportunities for dishonesty at the Steen if he were so inclined, and nothing was known against him. The whole affair was puzzling[2]. They were still working on it but weren't very hopeful[3]. Dalgliesh asked that any progress should be reported to him at once[4] and set off[5] with Sergeant Martin to examine Miss Bolam's flat[6].

Miss Bolam had lived on the fifth floor of a solid, redbrick block[7] near Kensington High Street. There was no difficulty over[8] the key. The resident caretaker[9] handed it over with formal and perfunctory[10] expressions of regret at Miss Bolam's death. She seemed to feel that some reference to the murder was necessary, but managed to give the impression that the company's tenants[11] usually had the good taste to quit this life in more orthodox fashion[12].

'There will be no undesirable publicity, I hope,' she murmured, as she escorted Dalgliesh and Sergeant Martin to the lift[13]. 'These flats are very select[14] and the company are most particular[15] about their tenants. We have never had trouble of this kind before.'

Dalgliesh resisted the temptation to say that Miss Bolam's murderer had obviously not recognized one of the company's tenants.

'The publicity is hardly likely to affect the flats,' he pointed out[16]. 'It's not as if the murder took place[17] here.' The caretaker was heard to murmur that she hoped not indeed!

1. preuve
2. curieuse
3. n'avaient pas beaucoup d'espoir
4. tout de suite
5. partit
6. appartement
7. immeuble
8. à récupérer
9. gardienne
10. de pure forme
11. locataires
12. manière
13. ascenseur
14. chics
15. exigeants
16. fit remarquer
17. avait eu lieu

They ascended[1] to the fifth floor together in the slow, old-fashioned[2] panelled[3] lift. The atmosphere was heavy with disapproval.

'Did you know Miss Bolam at all[4]?' Dalgliesh inquired. 'I believe she had lived here for some years.'

'I knew her to say good morning to, nothing more. She was a very quiet tenant. But then all our tenants are. She has been in residence for fifteen years, I believe. Her mother was the tenant previously and they lived here together. When Mrs Bolam died her daughter took over the tenancy[5]. That was before my time[6].'

'Did her mother die here?'

The caretaker closed her lips[7] repressively[8].

'Mrs Bolam died in a nursing home[9] in the country. There was some unpleasantness[10], I believe.'

'You mean that she killed herself?'

'I was told so[11]. As I said, it happened before I took this job. Naturally I never alluded[12] to the fact either to Miss Bolam or to any of the other tenants. It is not the kind of thing one would wish to talk about. They really do seem a most unfortunate[13] family.'

'What rent[14] did Miss Bolam pay?'

The caretaker paused before replying. This was obviously high on her list of questions that should not properly be asked. Then, as if reluctantly admitting the authority of the police, she replied:

'Our fourth and fifth floor two-bedroom flats are from £490 excluding rates[15].'

That was about half Miss Bolam's salary, thought Dalgliesh. It was too high a proportion for anyone without private means[16]. He had yet to see the dead woman's solicitor, but it looked as if

1. montèrent
2. démodé
3. lambrissé
4. un peu
5. a repris le bail
6. que je n'arrive
7. lèvres
8. comme si elle voulait s'empêcher de parler
9. maison de retraite médicalisée
10. des désagréments
11. c'est ce qu'on m'a dit
12. fait allusion
13. malheureuse
14. loyer
15. impôts locaux
16. sans fortune personnelle

Nurse Bolam's assessment[1] of her cousin's income was not far wrong[2].

He dismissed the caretaker[3] at the door of the flat and he and Martin went in together.

This prying[4] among the personal residue[5] of a finished life was a part of his job which Dalgliesh had always found a little distasteful[6]. It was too much like putting the dead at a disadvantage[7]. During his career he had examined with interest and with pity so many petty leavings[8]. The soiled underclothes[9] pushed hurriedly into drawers[10], personal letters which prudence would have destroyed, half-eaten meals, unpaid bills[11], old photographs, pictures and books which the dead would not have chosen to represent their taste to a curious or vulgar world, family secrets, stale[12] make-up in greasy jars[13], the muddle[14] of ill-disciplined or unhappy lives. It was no longer the fashion to dread an unshriven end[15] but most people, if they thought at all, hoped for time to clear away their debris[16]. He remembered from childhood the voice of an old aunt exhorting him to change his vest[17]. 'Suppose you got run over[18], Adam. What would people think?' The question was less absurd than it had seemed to a ten-year-old. Time had taught him that it expressed one of the major preoccupations of mankind, the dread of losing face[19].

But Enid Bolam might have lived each day as if expecting sudden death. He had never examined a flat so neat, so obsessively tidy. Even her few cosmetics, the brush and comb[20] on her dressing-table were arranged with patterned precision. The heavy double bed was made. Friday was obviously her day for changing the linen. The used sheets and

1. estimation
2. n'était pas éloignée de la réalité
3. lui fit signe de partir
4. fouille indiscrète
5. restes
6. désagréable
7. mettre le défunt dans une position désavantageuse
8. départs insignifiants
9. sous-vêtements sales
10. tiroirs
11. factures non payées
12. vieux
13. pots graisseux
14. désordre
15. les gens ne craignaient plus de mourir sans s'être confessés
16. ranger leur fouillis
17. maillot
18. et si tu te faisais renverser
19. la crainte de perdre la face
20. la brosse et le peigne

pillow-cases[1] were folded[2] into a laundry box[3] which lay open on a chair. The bedside table held nothing but a small travelling clock, a carafe of water and a Bible with a booklet[4] beside it appointing the passage to be read each day and expounding the moral[5]. There was nothing in the table drawer but a bottle of aspirin and a folded handkerchief[6]. A hotel room would have held as much individuality.

All the furniture was old and heavy. The ornate mahogany door[7] of the wardrobe swung open soundlessly to reveal a row of tightly packed clothes. They were expensive but unexciting. Miss Bolam had bought from that store which still caters mainly for country-house[8] dowagers[9]. There were well-cut skirts of indeterminate colour, heavy coats tailored to last[10] through a dozen English winters, woollen[11] dresses which could offend no one. Once the wardrobe was closed it was impossible accurately to recall a single garment[12]. At the back of them all, closeted from[13] the light, were bowls of fibre, planted no doubt with bulbs[14] whose Christmas flowering Miss Bolam would never see.

Dalgliesh and Martin had worked together for too many years to find much talking necessary and they moved about the flat almost in silence. Everywhere was the same heavy, old-fashioned furniture, the same ordered neatness[15]. It was hard to believe that these rooms had been recently lived in, that anyone had cooked a meal in this impersonal kitchen. It was very quiet. At this height[16] and muffled[17] by the solid Victorian walls the clamour[18] of traffic in Kensington High Street was a faint[19], distant throbbing[20]. Only the insistent ticking[21] of a

1. les draps et taies d'oreiller sales
2. pliés
3. bac à linge
4. brochure
5. expliquant la morale
6. mouchoir
7. la porte en acajou richement décorée
8. de province
9. douairières
10. conçus pour durer
11. en laine
12. vêtement
13. à l'abri de
14. bulbes
15. ordre
16. hauteur
17. étouffé
18. vacarme
19. faible
20. vrombissement
21. tic-tac

grandfather clock[1] in the hall stabbed[2] the still[3] silence. The air was cold and almost odourless except for the smell of the flowers. They were everywhere. There was a bowl of chrysanthemums on the hall table and another in the sitting-room. The bedroom mantelpiece[4] held a small jug[5] of anemones. On the kitchen dresser[6] was a taller brass[7] jug of autumn foliage[8], the gatherings[9] perhaps of some recent country walk. Dalgliesh did not like autumn flowers, the chrysanthemums which obstinately refuse to die, flaunting[10] their shaggy[11] heads even on a rotting[12] stem, scentless[13] dahlias fit only to be planted in neat rows in municipal parks. His wife had died in October and he had long recognized the minor bereavements[14] which follow the death of the heart. Autumn was no longer a good time of the year. For him the flowers in Miss Bolam's flat emphasized the general air of gloom[15], like wreaths[16] at a funeral.

The sitting-room was the largest room in the flat and here was Miss Bolam's desk. Martin fingered[17] it appreciatively[18].

'It's all good solid stuff, sir, isn't it? We've got a piece rather like this. The wife's mother left it to us. Mind you, they don't make furniture like it today. You get nothing for it[19], of course. Too big for modern rooms, I suppose. But it's got quality.

'You can certainly lean against it without collapsing[20],' said Dalgliesh.

'That's what I mean, sir. Good solid stuff. No wonder she hung on to it[21]. A sensible young woman on the whole[22], I'd say, and one who knew how to make herself comfortable.' He drew a second chair up to the desk where Dalgliesh was already seated,

1. horloge
2. poignardait
3. immobile
4. cheminée
5. pot
6. vaisselier
7. en cuivre
8. feuillage
9. récolte
10. exhibant
11. hirsutes
12. en train de pourrir
13. inodores
14. deuils
15. tristesse
16. couronnes
17. tâta
18. avec appréciation
19. et ça ne vaut plus rien
20. sans qu'ils s'écroulent
21. pas étonnant qu'elle les ait gardés
22. dans l'ensemble

planted his heavy thighs[1] in it, and did indeed look comfortable and at home.

The desk was unlocked. The top[2] rolled back[3] without difficulty. Inside was a portable typewriter and a metal box containing files of paper, each file neatly labelled[4]. The drawers and compartments of the desk held writing paper, envelopes and correspondence. As they expected, everything was in perfect order. They went through[5] the files together. Miss Bolam paid her bills as soon as they were due[6] and kept a running account of all her household expenditure[7].

There was much to be gone through. Details of her investments were filed under the appropriate heading[8]. At her mother's death the trustee securities[9] had been redeemed[10] and the capital reinvested in equities[11]. The portfolio[12] was skilfully balanced[13] and there could be little doubt that Miss Bolam had been well advised and had increased her assets considerably[14] during the past five years. Dalgliesh noted the name of her stockbroker[15] and solicitor. Both would have to be seen before the investigation was complete.

The dead woman kept few of her personal letters; perhaps there had been few worth keeping[16]. But there was one, filed under P[17], which was interesting. It was written in a careful hand on cheap[18] lined[19] paper from a Balham address, and read:

> Dear Miss Bolam,
>
> These are just a few lines to thank you for all you done for Jenny. It hasn't turned out[20] as we wished and prayed for but we shall know in His good time what His purpose is. I still feel

1. cuisses
2. couvercle
3. s'ouvrit
4. étiqueté avec soin
5. examinèrent
6. dans les temps
7. dépenses ménagères
8. rubrique
9. titres
10. rachetés
11. réinvesti en actions cotées en bourse
12. portefeuille
13. équilibré
14. ses avoirs avaient considérablement augmentés
15. agent de change
16. qui valaient la peine d'être gardées
17. classée sous la lettre P
18. pas cher
19. ligné
20. cela n'a pas marché

we did right to let them marry. It wasn't only to stop talk[1] as I think you know. He has gone for good[2], he writes. Her Dad and me didn't know that things had got that bad between them. She doesn't talk much to us but we shall wait patiently and maybe, one day, she will be our girl again. She seems very quiet and won't talk about it so we don't know whether she grieves[3]. I try not to feel bitterness[4] against him. Dad and I think it would be a good idea if you could get Jenny a post[5] in the health service. It is really good of you to offer and be interested after all that's happened. You know what we think about divorce so she must look to her job now for happiness[6]. Dad and I pray every night that she'll find it.

Thanking you again for all your interest and help. If you do manage[7] to get Jenny the post I'm sure she won't let you down[8]. She's learnt her lesson and it's been a bitter[9] one for us all. But His will be done[10].

Yours respectfully,
EMILY PRIDDY (Mrs)

1. mettre fin aux ragots
2. parti pour de bon
3. a du chagrin
4. rancœur
5. poste
6. trouver le bonheur dans son travail
7. si vous arrivez
8. elle ne vous décevra pas
9. amère
10. que sa volonté soit faite

It was extraordinary, thought Dalgliesh, that people still lived who could write a letter like that, with its archaic mixture of subservience[11] and self-respect[12], its unashamed[13] yet curiously poignant emotionalism[14]. The story it told was ordinary enough, but he felt detached from its reality. The letter could have been written fifty years ago; he almost expected to see the paper curling[15] with age and smell the

11. obséquiosité
12. estime de soi
13. sans gêne
14. sensiblerie
15. s'enrouler

tentative scent[1] of potpourri. It had no relevance, surely, to that pretty, ineffectual[2] child at the Steen.

'It's unlikely to have any importance,' he said to Martin. 'But I'd like you to go over to Balham and have a word with these people. We'd better know who the husband is. But, somehow, I don't think he'll prove to be Dr Etherege's mysterious marauder[3]. The man – or woman – who killed Miss Bolam was still in the building when we arrived. And we've talked to him.'

It was then that the telephone rang, sounding ominously[4] strident in the silence of the flat as if it were calling for the dead. Dalgliesh said:

'I'll take it. It will be Dr Keating with the PM report[5]. I asked him to ring me here if he got through with it[6].'

He was back with Martin within two minutes. The report had been brief. Dalgliesh said:

'Nothing surprising. She was a healthy[7] woman. Killed by a stab through the heart after being stunned, which we could see for ourselves, and *virgo intacta* which we had no reason to doubt. What have you got there?'

'It's her photograph album, sir. Pictures of Guide camps mostly[8]. It looks as if she went away[9] with the girls every year.'

Probably making that her annual holiday, thought Dalgliesh. He had a respect bordering on[10] simple wonder for those who voluntarily gave up[11] their leisure to[12] other people's children. He was not a man who liked children and he found the company of most of them insupportable after a very brief time. He took the album from Sergeant Martin. The photographs were small and technically unremark-

1. une faible odeur
2. inefficace
3. maraudeur
4. de façon inquiétante
5. rapport d'autopsie
6. dès qu'il a fini
7. en bonne santé
8. principalement
9. partait
10. proche de
11. renonçaient
12. pour s'occuper des loisirs de

able, taken apparently with a small box camera[1]. But they were carefully disposed on the page, each labelled in neat white printing[2]. There were Guides hiking[3], Guides cooking on primus stoves[4], erecting tents[5], blanket-swathed[6] around the camp-fire[7], lining up for kit inspection[8]. And in many of the photographs there was the figure of their captain, plump, motherly, smiling. It was difficult to connect this buxom[9], happy extrovert[10] with that pathetic corpse[11] on the record-room floor – or with the obsessional, authoritative administrator described by the staff of the Steen. The comments under some of the photographs were pathetic in their evocation of happiness remembered:

'The Swallows[12] dish up[13]. Shirley keeps an eye on[14] the spotted dick[15].'

'Valerie "flies up[16]" from the Brownies[17].'

'The Kingfishers[18] tackle the washing-up[19]. Snap[20] taken by Susan.'

'Captain helps the tide in[21]! Taken by Jean.'

This last showed Miss Bolam's plump shoulders rising from the surf[22], surrounded by some half-dozen of her girls. Her hair was down and hanging in flat swaths[23], wet and dank as seaweed[24], on either side of her laughing face. Together the two detectives looked at the photograph in silence. Then Dalgliesh said:

'There haven't been many tears shed[25] for her yet, have there? Only her cousin's and they were more shock than grief. I wonder whether the Swallows and the Kingfishers will weep[26] for her.'

They closed the album and went back to their search. It disclosed only one further[27] item of interest, but that was very interesting indeed. It was the

1. appareil photo
2. caractères d'imprimerie
3. en train de faire de la randonnée
4. en train de cuisiner sur des réchauds de camping
5. en train d'ériger des tentes
6. enveloppées dans des couvertures
7. autour du feu de camp
8. alignées pour une revue de détail
9. plantureuse
10. extravertie
11. cadavre
12. les Hirondelles
13. font le service
14. surveille
15. le pudding aux raisins
16. se sauve
17. les Jeannettes
18. les Martins-pêcheurs
19. s'attaquent à la vaisselle
20. photo instantanée
21. donne un coup de main à la marée
22. sortant des vagues
23. aplatis
24. algues
25. versées
26. pleureront
27. un dernier

carbon copy of a letter from Miss Bolam to her solicitor, dated the day before her death, and making an appointment to see him 'in connection with the proposed changes to my will which we discussed briefly on the telephone yesterday night'.

After the visit to Ballantyne Mansions there followed a hiatus[1] in the investigation, one of those inevitable delays[2] which Dalgliesh had never found it easy to accept. He had always worked at speed[3]. His reputation rested on the pace[4] as well as the success of his cases. He did not ponder too deeply the implications of this compulsive need to get on with the job[5]. It was enough to know that delay irritated him more than it did most men.

This hold up[6] was, perhaps, to be expected. It was hardly likely that a London solicitor would be in his office after mid-day on Saturday[7]. It was more dispiriting[8] to learn by telephone that Mr Babcock of Babcock and Honeywell had flown[9] with his wife to Geneva[10] on Friday afternoon to attend the funeral of a friend and would not be back in his City office until the following[11] Tuesday. There was now no Mr Honeywell in the firm, but Mr Babcock's chief clerk[12] would be in the office on Monday morning if he could help the superintendent. It was the caretaker speaking. Dalgliesh was not sure how far[13] the chief clerk could help him. He much preferred to see Mr Babcock. The solicitor was likely to be able to give a great deal of useful information about Miss Bolam's family as well as her financial affairs, but much of it would probably be given with at least a token show of resistance[14] and obtained only by the exercise of tact. It would be folly

1. coupure
2. retards
3. à vive allure
4. rythme
5. continuer à avancer
6. ralentissement
7. un samedi après-midi
8. décourageant
9. avait pris un avion
10. Genève
11. suivant
12. clerc
13. en quoi
14. une résistance symbolique

to jeopardize[1] success by a prior approach to[2] the clerk.

Until the details of the will were available[3] there was little point in[4] seeing Nurse Bolam again. Frustrated in his immediate plans Dalgliesh drove without his sergeant to call on[5] Peter Nagle. He had no clear aim[6] in view but that didn't worry him. The time would be well spent. Some of his most useful work was done in these unplanned[7], almost casual encounters when he talked, listened, watched, studied a suspect in his own home, or gleaned[8] the thin stalks of unwittingly dropped information[9] about the one personality which is central to any murder investigation – that of the victim.

Nagle lived in Pimlico on the fourth floor of a large, white, stuccoed[10] Victorian house near Ecleston Square. Dalgliesh had last visited this street three years previously[11] when it had seemed irretrievably[12] sunk into shabby decay[13]. But the tide had changed[14]. The wave[15] of fashion and popularity which flows so inexplicably in London, sometimes missing one district[16] while sweeping through its near neighbour[17], had washed the broad street bringing order and prosperity in its wake[18]. Judging by the number of house agents' boards[19], the property speculators[20], first as always to sniff[21] the returning tide[22], were reaping the usual profits[23]. The house on the corner looked newly painted. The heavy front door stood open. Inside, a board gave the names of the tenants, but there were no bells. Dalgliesh deduced that the flats were self-contained[24] and that, somewhere, there was a resident caretaker who would answer the front-door bell when the house was locked for the night. He

1. compromettre
2. en contactant d'abord
3. disponibles
4. ça n'avait presque aucun sens de
5. rendre visite à
6. but
7. non planifiées
8. glanait
9. les bribes d'information involontairement distribuées
10. en stuc
11. auparavant
12. irrémédiablement
13. en déclin
14. le vent avait changé
15. vague
16. quartier
17. quartier voisin
18. dans son sillage
19. panneaux d'agents immobiliers
20. spéculateurs immobiliers
21. flairer
22. le retour de la marée
23. engrangeaient les profits habituels
24. indépendants

could see no lift so set himself to climb the four
1. étages — flights[1] to Nagle's flat.

It was a light, airy house and very quiet. There was
no sign of life until the third floor where someone
was playing the piano and playing well; perhaps a
2. de sons aigus — professional musician, practising. The treble[2] cas-
3. s'estompa — cade of sound fell over Dalgliesh and receded[3] as
he reached the fourth floor. Here there was a plain
wooden door with a heavy brass knocker and a
card pinned above it on which was lettered the one
4. il frappa un petit coup — word – Nagle. He rapped[4] and heard Nagle shout
an immediate 'come in'.

The flat was surprising. He hardly knew what
he had expected, but it was certainly not this im-
5. atelier — mense, airy, impressive studio[5]. It ran the whole
length of the back of the house, the great north
6. sans rideaux — window, uncurtained[6], giving a panoramic view of
twisted chimney-pots and irregular sloping roofs.
7. écartés — Nagle was not alone. He was sitting, knees apart[7],
8. estrade — on a narrow bed which stood on a raised platform[8]
9. pelotonnée contre lui — at the east side of the room. Curled against him[9],
10. habillée — clad[10] only in a dressing-gown, was Jennifer Prid-
11. tasses — dy. They were drinking tea from two blue mugs[11];
12. plateau — a tray[12] holding the teapot[13] and a bottle of milk
13. théière — was on a small table beside them. The painting on
which Nagle had recently been working stood on
14. chevalet — an easel[14] in the middle of the room.

The girl showed no embarrassment at seeing Dal-
15. ôta — gliesh but swung[15] her legs from the bed and gave
him a smile which was frankly happy, almost wel-
16. coquetterie — coming, certainly without coquetry[16].

'Would you like some tea?' she asked.

Nagle said:

'The police never drink on duty and that includes tea. Better get your clothes on[1], kid. We don't want to shock the superintendent.'

The girl smiled again, gathered up[2] her clothes with one arm and the tea tray with the other and disappeared through a door at the far end of the studio. It was difficult to recognize in this confident sensual figure the tear-stained[3], diffident[4] child Dalgliesh had first seen at the Steen. He watched her as she passed. She was obviously naked except for the dressing-gown of Nagle's; her hard nipples[5] pointed the thin wool[6]. It came to Dalgliesh[7] that they had been making love. As she passed from view he turned to Nagle and saw in his eyes the transitory gleam[8] of amused speculation. But neither of them spoke.

Dalgliesh moved about the studio, watched by Nagle from the bed. The room was without clutter[9]. In its almost obsessional neatness it reminded him of Enid Bolam's flat with which it had otherwise nothing in common. The dais[10] with its plain wooden bed, chair and small table obviously served as a bedroom. The rest of the studio was taken up with[11] the paraphernalia of a painter, but there was none of that undisciplined muddle which the uninitiated associate with an artist's life. About a dozen large oils[12] were stacked[13] against the south wall and Dalgliesh was surprised by their power. Here was no[14] amateur indulging[15] his little talent. Miss Priddy was apparently Nagle's only model. Her heavy-busted[16], adolescent body gleamed at him from a diversity of poses, here foreshortened[17], there curiously elongated[18] as if the painter gloried in his technical competence. The most recent

1. vaut mieux te rhabiller
2. ramassa
3. au visage baigné de larmes
4. timide
5. tétons
6. fine couche de laine
7. Dalgliesh comprit
8. lueur
9. bien rangée
10. estrade
11. occupé par
12. peintures à l'huile
13. empilées
14. il ne s'agissait pas de
15. donnant libre cours à
16. à la poitrine plantureuse
17. selon une perspective tronquée
18. allongé

picture was on the easel. It showed the girl sitting astride[1] a stool[2] with the childish hands hanging relaxed between her thighs[3], the breasts bunched forward[4]. There was something in this flaunting[5] of technical expertise, in the audacious use of greens and mauve and in the careful tonal relationships[6] which caught at[7] Dalgliesh's memory.

'Who teaches you?' he asked. 'Sugg?'

'That's right.' Nagle did not seem surprised. 'Know his work?'

'I have one of his early[8] oils. A nude.'

'You made a good investment. Hang on to it[9].'

'I've every intention of doing so,' said Dalgliesh mildly[10]. 'I happen to like it. Have you been with him long?'

'Two years. Part time, of course. In another three years I'll be teaching him. If he's capable of learning, that is. He's getting an old dog[11] now and too fond of his own tricks[12].'

'You appear to have imitated some of them,' said Dalgliesh.

'You think so? That's interesting.' Nagle did not seem affronted[13]. 'That's why it will be good to get away[14]. I'm off to[15] Paris by the end of the month at the latest[16]. I applied for the Bollinger scholarship[17]. The old man put in a word for me[18] and last week I had a letter to say that it's mine.'

Try as he would[19] he could not entirely keep[20] the note of triumph from his voice. Underneath the assumption of nonchalance there was a spring[21] of joy. And he had reason to be pleased with himself. The Bollinger was no ordinary prize[22]. It meant, as Dalgliesh knew, two years in any European city with a generous allowance[23] and freedom for the

1. à califourchon
2. sur un tabouret
3. cuisses
4. la poitrine en avant
5. étalage
6. jeu des valeurs tonales
7. réveilla
8. premières
9. gardez-le précieusement
10. doucement
11. il se fait vieux
12. trop attaché à ses vieilles habitudes
13. offensé
14. partir
15. j'irai
16. au plus tard
17. bourse
18. a parlé en ma faveur
19. il avait beau essayer
20. cacher
21. bouffée
22. prix
23. allocation

student to live and work as he chose. The Bollinger trust[1] had been set up[2] by a manufacturer of patent medicines[3] who had died wealthy[4] and successful, but unsatisfied. His money had come from stomach powders[5] but his heart was in painting. His own talent was small and, to judge by the collection of paintings which he bequeathed[6] to the embarrassed trustees[7] of his local gallery, his taste had been on a par with[8] his performance. But the Bollinger scholarship[9] had ensured that artists should remember him with gratitude. Bollinger did not believe that art flourished in poverty or that artists were stimulated to their best efforts by cold garrets[10] and empty bellies. He had been poor in his youth and had not enjoyed it. He had travelled widely in his old age and been happy abroad. The Bollinger scholarship enabled young artists of promise to enjoy the second without enduring the first and it was well worth winning. If Nagle had been awarded[11] the Bollinger he was hardly likely to be much concerned now with the troubles of the Steen Clinic.

'When are you due to go?[12]' Dalgliesh asked.

'When I like. By the end of the month, anyway. But I may go earlier and without notice[13]. No sense in upsetting anyone[14].' He jerked his head[15] towards the far door as he spoke and added: 'That's why this murder is such a nuisance[16]. I was afraid it might hold things up[17]. After all, it was my chisel. And that wasn't the only attempt[18] made to implicate me. While I was in the general office waiting for the post someone phoned to ask me to go down for the laundry. It sounded like a woman. I'd got

1. fonds
2. créé
3. médicaments brevetés
4. riche
5. poudres contre les maux d'estomac
6. a léguées
7. administrateurs
8. comparable à
9. bourse
10. mansardes
11. avait remporté
12. quand est-il prévu que vous partiez ?
13. sans préavis
14. pas la peine de bouleverser qui que ce soit
15. fit un signe de la tête
16. m'embête
17. que ça ne retarde les choses
18. tentative

my coat on and was more or less on my way out[1], so I said I'd collect it when I got back.'

'So that's why you went to see Nurse Bolam on your return from the post and asked her whether the laundry was ready?'

'That's right.'

'Why didn't you tell her about the phone call at the time?'

'I don't know. There didn't seem any point[2]. I wasn't anxious to hang about[3] the LSD room. Those patients give me the creeps[4] with their moaning and muttering[5]. When Bolam said the stuff wasn't ready I thought it was Miss Bolam who had phoned and it wouldn't have done to have said so[6]. She was a bit too apt to[7] interfere with the nursing responsibilities, or so they thought[8]. Anyway, I didn't say anything about the call. I might have done but I didn't.'

'And you didn't tell me either when you were first interviewed.'

'Right again. The truth is that the whole thing struck me as a bit odd[9] and I wanted time to think about it. Well, I've thought, and you're welcome to the story[10]. You can believe it or not, as you like. It's all the same to me[11].'

'You seem to be taking it pretty calmly if you really believe that someone was trying to involve[12] you in the murder.'

'I'm not worrying. They didn't succeed[13] for one thing, and for another, I happen to believe that the chance[14] of an innocent man getting convicted[15] of murder in this country is practically nil[16]. You ought to[17] find that flattering[18]. On the other hand – given the jury system – the chances of the guilty

1. et j'allais sortir
2. je ne voyais pas l'intérêt
3. traîner dans
4. me font froid dans le dos
5. gémissements et grommellements
6. ce n'était pas la peine de le dire
7. elle avait un peu trop tendance à
8. du moins c'est ce que les infirmières pensaient
9. m'a semblé un peu étrange
10. et maintenant je vous en parle
11. ça m'est égal
12. impliquer
13. ils n'ont pas réussi
14. la possibilité
15. d'être reconnu coupable
16. quasiment nulle
17. vous devez
18. flatteur

getting off[1] are high. That's why I don't think you're going to solve this murder. Too many suspects. Too many possibilities.'

'We shall see. Tell me more about this call. When exactly did you receive it?'

'I can't remember. About five minutes before Shorthouse came into the general office, I think. It could have been earlier. Jenny may remember.'

'I'll ask her when she gets back[2]. What exactly did the voice say?'

'Just, "The laundry's ready if you'd fetch it now, please." I took it that Nurse Bolam was phoning. I replied that I was just going out with the post and would see to it[3] when I got back. Then I put down the receiver[4] before she had a chance to argue[5].'

'You were sure it was Nurse Bolam speaking?'

'I'm not sure at all. I naturally thought it was at the time because Nurse Bolam usually does phone about the laundry. As a matter of fact the woman spoke softly[6] and it could have been anyone.'

'But it was a woman's voice?'

'Oh, yes. It was a woman all right.'

'At any rate[7] it was a false message because we know that, in fact[8], the laundry wasn't sorted[9].'

'Yes. But what was the point of it? It doesn't add up[10]. If the idea was to lure me down to the basement[11] to frame me[12], the killer stood the risk[13] that I'd arrive at the wrong moment. Nurse Bolam, for example, wouldn't want me on the spot inquiring for the laundry if she were planning to be in the record-room slugging[14] her cousin. Even if Miss Bolam were dead before the call was made it still doesn't make sense. Suppose I'd nosed around[15] and found the body? The killer couldn't have want-

1. la probabilité que les coupables s'en tirent

2. reviendra

3. et que je m'en occuperais

4. j'ai raccroché

5. de répondre

6. à voix basse

7. en tout cas

8. en réalité

9. n'avait pas été trié

10. ça ne tient pas debout

11. m'attirer au sous-sol par la ruse

12. me faire accuser

13. prenait le risque

14. en train de cogner

15. et si j'étais allé fouiner

ed it discovered that soon! Anyway, I didn't go down until I got back from the post. Lucky for me I was out with it. The box is only just across the road, but I usually go down to Beefsteak Street to buy a *Standard*. The man there probably remembers me.'

Jennifer Priddy had returned during the last few words. She had changed into a plain woollen dress. Clasping a belt[1] round her waist[2], she said:

'It was the row over[3] your paper that finished poor old Cully[4]. You might have let him have it, darling, when he asked. He only wanted to check on his horses[5].'

Nagle said without rancour:

'Mean old devil. He'd do anything to save himself three-pence. Why can't he pay for it occasionally[6]? I'm no sooner in the door[7] before he puts out his hand[8] for it.'

'Still, you were rather unkind[9] to him, darling. It isn't as if you wanted it yourself. We only glanced at it downstairs then used it to wrap up[10] Tigger's food. You know what Cully is. The least upset[11] goes to his stomach.'

Nagle expressed his opinion of Cully's stomach with force and originality. Miss Priddy glanced at Dalgliesh as if inviting his shocked admiration of the vagaries[12] of genius and murmured:

'Peter! Really, darling, you are awful[13]!'

She spoke with coy[14] indulgence, the little woman administering a mild rebuke[15]. Dalgliesh looked at Nagle to see how he bore it[16], but the painter seemed not to have heard. He still sat, immobile, on the bed and looked down at them. Clad[17] now in brown linen trousers, thick blue jersey and san-

1. en attachant une ceinture
2. taille
3. dispute à propos de
4. qui a donné le coup de grâce à ce pauvre Cully
5. vérifier les résultats des courses de chevaux
6. de temps en temps
7. à peine je franchis la porte
8. il tend la main
9. peu aimable
10. emballer
11. la moindre contrariété
12. caprices
13. horrible
14. faussement effarouchée
15. reproche
16. comment il le prenait
17. vêtu

dals, he yet looked as formal and neat as he had in his porter's uniform, his mild eyes unworried[1], his long, strong arms relaxed.

Under his gaze the girl moved restlessly[2] about the studio, touching with happy possessiveness the frame[3] of a painting, running her fingers along the window ledge[4], moving[5] a jug of dahlias from one window to the next. It was as if she sought to[6] impose the soft nuances of femininity on this disciplined masculine workshop[7], to demonstrate that this was her home, her natural place. She was entirely unembarrassed[8] by the pictures of her naked body. It was possible that she gained satisfaction from this vicarious[9] exhibitionism. Suddenly Dalgliesh asked:

'Do you remember, Miss Priddy, whether anyone telephoned Mr Nagle while he was in the office with you?'

The girl looked surprised but said unconcernedly[10] to Nagle:

'Nurse Bolam phoned about the laundry, didn't she? I came in from the record-room – I'd only been gone a second – and heard you say that you were just on your way out and would go down when you came back.' She laughed[11]. 'After you put the receiver down you said something much less polite about the way the nurses expect you to be at their beck and call[12]. Remember?'

'Yes,' said Nagle shortly. He turned to Dalgliesh. 'Any more questions, Superintendent? Jenny'll have to be getting home soon[13] and I usually go part of the way[14]. Her parents don't know she sees me.'

'Only one or two. Have either of you any idea why Miss Bolam should send for[15] the group secretary?'

1. sereins
2. nerveusement
3. cadre
4. rebord de la fenêtre
5. déplaçait
6. cherchait à
7. atelier
8. elle n'était pas du tout gênée
9. par procuration
10. sans s'inquiéter
11. rit
12. à leur disposition
13. doit bientôt rentrer
14. fais un bout de chemin avec elle
15. a fait appeler

Miss Priddy shook[1] her head. Nagle said:

'It was nothing to do with us, anyway. She didn't know that Jenny poses for me. Even if she found out she wouldn't send for Lauder. She wasn't a fool. She knew he wouldn't concern himself with anything the staff did in their own time[2]. After all, she found out about Dr Baguley's affair[3] with Miss Saxon, but she wasn't daft[4] enough to tell Lauder.'

Dalgliesh did not ask whom Miss Bolam had told. He said:

'It was obviously something concerned with the administration of the clinic. Had anything unusual happened lately[5]?'

'Nothing but our famous burglary[6] and the missing fifteen quid[7]. But you know about that.'

'That's nothing to do with Peter,' said the girl with quick defensiveness. 'He wasn't even at the clinic when the fifteen pounds arrived.' She turned to Nagle. 'You remember, darling? That was the morning you got stuck[8] in the Underground. You didn't even know about the money!'

She had said something wrong. The flash of irritation in those large mud-brown eyes was momentary, but Dalgliesh did not miss it[9]. There was a pause before Nagle spoke, but his voice was perfectly controlled.

'I knew soon enough. We all did[10]. What with the fuss over[11] who sent it and the row over[12] who was to spend it, the whole damn group must have known.' He looked at Dalgliesh.

'Is that all?'

'No. Do you know who killed Miss Bolam?'

'I'm glad to say I don't. I shouldn't think[13] it was one of the psychiatrists. Those boys are the strong-

1. secoua
2. dans leur vie privée
3. liaison
4. bête
5. récemment
6. cambriolage
7. livres sterling
8. tu es resté bloqué
9. l'avait remarqué
10. tout le monde l'a su
11. avec toutes ces histoires à propos de
12. et les disputes à propos de
13. je ne pense pas que

est reason I know for staying sane[1]. But I can't see any of them actually killing. They haven't the nerve[2].'

Someone very different had said much the same thing.

As he reached the door, Dalgliesh paused and looked back at Nagle. He and the girl were sitting together on the bed as he had first seen them; neither of them made any move to see him out[3], but Jenny gave him her happy valedictory[4] smile.

Dalgliesh asked his last question:

'Why did you go for a drink[5] with Cully on the night of the burglary?'

'Cully asked me.'

'Wasn't that unusual?'

'So unusual that I went with him out of[6] curiosity to see what was up[7].'

'And what was?'

'Nothing really. Cully asked me to lend[8] him a quid[9] which I refused, and while the clinic was left empty someone broke in[10]. I don't see how Cully could have foreseen[11] that. Or maybe he did. Anyway, I can't see what it's got to do with the murder.'

Nor, on the face of it, could Dalgliesh. As he passed down the stairs he was vexed[12] by the thought of time passing, time wasted, the drag of hours[13] before Monday morning when the clinic would reopen and his suspects reassemble in the place where they were likely to be most vulnerable. But the last forty minutes had been well spent. He was beginning to trace the dominant thread in this tangled skein[14]. As he passed by the third-floor flat the pianist was playing Bach. Dalgliesh paused for a moment to listen. Contrapuntal music[15] was the

1. rester sain d'esprit
2. courage
3. l'accompagner à la porte
4. d'adieu
5. prendre un verre
6. par
7. ce qui se passait
8. prêter
9. livre
10. est entré par effraction
11. prévu
12. contrarié
13. les longues heures
14. démêler cet écheveau complexe
15. la musique contrapuntique

only kind he truly[1] enjoyed. But the pianist stopped suddenly with a crash[2] of discordant keys[3]. And then nothing. Dalgliesh passed down the stairs in silence and left the quiet house unseen[4].

When Dr Baguley arrived at the clinic for the Medical Committee meeting, the parking space reserved for doctors' cars was already occupied. Dr Etherege's Bentley was there parked next to Steiner's Rolls. On the other side of it was the battered[5] Vauxhall which proclaimed[6] that Dr Albertine Maddox had decided to attend.

Upstairs in the first-floor boardroom the curtains were drawn against the blue-black October sky. In the middle of the heavy mahogany table was a bowl of roses. Baguley remembered that Miss Bolam had always supplied[7] flowers for the meetings of the Medical Committee. Someone had decided to continue the practice. The roses were the slim[8], hothouse buds[9] of autumn, rigid and scentless[10] on their thornless stems[11]. In a couple of days they would open for their brief and barren[12] flowering[13]. In less than a week they would be dead. Baguley thought that so extravagant and evocative a flower was inappropriate to the mood[14] of the meeting. But the empty bowl would have been unbearably[15] poignant and embarrassing.

'Who supplied the roses?' he asked.

'Mrs Bostock, I think,' said Dr Ingram. 'She was up here getting the room ready[16] when I arrived.'

'Remarkable,' said Dr Etherege. He put out[17] a finger and stroked[18] one of the buds so gently that the stem did not even tremble. Baguley wondered whether the comment referred to the quality of the

1. véritablement
2. fracas
3. notes
4. sans être vu
5. cabossée
6. annonçait
7. apporté
8. minces
9. fleurs de serre en boutons
10. sans parfum
11. tiges sans épines
12. stérile
13. floraison
14. humeur
15. insupportablement
16. en train de préparer la salle
17. tendit
18. caressa

roses or to Mrs Bostock's perspicacity in supplying them[1].

'Miss Bolam was very fond of[2] flowers, very fond,' said the medical director. He looked round as if challenging his colleagues to disagree[3].

'Well,' he said. 'Shall we get started?[4]'

Dr Baguley, as honorary secretary, seated himself on the right of Dr Etherege. Dr Steiner took the chair next to him. Dr Maddox sat on Steiner's right. No other consultant was there. Dr McBain and Dr Mason-Giles were in the States[5] attending[6] a conference. The rest of the medical staff, torn[7] between curiosity and a disinclination[8] to interrupt their weekend break, had apparently decided to wait in patience for Monday. Dr Etherege had thought it proper to[9] telephone them all and let them know of the meeting. He gave their apologies formally and they were as gravely[10] received.

Albertine Maddox had been a surgeon and a highly successful one before she qualified as a psychiatrist. It was perhaps typical of her colleagues' ambivalence towards their specialty that Dr Maddox's double qualification enhanced[11] her standing[12] in their eyes. She represented the clinic on the Group Medical Advisory Committee, where she defended the Steen against the occasional snipings[13] of physicians and surgeons with a wit[14] and vigour which made her respected and feared. At the clinic she took no part in the Freudian versus eclectic controversy being, as Baguley observed, equally beastly[15] to both sides. Her patients loved her, but this did not impress her colleagues. They were used to[16] being loved by their patients and merely observed that Albertine was particularly

1. la perspicacité dont Mrs Bostock avait fait preuve en les fournissant
2. aimait beaucoup
3. comme pour défier ses collègues de le contredire
4. on commence ?
5. aux États-Unis
6. pour participer à
7. tiraillés
8. manque d'enthousiasme
9. avait jugé bon de
10. avec gravité
11. améliorait
12. sa réputation
13. railleries
14. esprit
15. vache
16. avaient l'habitude de

skilful in[1] handling a strong transference situation[2]. Physically she was a plump, grey-haired, unremarkable[3] woman who looked what she was, the comfortable[4] mother of a family. She had five children, the sons intelligent and prosperous, the girls well-married. Her insignificant-looking husband and the children treated her with a tolerant, faintly amused solicitude which never failed to astonish[5] her colleagues at the Steen to whom she was a formidable[6] personality. She sat now with Hector, her old Pekinese[7], squatting[8] malevolently[9] on her lap[10] looking as comfortably anticipatory[11] as a suburban housewife[12] at a matinée[13]. Dr Steiner said testily[14]:

'Really, Albertine, need you have brought Hector? I don't want to be unkind but that animal is beginning to smell[15]. You should have him put down[16].'

'Thank you, Paul,' replied Dr Maddox in her deep, beautifully modulated voice. 'Hector will be put down, as you so euphemistically[17] describe it, when he ceases to find life pleasant. I judge that he has not yet reached that state. It is not my habit to kill off living creatures simply because I find certain of their physical characteristics displeasing; nor, I may say, because they have become somewhat of a nuisance.'

Dr Etherege said quickly:

'It was good of you to find time to come tonight, Albertine. I'm sorry that the notice was so short[18].'

He spoke without irony, although he was as well aware[19] as were his colleagues that Dr Maddox only attended one committee meeting in[20] four on the grounds, which she made no effort to conceal[21], that her contract with the Regional Board contained no clause compelling her to[22] a

1. savait particulièrement bien
2. gérer les transferts délicats
3. ordinaire
4. à l'aise
5. étonner
6. redoutable
7. pékinois
8. assis
9. l'air malveillant
10. sur ses genoux
11. impatiente
12. ménagère
13. séance en matinée
14. d'un ton irrité
15. sentir mauvais
16. le faire piquer
17. par euphémisme
18. de vous avoir prévenue si tard
19. conscient
20. sur
21. cacher
22. l'obligeant à assister

monthly session of boredom[1] laced with claptrap[2], and that the company of more than one psychiatrist at a time made Hector sick[3]. The truth of this last assertion had been demonstrated too often to be safely challenged.

'I am a member of this committee, Henry,' replied Dr Maddox graciously. 'Is there any reason why I should not make the effort to attend?'

Her glance at Dr Ingram implied that not everyone present had an equal right. Mary Ingram was the wife of a suburban general practitioner and attended the Steen twice a week to give the anaesthetic[4] at ECT sessions. Not being either a psychiatrist or a consultant she was not normally present at meetings of the Medical Committee. Dr Etherege interpreted the glance correctly and said firmly[5]:

'Dr Ingram has been good enough to come along tonight at my request[6]. The main business[7] of the meeting is naturally concerned with Miss Bolam's murder, and Dr Ingram was in the clinic on Friday evening.'

'But is not a suspect, so I understand,' replied Dr Maddox. 'I congratulate her. It is gratifying that there is one member of the medical staff who has been able to produce a satisfactory alibi.'

She looked at Dr Ingram severely, her tone implying that an alibi was, in itself, suspicious and hardly becoming[8] to the most junior member of the staff since three senior consultants had been unable to produce one. No one asked how Dr Maddox knew about the alibi. Presumably she had been speaking to Sister Ambrose. Dr Steiner said pettishly[9]:

'It's ridiculous to talk about alibis as if the police could seriously suspect one of us! It's perfectly obvi-

1. ennui
2. mêlé d'âneries
3. malade
4. pratiquer les anesthésies
5. avec fermeté
6. demande
7. sujet principal
8. ne convenait guère
9. de mauvaise humeur

ous to me what happened. The murderer was lying in wait for her[1] in the basement. We know that. He may have been hidden[2] down there for hours, perhaps even since the previous day[3]. He could have slipped[4] past Cully with one of the patients or have pretended to be a relative or a hospital-car attendant[5]. He could even have broken in[6] during the night. That has been known, after all. Once in the basement there would be plenty of time to discover which key opened the record-room door and plenty of time to select a weapon. Neither the fetish nor the chisel were hidden.'

'And how do you suggest this unknown murderer left[7] the building?' asked Dr Baguley. 'We searched the place pretty thoroughly[8] before the police arrived and they went over it again. The basement and first-floor doors were both bolted on the inside, remember.'

'Climbed up[9] the lift shaft[10] by the pulley[11] ropes[12] and out through one of the doors leading to the fire-escape[13],' replied Dr Steiner, playing his trump card[14] with a certain panache. 'I've examined the lift and it's just possible. A small man – or a woman, of course – could squeeze[15] over the top of the box and get into the shaft. The ropes are quite thick[16] enough to support a considerable weight and the climb wouldn't be too difficult for anyone reasonably agile. They'd need to be slim, of course.' He glanced at his own rounding paunch[17] with complacency[18].

'It's a pleasant theory,' said Baguley. 'Unfortunately all the doors opening on the fire-escape were also bolted on the inside.'

1. l'attendait
2. il a pu se cacher
3. depuis la veille
4. s'être glissé
5. ambulancier
6. être entré par effraction
7. quitté
8. de fond en comble
9. en grimpant
10. cage d'ascenseur
11. poulie
12. câbles
13. escalier de secours
14. jouant sa carte maîtresse
15. se glisser
16. épais
17. bedaine
18. complaisance

'There is no building in existence which a desperate and experienced man cannot break into or get out of,' proclaimed Dr Steiner, as if from a plenitude of experience. 'He could have got out of a first-floor window and edged along the sill[1] until he could get a foothold[2] on the fire-escape. All I'm saying is that the murderer isn't necessarily one of the staff who happened to be on duty yesterday evening.'

'It could be I, for example,' said Dr Maddox.

Dr Steiner was undaunted[3].

'That, of course, is nonsense[4], Albertine. I make no accusations. I merely point out that the circle of suspects is less restricted than the police seem to think. They should direct their inquiries to Miss Bolam's private life. Obviously she had an enemy.'

But Dr Maddox was not to be diverted[5].

'Fortunately[6] for me,' she proclaimed, 'I was at the Bach recital at the Royal Festival Hall last night with my husband and dined there before the concert. And while Alasdair's testimony on my behalf[7] might be suspect, I was also with my brother-in-law[8] who happens to be a bishop[9]. A High Church[10] bishop,' she added complacently[11], as if incense[12] and chasuble set a seal[13] on episcopal virtue and veracity.

Dr Etherege smiled gently and said:

'I should be relieved if I could produce even an evangelical curate[14] to vouch for me[15] between six-fifteen and seven o'clock yesterday evening. But isn't all this theorizing a waste of time? The crime is in the hands of the police and there we must leave it. Our main concern[16] is to discuss its impli-

1. marcher sur le rebord de la fenêtre
2. prendre pied
3. imperturbable
4. absurde
5. poursuivit son raisonnement
6. heureusement
7. en ma faveur
8. beau-frère
9. évêque
10. fraction de l'Église d'Angleterre accordant une grande importance à l'autorité du prêtre, au rituel, etc.
11. avec suffisance
12. encens
13. scellaient
14. vicaire
15. répondre de moi
16. souci principal

cations for the work of the clinic and, in particular, the suggestion of the chairman and the group secretary that Mrs Bostock should carry on for the present as acting administrative officer. But we'd better proceed in order. Is it your pleasure that I sign the minutes[1] of the last meeting?'

There was the unenthusiastic but acquiescent mumble[2] which this question usually provokes and the medical director drew the minute book[3] towards him and signed. Dr Maddox said suddenly:

'What is he like?[4] This superintendent, I mean.'

Dr Ingram, who hadn't so far[5] spoken, surprisingly replied:

'He's about forty, I should think[6]. Tall and dark. I liked his voice and he has nice hands.' Then she blushed[7] furiously, remembering that, to[8] a psychiatrist, the most innocent remark could be embarrassingly revealing. That comment about nice hands was, perhaps, a mistake[9]. Dr Steiner, ignoring Dalgliesh's physical characteristics, launched into[10] a psychological assessment[11] of the superintendent to which his fellow psychiatrists gave the polite attention of experts interested in a colleague's theories. Dalgliesh, had he been present[12], would have been surprised and intrigued by the accuracy and percipience[13] of Dr Steiner's diagnosis. The medical director said:

'I agree that he's obsessional[14] and also that he's intelligent. That means that his mistakes will be the mistakes of an intelligent man – always the most dangerous. We must hope for all our sakes[15] that he makes none. The murder, and the inevitable publicity, are bound to have an effect on[16] the patients

1. le compte-rendu
2. murmure d'acquiescement peu enthousiaste
3. registre des délibérations
4. comment est-il ?
5. jusque-là
6. je dirais
7. rougit
8. pour
9. erreur
10. se lança dans
11. évaluation
12. s'il avait été présent
13. perspicacité
14. maniaque
15. dans notre intérêt
16. affecteront sans doute

and on the work of the clinic. And that brings us[1] to this suggestion about Mrs Bostock.'

'I have always preferred Bolam to Bostock,' said Dr Maddox. 'It would be a pity[2] if we lost one unsuitable AO – however[3] regrettably and fortuitously[4] – only to be saddled with another[5].'

'I agree,' said Dr Baguley. 'Of the two I personally always preferred Bolam. But this would only be a temporary arrangement presumably. The job will have to be advertised. In the meantime[6] someone's got to take over[7] and Mrs Bostock does at least[8] know the work.'

Dr Etherege said:

'Lauder made it plain[9] that the HMC[10] wouldn't favour putting in an outsider until the police have finished their investigation, even if they could find anyone willing to come. We don't want any additional upheaval[11]. There will be enough disturbance[12] to cope with[13]. And that brings me to the problem of the press. Lauder suggested, and I have agreed, that all inquiries are referred[14] to group headquarters and that no one here makes any statements[15]. It seems much the best plan. It's important in the interests of the patients that we don't have reporters running all over the clinic. Therapy is likely to suffer enough without that. Have I this Committee's formal confirmation of the decision?'

He had. No one evinced[16] any enthusiasm for coping with the press. Dr Steiner did not contribute to the general murmur of consent. His thoughts were still with the problem of Miss Bolam's successor. He said querulously[17]:

'I can't understand why Dr Maddox and Dr Baguley have this animus[18] against Mrs Bostock. I've

1. nous amène
2. ce serait dommage
3. même
4. fortuitement
5. pour en avoir une autre sur le dos
6. en attendant
7. doit prendre la relève
8. au moins
9. m'a clairement fait comprendre
10. comité de gestion de l'hôpital
11. bouleversement
12. perturbations
13. à gérer
14. doivent être adressées
15. aucune déclaration
16. personne ne manifesta
17. d'un ton récriminateur
18. animosité

noticed it before. It's ridiculous to compare her adversely[1] with Miss Bolam. There's no doubt which of them is – was – is – the more suitable administrator. Mrs Bostock is a highly intelligent woman, psychologically stable, efficient and with a real appreciation of the importance of the work we do here. No one could have said as much[2] of Miss Bolam. Her attitude to the patients was sometimes most unfortunate[3].'

'I didn't know that she came into contact much with the patients,' said Dr Baguley. 'Anyway, none of mine complained[4].'

'She made appointments occasionally and paid out travelling expenses. I can quite believe that your patients didn't remark[5] on her attitude. But mine are a rather different class. They're also more sensitive[6] to these things. Mr Burge, for example, mentioned the matter to me.'

Dr Maddox laughed unkindly[7].

'Oh, Burge! Is he still coming? I see that his new opus is promised for December. It will be interesting to see, Paul, whether your efforts have improved[8] his prose. If so[9], it's probably public money well spent.'

Dr Steiner burst into pained expostulation[10]. He treated a fair number[11] of writers and artists, some of them protégés of Rosa in search of a little free psychotherapy. Although he was sensitive to the arts his usually keen critical insight[12] failed[13] completely where his patients were concerned[14]. He could not bear to hear them criticized, lived in perpetual hope that their great talents would at last be recognized, and was roused to quick defensive anger on their behalf[15]. Dr Baguley thought that it

1. défavorablement
2. en dire autant
3. vraiment fâcheuse
4. ne s'est jamais plaint
5. n'ont pas fait de remarques
6. sensibles
7. de façon désagréable
8. amélioré
9. si c'est la cas
10. le docteur Steiner, affligé, se mit à protester
11. un certain nombre
12. sens critique habituellement développé
13. échouait
14. quand il s'agissait de ses patients
15. se mettait rapidement en colère quand il s'agissait de les défendre

was one of Steiner's more endearing[1] qualities; in many ways he was touchingly naïve[2]. He launched now into a muddled defence of[3] both his patient's character and his prose style, ending:

'Mr Burge is a most talented[4] and sensitive man, very distressed[5] by his inability to sustain[6] a satisfactory sexual relationship, particularly with his wives.'

This unfortunate solecism[7] seemed likely to provoke Dr Maddox to further unkindness[8]. It was certainly, thought Baguley, her night to be pro-eclectic.

Dr Etherege said mildly:

'Could we forget our professional differences for a moment and concentrate on the matter in hand[9]? Dr Steiner, have you any objection to accepting Mrs Bostock as a temporary administrative officer?'

Dr Steiner said grumpily[10]:

'The question is purely academic. If the group secretary wishes her to be appointed she will be appointed. This farce of appearing[11] to consult us is ridiculous. We have no authority either[12] to approve or[13] disapprove. That was made perfectly clear to me by Lauder when I approached him[14] last month about getting Bolam transferred.'

'I didn't know you had approached him,' said Dr Etherege.

'I spoke to him after the September meeting of the House Committee. It was merely a tentative suggestion[15].'

'And was met with a pretty positive brush off[16], no doubt,' said Baguley. 'You would have been wiser[17] to keep your mouth shut.'

'Or to have brought the matter before this Committee,' said Etherege.

1. attachantes
2. d'une naïveté touchante
3. il commença à défendre confusément
4. talentueux
5. tourmenté
6. maintenir
7. solécisme
8. méchanceté
9. revenir à nos moutons
10. d'un air bougon
11. faire semblant
12. ni
13. ni
14. je lui ai parlé
15. ce n'était qu'une simple suggestion
16. il vous a clairement envoyé balader
17. plus sage

'And with what result?' cried Steiner. 'What happened last time I complained about Bolam? Nothing! You all admitted that she was an unsuitable person to hold the post of administrative officer. You all agreed – well, most of you agreed – that Bostock – or even an outsider – would be preferable. But when it came to action not one of you was prepared to put your signature to a letter to the Hospital Management Committee. And you know very well why! You were all terrified of that woman. Yes, terrified!'

Amid[1] the murmur of outraged denial[2], Dr Maddox said:

'There was something intimidating about her[3]. It may have been that formidable[4] and self-conscious rectitude. You were as affected by it as anyone, Paul.'

'Possibly. But I did try[5] to do something about her. I spoke to Lauder.'

'I spoke to him, too,' said Etherege quietly, 'and possibly with more effect. I made it clear that this Committee realized that we had no control over the administrative staff, but I said that Miss Bolam appeared to me, speaking as a psychiatrist and as chairman of the Medical Committee, to be temperamentally unsuitable for her job[6]. I suggested that a transfer would be in her own interests. There could be no criticism of her efficiency and I made none. Lauder was non-committal[7], of course, but he knew perfectly well that I was entitled to make the point[8]. And I think he took it[9].'

Dr Maddox said:

'Allowing for[10] his natural caution, his suspicion[11] of psychiatrists and the usual speed[12] of his ad-

1. au milieu de
2. démenti indigné
3. elle avait quelque chose d'intimidant
4. redoutable
5. mais au moins j'ai essayé
6. ne me semblait pas être faite pour ce métier
7. est resté évasif
8. en droit d'exprimer ce point de vue
9. qu'il l'a compris
10. Compte tenu de
11. méfiance
12. vitesse

ministrative decisions, I suppose we should have been rid of[1] Miss Bolam within the next two years[2]. Someone has certainly speeded things up[3].'

Suddenly Dr Ingram spoke. Her pink, rather stupid face flushed unbecomingly[4]. She sat stiffly upright[5] and her hands, clasped[6] on the table in front of her, were shaking[7].

'I don't think you ought to say[8] things like that. It… it isn't right[9]. Miss Bolam is dead, brutally murdered. You sit here, all of you, and talk as if you didn't care[10]! I know she wasn't very easy to get on with[11] but she's dead, and I don't think this is the time to be unkind about her.'

Dr Maddox looked at Dr Ingram with interest and a kind of wonder as if she were faced by an exceptionally dull[12] child who had somehow succeeded in making an intelligent remark. She said:

'I see that you subscribe to the superstition that one should never tell the truth about the dead. The origins of that atavistic belief[13] have always interested me. We must have a talk about it sometime. I should like to hear your views.'

Dr Ingram, scarlet with embarrassment[14] and close to tears[15], looked as if the proposed talk were a privilege she would be happy to forgo[16]. Dr Etherege said:

'Unkind about her? I should be sorry to think that anyone here was being unkind. There are some things, surely, which don't need saying. There can't be a member of this Committee who isn't horrified at the senseless brutality of Miss Bolam's death and who wouldn't wish her back with us no matter what her defects as an administrator.'

1. on se serait débarrassé de
2. en l'espace de deux ans
3. accéléré les choses
4. de façon peu seyante
5. droite comme un piquet
6. jointes
7. tremblaient
8. vous devriez dire
9. correct
10. comme si vous vous en fichiez
11. n'était pas d'un abord facile
12. lent d'esprit
13. croyance atavique
14. rouge de honte
15. au bord des larmes
16. auquel elle serait heureuse de renoncer

The bathos[1] was too blatant[2] to be missed. As if conscious of their surprise and discomfiture[3], he looked up and said challengingly:

'Well, is there? Is there?'

'Of course not,' said Dr Steiner. He spoke soothingly[4], but the sharp little eyes slewed sideways[5] to meet Baguley's glance. There was embarrassment in that look, but Baguley recognized also the smirk[6] of malicious amusement[7]. The medical director wasn't playing this too cleverly. He had allowed Albertine Maddox to get out of hand[8] and his control over the Committee was less sure than formerly[9]. The pathetic thing about it, thought Baguley, was that Etherege was sincere. He meant every word[10]. He had – and so had they all, come to that – a genuine horror of violence. He was a compassionate[11] man shocked and saddened[12] by the thought of a defenceless woman brutally done to death. But his words sounded false. He was taking refuge in formality, deliberately trying to lower[13] the emotional tone of the meeting to one of platitudinous[14] convention. And he only succeeded in sounding insincere.

After Dr Ingram's outburst[15] the meeting seemed to lose heart. Dr Etherege made only spasmodic attempts to control it and the conversation ranged in a tired, desultory way from one subject to another[16] but, always and inevitably, returned to the murder. There was a feeling that the Medical Committee should express some common view. Groping from theory to theory[17] the meeting eventually[18] came to accept Dr Steiner's proposition. The killer had obviously entered the clinic earlier in the day when the system of booking people in and

1. déception
2. évidente
3. embarras
4. d'un ton apaisant
5. lancèrent un regard oblique
6. petit sourire suffisant
7. joie maligne
8. échapper à tout contrôle
9. avant
10. il y croyait
11. compatissant
12. affligé
13. abaisser
14. banale
15. explosion
16. allait d'un sujet à l'autre de manière décousue
17. passant d'une théorie à l'autre
18. finalement

out was not in force[1]. He had secreted himself in the basement, selected his weapons at leisure[2] and called Miss Bolam down by noting the number of her extension[3] from the card hung beside the telephone. He had made his way to the upper floors without being observed and left by one of the windows, managing to close it behind him before edging his way on to the fire-escape. That this procedure argued[4] considerable luck[5], coupled with unusual and remarkable agility, was not over-emphasized[6]. Under Dr Steiner's leadership the theory was elaborated. Miss Bolam's telephone call to the group secretary was dismissed[7] as irrelevant. She had undoubtedly wished to complain about some trifling misdemeanour[8], real or imagined, and which was quite unconnected[9] with her subsequent[10] death. The suggestion that the killer had swarmed up[11] the pulley in the lift shaft was generally discounted[12] as somewhat fanciful[13] although, as Dr Maddox pointed out[14], a man who could shut a heavy window while balancing on the outside sill[15], then swing himself some five feet[16] through space to reach the fire-escape, would hardly find the lift shaft an insuperable[17] problem.

Dr Baguley, wearying[18] of his part in the fabrication of this mythical killer, half-closed his eyes and gazed from under lowered lids[19] at the bowl of roses. Their petals had been opening gently and almost visibly in the warmth of the room. Now the red, green and pink swam together in an amorphous[20] pattern of colour which, as his gaze shifted[21], was reflected in the shining table. Suddenly he opened his eyes fully and saw Dr Etherege looking fixedly at him. There was concern in that sharp[22],

1. en vigueur
2. tranquillement choisi ses armes
3. numéro de son poste
4. impliquait
5. beaucoup de chance
6. on n'insista pas sur le fait que
7. rejeté
8. incartade sans importance
9. sans lien
10. ultérieure
11. grimpé à toute vitesse
12. réfutée
13. fantaisiste
14. fit remarquer
15. rebord
16. un mètre cinquante
17. insurmontable
18. las
19. paupières baissées
20. informe
21. se déplaçait
22. perçant

analytic regard; Dr Baguley thought that there was also pity. The medical director said:

'Some of our members have had enough. So, I think, have I. If no one has any urgent business to bring forward[1] I declare the meeting closed.'

Dr Baguley thought that it was not altogether by chance[2] that he and the medical director found themselves alone in the room, the last to leave. As he tested the windows to check that they were locked, Dr Etherege said:

'Well, James, have you come to a decision yet about succeeding me as medical director?'

'It's more a question of deciding whether or not to apply for the job[3] when it's advertised, surely?[4]' said Baguley. He asked: 'What about Mason-Giles or McBain?'

'M. G. isn't interested. It's maximum sessions[5], of course, and he doesn't want to give up his teaching hospital connection[6]. McBain is tied up with[7] the new regional unit for adolescents.'

It was typical of the medical director's occasional insensitivity[8] that he didn't try to soften[9] the fact that he had tried others first. He's scraping the bottom of the barrel[10], thought Baguley.

'And Steiner?' he asked. 'He'll be applying[11], I imagine?'

The medical director smiled.

'Oh, I don't think the Regional Board will appoint Dr Steiner. This is a multi-discipline clinic. We must have someone who can hold the place together. And there may be very great changes. You know my views. If there is to be a closer integration of psychiatry with general medicine a place like this may have to die for the greater good. We ought to

1. soumettre
2. pas tout à fait par hasard
3. poser ma candidature
4. n'est-ce pas ?
5. cela implique un nombre important de séances
6. renoncer à l'enseignement universitaire
7. s'occupe déjà de
8. manque de tact
9. atténuer
10. il n'a plus personne d'autre en vue
11. il va poser sa candidature

have access to beds. The Steen may find its natural home in a general hospital out-patient department[1]. I don't say it's probable. But it's possible.'

So that was the way the Board was thinking? Dr Etherege had his ear well to the ground[2]. A small outpatient unit with no registrars[3], no training function[4] and no link with a general hospital might well become anachronistic in the eyes of the planners[5]. Dr Baguley said:

'I don't mind where I see my patients as long as I get peace and quiet, a certain tolerance, and not too much of the hierarchical claptrap[6] and starched linen[7]. These proposed psychiatric units in general hospitals are all very well so long as the hospital appreciates[8] what we're going to need in staff and space. I'm too tired to do battle[9].'

He looked at the medical director.

'Actually, I had more or less decided not to apply[10]. I telephoned your room yesterday evening from the medical staff-room to ask if we could chat about it after the clinic.'

'Indeed? At what time?'

'At about six-twenty or six-twenty-five. There was no reply. Later, of course, we had other things to think about.'

The medical director said:

'I must have been in the library. I'm very glad I was if it means that you've had time to reconsider your decision[11]. And I hope that you will reconsider it, James.'

He turned out[12] the lights and they went downstairs together. Pausing at the foot[13], the medical director turned to Baguley and said:

1. service de consultation externe
2. était bien informé
3. chefs de clinique
4. stages
5. planificateurs
6. âneries
7. linge amidonné
8. se rend compte de
9. me battre
10. de ne pas présenter ma candidature
11. revenir sur votre décision
12. éteignit
13. en bas de l'escalier

'It was at about six-twenty that you telephoned? I find that very interesting, very interesting indeed.'

1. à peu près

'Well, about then[1], I suppose.'

2. saisi

3. regard

4. très doué pour le mettre en position de faiblesse

Dr Baguley realized with irritation and surprise that it was he, not the medical director, who sounded guilty and embarrassed. He was seized[2] by an intense desire to get out of the clinic, to escape from the blue, speculative gaze[3] which was so adept at putting him at a disadvantage[4]. But there was something else which must be said. At the door he forced himself to pause and face Dr Etherege. But despite his attempt at nonchalance his voice sounded forced, even belligerent:

'I'm wondering whether we ought to do something about Nurse Bolam.'

5. ce n'est pas de mon ressort

'In what way?' asked the medical director gently. Receiving no reply, he went on: 'All the staff know that they can ask to see me at any time. But I'm not inviting confidences. This is a murder investigation, James, and it's out of my hands[5]. Out of my hands completely. I think you would be wise to take the same attitude. Good night.'

CHAPTER SIX

Early Monday morning, the anniversary of his wife's death, Dalgliesh called in[1] at a small Catholic church behind the Strand[2] to light a candle[3]. His wife had been a Catholic. He had not shared her religion[4] and she had died before he could begin to understand what it meant to her or what importance this fundamental difference between them might have for their marriage. He had lit the first candle on the day she had died out of the need to formalize[5] an intolerable grief[6] and, perhaps, with a childish hope of somehow comforting her spirit[7]. This was the fourteenth candle. He thought of this most private action in his detached and secretive[8] life, not as superstition or piety[9], but as a habit which he could not now break even if he wished. He dreamed of his wife only seldom, but then with absolute clarity; waking[10] he could no longer accurately recall[11] her face. He pushed his coin[12] through the slot[13] and held his candle's wick[14] to the dying flame of a moist stump[15]. It caught immediately and the flame grew bright and clear. It had always been important to him that the wick should catch at once. He gazed through the flame for a moment

1. entra
2. quartier du centre de Londres célèbre pour ses théâtres
3. allumer un cierge
4. il ne pratiquait pas la même religion qu'elle
5. pour donner forme à
6. chagrin
7. réconforter son âme
8. secrète
9. piété
10. éveillé
11. se souvenir de
12. pièce
13. fente
14. mèche
15. la flamme mourante d'une bougie entamée

feeling nothing, not even anger[1]. Then he turned away.

The church was nearly empty, but it held for him an atmosphere of intense and silent activity which he sensed but could not share. As he walked to the door he recognized a woman, red-coated[2] and with a dark green scarf[3] over her head, who was pausing to dip[4] her fingers in the water stoup[5]. It was Fredrica Saxon, senior psychologist of the Steen Clinic. They reached the outer door together and he forced it open for her against the sudden swirl[6] of an autumn wind. She smiled at him, friendly and unembarrassed.

'Hullo. I haven't seen you here before.'

'I only come once a year,' Dalgliesh replied. He gave no explanation and she asked no questions. Instead she said:

'I wanted to see you. There's something I think you ought to know. Are you off duty[7]? If you aren't could you be unorthodox and talk to a suspect in a coffee bar? I'd rather not[8] come to your office and it isn't easy to ask for an interview at the clinic. I need some coffee anyway. I'm cold.'

'There used to be a place[9] round the corner,' said Dalgliesh. 'The coffee is tolerable and it's pretty quiet.'

The coffee bar had changed in a year. Dalgliesh remembered it as a clean but dull cafe with a row of deal tables[10] covered with plastic cloths[11] and a long service counter[12] embellished with a tea urn[13] and layers[14] of substantial[15] sandwiches under glass domes[16]. It had risen in the world[17]. The walls had been panelled[18] with imitation old oak[19] against which hung a formidable assortment of rapiers[20],

1. colère
2. en manteau rouge
3. foulard
4. plonger
5. bénitier
6. tourbillon
7. de repos
8. je préférerais ne pas
9. il doit y avoir un endroit normalement
10. rangée de tables en bois blanc
11. nappes en plastique
12. comptoir
13. fontaine à thé
14. couches
15. copieux
16. cloches en verre
17. il était bien mieux qu'avant
18. recouverts de panneaux
19. vieux chêne
20. rapières

ancient pistols and cutlasses[1] of uncertain authenticity. The waitresses looked like *avant-garde* débutantes earning their pin money[2] and the lighting[3] was so discreet as to be positively[4] sinister. Miss Saxon led the way to a table in the far corner[5].

'Just coffee?' asked Dalgliesh.

'Just coffee, please.'

She waited until the order had been given and then said:

'It's about Dr Baguley.'

'I thought it might be[6].'

'You were bound to hear something[7], I suppose. I'd rather tell you about it now than wait to be asked and I'd rather you heard it from me than from Amy Shorthouse.'

She spoke without rancour or embarrassment. Dalgliesh replied:

'I haven't asked about it because it doesn't seem relevant, but if you'd like to tell me it may be helpful.'

'I don't want you to get a wrong idea about it that's all. It would be so easy for you to imagine that we had a grudge[8] against Miss Bolam. We didn't, you know. At one time we even felt grateful[9] to her.'

Dalgliesh had no need to ask who she meant by that 'we'.

The waitress, uninterested, came with their coffee, pale foam[10] served in small transparent cups. Miss Saxon slipped[11] her coat from her shoulders and unknotted[12] her head scarf. Both of them wrapped their fingers round the hot cups[13]. She heaped the sugar[14] into her coffee then pushed the plastic bowl across the table to Dalgliesh. There was no tension about her, no awkwardness[15]. She

1. coutelas
2. argent de poche
3. l'éclairage
4. parfaitement
5. le coin du fond
6. c'est ce que je pensais
7. vous alliez forcément en entendre parler
8. rancune
9. reconnaissants
10. mousse
11. laissa glisser
12. dénoua
13. serraient leurs tasses dans leurs mains
14. mit beaucoup de sucre
15. gêne

had the directness[1] of a school child drinking coffee with a friend. He found her curiously peaceful to be with, perhaps because he did not find her physically attractive. But he liked her. It was difficult to believe that this was only their second meeting and that the matter that had brought them together was murder. She skimmed the froth[2] from her coffee and said, without looking up:

'James Baguley and I fell in love nearly three years ago. There wasn't any great moral struggle about it. We didn't invite love but we certainly didn't fight[3] against it. After all, you don't voluntarily give up[4] happiness unless[5] you're a masochist or a saint, and we aren't either[6]. I knew that James had a neurotic wife in the way one does get to know these things, but he didn't talk much about her. We both accepted that she needed him and that a divorce was out of the question. We convinced ourselves that we weren't doing her any harm[7] and that she need never know[8]. James used to say that loving me made his marriage happier for both of them. Of course, it is easier to be kind and patient when one is happy, so he may have been right. I don't know. It's a rationalization that thousands of lovers must use.

'We couldn't see each other very often, but I had my flat and we usually managed to have[9] two evenings a week together. Once Helen – that's his wife – went to stay with her sister and we had a whole[10] night together. We had to be careful at the clinic, of course, but we don't really see very much of each other there.'

'How did Miss Bolam find out about it?' asked Dalgliesh.

1. franchise
2. enleva la mousse
3. lutté
4. renonce à
5. sauf si
6. ni l'un ni l'autre
7. on ne lui faisait pas de mal
8. il valait mieux qu'elle ne sache pas
9. arrivions à passer
10. entière

'It was silly[1], really. We were at the theatre seeing Anouilh and she was sitting alone in the row[2] behind. Who would suppose that Bolam would want to see Anouilh, anyway? I suppose she was sent[3] a free[4] ticket. It was our second anniversary and we held hands[5] all through the play[6]. We may have been a little drunk[7]. Afterwards we left the theatre still hand in hand. Anyone from the clinic, anyone we knew, could have seen us. We were getting careless[8] and someone was bound to see us sooner or later[9]. It was just chance that it happened to be Bolam. Other people would probably have minded their own business[10].'

'Whereas[11] she told Mrs Baguley? That seems an unusually officious[12] and cruel thing to have done.'

'It wasn't, really. Bolam wouldn't see it that way. She was one of those rare and fortunate people who never for one moment doubt that they know the difference between right and wrong. She wasn't imaginative[13] so she couldn't enter into other people's feelings. If she were a wife whose husband was unfaithful[14] I'm sure that she would want to be told about it. Nothing would be worse than not knowing. She had the kind of strength that relishes a struggle[15]. I expect she thought it was her duty[16] to tell. Anyway, Helen came to the Steen to see her husband unexpectedly one Wednesday afternoon and Miss Bolam invited her into the AO's office and told her. I often wonder what exactly she said. I imagine that she said we were "carrying on"[17]. She could make practically anything sound vulgar.'

'She was taking a risk, wasn't she?' said Dalgliesh. 'She had very little evidence, certainly no proof[18].'

Miss Saxon laughed.

1. idiot
2. rangée
3. elle avait reçu
4. gratuit
5. on s'est tenu la main
6. pendant tout le spectacle
7. un peu éméchés
8. on faisait de moins en moins attention
9. tôt ou tard
10. ne se seraient probablement pas mêlés de nos affaires
11. alors que
12. particulièrement importun
13. elle manquait d'imagination
14. infidèle
15. aime l'adversité
16. devoir
17. que l'on « avait une liaison »
18. pas de preuves

'You're talking like a policeman. She had proof enough[1]. Even Bolam could recognize love when she saw it. Besides, we were enjoying ourselves together without a licence[2] and that was infidelity enough.'

The words were bitter but she did not sound resentful[3] or sarcastic. She was sipping[4] her coffee with evident satisfaction. Dalgliesh thought that she might have been talking about one of the clinic patients, discussing with detached and mild professional interest the vagaries[5] of human nature. Yet he did not believe that she loved easily or that her emotions were superficial. He asked what Mrs Baguley's reaction had been.

'That's the extraordinary thing, or at least it seemed so at the time. She took it wonderfully well. Looking back[6] I wonder whether we weren't all three mad, living in some kind of imaginary world that two minutes' rational thought would have shown us couldn't exist. Helen lives her life in a series of attitudes and the one she decided to adopt was the pose of the brave[7], understanding wife. She insisted on a divorce. It was going to be one of those friendly[8] divorces. That kind is only possible, I imagine, when people have ceased to care for each other[9], perhaps never have cared or been capable of caring. But that was the kind we were going to have. There was a great deal of[10] discussion. Everyone's happiness was to be safeguarded[11]. Helen was going to open a dress shop – it's a thing she's talked about for years. We all three got interested in it and looked for suitable premises[12]. It was pathetic really. We actually fooled ourselves[13] that it was all going to come right[14]. That's

1. suffisamment de preuves
2. sans en avoir l'autorisation
3. rancunière
4. sirotait
5. caprices
6. rétrospectivement
7. courageuse
8. à l'amiable
9. ne s'aiment plus
10. beaucoup de
11. assuré
12. locaux appropriés
13. avions l'illusion
14. que tout se passerait bien

why I said that James and I felt grateful to Enid Bolam. People at the clinic got to know that there was to be a divorce and that Helen would name me – it was all part of the policy of frankness and honesty – but very little was said to us. Bolam never mentioned the divorce to anyone. She wasn't a gossip[1] and she wasn't malicious[2] either. Somehow her part in it got about in the way these things do. I think Helen may have told someone, but Miss Bolam and I never talked about it ever.

'Then the inevitable happened. Helen began to crack[3]. James had left her with the Surrey house and was living with me in the flat. He had to see her fairly often. He didn't say very much at first, but I knew what was happening. She was ill, of course, and we both knew it. She had played out the role of the patient, uncomplaining[4] wife and, according to the novels and the films, her husband should, by now, have been returning to her. And James wasn't. He kept most of it from me, but I had some idea what it was doing to him, the scenes, the tears[5], the entreaties[6], the threats of suicide[7]. One minute she was going through with the divorce[8], the next she would never give him his freedom. She couldn't, of course. I see that now. It wasn't hers to give[9]. It's degrading[10] to talk about a husband as if he's a dog chained up[11] in the back yard[12]. All the time that this was happening I was realizing more and more that I couldn't go on. Something that had been a slow process over the years came to a head[13]. There's no point[14] in talking about it or trying to explain. It isn't relevant to your inquiry, is it? Nine months ago I started to receive instruction with the hope of being received into the Cath-

1. commère
2. méchante
3. a commencé à craquer
4. résignée
5. larmes
6. supplications
7. menaces de suicide
8. acceptait de divorcer
9. elle ne pouvait pas la lui donner
10. dégradant
11. enchaîné
12. dans la cour
13. au point critique
14. il ne sert à rien

olic Church. When that happened Helen withdrew her petition[1] and James went back to her. I think he no longer cared what happened to him or where he went. But you can see, can't you, that he had no reason to hate Bolam. I was the enemy.'

Dalgliesh thought that there could have been very little struggle. Her rosy, healthy[2] face with the broad and slightly tip-tilted[3] nose, the wide cheerful[4] mouth, was ill-suited[5] to tragedy. He recalled how Dr Baguley had looked, seen in the light of Miss Bolam's desk lamp. It was stupid and presumptuous to try to assess suffering[6] by the lines on a face or the look in the eyes. Miss Saxon's mind was probably as tough[7] and resilient[8] as her body. It did not mean that she felt less because she could withstand[9] more. But he felt profoundly sorry for Baguley, rejected by his mistress[10] at the moment of the greatest trial[11] in favour of a private happiness which he could neither share nor understand. Probably no one could fully know the magnitude[12] of that betrayal[13]. Dalgliesh did not pretend to understand Miss Saxon. It wasn't hard to imagine what some people at the clinic would make of it. The facile explanations came easily to mind. But he could not believe that Fredrica Saxon had taken refuge in religion from her own sexuality or had ever refused to face reality.

He thought of some of the things she had said about Enid Bolam.

'Who would suppose that Bolam would want to see Anouilh? I suppose she was sent a free ticket… Even Bolam could recognize love when she saw it… She could make practically anything sound vulgar.' People did not automatically become kind[14]

1. retira sa demande de divorce
2. en bonne santé
3. retroussé
4. joyeuse
5. ne convenait guère
6. évaluer la souffrance
7. solide
8. résistant
9. supporter
10. maîtresse
11. épreuve
12. ampleur
13. trahison
14. gentils

because they had become religious. Yet there had been no real malice in her words. She spoke what she thought and would be equally detached about her own motives. She was probably the best judge of character in the clinic. Suddenly, and in defiance of orthodoxy[1], Dalgliesh asked:

'Who do you think killed her, Miss Saxon?'

'Judging by character and the nature of the crime and taking no account of[2] mysterious telephone calls from the basement, creaking[3] lifts, and apparent alibis?'

'Judging by character and the nature of the crime.'

She said without hesitation and with no apparent reluctance[4]:

'I'd have said it was[5] Peter Nagle.'

Dalgliesh felt a stab of disappointment[6]. It was irrational to have thought that she might actually know.

'Why Nagle?' he asked.

'Partly because I think this was a masculine crime. The stabbing[7] is significant. I can't see a woman killing in just that way. Faced with[8] an unconscious[9] victim I think a woman would strangle[10]. Then there's the chisel. To use it with such expertise suggests an identification of the weapon with the killer. Why use it otherwise[11]? He could have struck her[12] again and again with the fetish.'

'Messy[13], noisy and less sure,' said Dalgliesh.

'But the chisel was only sure in the hands of a man who had confidence in his ability to use it, someone who is literally "good with his hands". I can't see Dr Steiner killing in that way, for instance. He couldn't even knock in a nail[14] without breaking the hammer[15].'

1. au mépris de l'orthodoxie
2. sans tenir compte de
3. qui craquent
4. réticence
5. je dirais que c'est
6. éprouva une vive déception
7. l'agression à l'arme blanche
8. face à
9. inconsciente
10. l'étranglerait
11. sinon
12. la frapper
13. salissant
14. enfoncer un clou
15. marteau

Dalgliesh was inclined to agree that Dr Steiner was innocent. His clumsiness[1] with tools had been mentioned by more than one member of the clinic staff. Admittedly[2] he had lied[3] in denying[4] that he knew where the chisel was kept, but Dalgliesh judged that he had acted from fear rather than guilt. And his shame-faced[5] confession of falling asleep while awaiting Mr Burge had the ring of truth[6].

Dalgliesh said:

'The identification of the chisel with Nagle is so certain that I think we were meant to suspect him. And you do?'

'Oh, no! I know he couldn't have done it. I only answered the question as you posed it. I was judging by character and the nature of the crime.'

They had finished their coffee now and Dalgliesh thought that she would want to go. But she seemed in no hurry. After a moment's pause, she said:

'I have one confession to make; on another person's behalf[7] actually[8]. It's Cully. Nothing important but something you ought to know and I promised I'd tell you about it. Poor old Cully is scared out of his wits[9] and they aren't plentiful[10] at the best of times.'

'I knew he was lying[11] about something,' said Dalgliesh. 'He saw someone passing down the hall, I suppose.'

'Oh, no! Nothing as useful as that. It's about the missing rubber apron[12] from the art therapy department. I gather[13] you thought that the murderer might have worn[14] it. Well, Cully borrowed it[15] from the department last Monday to wear while he emulsion-painted his kitchen. You know what a mess paint makes. He didn't ask Miss Bolam if he could

1. maladresse
2. il est vrai que
3. menti
4. en niant
5. plein de honte
6. semblait sincère
7. de la part de quelqu'un d'autre
8. à vrai dire
9. la peur a fait perdre la tête à ce pauvre Cully
10. qui n'est déjà pas brillant
11. mentait
12. tablier en caoutchouc
13. j'imagine que
14. porté
15. l'a emprunté

take it because he knew what the answer would be and he couldn't ask Mrs Baumgarten because she's away sick[1]. He meant to bring it back[2] on Friday but when Sister was checking the inventory[3] with your sergeant and they asked him if he'd seen it he lost his head and said "no". He's not very bright[4] and he was terrified that you'd suspect him of the murder if he owned up[5].'

Dalgliesh asked her when Cully had told her of this.

'I knew he had the apron because it just happened that I saw him take it. I guessed[6] that he'd be in a state[7] about it so I went round to see him yesterday morning. His stomach gets upset when he worries and I thought someone had better keep an eye on him.'

'Where is the apron now?' asked Dalgliesh.

Miss Saxon laughed.

'Disposed about[8] London in half a dozen litter baskets[9] if they haven't been emptied[10]. Poor old Cully daren't[11] put it in his own dustbin[12] in case it was searched by the police and couldn't burn it because he lives in a council flat[13] with electric heating[14] and no stove[15]. So he waited until his wife was in bed, then sat up[16] until eleven cutting it into pieces with the kitchen scissors. He put the pieces into a number of paper bags, shoved[17] the bags into a hold-all[18], and took a 36 bus up the Harrow Road until he was well away from his home ground[19]. Then he slipped one of the bags into each litter bin he came across[20] and dropped the metal buttons down the gutter grating[21]. It was a formidable undertaking[22] and the poor fellow could hardly creep home[23] what with[24] fear, tiredness – he'd

1. elle était en congé maladie
2. il allait le rapporter
3. faisait l'inventaire
4. intelligent
5. avouait
6. j'ai compris
7. dans tous ses états
8. jeté en morceaux quelque part à
9. poubelles
10. vidées
11. n'a pas osé
12. poubelle
13. logement social
14. chauffage électrique
15. poêle
16. est resté debout
17. il a mis
18. fourre-tout
19. de chez lui
20. qu'il trouvait
21. à travers le grillage du caniveau
22. une entreprise redoutable
23. rentrer sans bruit à la maison
24. entre

lost the last bus – and the belly-ache. He wasn't in too good a shape[1] when I called next morning, but I did manage to convince him that it wasn't a matter of life and death[2] – particularly death. I told him I'd let you know about it.'

'Thank you,' said Dalgliesh gravely. 'You haven't any other confessions to pass on, I suppose? Or have you a conscientious objection[3] to handing over[4] an unfortunate[5] psychopath to justice?'

She laughed, pulling on her coat and trying the scarf over her dark, springing[6] hair.

'Oh, no! If I knew who did it I'd tell you. I don't like murder and I'm quite law-abiding[7], really. But I didn't know we were talking about justice. That's your word. Like Portia, I feel that in the course of justice[8] none of us would see salvation. Please, I would much rather pay for my own coffee.'

She doesn't want to feel I bought information from her, thought Dalgliesh, not even a shilling's worth[9]. He resisted the temptation to say that the coffee could come from expenses[10], wondering a little at this impulse to sarcasm which she aroused[11] in him. He liked her, but there was something about her certainty, her self-sufficiency[12], which he found irritating. Perhaps what he felt was envy[13].

As they left the cafe he asked her whether she was on her way to[14] the Steen.

'Not today. I don't have a session on Monday mornings. But I shall be there tomorrow.'

She thanked him formally for the coffee and they parted[15]. He turned eastwards[16] towards the Steen and she disappeared in the direction of the Strand. As he watched her slim, dark figure swinging out of sight[17] he pictured Cully creeping through the

1. en très bonne forme
2. une question de vie ou de mort
3. êtes-vous moralement opposée
4. au fait de livrer
5. malheureux
6. bouclés
7. je respecte la loi
8. si justice était faite
9. même pour un shilling
10. il passerait le café dans sa note de frais
11. provoquait
12. indépendance
13. jalousie
14. elle allait à
15. ils se séparèrent
16. il se dirigea vers l'est
17. disparaître d'un pas alerte

night with his pathetic bundle[1], half petrified with fright[2]. He was not surprised that the old porter had confided so fully in Fredrica Saxon; in Cully's place, he would probably have done the same. She had, thought Dalgliesh, given him a great deal of interesting information. But what she hadn't been able to give him was an alibi for Dr Baguley or for herself.

Mrs Bostock, shorthand-notebook at the ready[3], sat beside Dr Etherege's chair, her elegant legs crossed at the knees and her flamingo head[4] lifted to receive, with becoming gravity, the medical director's instructions.

'Superintendent Dalglicsh has telephoned to say that he will be here shortly[5]. He wants to see certain members of the staff again and has asked for an interview with me before lunch.'

'I don't see how you can fit him in[6] before lunch, Doctor,' said Mrs Bostock repressively[7]. 'There's the Professional Staff Committee at two-thirty and you haven't had time to look at the agenda. Dr Talmage from the States is booked for twelve-thirty and I was hoping for an hour's dictation from eleven a.m.'

'That will have to wait. The superintendent will be taking up a great deal of your own time, I'm afraid. He has some questions about the working of the clinic[8].'

'I'm afraid I don't quite understand, Doctor. Do you mean he's interested in the general administrative arrangements?' Mrs Bostock's tone was a nice blend[9] of surprise and disapproval.

'Apparently so[10],' replied Dr Etherege. 'He mentioned the appointments diary[11], the diagnostic in-

1. paquet
2. peur
3. carnet de sténo fin prêt
4. tête de flamand rose
5. sous peu
6. trouver du temps pour lui
7. d'un ton tranchant
8. la façon dont la clinique fonctionne
9. mélange
10. apparemment
11. le carnet de rendez-vous

dex, the arrangements for registering incoming and outgoing post, and the medical record system. You had better deal with him personally. If I want to dictate I'll send for[1] Miss Priddy.'

'I'll do what I can to help, naturally,' said Mrs Bostock. 'It's unfortunate that he should have picked one of our busiest mornings[2]. It would be simpler to arrange a programme for him if I knew what he had in mind[3].'

'We should all like to know that, I imagine,' replied the medical director. 'I should just answer his questions as fully as you can[4]. And please get Cully to ring me as soon as he wants to come up.'

'Yes, Doctor,' said Mrs Bostock, recognizing defeat. And took her leave[5].

Downstairs, in the ECT room, Dr Baguley twitched himself into[6] his white coat, helped by Nurse Bolam.

'Mrs King will be here for her LSD treatment on Wednesday as usual. I think it will be best if we give it in one of the PSW rooms on the third floor. Miss Kettle isn't in[7] on Wednesday evenings, is she? Have a word with her[8]. Alternatively[9] we could use Mrs Kallinski's room or one of the small interviewing rooms at the back.'

Nurse Bolam said:

'It won't be so convenient for you, Doctor. It means coming up two flights[10] when I phone.'

'That isn't going to kill me. I may look in my dotage[11] but I still have the use of my legs.'

'There's the question of a bed, Doctor. I suppose we could put up one of the recovery stretchers[12] from the ECT clinic'

1. j'appellerai
2. une de nos matinées les plus chargées
3. ce à quoi il pense
4. de la façon la plus détaillée
5. prit congé
6. mit
7. ne travaille pas
8. parlez-en avec elle
9. sinon
10. étages
11. avoir l'air d'être gâteux
12. brancards

'Get Nagle to see to it[1]. I don't want you alone in that basement.'

'I'm not in the least frightened[2], really, Dr Baguley.'

Dr Baguley lost his temper[3].

'For God's sake[4], use your brain[5], Nurse. Of course you're frightened! There's a murderer loose[6] somewhere in this clinic and no one – except one person – is going to be happy about staying alone for any length of time[7] in the basement. If you really aren't frightened then have the good sense[8] to conceal[9] the fact, especially from the police. Where's Sister? In the general office?'

He picked up the receiver and dialled jerkily[10].

'Sister? Baguley here. I've just told Nurse Bolam that I don't feel happy about using[11] the basement room for LSD this week.'

Sister Ambrose's voice came back clearly:

'Just as you like[12], Doctor, of course. But if the basement is more convenient and we could get a relief nurse from one of the general hospitals in the group for the ECT clinic, I should be quite happy to stay downstairs with Nurse Bolam. We could special Mrs King together.'

Dr Baguley said shortly:

'I want you in the ECT clinic as usual, Sister, and the LSD patient will go upstairs. I hope that's finally understood[13].'

In the medical director's room two hours later, Dalgliesh placed three black metal boxes on Dr Etherege's desk. The boxes, which had small round holes punched[14] in each of the shorter sides,

1. demandez à Nagle de s'en occuper
2. cela ne me fait vraiment pas peur
3. perdit patience
4. bon sang
5. réfléchissez
6. en liberté
7. pour quelque durée que ce soit
8. bon sens
9. cacher
10. composa le numéro nerveusement
11. je préfère ne pas utiliser
12. comme vous voudrez
13. je veux que les choses soient claires une fois pour toutes
14. qui étaient perforées

were packed with[1] buff-coloured[2] cards. It was the clinic diagnostic index. Dalgliesh said:

'Mrs Bostock has explained this to me. If I've understood her correctly, each of these cards represents a patient. The information on the case record is coded and the patient's code punched[3] on the card. The cards are punched with even rows[4] of small holes and the space between each hole is numbered. By punching any number with the hand machine I cut out the card between the two adjacent holes to form an oblong slit[5]. If this metal rod[6] is then inserted through, say, hole number 20 on the outside of the box, and pushed right through the cards, and the box is rotated[7], any card which has been punched through that number will stand out[8]. It is, in fact, one of the simplest of the many punch-card systems on the market.'

'Yes. We use it principally as a diagnostic index and for research.' If the medical director was surprised at Dalgliesh's interest he made no sign. The superintendent went on:

'Mrs Bostock tells me that you don't code from the case record until the patient has completed treatment[9] and that the system was started in 1952. That means that patients at present attending won't yet have a card – unless[10], of course, they were treated here earlier – and that patients who completed treatments before 1952 aren't included.'

'Yes. We should like to include the earlier cases, but it's a question of staff time. The coding and punching are time-consuming and it's the kind of job that gets put on one side[11]. At present we're coding the February 1962 discharges[12], so we're quite a bit behind[13].'

1. remplies de
2. couleur chamois
3. perforé
4. rangées régulières
5. incision oblongue
6. baguette en métal
7. on fait pivoter la boîte
8. sortira
9. a fini son traitement
10. à moins que
11. qu'on met de côté
12. les patients qui ont terminé leur traitement en 1962
13. nous avons pris du retard

'But once the patient's card is punched you can select any diagnosis or category of patient at will[1]?'

'Yes, indeed.' The medical director gave his slow sweet smile.

'I won't say that we can pick out[2] immediately all the indigenous depressives[3] with blue-eyed grandmothers who were born in wedlock[4] because we haven't coded information about grandparents. But anything coded can be extracted[5] without trouble.'

Dalgliesh laid a slim manilla file on the desk.

'Mrs Bostock has lent me[6] the coding instructions. I see that you code sex, age, marital status[7], address by local authority area[8], diagnosis[9], consultant who treated the patient, dates of first and subsequent attendances and a considerable amount of detail about symptoms, treatment and progress. You also code social class. I find that interesting.'

'It's unusual, certainly,' replied Dr Etherege. 'Chiefly[10], I suppose, because it can be a purely subjective assessment. But we wanted it because it's sometimes useful in research. As you see we use the Registrar-General's classes. They're accurate enough[11] for our purposes[12].'

Dalgliesh ran the thin metal rod through his fingers.

'So I could select, for example, the cards of patients in class one who were treated eight to ten years ago, were married with a family, and were suffering from, say[13], sexual aberration, kleptomania, or any other socially unacceptable personality disorder[14].'

'You could,' admitted the medical director quietly. 'But I can't see why you should want to.'

1. à volonté
2. repérer
3. dépressifs endogènes
4. nés de parents mariés
5. extrait
6. m'a prêté
7. situation familiale
8. selon la commune
9. diagnostic
10. principalement
11. suffisamment précis
12. buts
13. disons
14. tout autre trouble de la personnalité socialement inacceptable

'Blackmail[1], Doctor. It occurs to me[2] that we have here a neatly contrived apparatus[3] for the pre-selection of a victim. You push through the rod and out pops your card[4]. The card bears[5] a number on the top right-hand corner[6]. And down in the basement record-room the medical record is filed and waiting.'

The medical director said:

'This is nothing but guesswork[7]. There isn't a shred of evidence[8].'

'There's no proof, certainly, but it's a reasonable possibility. Consider the facts. On Wednesday afternoon Miss Bolam saw the group secretary after the House Committee meeting and told him all was well at the clinic. At twelve-fifteen on Friday morning she telephoned to ask for an urgent visit because "something is going on here that he ought to know about". It was something serious and continuing[9] and something that started before her time here, that is more than three years ago.'

'Whatever it was[10] we've no evidence that it was the reason for her death.'

'No.'

'In fact, if the murderer wanted to prevent[11] Miss Bolam seeing Lauder he left it rather late[12]. There was nothing to stop the group secretary turning up here[13] any time after one o'clock.'

Dalgliesh said:

'She was told over the telephone that he couldn't arrive until after the JCC[14] meeting that evening. That leads us to ask[15] who could have overheard[16] the telephone call. Cully was officially on the board[17], but he was unwell[18] most of the day and, from time to time, other members of the staff

1. pour faire chanter quelqu'un
2. je réalise
3. appareil soigneusement conçu
4. votre carte sort
5. porte
6. dans le coin en haut à droite
7. ce n'est qu'une simple hypothèse
8. il n'y a pas la moindre preuve
9. permanent
10. quoi qu'il en soit
11. empêcher
12. a attendu bien longtemps
13. de venir ici
14. commission mixte de consultation
15. cela nous amène à nous demander
16. entendu
17. au standard
18. mal en point

took over[1], sometimes only for a few minutes. Nagle, Mrs Bostock, Miss Priddy and even Mrs Shorthouse all say that they helped on the board. Nagle thinks he took over for a short time at midday before he went out for his lunchtime beer, but says that he can't be sure. Nor can Cully[2]. No one admits to having put through[3] this particular call.'

'They might not know if they had,' replied Dr Etherege. 'We're insistent that[4] the operator doesn't listen in to calls[5]. That, after all, is important in our work. Miss Bolam may have merely asked for group offices. She must put through calls fairly often to the finance and supplies departments[6] as well as the group secretary. The operator couldn't know there was anything special about this call. She might even have asked for an outside line[7] and put through the call herself. That is possible, of course, with the PABX[8] system.'

'But it could still be overheard by the person on the board.'

'If he plugged in[9] I suppose it could.'

Dalgliesh said: 'Miss Bolam told Cully late in the afternoon that she was expecting Mr Lauder and she may have mentioned the visit to other people. We don't know. No one will admit to having been told except Cully. In the circumstances, that isn't perhaps surprising. We're not going to get much further[10] with it at present. What I must do now is to find out what Miss Bolam wanted to tell Mr Lauder. One of the first possibilities to be considered in a place like this must be blackmail[11]. God knows that's continuing and it's serious enough.'

The medical director did not speak for a moment. Dalgliesh wondered whether he was contemplating[12]

1. ont pris sa relève
2. Cully non plus
3. transmis
4. nous insistons pour que
5. n'écoute pas les conversations téléphoniques
6. services des finances et de l'approvisionnement
7. ligne extérieure
8. autocommutateur privé
9. s'il se connectait
10. nous n'allons pas avancer beaucoup
11. chantage
12. envisageait

1. de protester une nouvelle fois
2. inquiétude
3. incrédulité
4. après avoir élaboré cette théorie
5. mener à bien
6. ligne de conduite
7. très injuste
8. vous vous rendez compte
9. on commence ?
10. concerne seulement les névroses de l'aristocratie et de la haute bourgeoisie
11. il inspecta
12. le maître chanteur
13. choisir
14. revenus réguliers
15. plus intéressant
16. succomber
17. passer

a further remonstrance[1], selecting appropriate words to express concern[2] or disbelief[3]. Then he said quietly:

'Of course it's serious. There's no point in wasting time discussing just how serious. Obviously, having thought up this theory[4], you have to carry through[5] your investigation. Any other course of action[6] would be most unfair[7] to the members of my staff. What do you want me to do?'

'To help me select a victim. Later, perhaps, to make some telephone calls.'

'You appreciate[8], Superintendent, that the case records are confidential?'

'I'm not asking to see a single case record. But if I did I don't think either you or the patient need worry. Shall we get started?[9] We can take out our class 1 patients. Perhaps you would call out the codes for me.'

A considerable number of the Steen patients were in class 1. 'Upper-class neuroses catered for only[10],' thought Dalgliesh. He surveyed[11] the field for a moment and then said:

'If I were the blackmailer[12] would I choose a man or a woman? It would depend on my own sex probably. A woman might pick on[13] a woman. But, if it's a question of a regular income[14] a man is probably a better bet[15]. Let's take out the males next. I imagine our victim will live out of London. It would be risky to select an ex-patient who could too easily succumb[16] to the temptation to pop[17] into the clinic and let you know what was going on. I think I'd select my victim from a small town or village.'

The medical director said:

'We only coded the country if it were an out-London address. London patients are coded by borough[1]. Our best plan will be to take out all the London addresses and see what's left[2].'

This was done. The number of cards still in the survey was now only a few dozen. Most of the Steen patients, as might be expected[3], came from the county[4] of London. Dalgliesh said:

'Married or single? It's difficult to decide whether one or the other would be most vulnerable. Let's leave it open and start on the diagnosis. This is where I need your help particularly, Doctor. I realize this is highly confidential information. I suggest that you call out the codes for the diagnoses or symptoms which might interest a blackmailer. I don't want details.'

Again the medical director paused. Dalgliesh waited patiently, metal rod in hand, while the doctor sat in silence, the code book open before him. He seemed not to be seeing it. After a minute he roused himself[5] and focused his eyes on the page. He said quietly:

'Try codes 23, 68, 69 and 71.'

There were now only eleven cards remaining. Each of them bore[6] a case record number on the top right-hand margin[7]. Dalgliesh made a note[8] of the numbers, and said:

'This is as far as we can go[9] with the diagnostic index. We must now do what I think our blackmailer did, have a look at the case records, and learn more of our prospective[10] victims. Shall we go down to the basement?'

The medical director got up without a word. As they went down the stairs they passed Miss Kettle

1. arrondissement
2. ce qui reste
3. comme prévu
4. comté
5. se ressaisit
6. portait
7. dans la marge en haut à droite
8. prit note
9. on ne peut pas aller plus loin
10. potentielles

on her way up[1]. She nodded[2] to the medical director and gave Dalgliesh a brief, puzzled[3] glance as if wondering whether he were someone she had met and ought to[4] recognize. In the hall Dr Baguley was talking with Sister Ambrose. They broke off[5] and turned to watch with grave, unsmiling[6] faces as Dr Etherege and Dalgliesh made their way to[7] the basement stairs. At the other end of the hall the grey outline[8] of Cully's head could be seen through the glass of the reception kiosk. The head did not turn and Dalgliesh guessed that Cully, absorbed in his contemplation of the front door, had not heard them.

The record-room was locked, but no longer sealed. In the porters' rest-room Nagle was putting on his coat, evidently on his way out to an early lunch. He made no sign as the medical director took the record-room key from its hook[9], but the flash of interest in his mild, mud-brown eyes was not lost on Dalgliesh[10]. They had been well observed. By early afternoon everyone in the clinic would know that he had examined the diagnostic index with the medical director and then visited the record-room. To one person that information would be of crucial interest. What Dalgliesh hoped was that the murderer would become frightened and desperate; what he feared was that he would become more dangerous.

Dr Etherege switched on the light in the record-room and the fluorescent tubes flickered[11], yellowed and blazed into whiteness[12]. The room stood revealed[13]. Dalgliesh smelt[14] again its characteristic smell, compounded of mustiness[15], old paper and the tang[16] of hot metal. He watched

1. qui montait
2. fit un signe de la tête
3. perplexe
4. était censée
5. s'interrompirent
6. sérieux
7. se dirigeaient vers
8. contour
9. crochet
10. Dalgliesh remarqua une lueur d'intérêt dans ses doux yeux marrons
11. les tubes fluorescents s'allumèrent
12. émettant une forte lumière blanche
13. apparut dans toutes ses dimensions
14. sentit
15. odeur de renfermé
16. odeur forte

without betraying any emotion while the medical director locked the door on the inside and slipped the key in his pocket.

There was no sign now that the room had been the scene of murder. The torn[1] records had been repaired and replaced on the shelves[2], the chair and table placed upright[3] in their usual position.

The records were tied together with string[4] in bundles of ten[5]. Some of the files had been stored[6] for so long that they seemed to adhere to each other. The string bit into[7] the bulging[8] manilla covers[9]; across their tops[10] was a thin patina of dust[11]. Dalgliesh said:

'It should be possible to tell which of these bundles have been untied[12] since the records were weeded out[13] and brought down for storage[14]. Some of them look as if they haven't been touched for years. I realize that a bundle may have been untied to extract a record for a perfectly innocent purpose, but we may as well make a start with files from those bundles which have obviously been untied within[15] the last year or so[16]. The first two numbers are in the eight thousand range. These seem to be on the top shelf[17]. Have we a ladder[18]?'

The medical director disappeared behind the first row of shelves and reappeared with a small stepladder[19] which he manoeuvred with difficulty into the narrow aisle[20]. Looking up at Dalgliesh as the detective mounted, he said:

'Tell me, Superintendent. Does this touching confidence[21] mean that you have eliminated me from your list of suspects? If it does[22] I should be interested to know by what process of deduction you came to that conclusion. I can't flatter myself[23] that

1. déchirés
2. étagères
3. redressées
4. attachés avec des cordes
5. par tas de dix
6. conservés
7. rongeait
8. pleines à craquer
9. couvertures cartonnées
10. au-dessus
11. poussière
12. ouverts
13. triés
14. emmenés au sous-sol pour y être entreposés
15. à partir de
16. à peu près
17. étagère du haut
18. échelle
19. escabeau
20. allée
21. confiance touchante
22. si c'est le cas
23. je ne crois pas pouvoir me vanter

you believe me incapable of murder. No detective would accept that, surely, of any man.'

'And no psychiatrist possibly,' said Dalgliesh. 'I don't ask myself whether a man is capable of murder, but whether he is capable of this particular murder. I don't think you're a petty blackmailer[1]. I can't see how you could have known about Lauder's proposed visit. I doubt whether you've either the strength or skill[2] to kill in that way. Lastly, I think you're probably the one person here whom Miss Bolam wouldn't have kept waiting. Even if I'm wrong[3] you can hardly refuse to co-operate, can you?'

He was deliberately curt[4]. The bright blue eyes were still gazing into his, inviting a confidence which he did not want to give but found it difficult to resist. The medical director went on:

'I have only met three murderers. Two of them are buried in quicklime[5]. One of the two hardly knew what he was doing and the other couldn't have stopped himself. Are you satisfied, Superintendent, with that solution?'

Dalgliesh replied:

'No man in his senses would be[6]. But I don't see how that affects what I'm trying to do now: catch[7] this murderer before he – or she – kills again.'

The medical director said no more. Together they found the eleven case records they sought[8] and took them up to Dr Etherege's room. If Dalgliesh had expected the medical director to make difficulties over the next stage of the investigation he was agreeably surprised. The hint[9] that this killer might not stop at one victim had struck home[10]. When

1. je ne crois pas que vous soyez capable d'un petit chantage mesquin
2. habileté
3. je me trompe
4. cassant
5. enterrés dans la chaux vive
6. il faudrait être fou pour l'être
7. attraper
8. cherchaient
9. l'allusion
10. avait fait mouche

Dalgliesh explained what he wanted the medical director did not protest. Dalgliesh said:

'I'm not asking for the names of these patients. I'm not interested in what was wrong with them[1]. All I want you to do is to telephone each of them and ask tactfully[2] whether they rang the clinic recently, probably on Friday morning. You could explain that someone made a call which it's important to trace[3]. If one of these patients did ring[4] I want the name and address. Not the diagnosis. Just the name and address.'

'I must ask the patient's consent[5] before I give that information.'

'If you must,' said Dalgliesh. 'I leave that to you[6]. All I ask is to get that information.'

The medical director's stipulation[7] was a formality and both of them knew it. The eleven case records were on the desk and nothing but force could keep the addresses from Dalgliesh[8] if he wanted them. He sat at some distance from Dr Etherege in one of the large, leather-covered[9] chairs, and prepared to watch, with professional interest, his unusual collaborator at work. The medical director picked up his receiver and asked for an outside line. The patients' telephone numbers had been noted on the case records and the first two tries[10] at once reduced the eleven possibles to nine. In each case the patient had changed his address since his attendance[11]. Dr Etherege apologized for disturbing the new subscribers[12] to the numbers concerned and dialled for the third time[13]. The third number answered and the medical director asked if he might speak to Mr Caldecote. There was a prolonged

1. leurs problèmes

2. avec tact

3. en retrouver la trace

4. a effectivement appelé

5. consentement

6. je vous laisse le soin d'en décider

7. condition

8. empêcher Dalgliesh d'accéder aux adresses

9. en cuir

10. essais

11. visite

12. les nouveaux abonnés

13. composa un troisième numéro

crackling[1] from the other end[2] and Dr Etherege made the appropriate response.

'No, he hadn't heard. How very sad. Really? No, it was nothing important. Just an old acquaintance[3] who would be driving through Wiltshire and hoped to meet Mr Caldecote again. No, he wouldn't speak to Mrs Caldecote. He didn't want to distress her.'

'Dead?' asked Dalgliesh, as the receiver was replaced.

'Yes. Three years ago, apparently. Cancer, poor fellow. I must note that on his record.'

He did so while Dalgliesh waited.

The next number was difficult to get and there was much talk with the exchange[4]. When at last the number was rung there was no reply.

'We seem to be having no success, Superintendent. It was a clever[5] theory of yours, but, it appears, more ingenious[6] than true.'

'There are still seven more patients to try,' said Dalgliesh quietly. The medical director murmured something about a Dr Talmage whom he was expecting, but referred to[7] the next file and dialled again. This time the patient was at home and, apparently, not in the least[8] surprised to hear from[9] the medical director of the Steen. He poured out a lengthy account[10] of his present psychological condition to which Dr Etherege listened with patient sympathy and made appropriate replies. Dalgliesh was interested and a little amused at the skill with which the call was conducted. But the patient had not recently telephoned the clinic. The medical director put down the receiver and spent some time noting what the patient had told him on the case record.

1. grésillement
2. bout
3. connaissance
4. central téléphonique
5. brillante
6. ingénieuse
7. prit
8. pas du tout
9. recevoir un appel de
10. il donna un long compte-rendu

'One of our successes, apparently. He wasn't at all surprised that I telephoned. It's rather touching the way patients take it for granted[1] that their doctors are immensely concerned for their welfare[2] and are thinking of them personally at all times of the day and night. But he didn't phone. He wasn't lying, I assure you. This is very time-consuming, Superintendent, but I suppose we must go on.'

'Yes, please. I'm sorry, but we must go on.'

But the next call brought success. At first it sounded like another failure. From the conversation Dalgliesh gathered[3] that the patient had recently been taken to hospital and that it was his wife who had answered. Then he saw the medical director's face change, and heard him say:

'You did?[4] We knew that someone had telephoned and were trying to trace the call[5]. I expect you've heard about the very dreadful[6] tragedy that we've had here recently. Yes, it is in connection with that.' He waited while the voice spoke at some length[7] from the other end. Then he put down the receiver and wrote briefly on his desk jotting pad[8]. Dalgliesh did not speak. The medical director looked up at him with an expression half puzzled, half surprised.

'That was the wife of a Colonel Fenton of Sprigg's Green in Kent. She telephoned Miss Bolam about a very serious matter at about midday last Friday. She didn't want to talk to you on the phone about it and I thought it better not to press her[9]. But she'd like to see you as soon as possible. I've written down the address.'

'Thank you, Doctor,' said Dalgliesh, and took the proffered paper[10]. He showed neither surprise nor

1. trouvent tout à fait naturel
2. bien-être
3. comprit
4. c'est vrai ?
5. savoir qui avait téléphoné
6. affreuse
7. longuement
8. bloc-notes
9. insister
10. le papier qu'il lui tendait

1. soulagement
2. battait fort
3. secoua
4. au-delà de
5. quelconque
6. qui traînaient
7. les gens qui travaillaient à Londres
8. n'avait pas de cachet
9. à la retraite
10. avaient des carrés de
11. choux et choux de Bruxelles
12. épars
13. dont les tiges avaient été abîmées par de récentes cueillettes
14. traîtrise
15. en grès
16. châtaigniers
17. cimetière
18. cela ne le rendait pas désagréable à voir
19. tondue
20. tombes
21. arracher les mauvaises herbes des chemins de gravier
22. haie de lauriers
23. presbytère
24. annexes
25. en bois
26. affreux

relief[1], but his heart was singing[2]. The medical director shook[3] his head as if the whole thing were beyond[4] his understanding. He said:

'She sounds rather a formidable old lady and very formal. She said that she would be very glad if you would take afternoon tea with her.'

Just after four o'clock Dalgliesh drove slowly into Sprigg's Green. It revealed itself as an undistinguished[5] village lying between the Maidstone and Canterbury roads. He could not remember having passed through it before. There were few people about[6]. The village, thought Dalgliesh, was too far from London to tempt the commuter[7] and had no period charm[8] to attract retired[9] couples or artists and writers in search of country peace with a country cost of living. Most of the cottages were obviously lived in by farm workers, their front gardens clumped with[10] cabbages and brussels sprouts[11], straggly[12] and stem-scarred from recent pickings[13], their windows shut close against the treachery[14] of an English autumn. Dalgliesh passed the church, its short flint-and-stone[15] tower and clear glass windows only half-visible behind the surrounding chestnut trees[16]. The churchyard[17] was untidy but not offensively so[18]. The grass had been mown[19] between the graves[20] and some attempt made to weed the gravel paths[21]. Separated from the churchyard by a tall laurel hedge[22] stood the vicarage[23], a sombre Victorian house built to accommodate a Victorian-size family and its appendages[24]. Next came the green itself, a small square of grass bounded by a row of weather-boarded[25] cottages and faced by a more than usually hideous[26] modern pub and petrol station[1]. Outside the King's Head[2] was a concrete bus shelter[3] where a group of women waited dispiritedly[4]. They gave Dalgliesh a brief and uninterested glance as he passed. In spring, no doubt, the surrounding cherry orchards[5] would lend[6] their charm even to Sprigg's Green. Now, however, there was a chill dampness[7] in the air, the fields looked perpetually sodden[8], a slow mournful[9] procession of cows being driven to the evening milking[10] churned the road verges to mud[11]. Dalgliesh slowed to a walking pace[12] to pass them, keeping his watch for Sprigg's Acre. He did not want to ask the way.

He was not long in finding it. The house lay a little back from the road and was sheltered from it by a six-foot[13] beech[14] hedge which shone golden[15] in the fading light[16]. There appeared to be no drive[17] and Dalgliesh edged[18] his Cooper Bristol carefully on to the grass verge[19] before letting himself in through the white gates of the garden. The house lay before him, rambling[20], low built and thatched[21], with an air of comfort and simplicity. As he turned from latching the gate[22] behind him a woman turned the corner of the house and came down the path to meet him. She was very small. Somehow this surprised Dalgliesh. He had formed a mental picture of a stout, well-corseted[23] colonel's wife condescending to see him, but at her own time and place. The reality was less intimidating and more interesting. There was something gallant and a little pathetic in the way she came down the path towards him. She was wearing a thick skirt and a tweed jacket and was hatless, her thick white hair lifting[24] with the evening breeze. She wore gardening

1. station service
2. nom de pub très répandu
3. abri de bus en béton
4. avec découragement
5. cerisaies
6. donner
7. humidité glaciale
8. détrempés
9. lugubre
10. traite
11. transformait les accotements de la route en boue
12. se mit au pas
13. d'un mètre quatre-vingts
14. de hêtres
15. qui avait un éclat doré
16. dans la lumière tombante
17. allée
18. rangea
19. bande d'herbe
20. pleine de coins et de recoins
21. avec un toit de chaume
22. après avoir fermé le loquet du portail
23. à forte poitrine
24. se soulevant

gloves, incongruously large with vast gauntlets[1] which made the trowel[2] she carried look like a child's toy. As they met she pulled off[3] the right glove and held out[4] her hand to him, looking up at him with anxious eyes which lightened, almost imperceptibly, with relief. But when she spoke her voice was unexpectedly firm.

'Good afternoon. You must be Superintendent Dalgliesh. My name is Louise Fenton. Did you come by car? I thought I heard one.'

Dalgliesh explained where he had left it and said that he hoped that it would not be in anyone's way.

'Oh, no! Not at all. Such an unpleasant way to travel. You could have come by train quite easily to Marden and I would have sent the trap[5] for you. We haven't a car. We both dislike them very much. I'm sorry you had to sit in one all the way from London.'

'It was the fastest way,' said Dalgliesh, wondering if he should apologize for living in the twentieth century. 'And I wanted to see you as soon as possible.'

He was careful to keep the urgency from his voice, but he could see the sudden tensing[6] of her shoulders[7].

'Yes. Yes, of course. Would you like to see the garden before we go in? The light is fading but we might just have time.'

An interest in the garden was apparently expected and Dalgliesh acquiesced[8]. A light east wind, rising as the day died, whipped[9] uncomfortably around his neck and ankles[10]. But he never hurried[11] an interview. This one promised to be difficult for Mrs Fenton and she was entitled[12] to take

1. avec d'immenses manchettes
2. truelle
3. enleva
4. tendit
5. cabriolet
6. tension
7. épaules
8. acquiesça
9. fouettait
10. son cou et ses chevilles
11. hâtait
12. autorisée

her time. He wondered at his own impatience even as he concealed[1] it. For the last two days he had been irked[2] by a foreboding[3] of tragedy and failure which was the more disturbing because it was irrational. The case was young yet[4]. His intelligence told him that he was making progress. Even at this moment he was within grasp of[5] motive, and motive, he knew, was crucial to this case. He hadn't failed yet in his career at the Yard and this case, with its limited number of suspects and careful contriving[6], was an unlikely candidate for a first failure. Yet he remained worried, vexed[7] by this unreasonable fear that time was running out[8]. Perhaps it was the autumn. Perhaps he was tired. He turned up his coat collar[9] and prepared himself to look interested and appreciative.

They passed together through a wrought-iron[10] gate at the side of the house and entered the main garden. Mrs Fenton was saying:

'I love the garden dearly[11], but I'm not much good at it. Things don't grow for me[12]. My husband has the green fingers[13]. He's in Maidstone Hospital at present having an operation for hernia. It's all been very successful I'm happy to say. Do you garden[14], Superintendent?'

Dalgliesh explained that he lived in a flat high above the Thames in the City and had recently sold his Essex cottage.

'I really know very little about gardening,' he said.

'Then you will enjoy looking at ours,' replied Mrs Fenton, with gentle if[15] illogical persistence.

There was, indeed, plenty[16] to see even in the fading light of an autumn day. The colonel had given his imagination full play[17], compensating per-

1. cachait
2. agacé
3. pressentiment
4. ne faisait que commencer
5. sur le point de saisir
6. planification méticuleuse
7. vexé
8. le temps venait à manquer
9. releva le col de son manteau
10. en fer forgé
11. j'aime beaucoup notre jardin
12. grâce à moi
13. la main verte
14. est-ce que vous jardinez
15. mais
16. beaucoup
17. donné libre cours à son imagination

haps for the enforced regimentation[1] of much of his life by indulgence in[2] a picturesque and undisciplined profusion. There was a small lawn surrounding a fish pond[3] and edged[4] with crazy paving[5]. There was a succession of trellis archways[6] leading from one carefully tended plot to another[7]. There was a rose garden with a sundial[8] where a few last roses still gleamed[9] white on their leafless sterns[10]. There were hedges of beech, yew[11] and hawthorn[12] as gold and green backcloths[13] to the banked chrysanthemums[14]. At the bottom of the garden ran[15] a small stream[16], crossed[17] every ten yards[18] by wooden bridges which were a monument to the colonel's industry[19], if not to his taste. The appetite had grown by what it fed on[20]. The colonel, having once successfully bridged his brook[21], had been unable to resist further efforts. Together they stood for a moment on one of the bridges. Dalgliesh could see the colonel's initials cut into the wood of the handrail[22]. Beneath their feet the little stream, already half choked[23] with the first fallen leaves, made its own sad music. Suddenly, Mrs Fenton said:

'So somebody killed her. I know I ought to feel pity for her whatever she did. But I can't. Not yet. I should have realized that Matthew wouldn't be the only victim. These people never stop at one victim, do they? I suppose someone couldn't stand it any more and took that way out[24]. It's a very terrible thing, but I can understand it. I read about it in the papers, you know, before the medical director telephoned. Do you know, Superintendent, for a moment I was glad? That's a terrible thing to say,

1. réglementation forcée
2. en se livrant à
3. bassin
4. bordé
5. dallage irrégulier
6. treillage en voûte
7. menant d'une parcelle bien entretenue à l'autre
8. cadran solaire
9. brillaient
10. tiges
11. ifs
12. aubépines
13. toiles de fond
14. massifs de chrysanthèmes
15. coulait
16. ruisseau
17. traversé
18. dix mètres
19. application
20. l'appétit était venu en mangeant
21. ruisseau
22. rampe
23. obstrué
24. porte de sortie

but it's true. I was glad she was dead. I thought that now Matthew needn't worry any more.'

Dalgliesh said gently:

'We don't think that Miss Bolam was blackmailing your husband. It's possible that she was, but not likely. We think she was killed because she had found out what was happening and meant to stop it. That's why it's so important that I talk to you.'

Mrs Fenton's knuckles[1] whitened[2]. The hands grasping the bridge began to shake. She said:

'I'm afraid I've been very stupid. I mustn't waste any more of your time. It's getting cold, isn't it? Shall we go indoors?'

They turned towards the house, neither of them speaking. Dalgliesh shortened his stride[3] to the slow pace of the thin, upright figure at his side. He glanced at her anxiously. She was very pale and he thought he saw her lips moving soundlessly. But she walked firmly. She was going to be all right. He told himself that he mustn't hurry things. In half an hour, perhaps less, he would have the motive securely in his hands like a bomb that would blow the whole case wide open[4]. But he must be patient. Once again he was touched by an indefinable unrest[5] as if, even at this moment of imminent triumph, his heart held the sure knowledge of failure. The dusk[6] closed in around them. Somewhere a bonfire[7] smouldered[8], filling his nostrils[9] with acrid[10] smoke. The lawn was a wet sponge[11] under his feet.

The house welcomed them, blessedly[12] warm and smelling faintly[13] of home-baked[14] bread. Mrs Fenton left him to put her head into a room at the far end of the hall. He guessed that tea was being or-

1. articulations
2. blanchirent
3. fit de plus petits pas
4. faire exploser l'affaire
5. agitation
6. crépuscule
7. feu de jardin
8. couvait
9. narines
10. âcre
11. éponge humide
12. merveilleusement
13. légèrement
14. fait maison

dered. Then she led him into the drawing-room[1] to the comfort of a wood fire which threw immense shadows over the chintz-covered chairs and sofa and the faded[2] carpet. She switched on a huge standard lamp at the side of the fireplace and tugged[3] the curtains across the windows, shutting out[4] desolation and decay[5]. Tea arrived, the tray set on a low table by a stolid[6] and aproned maid[7] almost as old as her mistress who carefully avoided looking at Dalgliesh. It was a good tea. Dalgliesh saw with an emotion which was too like compassion to be comfortable that trouble had been taken on his behalf[8]. There were fresh-baked[9] scones, two kinds of sandwiches, homemade cakes and an iced sponge[10]. There was too much of everything, a schoolboy's tea[11]. It was as if the two women, faced with their unknown and most unwelcome visitor, had sought relief from uncertainty in the provision of this embarrassingly liberal feast[12]. Mrs Fenton herself seemed surprised at the variety which faced her[13]. She manoeuvred cups on the tray like an anxious, inexperienced hostess. It was only when Dalgliesh was provided with his tea and sandwich that she spoke again about the murder.

'My husband attended the Steen Clinic for about four months, nearly[14] ten years ago, soon after he left the army. He was living in London at the time and I was in Nairobi staying with my daughter-in-law[15] who was expecting her first baby[16]. I never knew about my husband's treatment until he told me a week ago.'

She paused and Dalgliesh said:

'I ought to say now that we aren't, of course, interested in what was wrong with Colonel Fenton. That

1. salon
2. aux teintes passées
3. tira
4. pour laisser dehors
5. déclin
6. flegmatique
7. bonne
8. que tout avait été préparé soigneusement pour lui
9. qui sortaient du four
10. gâteau de Savoie glacé
11. goûter
12. ce festin si copieux qu'il en était embarrassant
13. devant ses yeux
14. environ
15. belle-fille
16. qui attendait son premier enfant

is a confidential medical matter and it isn't the concern of the police[1]. I didn't ask Dr Etherege for any information and he wouldn't have given it to me if I had. The fact that your husband was being blackmailed may have to come out – I don't think that can be avoided – but his reason for going to the clinic and the details of his treatment are no one's business but his and yours[2].'

Mrs Fenton replaced[3] her cup on the tray with infinite care[4]. She looked into the fire and said:

'I don't think it is my business, really. I wasn't upset because he didn't tell me. It's so easy to say now that I would have understood and would have tried to help, but I wonder. I think he was wise not to speak about it. People make such a fuss about absolute honesty in marriage, but it isn't very sensible[5] to confess hurtful[6] things unless you really mean to hurt[7]. I wish Matthew had told me about the blackmail, though. Then he really needed help. Together I'm sure we could have thought of something.'

Dalgliesh asked how it had started.

'Just two years ago, Matthew says. He had a telephone call. The voice reminded him about his treatment at the Steen and actually quoted[8] some of the very intimate details Matthew had told the psychiatrist. Then the voice suggested that he would like to help other patients who were trying to overcome[9] similar difficulties. There was a lot of talk about the dreadful social consequences of not getting cured[10]. It was all very subtle and clever, but there wasn't the least doubt what the voice was after[11]. Matthew asked what he was expected to do and was told to send fifteen pounds in notes[12]

1. cela ne regarde pas la police

2. ne regarde que lui et vous

3. reposa

4. avec beaucoup de soin

5. raisonnable

6. blessantes

7. sauf si l'on souhaite réellement blesser

8. cité

9. surmonter

10. être soigné

11. ce que voulait la voix

12. en billets de banque

to arrive by the first post[1] on the first day of every month. If the first was a Saturday or Sunday, the letter was to arrive[2] on Monday. He was to address the envelope in green ink[3] to the administrative secretary and enclose[4] with the money a note to say that it was a donation[5] from a grateful patient. The voice said that he could be sure that the cash would go where it could do most good.'

'It was a clever enough plan,' said Dalgliesh. 'Blackmail would be difficult to prove and the amount was nicely calculated. I imagine that your husband would have been forced to take a different line[6] if the demand had been too exorbitant.'

'Oh, he would! Matthew would never let us be ruined. But you see, it was such a small amount really. I don't mean that we could afford[7] to lose fifteen pounds a month, but it was a sum which Matthew could just find by personal economies without making me suspicious. And the demand never rose[8]. That was the extraordinary thing about it. Matthew said that he always understood a blackmailer was never satisfied but kept increasing the demand until the victim couldn't pay another penny. It wasn't like that at all. Matthew sent the money to arrive on the first day of the next month and he had another call. The voice thanked him for his kind donation and made it quite clear that no more than fifteen pounds was expected. And no more ever was. The voice said something about sharing the sacrifice equally. Matthew said he could almost persuade himself that the thing was genuine. About six months ago he decided to miss a month[9] and see what happened. It wasn't very pleasant. There was another call and the menace was

1. courrier
2. devait arriver
3. encre
4. joindre
5. don
6. réagir différemment
7. nous permettre
8. le montant n'a jamais été augmenté
9. laisser passer un mois sans payer

unmistakable[1]. The voice talked about the need to save patients from social ostracism[2] and said how distressed the people of Sprigg's Green would be to hear about his lack[3] of generosity. My husband decided to go on. If the village really got to know, it would mean leaving this house. My family have lived here for two hundred years and we both love it. Matthew would be heartbroken[4] to leave the garden. And then there's the village. Of course, you haven't seen it at its best, but we love it. My husband is a churchwarden[5]. Our small son, who was killed in a road accident, is buried[6] here. It isn't easy to pull up your roots[7] at seventy.'

No, it wouldn't be easy. Dalgliesh didn't question her assumption that discovery would mean that they must leave. A younger, tougher[8], more sophisticated couple would no doubt ride the publicity[9], ignore the innuendoes[10] and accept the embarrassed sympathy[11] of their friends in the sure knowledge[12] that nothing lasts for ever[13] and that few things in village life are as dead as last year's scandal. Pity[14] was less easy to accept. It was probably the fear of pity that would drive most victims to retreat[15]. He asked what had brought the matter to a head[16]. Mrs Fenton replied:

'Two things, really. The first is that we needed more money. My husband's younger brother died unexpectedly a month ago and left his widow[17] rather badly off[18]. She is an invalid[19] and not likely to live more than a year or two, but she is very happily settled in a nursing-home[20] near Norwich and would like to stay there. It was a question of helping with the fees[21]. She needed about another five pounds a week[22] and I couldn't understand

1. manifeste
2. ostracisme social
3. manque
4. cela briserait le cœur de Matthew
5. bedeau
6. enterré
7. se déraciner
8. plus solide
9. resterait indifférent à cette publicité
10. ignorerait les sous-entendus
11. témoignages de sympathie embarrassés
12. en sachant parfaitement
13. rien ne dure éternellement
14. la pitié
15. battre en retraite
16. changement
17. veuve
18. plutôt mal lotie
19. très malade
20. maison de retraite
21. frais
22. cinq livres de plus par semaine

why Matthew seemed so worried about it. It would mean careful planning[1], but I thought we ought to be able to manage it. But he knew, of course, that we couldn't if he had to go on sending the fifteen pounds to the Steen. Then there was his operation. It wasn't a very serious one, I know, but any operation is a risk at seventy and he was afraid that he might die and the whole story come out[2] without his being able to explain. So he told me. I was very glad[3] he did. He went into hospital perfectly happy as a result and the operation went very well. Really very well indeed. Could I give you some more tea, Superintendent?'

Dalgliesh passed her his cup and asked what action she had decided to take. They were now coming to the crux of the story[4], but he was careful neither to hurry her nor to appear over-anxious. His comments and questions might have been those of any afternoon guest, dutifully[5] taking a polite share in[6] his hostess's conversation. She was an old lady who had been through a severe strain[7] and was faced with one even greater. He guessed a little of what this revelation to a stranger must be costing her[8]. Any formal expression of sympathy would have been a presumption[9], but at least he could help with patience and understanding.

'What did I decide to do? Well, that was the problem, of course. I was determined that the blackmailing should be stopped, but I wanted to spare us[10] both if I could. I'm not a very intelligent woman – it's no use shaking your head, if I were this murder wouldn't have happened – but I thought it out very carefully[11]. It seemed to me that the best thing was to visit the Steen Clinic and see someone in authority.

1. gestion minutieuse
2. que toute l'histoire soit révélée
3. très contente
4. la clé de l'histoire
5. consciencieusement
6. participant poliment à
7. rude épreuve
8. devait lui coûter
9. impertinent
10. nous épargner
11. j'y ai réfléchi soigneusement

I could explain what was happening, perhaps even without mentioning my name, and ask them to make their own investigation and put a stop to the blackmail. After all, they would know about my husband, so I wouldn't be confiding[1] his secret to anyone new and they would be just as anxious to avoid publicity as I was. It wouldn't do the clinic any good if this came out, would it? They could probably find out who was responsible without a great deal of difficulty. Psychiatrists are supposed to understand people's characters after all, and it must be someone who was at the clinic when my husband attended. And, then, being a woman would narrow the field[2].'

'Do you mean the blackmailer was a woman?' asked Dalgliesh, surprised.

'Oh, yes! At least, the voice on the telephone was a woman's voice, my husband says.'

'Is he quite sure of that?'

'He didn't express any doubt to me. It wasn't only the voice, you see. It was some of the things she said. Things like it not being only[3] members of my husband's sex who had these illnesses[4], and had he ever thought what unhappiness[5] they could cause to women, and so on. There were definite references to her being a woman[6]. My husband remembers the telephone conversations very clearly and he will be able to tell you what the remarks were. I expect you will want to see him as soon as possible, won't you?'

Touched by the obvious anxiety in her voice, he replied:

'If his doctor thinks Colonel Fenton is well enough to have a brief talk with me I should like to see him

1. je n'étais donc pas en train de confier

2. le fait qu'il s'agisse d'une femme faciliterait l'enquête

3. du genre qui n'est pas réservé qu'aux

4. maladies

5. peine

6. au fait qu'il s'agissait d'une femme

on my way back[1] to London tonight. There are one or two points – this matter of the blackmailer's sex is one – that only he can help with. I shan't bother him[2] more than necessary.'

'I'm sure he will be able to see you. He has a little room of his own[3] – an amenity bed[4] they call them – and he's doing very well. I told him that you were coming today so he won't be surprised to see you. I don't think I'll come too, if you don't mind. I think he would rather[5] see you alone. I shall write a note for you to take.'

Dalgliesh thanked her and said:

'It's interesting that your husband should say it was a woman. He could be right, of course, but it could be a clever deception[6] on the blackmailer's part and difficult to disprove[7]. Some men are able to mimic[8] a woman's voice very convincingly[9] and the casual references[10] to establish sex would be even more effective[11] than a disguised[12] voice. If the colonel had decided to prosecute[13] and the matter had come to court[14], it would have been very difficult to convict[15] a man of this particular crime unless the evidence[16] was very strong. And as far as I can see[17] the evidence would be almost non-existent. I think we'll keep a very open mind on[18] the question of the blackmailer's sex. But I'm sorry. I interrupted.'

'It was rather an important point to establish, wasn't it? I hope that my husband will be able to help with it. Well, as I was saying, I decided that the best move was to visit the clinic. I went up to London last Friday morning on an early train. I had to see my chiropodist[19] and there were one or two things Matthew needed in hospital. I decided

1. sur le chemin du retour
2. je ne l'importunerai pas
3. pour lui tout seul
4. dans un hôpital, catégorie de lits réservés aux malades qui paient pour avoir plus de confort et d'intimité
5. il préférerait
6. tromperie
7. difficile d'en prouver la fausseté
8. imiter
9. de façon très convaincante
10. petites remarques
11. efficaces
12. déguisée
13. intenter une action en justice
14. devant le juge
15. condamner
16. les preuves
17. d'après ce que j'ai compris
18. ce n'est pas la peine de rester sur nos positions quant à
19. pédicure

to shop first. I should have gone direct to the clinic, of course. That was another mistake. It was cowardice[1], really. I wasn't looking forward to it[2] and I tried to behave as if it were nothing so very special, just a casual visit I could fit in[3] between the shopping and the chiropodist. In the end I didn't go at all. I telephoned instead. You see, I told you I wasn't very intelligent.'

Dalgliesh asked what had led to[4] the change of plan.

'It was Oxford Street[5]. I know that sounds silly[6], but it happened that way. I hadn't been up to London alone for a very long time and I had forgotten how dreadful it is now. I used to love it when I was a girl. It seemed a gracious city then. Now the skyline[7] has changed and the streets seem full of freaks[8] and foreigners[9]. One shouldn't resent them[10], I know – the foreigners, I mean. It's just that I felt so alien[11]. And then there were the cars. I tried to cross[12] Oxford Street and was stranded[13] among them on one of the islands[14]. Of course, they weren't killing anyone or knocking anyone down[15]. They couldn't. They couldn't even move. But they smelt so horrible that I had to hold my handkerchief to my nose and I felt so faint[16] and ill. When I reached the pavement[17] I went into one of the stores[18] to find the women's rest-room[19]. It was on the fifth floor and it took me a long time to get to the right lift. The crowds[20] were dreadful and we were all squashed in together[21]. When I got to the rest-room all the chairs were taken. I was standing against the wall wondering whether I could summon[22] enough energy to queue for my lunch when I saw the row of telephone boxes[23].

1. lâcheté
2. je ne mourais pas d'envie d'y aller
3. caser
4. ce qui avait déterminé
5. une des grandes artères commerçantes de Londres
6. stupide
7. le profil de la ville
8. des excentriques
9. des étrangers
10. il ne faut pas leur en vouloir
11. tellement étrangère à tout cela
12. traverser
13. coincée
14. îlots
15. ne renversaient personne
16. faible
17. trottoir
18. magasins
19. toilettes
20. la foule
21. écrasés les uns contre les autres
22. rassembler
23. cabines téléphoniques

Suddenly I realized that I could telephone the clinic and save myself the journey and the ordeal[1] of telling my story face to face. It was stupid of me, I see that now, but at the time it seemed a very good idea. It would be easier to conceal my identity on the telephone and I felt that I should be able to explain more fully. I also gained a great deal of comfort from the thought that, if the conversation became too difficult, I could always ring off[2]. You see, I was being very cowardly[3] and my only excuse is that I was very tired, far more tired than I imagined possible. I expect you will say that I ought to have gone straight to the police, to Scotland Yard. But Scotland Yard is a place I associate with detective stories and murders. It hardly seems possible that it actually exists and you can call there and tell your story. Besides, I was still very anxious to avoid publicity. I didn't think the police would welcome someone who wanted help, but wasn't prepared to co-operate by telling the whole story or being willing to prosecute[4]. All I wanted, you see, was to stop the blackmailer. It wasn't very public-spirited of me[5], was it?'

'It was very understandable,' replied Dalgliesh. 'I thought it very possible that Miss Bolam got the warning[6] by telephone. Can you remember what you said to her?'

'Not very clearly. I'm afraid. When I had found the four pennies for the call and looked up the number in the directory[7] I spent a few minutes deciding what I would say. A man's voice answered and I asked to speak to the administrative secretary. Then there was a woman's voice which said, "Administrative officer speaking." I hadn't expected to

1. épreuve
2. raccrocher
3. lâche
4. engager des poursuites judiciaires
5. je n'ai pas fait preuve de beaucoup d'esprit civique
6. avertissement
7. annuaire

hear a woman and I suddenly got it into my mind[1] that I was speaking to the blackmailer. After all, why not? So I said that someone from the clinic, and probably she, had been blackmailing my husband and that I was telephoning to say that she wouldn't get another penny from now on[2] and that if we received any more telephone calls we should go straight to the police. It all came out in a rush[3]. I was shaking rather badly and had to lean against the wall[4] of the telephone box for support. I must have sounded[5] a little hysterical. When she could get a word in[6] she asked me whether I was a patient and who was treating me and said something about asking one of the doctors to have a word with me. I suppose she thought I was out of my mind[7]. I replied that I had never attended the clinic and that, if ever I needed treatment, which God forbid[8], I should know better than to go to a place where a patient's indiscretions[9] and unhappiness were made an opportunity for blackmail. I think I ended up by saying that there was a woman involved[10], that she must have been at the clinic for nearly ten years, and that, if the administrative officer wasn't the person concerned, I hoped that she would make it her duty to[11] discover who was. She tried to get[12] me to leave my name or to come to see her, but I rang off.'

'Did you give her any details about how the blackmail was organized?'

'I told her that my husband had sent fifteen pounds a month in an envelope addressed in green ink. That's when she became suddenly very anxious that I should visit the clinic or at least leave my name. It was rude[13] of me to ring off without end-

1. j'ai pensé
2. dorénavant
3. tout s'est passé très vite
4. m'appuyer contre la paroi
5. j'ai dû avoir l'air
6. dès qu'elle a pu placer un mot
7. j'avais perdu la tête
8. Dieu m'en garde
9. erreurs
10. il s'agissait d'une femme
11. se ferait un devoir de
12. convaincre
13. impoli

ing the conversation, but I suddenly became frightened. I don't know why. And I had said all that I meant to say. One of the chairs in the rest-room was vacant by then, so I sat down for half an hour until I felt better. Then I went straight to Charing Cross[1] and had some coffee and sandwiches in the buffet there and waited for my train home. I read about the murder in the paper[2] on Saturday and I'm afraid I took it for granted[3] that one of the other victims – for there must have been others, surely – had taken that way out[4]. I didn't connect the crime with my telephone call, at least, not at first. Then I began to wonder whether it might not be my duty to let the police know what had been going on at that dreadful place. Yesterday I talked to my husband about it and we decided to do nothing in a hurry[5]. We thought it might be best to wait and see whether we received any further calls from the blackmailer. I wasn't very happy about our silence. There haven't been many details of the murder in the papers, so I don't know what exactly happened. But I did realize that the blackmail might be in some way connected with the crime and that the police would wish to know about it. While I was still worrying about what to do, Dr Etherege telephoned. You know the rest. I'm still wondering how you managed to trace me[6].'

'We found you in the same way as the blackmailer picked out Colonel Fenton, from the clinic diagnostic index and the medical record. You mustn't think that they don't look after[7] their confidential papers at the Steen. They do. Dr Etherege is very distressed indeed about the blackmail. But no sys-

1. une des grandes gares londoniennes
2. dans le journal
3. il m'est paru naturel
4. choisi cette solution
5. dans la précipitation
6. vous avez réussi à me trouver
7. ils ne font pas attention à

tem is completely proof against[1] clever and deliberate wickedness[2].'

'You will find him, won't you?' she asked. 'You will find him?'

'Thanks to you, I think we shall,' Dalgliesh replied. As he held out[3] his hand to say goodbye, she suddenly asked:

'What was she like, Superintendent? I mean the woman who was murdered. Tell me about Miss Bolam.'

Dalgliesh said:

'She was forty-one years old. Not married. I never saw her alive[4], but she had light brown hair[5] and blue-grey eyes. She was rather stout[6], wide browed[7], thin mouthed[8]. She was an only child[9] and both her parents were dead. She lived rather a lonely[10] life, but her church meant a great deal to her[11] and she was a Guide captain. She liked children and flowers. She was conscientious and efficient, but not very good at understanding people. She was kind when they were in trouble[12] but they thought her rigid, humourless[13] and censorious[14]. I think they were probably right. She had a great sense of duty[15].'

'I am responsible for her death. I have to accept that.'

Dalgliesh said gently:

'That's nonsense[16], you know. Only one person is responsible and, thanks to you, we shall get him.'

She shook[17] her head.

'If I had come to you in the first place[18] or even had the courage to turn up[19] at the clinic instead of telephoning she would be alive today.'

1. à l'épreuve de
2. méchanceté
3. tendit
4. de son vivant
5. cheveux châtain clair
6. corpulente
7. avait un front large
8. avait des lèvres minces
9. enfant unique
10. solitaire
11. comptait beaucoup pour elle
12. avaient des ennuis
13. dépourvue d'humour
14. sévère
15. devoir
16. ne dites pas des absurdités
17. secoua
18. d'abord
19. aller

Dalgliesh thought that Louise Fenton deserved[1] better than to be pacified[2] with easy lies[3]. And they would have brought[4] no comfort. Instead he replied:

'I suppose that could be true. There are so many "ifs[5]". She would be alive today if her group secretary had cancelled[6] a meeting and hurried[7] to the clinic, if she herself had gone at once to see him, if an old porter hadn't had stomach-ache. You did what you thought right and no one can do more.'

'So did she[8], poor woman,' replied Mrs Fenton. 'And look where it led her[9].'

She patted[10] Dalgliesh briefly on the shoulder, as if it were he who needed the comfort and reassurance.

'I didn't mean to bore you[11]. Please forgive me[12]. You've been very patient and kind. Might I ask one more question? You said that, thanks to me, you would get this murderer. Do you know now who it is?'

'Yes,' said Dalgliesh. 'I think I now know who it is.'

1. méritait
2. calmée
3. mensonges
4. apporté
5. si
6. annulé
7. s'était dépêché d'aller
8. elle aussi
9. voyez où ça l'a menée
10. tapota
11. je n'avais pas l'intention de vous ennuyer
12. pardonnez-moi

CHAPTER SEVEN

Back in his office at the Yard just over two hours later, Dalgliesh talked over the case with Sergeant Martin. The file lay open on the desk before him.

'You got corroboration[1] of Mrs Fenton's story all right, sir?'

'Oh, yes. The colonel was quite forthcoming[2]. Now that he's recovered[3] from the twin ordeals[4] of his operation and the confession to his wife, he's inclined[5] to take both experiences rather lightly[6]. He even suggested that the request for money could have been genuine and that it was reasonable to assume that it was. I had to point out that a woman has been murdered before he faced the realities of the situation. Then he gave me the full story[7]. It agreed with what Mrs Fenton had told me except for one interesting addition. I give you three guesses[8].'

'Would it be about the burglary? It was Fenton I suppose?'

'Damn you Martin, you might make an effort sometimes to look surprised. Yes, it was our colonel. But he didn't take the fifteen pounds. I wouldn't have blamed him if he had[9]. The money was his after all. He admits himself that he would have taken it back[10] if he'd seen it, but, of course, he didn't. He was there for quite another purpose,

1. confirmation
2. ouvert
3. il s'est remis
4. double épreuve
5. il a tendance
6. à la légère
7. il m'a raconté toute l'histoire
8. je vous laisse trois chances de deviner de quoi il s'agit
9. je n'aurais pas pu le lui reprocher, si c'était lui
10. il l'aurait repris

to get hold of[1] that medical record. He was a bit out of his depth[2] in most things but he did realize that the medical record was the only real evidence of what happened when he was a patient at the Steen. He mucked up[3] his burglary attempt of course despite having practised glass-cutting in his greenhouse, and made an undignified[4] exit when he heard Nagle and Cully arriving. He got nowhere near the record he wanted[5]. He assumed it was in one of the files in the general office and managed to prise those open[6]. When he saw that the records were filed numerically[7] he knew he couldn't succeed. He had long forgotten his clinic number. I expect he put it firmly out of his mind[8] when he felt he was cured.'

'Well, the clinic did that for him, anyway.'

'He doesn't admit it I can tell you. I believe that's not uncommon with psychiatric patients. It must be rather disheartening[9] for psychiatrists. After all, you don't get surgical patients claiming that they could have performed their own operation[10] given half a chance[11]. No, the colonel isn't feeling particularly grateful to the Steen, nor inclined to give the clinic much credit for keeping him out of trouble[12]. I suppose he could be right. I don't imagine that Dr Etherege would claim that you can do a great deal for a psychiatric patient in four months which was the length of time Fenton attended. His cure – if you can call it that – probably had something to do with leaving the army. It's difficult to judge whether he welcomed that[13] or dreaded it[14]. Anyway, we'd better resist the temptation to be amateur psychologists.'

'What sort of man is the colonel, sir?'

1. mettre la main sur
2. dépassé
3. il a raté
4. manquant de dignité
5. il n'est pas du tout arrivé à trouver le dossier qu'il cherchait
6. a réussi à les forcer
7. par ordre numérique
8. l'avait délibérément oublié
9. décourageant
10. ils se seraient opérés eux-mêmes
11. si on leur en avait laissé la chance
12. pour lui avoir épargné des ennuis
13. s'il s'en réjouissait
14. ou s'il en avait peur

'Small. Probably looks smaller because of his illness. Sandy hair[1]; bushy eyebrows[2]. Rather like a small fierce[3] animal glaring out[4] from its hole[5]. A much weaker[6] personality than his wife, I'd say, despite[7] Mrs Fenton's apparent frailty[8]. Admittedly it's difficult to be at one's best[9] lying in a hospital bed wearing a striped bedjacket[10] and with a formidable Sister warning one to be a good boy[11] and not talk too long. He wasn't very helpful about the telephone voice. He says that it sounded like a woman and it never occurred to him that it mightn't be. On the other hand he wasn't surprised when I suggested that the voice could have been disguised. But he's honest, and, obviously, he can't go further than that. He just doesn't know. Still, we've got the motive. This is one of those rare cases in which knowing why is knowing who.'

'Are you applying for a warrant?[12]'

'Not yet. We're not ready. If we don't go carefully[13] now the whole case could come apart[14] in our hands.'

Again he was visited by[15] the chilling[16] presentiment of disaster. He found himself analysing the case as if he had already failed. Where had it gone wrong? He had shown his hand[17] to the murderer when he had taken the clinic diagnostic index so openly into the medical director's room. That fact would be round the clinic[18] quickly enough. He had meant it to be[19]. There came a time when it was useful to frighten[20] your man. But was this killer the kind who could be frightened into betraying himself[21]? Had it been an error of judgement to move so openly? Suddenly Martin's plain[22], honest face looked irritatingly bovine[23] as he stood

1. d'un blond roux
2. sourcils broussailleux
3. féroce
4. lançant des regards furieux
5. depuis son terrier
6. moins forte
7. malgré
8. fragilité
9. en pleine forme
10. chemise d'hôpital rayée
11. l'enjoignant d'être sage
12. vous allez demander un mandat ?
13. avec précaution
14. se désagréger
15. il avait à nouveau
16. qui donne des frissons
17. avait montré son jeu
18. ferait le tour de la clinique
19. il l'avait voulu
20. effrayer
21. qu'on pouvait amener à se trahir en lui faisant peur
22. banal
23. bovin

there unhelpfully[1] waiting for instructions. Dalgliesh said:

'You went to the Priddys' place[2], I suppose. Well, let's have the dirt about that[3]. The girl is married, I suppose?'

'There's no doubt about that, sir. I was there earlier this evening and I had a chat[4] with the parents. Luckily[5] Miss Priddy was out, fetching fish and chips for supper. They're in quite poor circumstances[6].'

'That's a *non sequitur*[7]. However, go on.'

'There isn't much to report. They live in one of those terrace houses[8] leading down[9] to the southern railway line[10] in Balham. Everything's very comfortable and neat but there's no television or anything like that. I suppose their religion's against it. Both the Priddys are over sixty I reckon[11]. Jennifer's the only child and her mother must have been more than forty when she was born. It's the usual story about the marriage. I was surprised they told me but they did. The husband's a warehouseman[12]; used to work with the girl at her last job. Then there was a baby on the way[13] so they had to get married.'

'It's almost pitiably[14] common. You'd think that her generation[15], who think they know all the answers about sex, would make themselves familiar with[16] a few basic facts. However, we're told these little mishaps[17] don't worry anyone these days.'

Dalgliesh was shocked by the bitterness[18] in his own voice. Was it really necessary, he wondered, to protest quite so vehemently about so common a little tragedy? What was happening to him? Martin said stolidly:

1. sans aider
2. vous êtes allé chez les Priddy
3. racontez-moi tout
4. j'ai discuté
5. heureusement
6. ils n'ont pas beaucoup d'argent
7. je ne vois pas le rapport
8. rangées de maisons
9. qui mènent
10. voie ferrée
11. je pense
12. manutentionnaire
13. un bébé en route
14. lamentablement
15. les jeunes de sa génération
16. se seraient informés sur
17. mésaventures
18. amertume

'They worry people like the Priddys. These kids get themselves into trouble[1] but it's usually the despised[2] older generation who have to cope[3]. The Priddys did their best[4]. They made the kids marry of course. There isn't much room in the house[5] but they gave up the first floor[6] and made it into a small flat for the young couple. Very nicely done it was too. They showed me.'

Dalgliesh thought how much he disliked the expression 'young couple' with its cosy undertones of dewy-eyed domesticity[7], its echo of disillusion[8].

'You seem to have made a hit[9] in your brief visit,' he said.

'I liked them, sir. They're good people. The marriage didn't last[10] of course, and I think that they wonder now whether they did the right thing in forcing it. The chap[11] left Balham over two years ago and they don't know where he is now. They told me his name and I saw his photograph. He's got nothing to do with the Steen Clinic, sir.'

'I didn't think he had. We hardly expected to discover that Jennifer Priddy was Mrs Henry Etherege. Neither her parents nor her husband have anything to do with this crime.'

Nor had they, except that their lives, like flying tangents[12], had made brief contact with the circle of death. Every murder case produced such people. Dalgliesh had sat more times than he could remember in sitting-rooms, bedrooms, pubs and police stations talking to people who had come, however briefly, in touch[13] with murder. Violent death was a great releaser of[14] inhibitions, the convulsive kick which spun open the top of so many ant hills[15]. His job, in which he could deceive himself that non-

1. ces gamins s'attirent des ennuis
2. méprisée
3. s'en charger
4. ont fait de leur mieux
5. la maison n'est pas bien grande
6. ils leur ont cédé le premier étage
7. la vie de famille innocente et chaleureuse qu'elle évoquait
8. désillusion
9. vous semblez avoir remporté un franc succès
10. n'a pas duré
11. type
12. tangentes
13. qui étaient entrés en contact, ne fût-ce que brièvement
14. débloquait facilement
15. coup de pied dans la fourmilière

involvement[1] was a duty, had given him glimpses into[2] the secret lives of men and women whom he might never see again except as half-recognized faces in a London crowd. Sometimes he despised[3] his private image, the patient, uninvolved[4], uncensorious[5] inquisitor[6] of other people's misery and guilt. How long could you stay detached, he wondered, before you lost your own soul[7]?

'What happened to the child?' he asked suddenly.

'She had a miscarriage[8], sir,' answered Martin.

'Of course,' thought Dalgliesh. 'She would.' Nothing could go right for such as the Priddys. Tonight he felt that he, too, was tainted with their ill luck[9]. He asked what Martin had learned about Miss Bolam.

'Not much that we didn't know already. They went to the same church and Jennifer Priddy used to be a Girl Guide in Bolam's company. The old people spoke of her with a great deal of[10] respect. She was helpful to them when the baby was on the way – I got the impression that she paid to have the house converted – and when the marriage failed she suggested that the Priddy child should work at the Steen. I think the old people were glad to think that someone was keeping an eye on Jenny. They couldn't tell me much about Miss Bolam's private life, at least nothing that we don't know. There was one odd[11] thing though. It happened when the girl got back with the supper[12]. Mrs Priddy asked me to stay and have a meal with them but I said I'd better be getting back. You know what it is with fish and chips. You just buy the right number of pieces and it isn't easy to fit in an extra[13]. Anyway, they called the girl in to say "goodbye" and she came in from

1. neutralité
2. lui avait laissé entrevoir
3. méprisait
4. neutre
5. indulgent
6. enquêteur
7. âme
8. elle a fait une fausse couche
9. malchance
10. beaucoup de
11. bizarre
12. souper
13. une personne supplémentaire

the kitchen looking like death[1]. She only stayed a second or two and the old people didn't seem to notice anything. But I did. Something had scared the kid properly[2].'

'Finding you there, perhaps. She may have thought that you'd mentioned her friendship with Nagle.'

'I don't think it was that, sir. She looked into the sitting-room when she first got back from the shop and said "good evening" without turning a hair[3]. I explained that I was just having a chat with her parents because they were friends of Miss Bolam and might be able to tell us something useful about her private life. It didn't seem to worry her. It was about five minutes later that she came back looking so odd.'

'No one arrived at the house or telephoned during that time?'

'No. I heard no one anyway. They aren't on the phone[4]. I suppose it was something that occurred to her[5] while she was alone in the kitchen. I couldn't very well ask her. I was on my way out and there wasn't anything you could put tongue to[6]. I just told them all that if they thought of anything that might help they should let us know at once.'

'We've got to see her again, of course, and the sooner the better[7]. That alibi's got to be broken[8] and she's the only one who can do it. I don't think the girl was consciously lying[9], or even deliberately withholding[10] evidence. The truth simply never occurred to her.'

'Nor to me, sir, until we got the motive. What do you want to do now? Let him sweat[11] a bit?'

1. extrêmement pâle
2. quelque chose lui avait fait une peur bleue
3. sans sourciller
4. ils n'ont pas le téléphone
5. qui lui est venu à l'esprit
6. rien à dire
7. le plus tôt possible
8. démoli
9. mentait consciemment
10. dissimulait
11. se faire du mauvais sang

'I daren't, Martin. It's too dangerous. We've got to press on[1]. I think we'll go now and have a little chat with Nagle.'

But when they reached the Pimlico house twenty minutes later they found the flat locked and a folded scrap of paper[2] wedged[3] under the knocker[4]. Dalgliesh smoothed it out[5] and read aloud[6]. 'Darling. Sorry I missed you[7]. I must speak to you. If I don't see you tonight I'll be at the clinic early. Love, Jenny.'

'Any point in waiting for him[8], sir?'

'I doubt it[9]. I think I can guess where he is. Cully was on the board when we did our phoning this morning but I made sure that Nagle, and probably everyone else at the Steen, knew that I was interesting myself in the medical records. I asked Dr Etherege to put them back[10] after I left. Nagle goes into the Steen on one or two evenings in the week to see to[11] the boiler[12] and turn off[13] the art therapy department kiln[14]. I imagine that he's there tonight, taking the opportunity of seeing which records have been moved. We'll look in[15] anyway.'

As the car moved northwards[16] towards the river, Martin said:

'It's easy to see that he needed the cash. You couldn't rent[17] a flat like that on[18] a porter's pay[19]. And then there would be his painting gear[20].'

'Yes. The studio is pretty impressive[21]: I should like you to have seen it. And there were the lessons from Sugg. Nagle may have got those on the cheap[22] but Sugg doesn't teach for nothing. I don't think the blackmailing was particularly lucrative[23]. That's where he was clever. There was probably more than one victim and the amounts were nicely

1. continuer
2. un bout de papier plié
3. coincé
4. heurtoir
5. le déplia
6. à voix haute
7. désolée de voir que je t'ai raté
8. ça vaut la peine de l'attendre ?
9. je ne crois pas
10. de les remettre à leur place
11. pour s'occuper de
12. chaudière
13. éteindre
14. four
15. on va passer voir
16. en direction du nord
17. louer
18. avec
19. salaire
20. matériel de peinture
21. impressionnant
22. à moindre coût
23. lucratif

calculated. But even if he only made fifteen to thirty pounds a month, tax free[1], it would be enough to carry him over[2] until he won the Bollinger or made his name[3].'

'Is he any good[4]?' asked Sergeant Martin. There were subjects on which he never expressed an opinion but took it for granted that his Super was an expert.

'The trustees of the Bollinger Trust[5] think so apparently.'

'There's not much doubt is there[6], sir?' And Martin was not referring to Nagle's talent for painting. Dalgliesh said irritably[7]:

'Of course there's doubt. There always is at this stage[8] of an investigation. But consider what we know. The blackmailer instructed[9] that the cash should be sent in a distinctively addressed envelope, presumably so that he could pick it out[10] before the post was opened. Nagle gets to the clinic first and is responsible for sorting[11] and distributing the post. Colonel Fenton was asked to send the money so that it arrived on the first of each month. Nagle came to the clinic on 1st May although[12] he was ill[13] and had to be taken home later. I don't think it was anxiety about the Duke's visit that brought him in[14]. The only time he didn't manage to get first to work was the day he got stuck[15] in the tube[16] and that was the day Miss Bolam received fifteen pounds from an unknown grateful patient.

'And now we come to the murder and theory replaces fact. Nagle was helping on the switchboard that morning because of Cully's belly-ache. He listens to Mrs Fenton's call. He knows what Miss Bolam's reaction will be and, sure enough, he is asked

1. exempts d'impôts
2. cela pouvait lui suffire
3. se faire un nom
4. doué
5. les administrateurs du fonds Bollinger
6. n'est-ce pas ?
7. avec irritation
8. stade
9. avait demandé
10. l'identifier et la récupérer
11. du tri
12. même si
13. malade
14. je ne pense pas qu'il soit allé à la clinique parce qu'il était inquiet à propos de la visite du duc
15. bloqué
16. métro

to put through a call to[1] the group offices. He listens again and learns that Mr Lauder will be at the Steen after the JCC meeting. Sometime before then Miss Bolam has got to die. But how? He can't hope to entice her[2] away from the Steen. What excuse could he use and how could he provide himself with[3] an alibi? No, it must be done in the clinic. And perhaps that isn't such a bad plan after all. The AO isn't popular[4]. With luck there will be plenty[5] of suspects to keep the police occupied, some of them with pretty good reasons for wishing Miss Bolam dead.

'So he makes his plans. It was obvious, of course, that the phone call to Miss Bolam wasn't necessarily made from the basement. Nearly all the rooms have telephones. But if the murderer wasn't in the record-room waiting for her how could he ensure that she would stay there until he could get down? That's why Nagle chucked the records about[6]. He knew Miss Bolam well enough to be fairly sure that she couldn't bear not to pick them up[7]. Dr Baguley thought that her first reaction might be to phone for Nagle to help. She didn't, of course, because she was expecting him to appear any minute. Instead she made a start on[8] the job herself, giving him the two or three minutes that he needed.

'This is what I think happened. At about ten past six he goes down to the porters' rest-room to put on his outdoor coat. It's then that he unlocks the record-room door and throws[9] the files on the floor. He leaves the light on[10] and shuts the door but doesn't bolt it[11]. Then he unlocks the back door. Next[12] he goes into the general office to collect the outgoing post[13]. Miss Priddy is there but periodically[14]

1. appeler
2. l'attirer
3. trouver
4. n'est pas beaucoup aimée
5. beaucoup
6. a éparpillé tous les dossiers par terre
7. elle ne résisterait pas à la tentation de les ramasser
8. commença
9. jette
10. allumée
11. mais pas à clé
12. ensuite
13. le courrier à expédier
14. de temps en temps

visits the adjoining[1] filing-room[2]. He only needs half a minute to telephone Miss Bolam and to ask her to come down to the record-room as he has something serious to show her. We know how she reacted to that message. Before Nagle has a chance to replace[3] the receiver Jennifer Priddy is back. He keeps his head[4], depresses the receiver rest[5], and pretends to[6] be speaking to Nurse Bolam about the laundry. Then, without wasting any more time, he leaves with the post. He has only to take it to the box across the road. Then he darts[7] down the mews[8], enters the basement by the unlocked back door, slips the chisel in his pocket, collects Tippett's fetish and enters the record-room. Miss Bolam is there as he expects, kneeling[9] to pick up[10] the torn[11] and scattered[12] files. She looks up at him, ready no doubt to ask where he's been. But before she has time to speak he strikes[13]. Once she's unconscious he can take his time over the stabbing[14]. There mustn't be any mistake, and there isn't. Nagle paints from the nude[15] and his knowledge of anatomy is probably as good as that of most psychiatrists. And he was handy with that chisel[16]. For this most important job he chose a tool he had confidence in and knew how to use[17].' Martin said:

'He couldn't have got down to the basement in time if he'd walked to the corner of Beefsteak Street for his *Standard*. But the newsboy[18] there couldn't swear[19] that he'd seen him. He was carrying a paper when he returned to the Steen but he could have got that in his lunch hour and kept it in his pocket.'

'I think he did,' said Dalgliesh. 'That's why he wouldn't let Cully see it to check the racing

1. à côté
2. pièce pour les archives
3. reposer
4. il garde la tête froide
5. appuie sur le commutateur
6. fait semblant de
7. file
8. la ruelle
9. à genoux
10. en train de ramasser
11. déchirés
12. éparpillés
13. il frappe
14. pour la poignarder
15. fait des études de nus
16. il savait très bien se servir de ce ciseau à bois
17. qu'il savait bien utiliser
18. le crieur de journaux
19. jurer

1. les résultats des courses
2. de midi
3. envelopper
4. avant de le brûler
5. sur ses talons
6. monté
7. il aurait fait attention à ne pas
8. très probablement
9. cambriolage
10. voleur
11. qu'il y avait droit
12. effraction
13. il valait mieux éviter que la police commence
14. intrus
15. mettre la main
16. le fait d'avoir piqué
17. a compliqué les choses
18. c'était particulièrement bien trouvé
19. le faire monter
20. avant de se glisser dehors

results[1]. Cully would have seen at once that it was the midday[2] edition. Instead Nagle takes it downstairs and later uses it to wrap up[3] the cat's food before burning it[4] in the boiler. He wasn't in the basement alone for long, of course. Jenny Priddy was hard on his heels[5]. But he had time to bolt the back door again and visit Nurse Bolam to ask if the clean laundry was ready to be carried upstairs[6]. If Priddy hadn't come down Nagle would have joined her in the general office. He would take care not to[7] be alone in the basement for more than a minute. The killing had to be fixed for the time when he was out with the post.' Martin said:

'I wondered why he didn't unbolt the basement door after the killing but like as not[8] he couldn't bring himself to draw attention to it. After all, if an outsider could have gained access that way it wouldn't take long for people to start thinking "and so could Nagle". He took that fifteen quid no doubt after Colonel Fenton's break-in[9]. The local boys always did think it odd that the thief[10] knew where to find it. Nagle thought he had a right to it[11] I suppose.'

'More likely he wanted to obscure the reason for the breaking[12], to make it look like a common burglary. It wouldn't do for the police to start[13] wondering why an unknown intruder[14] should want to get his hands[15] on the medical records. Pinching[16] that fifteen pounds – which only Nagle had the chance to do – confused the issue[17]. So did that business with the lift, of course. That was a nice touch[18]. It would only take a minute to wind it up[19] to the second floor before he slipped out[20] of the basement door and there was a reasonable chance that someone would hear it and remember.'

Sergeant Martin thought that it all hung together very well[1] but that it was going to be the devil to prove[2] and said so[3].

'That's why I showed my hand[4] at the clinic yesterday. We've got to get him rattled[5]. That's why it's worth looking in[6] at the Steen tonight. If he's there we'll put on the pressure a bit. At least we know now where we're going.'

Half an hour before Dalgliesh and Martin called at the Pimlico flat, Peter Nagle let himself into[7] the Steen by the front door and locked it behind him. He did not put on the lights but made his way to[8] the basement with the aid of his heavy torch. There wasn't much to be done: just the kiln[9] to be turned off, the boiler inspected. Then there was a little matter of his own[10] to be attended to[11]. It would mean entering the record-room but that warm, echoing place of death[12] had no terror for him. The dead[13] were dead, finished, powerless, silenced[14] for ever. In a world of increasing uncertainty that much was certain. A man with the nerve to kill had much that he might reasonably fear. But he had nothing to fear from the dead.

It was then that he heard the front-door bell[15]. It was a hesitant, tentative[16] ring but it sounded unnaturally loud[17] in the silence of the clinic. When he opened the door the figure of Jenny slid through[18] so quickly that she seemed to pass by him like a wraith[19], a slim ghost[20] born of the darkness[21] and mist[22] of the night. She said breathlessly[23]:

1. tout ça se tenait très bien
2. très difficile à prouver
3. et le dit
4. j'ai dévoilé mon jeu
5. il faut qu'il perde son sang-froid
6. ça vaut la peine d'aller faire un tour
7. était rentré dans
8. se dirigea vers
9. four
10. petite chose personnelle
11. à faire
12. cet endroit qui sentait la mort
13. les morts
14. réduits au silence
15. sonnette
16. timide
17. étrangement fort
18. se glissa
19. apparition
20. fantôme
21. obscurité
22. brume
23. en haletant

'I'm sorry darling, I had to see you. When you weren't at the studio I thought you might be here.'

'Did anyone see you at the studio?' he asked. He felt that the question was important without knowing why.

She looked up at him surprised.

'No. The house seemed empty. I didn't meet anyone. Why?'

'Nothing. It doesn't matter. Come on downstairs. I'll light[1] the gas stove[2]. You're shivering[3].'

They went down to the basement together, their footsteps[4] echoing in the eerie[5], presageful[6] calm of a house which, with tomorrow[7], would awaken[8] to voices, movement and the ceaseless hum[9] of purposeful[10] activity. She began walking on tiptoe[11] and when she spoke it was in whispers[12]. At the top of the stairs she reached for his hand[13] and he could feel hers trembling. Halfway down there was a sudden faint noise and she started[14].

'What is it? What's that noise?'

'Nothing. Tigger in his scratch tin[15] I imagine.'

When they were in the rest-room and the fire was lit he threw himself[16] into one of the armchairs and smiled up at her. It was the devil of a nuisance[17] that she should turn up now but somehow he must hide his irritation. With any luck[18] he could get rid of her fairly quickly. She would be out of the clinic well before ten.

'Well?' he asked.

Suddenly she was on the rug[19] at his feet and clasping his thighs[20]. Her pale eyes searched his in passionate entreaty[21].

'Darling, I've got to know! I don't mind what you've done as long as I know[22]. I love you and I

1. je vais allumer
2. gazinière
3. tu trembles
4. pas
5. inquiétant
6. plein de présages
7. le lendemain
8. s'éveillerait
9. bourdonnement incessant
10. réfléchie
11. sur la pointe des pieds
12. en murmurant
13. elle prit sa main
14. sursauta
15. bac
16. se jeta
17. extrêmement pénible
18. avec un peu de chance
19. tapis
20. et serra ses cuisses
21. supplication
22. pourvu que je sache

want to help. Darling, you must tell me if you're in any trouble[1].'

It was worse than he feared. Somehow she had got hold of[2] something. But how, and what? Keeping his voice light he asked:

'What sort of trouble for God's sake? You'll be saying next that I killed her.'

'Oh, Peter, please don't joke[3]! I've been worried. There is something wrong, I know there is. It's the money isn't it? You took that fifteen pounds.'

He could have laughed aloud[4] with relief. In a surge[5] of emotion he put his arms round her and drew her down upon him, his voice muffled[6] in her hair.

'You silly kid. I could have helped myself to the petty cash[7] any time if I wanted to steal[8]. What the hell started you off on this nonsense?[9]'

'That's what I've been telling myself. Why should you take it? Oh, darling, don't be angry with me. I've been so worried. You see, it was the paper.'

'What paper, for God's sake.' It was all he could do not to shake her into coherence[10]. He was glad that she could not see his face. So long as[11] he need not meet her eyes he could fight his anger and the fatal, insidious panic. What in God's name was she trying to say?

'The *Standard*. That sergeant came to see us this evening. I'd been to fetch the fish and chips. When I was unwrapping them[12] in the kitchen I looked at the paper they were wrapped in. It was Friday's *Standard* and it had a large picture[13] of that air crash[14], all over the front page[15]. Then I remembered that we had used your *Standard* to wrap up

1. si tu as des ennuis

2. elle avait réussi à apprendre

3. ne plaisante pas

4. éclater de rire

5. accès

6. étouffée

7. j'aurais pu prendre l'argent de la petite caisse

8. voler

9. qu'est-ce qui a bien pu te faire croire une telle bêtise ?

10. pour l'empêcher de penser avec cohérence

11. tant que

12. pendant que je le déballais

13. photo

14. accident d'avion

15. qui faisait la une

Tigger's food and the front page was different. I hadn't seen that picture before.'

He tightened his hold on her[1] and said very quietly:

'Did you say anything about this to the police?'

'Darling, of course I didn't! Suppose it made them suspect you! I didn't say anything to anyone; but I needed to see you. I don't care about the fifteen pounds. I don't care if you did meet her in the basement. I know you didn't kill her. All I want is for you to trust me[2]. I love you and I want to help. I can't bear it if you keep things from me[3].'

That's what they all said but there wasn't one in a million who really wanted to know the truth about a man. For a second he was tempted to tell her, spit[4] the whole brutal story into her silly pleading[5] face and watch the sudden draining away of pity and love[6]. She could probably bear to know about Bolam. What she couldn't bear would be the knowledge that he hadn't blackmailed for her sake[7], that he hadn't acted to preserve their love, that there wasn't any love to preserve and never had been. He would have to marry her, of course. He had always known that it might be necessary. Only she could effectively witness[8] against him and there was one sure way to stop her tongue[9]. But time was short[10]. He planned to be in Paris by the end of the week. Now it looked as if he wouldn't be travelling alone. He thought quickly. Shifting[11] her weight to the arm[12] of the chair but still keeping his arms[13] around her, his face resting[14] against her cheek he said softly:

'Listen darling. There's something you've got to know. I didn't tell you before because I didn't want

1. la serra plus fortement
2. que tu me fasses confiance
3. si tu me caches des choses
4. cracher
5. suppliant
6. regarder l'amour et la pitié disparaître soudainement
7. pour elle
8. témoigner
9. l'empêcher de parler
10. le temps pressait
11. en déplaçant
12. accoudoir
13. bras
14. posé

to worry you. I did take the fifteen quid. It was a bloody stupid thing[1] to do but there's no sense in[2] worrying about that now. I suppose Miss Bolam might have guessed. I don't know. She didn't say anything to me and it wasn't I who phoned her. But I was in the basement after she was killed. I left the back door open and came back that way. I get sick[3] of that old fool Cully booking me in and out[4] as if I were as nutty[5] as a patient and asking for the paper as soon as I appear. Why can't he buy his own, the mean old devil. I thought I'd fool him for once[6]. When I came in at the basement door I saw that there was a light in the record-room and the door was ajar, so I went to look. I found her body. I knew that I daren't be found there, particularly if they ever discovered about the fifteen quid, so I said nothing and left again by the back door and came in as usual by the front. I've kept quiet ever since[7]. I must, darling. I've got to take up[8] the Bollinger by the end of this week and the police wouldn't let me go if they started suspecting me. If I don't get away now I'll never have the chance again as long as I live.'

That at least was true. He had to get away now. It had become an obsession. It wasn't only the money, the freedom, the sun and the colours. It was the final vindication[9] of the lean, pallid years[10] of struggle[11] and humiliation. He had to take up the Bollinger. Other painters could fail[12] here and still succeed[13] in the end. But not he.

And, even now, he might fail. It was a thin story[14]. He was struck[15], as he spoke, by the inconsistencies[16], the improbabilities. But it hung together[17] – just[18]. He couldn't see how she could prove it false[19].

1. une connerie
2. ce n'est pas la peine de
3. j'en ai ras-le-bol
4. qui contrôle mes allées et venues
5. cinglé
6. j'ai eu envie de le mener en bateau pour une fois
7. je n'ai plus ouvert ma bouche depuis
8. recevoir
9. légitimation
10. pâles années de vaches maigres
11. combats
12. échouer
13. réussir
14. une histoire peu crédible
15. frappé
16. incohérences
17. ça se tenait
18. plus ou moins
19. prouver que c'était faux

And she wouldn't want to try. But he was surprised by her reaction.

'By the end of this week! You mean, you're going to Paris almost at once. What about the clinic... your job?'

'For God's sake, Jenny, what the hell does that matter? I shall leave without notice[1] and they'll find someone else. They'll have to do without me.'

'And me?'

'You're coming with me of course. I always meant that you should. Surely you knew that?'

'No,' she said, and it seemed to him that her voice held a great sadness. 'No, I never knew that.'

He tried to assume a tone of confidence tinged with[2] slight[3] reproach.

'I never discussed it because I thought there were some things we didn't need to say. I know the time's short but it'll be easier if you don't have to stick around[4] too long at home waiting. They'd only get suspicious. You've got a passport, haven't you? Didn't you go to France with the Guides that Easter[5]? What I suggest is that we marry by special licence[6] as soon as possible – after all we've got the money now – and write to your parents when we get to Paris. You do want to come, don't you, Jenny?'

Suddenly she was shaking in his arms and he felt the warm wetness[7] of her tears stinging his face[8].

'I thought you meant to go without me. The days went by[9] and you never said anything. Of course, I want to come. I don't care what happens as long as we're together. But we can't get married. I never told you because I was afraid you'd be angry and

1. sans prévenir
2. teinté de
3. petite
4. rester
5. à Pâques
6. avec dispense
7. humidité
8. larmes qui lui piquaient le visage
9. passaient

you've never asked me anything about myself. I can't get married because I'm married already.'

The car had turned into Vauxhall Bridge Road but traffic was heavy[1] and they were making poor time[2]. Dalgliesh sat back in his seat as if all day were before[3] him, but inwardly[4] he was fidgeting with anxiety[5]. He could discover no rational cause for this impatience. The call at the Steen was merely speculative. The chances[6] were that Nagle, if indeed he had called at the clinic, would have left before they arrived. Probably he was even now putting down[7] his evening pint in some Pimlico pub. At the next corner[8] the traffic lights[9] were against them and the car slowed to a halt[10] for thc third time in a hundred yards. Suddenly Martin said:

'He couldn't have got away with it[11] for long, even by killing Bolam. Sooner or later Mrs Fenton – or another victim maybe – would have turned up[12] at the Steen.'

Dalgliesh replied:

'But he might well have got away with it for long enough to take up the Bollinger. And even if the blackmailing came to light[13] before he got away[14] – what could we prove? What can we prove now, come to that[15]? With Bolam dead what jury could be sure beyond reasonable doubt[16] that she wasn't the blackmailer? Nagle's only got to say that he remembers seeing the odd envelope addressed in green ink and that he placed it with the AO's post. Fenton will confirm that he thought the telephone calls came from a woman. And blackmailers do occasionally come to a violent end. Nagle wouldn't go on with it after Mrs Fenton's call. Even that would

1. il y avait beaucoup de circulation
2. ils n'avançaient pas
3. devant
4. secrètement
5. rongé d'inquiétude
6. le plus probable
7. en train d'avaler
8. angle
9. les feux
10. s'arrêta
11. il ne s'en serait pas tiré
12. se serait présentée
13. était découvert
14. avant son départ
15. si on y pense
16. sans le moindre doute

help his case. Bolam dies and the blackmailing stops. Oh, I know all the arguments against it! But what can anyone prove?'

Martin said stolidly[1]:

'He'll try to be too clever[2]. They always do. The girl's under his thumb[3] of course, poor little devil. If she sticks to her story[4] that he wasn't alone long enough to make that call...

'She'll stick all right, Sergeant.'

'I'm pretty sure he doesn't know about the husband. If she looks dangerous he probably thinks that he can stop her tongue[5] by marrying her.'

Dalgliesh said quietly:

'What we've got to do is to pull him in[6] before he finds out that he can't.'

1. flegmatiquement
2. malin
3. sous sa coupe
4. si elle reste fidèle à sa version
5. lui clouer le bec
6. le coincer

In the porters' room at the Steen, Nagle was writing a letter. He wrote easily. The glib[7] and lying[8] phrases[9] flowed[10] with unexpected ease[11]. He would have died rather than send such a letter. It would have been unbearable to think that any eyes could see this spate[12] of emotional clap-trap[13] and recognize it as his. But the letter never would be read except by Jenny. Within thirty minutes it would be thrust[14] into the boiler, its purpose served and the oily phrases only an uncomfortable memory. In the meantime he might as well make it convincing. It was easy enough to guess what Jenny would want him to say. He turned over[15] the paper and wrote:

> By the time you read[16] this we shall be in France together. I know that this will cause you very great unhappiness, but please believe me when I say that we can't live with-

7. enjôleuses
8. mensongères
9. expressions
10. coulaient
11. facilité
12. avalanche
13. baratin émotionnel
14. plongée
15. retourna
16. quand vous lirez

out each other. I know that one day we shall be free to marry. Until then Jenny will be safe[1] with me and I shall spend[2] my life trying to make her happy. Please try to understand and to forgive.

It was a good ending[3], he thought. It would appeal to[4] Jenny, anyway, and no one else was going to see it. He called to her and pushed the paper across the table.

'Will this do?[5]'

She read it in silence.

'I suppose so.'

'Damn it all kid[6], what's wrong with it?' He felt a surge of anger that his careful effort should be found inadequate. He had expected, and had braced himself to meet[7], her astonished gratitude. She said quietly:

'Nothing's wrong with it.'

'You'd better write your bit then. Not on the end. Take a fresh sheet[8].'

He slid[9] the paper across the table at her, not meeting her eyes[10]. This was taking time, and he could not be sure how much time there was.

'Better make it short,' he said.

She took up the pen but made no effort to write.

'I don't know what to say.'

'There isn't much you need say. I've said it all.'

'Yes,' she said with great sadness. 'You've said it all.'

He kept[11] the rising[12] irritation from his voice and told her:

'Just write that you're sorry to cause them unhappiness, but you can't help yourself[13]. Something

1. en sécurité
2. passerai
3. fin
4. elle plairait à
5. est-ce que ça ira ?
6. bon sang !
7. s'était préparé à
8. feuille blanche
9. fit glisser
10. sans la regarder
11. refréna
12. montante
13. tu ne peux pas t'en empêcher

like that. Damn it all, you're not going to the end[1] of the world. It's up to them[2]. If they want to see you I shan't stop them[3]. Don't pile the agony on too much[4]. I'm going upstairs to mend[5] that lock[6] in Miss Saxon's room. When I come down we're going to celebrate. There's only beer, but tonight you'll drink beer, my darling, and like it[7].'

He took a screwdriver[8] from the tool box and went out quickly before she had time to protest. His last glimpse was of[9] her frightened face staring after him[10]. But she didn't call him back.

Upstairs it was a moment's work only to slip on[11] a pair of rubber gloves and prise open[12] the door of the dangerous-drugs[13] cupboard. It gave[14] with a terrifyingly loud crack[15] so that he stood rooted[16] for a moment half expecting to hear her call. But there was no sound. He remembered clearly that scene some six months ago when one of Dr Baguley's patients had become violent and disorientated. Nagle had helped to control him while Baguley had called to Sister for paraldehyde[17]. Nagle recalled the words[18]:

'We'll give it in beer[19]. It's pretty filthy stuff[20] but they can hardly taste it[21] in beer. Odd that. Two drams[22], Sister, to 2 cc.'

And Jenny, who disliked beer, would taste it even less.

Quickly he put the screwdriver and the small blue bottle of paraldehyde in his jacket pocket and slipped out, lighting his way with the torch. All the clinic curtains were drawn[23], but it was important to show as little light as possible. He needed at least another undisturbed half-hour.

1. à l'autre bout
2. ça dépend d'eux
3. je ne les en empêcherai pas
4. ne dramatise pas à l'excès
5. réparer
6. serrure
7. et tu aimeras ça
8. tournevis
9. il aperçut
10. qui le fixait
11. enfiler
12. forcer
13. médicaments dangereux
14. céda
15. craquement
16. immobile
17. paraldéhyde
18. se souvenait des mots
19. on le mélangera à la bière
20. ça a un goût affreux
21. ils peuvent à peine le sentir
22. deux petits verres
23. tirés

She looked up in surprise at his quick reappearance. He went over to her and kissed the back of her neck[1].

'I'm sorry sweetie[2], I shouldn't have left you. I'd forgotten that you might be nervous. The lock can wait, anyway. How's the letter going?'

She pushed it over to him. He turned his back on her to read the few carefully penned[3] lines deliberately, taking his time. But his luck had held[4]. It was as neat[5] and convincing a suicide note[6] as was ever read in a Coroner's court[7]. He couldn't have dictated anything better. He felt a surge of confidence and excitement as he did when a painting was going well. Nothing could spoil[8] it now. Jenny had written:

> I can't say I'm sorry for what I've done. I haven't any choice. I feel so happy and it would all be perfect if I didn't know that I'm making you miserable[9]. But it's the only and best thing for me. Please try to understand. I love you very much. Jenny.

He put the letter back on the table and went to pour out[10] the beer, his actions hidden[11] by the open door of the cupboard. God, the stuff did stink[12]! Quickly he added[13] the foaming light ale[14] and called to her.

'Are you happy?'

'You know I am.'

'Then let's drink to it. To us, darling.'

'To us.'

She grimaced[15] as the liquid met her lips[16]. He laughed[17].

1. lui embrassa la nuque
2. chérie
3. écrites avec soin
4. la chance ne l'avait pas abandonné
5. soignée
6. lettre de suicide
7. qui n'ait jamais été lue à des jurés
8. gâcher
9. je vais vous rendre malheureux
10. verser
11. cachées
12. puait vraiment
13. ajouta
14. la bière blonde et mousseuse
15. elle fit une grimace
16. lèvres
17. rit

'You look as if you're drinking poison. Knock it back, girl[1]. Like this!'

He opened his throat and drained[2] his own glass. Laughing, she shuddered[3] slightly and gulped down[4] her ale. He took the empty glass from her and folded her in his arms[5]. She clung to him[6], her hands like a cold compress on the back of his neck. Releasing himself[7] he drew her down beside him on to the armchair. Then, clasped together[8] they slid to the floor[9] and lay[10] together on the rug[11] in front of the gas fire. He had turned off the light and her face shone[12] in the fierce[13] red glow[14] of the fire as if she lay in the full sun. The hiss[15] of the gas was the only sound in the silence.

He pulled[16] a cushion[17] from one of the armchairs and pushed it under her head. Only one cushion; he had a use for the other. It could rest on the bottom of the gas stove. She would be less likely to wake[18] if he made her comfortable on that last brief slide[19] from unconsciousness[20] to death. He put his left arm around her and they lay tight clasped without speaking. Suddenly she turned her face to his and he felt her tongue[21], wet and slippery[22] as a fish, infiltrating between his teeth. Her eyes, their pupils black in the gaslight, were heavy with desire[23]. 'Darling,' she whispered. 'Darling.' Christ, he thought, not that. He couldn't make love to her now. It would keep her quiet but it wasn't possible. There wasn't time. And surely the police pathologist could tell how recently that had happened to a woman. He thought for the first time with relief of her obsession with safety and whispered, 'We can't darling. I haven't got anything with me. We can't risk it now.'

1. allez, bois-la cul sec
2. vida
3. frissonna
4. avala
5. la prit dans ses bras
6. elle se cramponna à lui
7. en se libérant
8. enlacés
9. glissèrent par terre
10. restèrent allongés
11. tapis
12. brillait
13. violente
14. lumière
15. sifflement
16. tira
17. coussin
18. se réveiller
19. passage
20. inconscience
21. langue
22. glissante
23. pleins de désir

She gave a little murmur of acquiescence and nuzzled against him[1], moving her left leg over his thighs[2]. It lay there, heavy and inert, but he dare not move nor speak in case he broke that insidious drop[3] into unconsciousness. She was breathing[4] more deeply now, hotly and irritatingly into his left ear. God, how much longer was it going to take! Holding[5] his own breath he listened. Suddenly she gave a little snort[6] like a contented[7] animal. Under his arm he sensed a change in the rhythm of her breathing. There was an almost physical release of tension as her body relaxed. She was asleep.

Better give her a few minutes, he thought. There wasn't much time to spare[8], but he dare not hurry. It was important that there were no bruises[9] on her body and he knew he couldn't face a struggle. But there could be no turning back[10] now. If she woke and resisted it would still have to be done.

So he waited, lying so still[11] that they might both have been dead bodies stiffening[12] together into a final stylized embrace[13]. After a little time he raised himself cautiously on his right elbow[14] and looked at her. Her face was flushed[15], her mouth with its short upper[16] lip curved against the white childish teeth was half open. He could smell the paraldehyde on her breath. He watched her for a moment, noting the length of the pale lashes[17] against her cheeks[18], the upward slant of the eyebrows[19] and the shadows under the broad cheek bones[20]. Strange that he had never got round to drawing[21] her face. But it was too late to think of that now.

He murmured to her as he lifted[22] her gently[23] across the room to the black mouth of the gas oven.

1. se blottit contre lui
2. cuisses
3. chute
4. elle respirait
5. en retenant
6. elle poussa un petit grognement
7. satisfait
8. à perdre
9. bleus
10. il ne pouvait plus revenir en arrière
11. immobile
12. raidissant
13. étreinte
14. coude
15. rouge
16. supérieure
17. cils
18. joues
19. les sourcils arqués vers le haut
20. pommettes
21. il n'avait jamais réussi à dessiner
22. souleva
23. doucement

'It's all right, Jenny darling. It's only me. I'm making you comfortable. It's all right, darling.'

But it was himself that he was reassuring.

There was plenty of room in the large, old-fashioned oven, even with the cushion. The bottom of the oven was only a few inches[1] from the ground[2]. Feeling for her shoulder blades[3] he edged her gently forward. As the cushion took the weight of her head he looked to make sure that the gas jets were still unimpeded[4]. Her head rolled[5] gently sideways[6] so that the half-open mouth, moist[7] and vulnerable as a baby's[8], hung just above them, poised[9] and ready to suck up[10] death. As he slid his hands from under her body she gave a little sigh[11] as if she were comfortable at last.

He gave one last look at her, satisfied with his handiwork[12].

And now it was time to hurry. Feeling in his pocket for the rubber gloves, he moved with fantastic speed, treading lightly[13], his breath coming in shallow gasps[14] as if he could no longer bear[15] the sound of his own breathing. The suicide note was on the table. He took the screwdriver and wrapped her right hand gently round it, pressing the palm around the shining handle, the right finger-tip[16] against the base of the blade[17]. Was that how she would have held[18] it? Near enough. He placed the screw-driver on top of the suicide note.

Next he washed up his own glass and put it back in the cupboard, holding the dish-cloth[19] in front of the gas fire for a second until the damp stain[20] had evaporated. He turned off the fire. No need to worry about prints[21] here. There was nothing to show when last it had been lit[22]. He wondered

1. quelques centimètres
2. sol
3. omoplates
4. n'étaient pas obstrués
5. roula
6. sur le côté
7. humide
8. comme celle d'un enfant
9. suspendue
10. absorber
11. soupir
12. ouvrage
13. en marchant d'un pas léger
14. en respirant à petits coups
15. supporter
16. bout du doigt
17. lame
18. tenu
19. torchon
20. tache humide
21. empreintes
22. qui indiquait quand il avait été allumé pour la dernière fois

briefly about the paraldehyde bottle and Jenny's glass, but decided to leave them on the table with the note and the screwdriver. The natural thing would surely be for her to drink sitting at the table and then to move to the stove when she felt the first signs of drowsiness[1]. He wiped[2] his own prints from the bottle and clasped[3] her left hand around it, her right-hand index finger and thumb[4] on the stopper[5]. He was almost afraid to touch her, but she was now deeply asleep. Her hand was very warm to his touch and so relaxed that it felt boneless[6]. He was repelled[7] by its limp flaccidity[8], by this touch which was without communication, without desire. He was glad when he had dealt similarly with the drinking glass and the bottle of beer. It would only be necessary now to touch her once again.

Last of all he took his own letter to the Priddys and the pair of gloves and threw them into the boiler. There was only the gas tap[9] to turn on. It was on the right of the stove and within easy reach[10] of her limp right arm. He lifted the arm, pressed her index finger and thumb against the tap, and turned it on. There was the soft hiss of escaping gas. How long, he wondered, was it likely to take? Not long surely? Perhaps only a matter of minutes. He put out the light and backed out[11], closing the door behind him.

It was then that he remembered the front-door keys. They must be found on her. His heart struck cold[12] as he realized how fatal that one mistake could have been. He edged into the room again by the light of his torch. Taking the keys from his pocket and holding his breath[13] against the gas, he placed them in her left hand. He had reached the

1. somnolence
2. effaça
3. referma
4. pouce
5. bouchon
6. qu'elle semblait ne pas avoir d'os
7. il éprouvait du dégoût
8. flaccidité molle
9. robinet
10. à portée
11. sortit à reculons
12. il eut un coup au cœur
13. retenant sa respiration

door before he heard Tigger's mew[1]. The cat must have been sleeping under the cupboard. It was moving slowly round the body now, putting out a tentative[2] paw[3] towards the girl's right foot. Nagle found that he could not bear to go near her again.

'Come here Tigger,' he whispered. 'Come here boy.'

The cat turned its great amber[4] eyes on him and seemed to be considering, but without emotion and without haste[5]. Then it came slowly across to the door. Nagle hooked[6] his left foot under the soft belly and lifted the cat through the door in one swift[7] movement.

'Come out of it, you bloody fool. D'you want to lose all nine lives at one go[8]? That stuff[9]'s lethal.'

He closed the door, and the cat, suddenly active, shot away[10] into the dark.

Nagle made his way without lights to the back door, felt for[11] the bolts and let himself out. He paused for a moment, back against the door, to check that the mews was empty. Now that it was over he had time to note the signs of strain[12]. His forehead[13] and hands were wet with sweat[14] and he had difficulty with his breathing[15]. He drew in deep gasps[16] of the damp[17] and blessedly[18] cool night air. The fog wasn't thick[19], hardly[20] more than a heavy mist, through which the street lamp which marked the end of the mews gleamed like a yellow smudge[21] in the darkness. That gleam, only forty yards[22] away, represented safety[23]. Yet all at once it seemed unattainable[24]. Like an animal in its lair[25] he gazed in horrified fascination at the dangerous beacon[26] and willed his legs to move. But their power had gone. Crouching[27] in the darkness and

1. miaulement
2. timide
3. patte
4. ambrés
5. hâte
6. glissa
7. rapide
8. d'un coup
9. truc
10. fila
11. chercha en tâtonnant
12. tension
13. front
14. sueur
15. des difficultés à respirer
16. avala de grandes bouffées
17. humide
18. délicieusement
19. dense
20. à peine
21. tache
22. cinquante mètres
23. salut
24. inaccessible
25. tanière
26. fanal
27. accroupi

shelter[1] of the doorway, his back pressed against the wood, he fought off[2] panic. After all, there was no great hurry. In a moment he would leave this spurious[3] sanctuary and put the mews behind him. Then it was only a matter of re-entering the square from the other side and waiting until there was a casual passer-by to witness his vain hammering at the front door[4]. Even the words he would speak were ready. 'It's my girl. I think she's in there, but she won't open up. She was with me earlier this evening and when she'd gone I found the keys were missing. She was in a queer state[5]. Better get a copper[6]. I'm going to smash[7] this window.'

Then the crash of broken glass, the dash[8] to the basement and the chance to lock the back door again before the hurrying footsteps were at his heels[9]. The worst was over. From now on it was all so easy. By ten o'clock the body would have been removed, the clinic empty. In a moment he would move on to the final act. But not yet. Not quite yet.

Along the Embankment[10] the traffic was almost stationary. There seemed to be some kind of function[11] on at the Savoy. Suddenly Dalgliesh said:

'There's no guard at the clinic now, of course?'

'No, sir. You remember I asked you this morning if we need keep a man there and you said no.'

'I remember.'

'After all, sir, it hardly seemed necessary. We'd examined the place thoroughly[12] and there aren't all those men to spare[13].'

'I know, Martin,' replied Dalgliesh testily[14]. 'Surprisingly enough those were the reasons for my decision.' The car came to a stop once more. Dalgliesh

1. abri
2. essaya de vaincre
3. faux
4. le voit tambouriner contre la porte d'entrée
5. dans un état étrange
6. flic
7. briser
8. course folle
9. sur ses talons
10. nom abrégé du « Victoria Embankment », rue de la rive nord de la Tamise à Londres
11. réception
12. de fond en comble
13. à disposition
14. d'un ton irrité

put his head out of the window. 'What the hell does he think he's doing?'

'I think he's doing his best, sir.'

'That's what I find so depressing. Come on, Sergeant. Get out! We'll do the rest on foot[1]. I'm probably being a bloody fool, but when we get to the clinic, we'll cover both exits. You go round to the back.'

If Martin felt surprise it was not his nature to show it. Something seemed to have got into the old man. As like as not[2] Nagle was back in his flat and the clinic locked and deserted. A couple of fools they'd look creeping up on[3] an empty building. Still, they'd know soon enough. He bent[4] his energies to keeping up with[5] the superintendent.

Nagle never knew how long he waited in the doorway[6], bent almost double[7] and panting[8] like an animal. But after a time[9], calmness returned and with it the use of his legs. He moved stealthily[10] forward, hoisted himself[11] over the rear railings and set off down the mews. He walked like an automation[12], hands stiffly by his sides, his eyes closed. Suddenly he heard the foot-fall[13]. Opening his eyes, he saw silhouetted against the street lamp a familiar bulky[14] figure. Slowly, inexorably, it moved towards him through the mist. His heart leapt[15] in his chest[16] then settled into a regular tumultuous throbbing[17] that shook his whole body. His legs felt heavy and cold as death, checking[18] that first fatal impulse to flight[19]. But at least his mind worked. While he could think there was hope. He was cleverer than they. With luck they wouldn't even think of entering the clinic. Why should they? And surely

1. à pied
2. très probablement
3. en train de s'approcher à pas de loup de
4. rassembla
5. pour ne pas se laisser distancer par
6. dans l'embrasure de la porte
7. presque plié en deux
8. haletant
9. au bout d'un moment
10. furtivement
11. se hissa
12. robot
13. bruit de pas
14. corpulente
15. bondit
16. poitrine
17. rythme
18. réfrénant
19. sa furieuse envie de s'enfuir

she would be dead by now! With Jenny dead they could suspect what they liked. They'd never prove a thing.

The torch shone full on his face. The slow unemphatic[1] voice spoke:

'Good evening, lad[2]. We were hoping to meet you. Going in or coming out?'

Nagle did not reply. He stretched his mouth into the semblance of a smile. He could only guess how he looked in that fierce light: a death's head, the mouth agape[3] with fright, the eyes staring.

It was then that he felt the tentative rub[4] against his legs. The policeman bent and scooped up[5] the cat, holding it between them. Immediately it began to purr[6], throbbing its contentment[7] at the warmth of that huge hand.

'So here's Tigger. You let him out, did you? You and the cat came out together.'

Then, instantaneously, they were both aware of it[8] and their eyes met. From the warmth of the cat's fur[9] there rose[10] between them, faint[11] but unmistakable[12], the smell of gas.

The next half-hour passed for Nagle in a confused whirl[13] of noise and blinding[14] lights out of which a few vivid tableaux sprang into focus[15] with unnatural clarity and stayed fixed in his mind for the rest of his life. He had no memory of the sergeant dragging him[16] back over the iron railings[17], only of the grip[18], firm as a tourniquet[19], numbing[20] his arm and the hot rasp[21] of Martin's breath in his ear. There was a smash[22] and the sad, delayed tinkle[23] of broken glass as someone kicked out the windows of the porters' room, the shrill screech[24] of

1. posée
2. mon vieux
3. grande ouverte
4. frottement
5. ramassa
6. ronronner
7. vibrant de satisfaction
8. ils s'en rendirent compte
9. fourrure
10. montait
11. légère
12. évidente
13. tourbillon
14. aveuglantes
15. apparaissaient
16. le tirant
17. grille
18. poigne
19. garrot
20. qui engourdissait
21. crissement
22. fracas
23. tintement
24. bruit strident

a whistle[1], a confusion of running feet on the clinic stairs, a blaze of lights hurting his eyes. In one of the tableaux Dalgliesh was crouched[2] over the girl's body, his mouth wide-stretched as a gargoyle's[3], clamped over her mouth as he forced his breath into her lungs[4]. The two bodies seemed to be fighting, locked in an obscene embrace like the rape of the dead[5]. Nagle didn't speak. He was almost beyond thought, but instinct warned him that he must say nothing. Pinned[6] against the wall by strong arms and watching fascinated the feverish heave of Dalgliesh's shoulders[7], he felt tears start in his eyes. Enid Bolam was dead, and Jenny was dead, and he was tired now, desperately tired. He hadn't wanted to kill her. It was Bolam who had forced him into all the trouble and danger of murder. She and Jenny between them had left him no choice. And he had lost Jenny. Jenny was dead. Faced with the enormity, the unfairness of what they had made him do, he felt without surprise the tears of self-pity[8] flow[9] in a warm stream[10] down his face.

The room was suddenly full. There were more uniformed men, one of them burly as a Holbein[11], pig-eyed[12], slow-moving. There was the hiss[13] of oxygen, a murmur of consulting voices. Then they were edging[14] something on to a stretcher[15] with gentle, experienced hands, a red-blanketed shape which rolled sideways as the poles[16] were lifted. Why were they carrying it so carefully? It couldn't feel jolting[17] any more.

Dalgliesh didn't speak until Jenny had been taken away. Then, without looking at Nagle, he said:

'Right, Sergeant. Get him down to the station. We can hear his story there.'

1. sifflet
2. accroupi
3. comme celle d'une gargouille
4. poumons
5. viol d'un cadavre
6. immobilisé
7. les épaules de Dalgliesh qui se contractaient
8. apitoiement
9. couler
10. flux
11. ayant la carrure d'un personnage de Holbein
12. aux yeux porcins
13. sifflement
14. posaient
15. brancard
16. poignées
17. sentir les secousses

Nagle moved his mouth. His lips were so dry that he heard them crack. But it was some seconds before the words would come and then there was no stopping them. The carefully rehearsed[1] story tumbled out in a spate[2], bald[3] and unconvincing:

'There's nothing to tell. She came to see me at my flat and we spent the evening together. I had to tell her that I was going away without her. She took it pretty badly[4], and after she'd left I found that the clinic keys were missing. I knew she was in a bit of a state[5] so I thought I'd better come along. There's a note on the table. She's left a note. I could see she was dead and I couldn't help, so I came away. I didn't want to be mixed up[6] in it. I've got the Bollinger to think of. It wouldn't look good[7] getting mixed up with a suicide.'

Dalgliesh said:

'You'd better not say anything else for the present. But you'll have to do better than that[8]. You see, it isn't quite[9] what she has told us. That note on the table isn't the only one she left.'

With slow deliberation[10] he took from his breast pocket a small folded sheet[11] of paper and held it an inch[12] from Nagle's fascinated, fear-glazed[13] eyes:

'If you were together this evening in your flat, how do you explain this note which we found under your door knocker[14]?'

It was then that Nagle realized with sick despair[15] that the dead, so impotent and so despised[16], could bear witness[17] against him after all. Instinctively he put out[18] his hand for[19] the note, then dropped[20] his arm. Dalgliesh replaced the note in his pocket. Watching Nagle closely[21], he said:

1. soigneusement préparée
2. se déversa comme un torrent
3. plate
4. mal
5. dans tous ses états
6. mêlé
7. ce ne serait pas bien
8. trouver mieux à nous raconter
9. exactement
10. lentement et de façon réfléchie
11. feuille pliée
12. à quelques centimètres
13. rendus vitreux à cause de la peur
14. heurtoir
15. désespoir nauséeux
16. méprisés
17. témoigner
18. tendit
19. pour prendre
20. laissa tomber
21. de près

'So you rushed here tonight because you were concerned for her safety? Very touching! In that case let me put your mind at rest[1]. She's going to live.'

'She's dead,' said Nagle dully[2]. 'She killed herself.'

'She was breathing when we'd finished with her. Tomorrow, if all goes well, she'll be able to tell us what happened. And not only what happened here tonight. We shall have some questions about Miss Bolam's murder.'

Nagle gave a shout of harsh laughter[3]:

'Bolam's murder! You'll never get me[4] for that! And I'll tell you why, you poor boobs[5]. Because I didn't kill her! If you want to make fools of yourselves[6], go ahead[7]. Don't let me stop you. But I warn you[8]. If I'm arrested for Bolam's murder I'll make your names stink in every newspaper[9] in the country.'

He held out his wrists[10] to Dalgliesh.

'Come on, Superintendent! Go ahead and charge me[11]. What's stopping you? You've worked it all out[12] very cleverly, haven't you? You've been too clever by half[13], you bloody supercilious copper[14]!'

'I'm not charging you,' said Dalgliesh. 'I'm inviting you to come to headquarters to answer some questions and to make a statement[15]. If you want a solicitor[16] present you're entitled to have one[17].'

'I'll have one all right. But not just at the moment. I'm in no hurry, Superintendent. You see, I'm expecting a visitor. We arranged to meet here at ten and it's nearly that now. I must say we'd planned to have the place to ourselves and I don't think my visitor will be particularly pleased to see you. But if you want to meet Miss Bolam's killer you'd better

1. soyez rassuré
2. d'une voix terne
3. éclata de rire
4. vous n'arriverez jamais à m'accuser
5. nigauds
6. vous rendre ridicules
7. allez-y
8. je vous préviens
9. vos noms feront la une de tous les journaux
10. poignets
11. inculpez-moi
12. vous avez tout compris
13. vous avez été un peu trop malin
14. sale flic arrogant
15. faire une déclaration
16. avocat
17. vous y avez droit

stick around[1]. It won't be long. The person I'm expecting has been trained to be on time[2].'

Suddenly all his fear seemed to have left him. The large brown eyes were expressionless again, muddy pools[3] in which only the black iris burned[4] with life. Martin, still clasping Nagle's arms, could feel the muscles bracing[5], could sense the physical return of confidence. But before anyone had time to speak their ears caught simultaneously the sound of footsteps. Someone had come in by the basement door and was moving quietly down the passage.

Dalgliesh moved to the door in one silent stride[6] and braced himself[7] against it. The footsteps, timid, hesitant, stopped outside. Three pairs of eyes watched as the door-knob[8] turned, first right, then left. A voice called softly:

'Nagle! Are you there, Nagle! Open the door.'

With a single movement Dalgliesh stepped to one side[9] and crashed open[10] the door. The slight[11] figure moved forward involuntarily under the blaze[12] of the fluorescent lights. The immense grey eyes widened[13] and slewed[14] from face to face, the eyes of an uncomprehending[15] child. Whimpering[16], she clutched[17] a handbag[18] to her breast in a sudden protective gesture as if she were shielding[19] a baby. Wrenching himself[20] from Martin's grip[21] Nagle snatched[22] it from her and tossed[23] it to Dalgliesh. It fell plumply[24] into the detective's hands, the cheap plastic sticking[25] warmly to his fingers. Nagle tried to keep his voice level, but it cracked with excitement and triumph.

'Take a look inside, Superintendent. It's all there. I'll tell you what you'll find. A signed confession

1. restez dans les parages
2. à l'heure
3. flaques de boue
4. brûlait
5. se contracter
6. enjambée
7. s'arc-bouta
8. poignée
9. se mit sur le côté
10. ouvrit grand
11. mince
12. éclat
13. s'agrandirent
14. passèrent
15. ahuri
16. en gémissant
17. serra
18. sac à main
19. protégeait
20. en se dégageant
21. étreinte
22. saisit
23. lança
24. en plein
25. collant

of Enid Bolam's murder and one hundred pounds in notes[1], a first payment on account to keep my mouth shut.'

He turned to his visitor.

'Sorry, kid. I didn't plan it this way. I was willing enough to keep quiet about what I'd seen, but things have changed since Friday night. I've got troubles of my own to worry about now and no one's going to pin[2] a murder charge on me. Our little arrangement's off.'

But Marion Bolam had fainted[3].

Two months later a magistrate's court committed Marion Grace Bolam for trial[4] on a charge of[5] her cousin's murder. A capricious autumn had hardened[6] into winter and Dalgliesh walked back alone to headquarters under a grey blanket of sky which sagged[7] with its weight of snow. The first moist flakes[8] were already falling, melting[9] gently against his face. In his chief's office the lights were lit and the curtains drawn, shutting out the glittering[10] river, the necklace[11] of light along the Embankment and all the cold inertia of a winter afternoon. Dalgliesh made his report briefly. The AC[12] listened in silence, then said:

'They'll try for diminished[13] responsibility, I suppose. How did the girl seem?'

'Perfectly calm, like a child who knows she's been naughty and is on her best behaviour[14] in the hope that the grown-ups[15] will overlook it[16]. She feels no particular guilt, I suspect, except the usual female guilt at being found out.'

'It was a perfectly straightforward[17] case,' said the AC. 'The obvious suspect, the obvious motive.'

1. en billets de banque
2. coller
3. s'était évanouie
4. mit Marion Bolam en accusation
5. pour
6. s'était durci
7. s'affaissait
8. flocons humides
9. et fondaient
10. scintillante
11. collier
12. Assistant Commissioner = préfet de police adjoint
13. atténuée
14. se conduit très bien
15. adultes
16. fermeront les yeux
17. très clair

'Too obvious for me, apparently,' said Dalgliesh bitterly. 'If this case doesn't cure me of conceit[1], nothing will. If I'd paid more attention to the obvious I might have questioned why she didn't get back to Rettinger Street until after eleven when the television service was closing down. She'd been with Nagle, of course, arranging the blackmail payments. They met in St James's Park, apparently. He saw his chance all right when he went into that record-room and found her bending over[2] her cousin's body. He must have been on her before she heard a sound. He took over[3] from there with his usual efficiency. It was he who put the fetish so carefully on the body, of course. Even that detail misled[4] me. Somehow I couldn't see Marion Bolam making that final contemptuous[5] gesture. But it was an obvious crime, all right. She hardly made an attempt at concealment[6]. The rubber gloves she wore were stuffed back[7] in her uniform pocket. The weapons she chose were the ones nearest to hand[8]. She wasn't trying to incriminate anyone else. She wasn't even trying to be clever. At about six-twelve she telephoned the general office and asked Nagle not to come down yet for the laundry; he couldn't resist lying about that call, incidentally, which gave me another opportunity for being over-subtle[9]. Then she rang for her cousin. She couldn't be absolutely sure that Enid would come alone and the excuse had to be valid so she threw the medical records on the floor. Then she waited in the record-room for her victim, fetish in hand and chisel in her uniform pocket. It was unfortunate for her that Nagle returned secretly to the clinic when he was out with the post. He'd over-heard Miss Bolam's call to

1. suffisance
2. penchée sur
3. il a pris la situation en main
4. induit en erreur
5. plein de mépris
6. elle n'a même pas essayé de le cacher
7. fourrés
8. à portée de main
9. trop subtil

the group secretary and wanted to get his hands on the Fenton record. It seemed safer to chuck[1] it in the basement furnace[2]. Coming upon[3] the murder forced him to change his plan and he didn't get another chance once the body was discovered and the record-room sealed. Nurse Bolam, of course, had no choice of time. She discovered on Wednesday night that Enid intended to alter her will. Friday was the earliest evening when there was a lysergic acid session and she would have the basement to herself. She couldn't act earlier; she daren't act later.'

'The murder was highly convenient for Nagle,' said his chief. 'You can't blame yourself[4] for concentrating on him. But if you insist on indulging in self-pity don't let me spoil[5] your fun.'

'Convenient, perhaps, but not necessary,' Dalgliesh replied. 'And why should he have killed Bolam? His one aim, apart from making easy money, was to take up the Bollinger and get away to Europe without fuss[6]. He must have known that it would be difficult to pin[7] the Fenton blackmail on him even if the group secretary decided to call in the police. And, in fact, we still haven't enough evidence to charge him. But murder is different. Anyone connected with murder is likely to have his private plans disorganized. Even the innocent can't so easily shake off[8] that contaminating dust[9]. To kill Bolam only increased his danger. But to kill Priddy was a different matter. At one stroke[10] he could safeguard[11] his alibi, get rid of an encumbrance[12] and give himself the hope of marrying the heiress[13] of nearly thirty thousand. He knew he'd have little chance with Marion Bolam if she learned that Prid-

1. jeter
2. chaudière
3. en tombant sur
4. vous ne devez pas vous en vouloir
5. gâcher
6. discrètement
7. coller
8. se débarrasser de
9. poussière
10. d'un seul coup
11. préserver
12. embarras
13. héritière

dy had been his mistress. She wasn't Enid Bolam's cousin for nothing.'

The AC said:

'At least we've got him as an accessory[1] after the fact and that should put him away for quite a time. I'm not sorry that the Fentons will be spared the ordeal of giving evidence[2]. But I doubt whether the charge of attempted murder[3] will stick[4] – not unless Priddy changes her mind[5]. If she persists in supporting his story we'll get nowhere.'

'She won't change her mind, sir,' said Dalgliesh bitterly.

'Nagle doesn't want to see her, of course, but nothing makes any difference. All she thinks about is planning their life together when he comes out. And God help her when he does.'

The AC shifted[6] his immense bulk[7] irritably[8] in his chair, closed the file and pushed it across the table to Dalgliesh. He said:

'There's nothing that you or anyone else can do about that. She's the kind of woman who pursues her own destruction[9]. I've had that artist, Sugg, on to me[10] by the way. Extraordinary ideas about judicial procedure these people have! I told him that it's out of our hands[11] now and referred him[12] to the proper quarter[13]. He wants to pay for Nagle's defence, if you please[14]! Said that if we've made a mistake the world will lose a remarkable talent.'

'It will be lost, anyway,' replied Dalgliesh. Thinking aloud, he added: 'I wonder just how good an artist would have to be before one let him get away with[15] a crime like Nagle's. Michelangelo? Velazquez? Rembrandt?'

1. complice
2. l'épreuve de venir témoigner leur soit épargnée
3. tentative de meurtre
4. puisse tenir
5. change d'avis
6. bougea
7. masse
8. avec irritation
9. qui cherche sa propre destruction
10. qui est venu me voir
11. ce n'est plus de notre ressort
12. je l'ai envoyé
13. ceux qui sont concernés
14. si possible
15. lui pardonnerait

'Oh, well,' said the AC easily. 'If we had to ask ourselves that question we wouldn't be policemen.'

Back in Dalgliesh's office Sergeant Martin was putting away[1] papers. He took one look at his super[2]'s face, pronounced a stolid[3] 'Good night, sir', and left. There were some situations which his uncomplicated nature found it prudent to avoid. The door had hardly closed behind him when the telephone rang. It was Mrs Shorthouse.

'Hullo!' she yelled[4]. 'Is that you? I had the devil of a job getting through to you[5]. Saw you in court today. Don't suppose you noticed me, though. How are you?'

'Well, thank you, Mrs Shorthouse.'

'Don't suppose we'll be meeting again, so I thought I'd give you a ring to say cheerio[6] and tell you the news. Things have been happening[7] at the clinic, I can tell you. Miss Saxon's leaving for one thing[8]. She's going to work in a home[9] for subnormal kids up north[10]. Run by the RCs it is[11]. Fancy going off to work[12] in a convent! No one at the Steen ever did that before.'

Dalgliesh said he could well believe it.

'Miss Priddy's been transferred to one of the group's chest clinics[13]. Mr Lauder thought the change would do her good[14]. She's had a terrible row[15] with her people[16] and she's living alone now in a bed-sitter[17] in Kilburn. But you know all about that, no doubt. Mrs Bolam's gone to an expensive nursing-home[18] near Worthing. All on her share of Cousin Enid's money[19], of course. Poor sod[20]. I'm surprised she could bring herself[21] to touch a penny of it.'

1. était en train de ranger
2. chef
3. flegmatique
4. cria
5. ça a été très difficile de vous joindre
6. bye-bye
7. il se passe des choses
8. pour commencer
9. foyer
10. dans le Nord
11. dirigé par des religieuses
12. quelle idée d'aller travailler
13. centres de pneumologie
14. lui ferait du bien
15. dispute
16. ses vieux
17. studette
18. clinique privée
19. payée avec l'argent de sa cousine
20. la pauvre !
21. se décider

Dalgliesh wasn't surprised, but did not say so. Mrs Shorthouse went on:

'And then there's Dr Steiner. He's getting married to his wife.'

'What did you say, Mrs Shorthouse?'

'Well, re-married. Fixed it up very sudden they did[1]. They got divorced and now they're getting married again. What d'you think of that?'

Dalgliesh said that it was a question of what Dr Steiner thought of it.

'Oh, he's as pleased[2] as a dog with a new collar. And a collar is just about[3] what he's getting, if you ask me[4]. There's a rumour that the Regional Board may close the clinic and move everyone to a hospital out-patient department. Well, you can't wonder![5] First a stabbing and then a gassing, and now a murder trial. Not nice really. Dr Etherege says it's upsetting[6] for the patients, but I haven't noticed it to speak of[7]. The numbers haven't half gone up[8] since last October. That would have pleased Miss Bolam. Always worrying about the numbers she was. Mind you there are those who say we wouldn't have had that trouble[9] with Nagle and Priddy if you'd picked on the right one first go[10]. It was a near thing all right[11]. But what I say is, you did your best and there's no harm done[12] to speak of.'

No harm to speak of! So these, thought Dalgliesh bitterly, as he replaced the receiver, were the concomitants of failure[13]. It was enough to taste his sour[14], corroding[15] self-pity without enduring[16] the AC's moralizing[17], Martin's tact, Amy Shorthouse's condolences. If he were to break free from[18] this pervasive gloom[19] he needed a respite[20] from crime and death, needed to walk for one brief evening

1. ils ont décidé tout ça très vite
2. content
3. exactement
4. si vous voulez mon avis
5. c'est pas étonnant !
6. perturbant
7. je n'ai rien remarqué
8. le nombre de patients n'a pas diminué
9. souci
10. si vous aviez trouvé tout de suite le coupable
11. vous avez réussi de justesse
12. pas de dégâts
13. c'était une preuve de son échec
14. aigre
15. corrosif
16. subir
17. leçon de morale
18. pour se libérer de
19. tristesse envahissante
20. s'éloigner momentanément

1. il se rendit compte
2. ironiquement
3. un souci d'un genre différent
4. freiné
5. prudence
6. ses fonctions
7. l'engageait
8. il avait sûrement le droit

out of the shadow of blackmail and murder. It came to him[1] that what he wanted was to dine with Deborah Riscoe. At least, he told himself wryly[2], it would be a change of trouble[3]. He put his hand on the receiver and then paused, checked[4] by the old caution[5], the old uncertainties. He was not even sure that she would wish to take a call at the office, what exactly her place[6] was at Hearne and Illingworth. Then he remembered how she had looked when last they met and he lifted the receiver. He could surely dine with an attractive woman without this preparatory morbid self-analysis. The invitation would commit him[7] to nothing more crucial than seeing that she had a pleasant evening and paying the bill. And a man was surely entitled[8] to call his own publishers.

Imprimé en Italie par La Tipografica Varese Srl
Dépôt légal : octobre 2014
311726-03/11029469-octobre 2014